A CHRISTMAS HE CAN'T REFUSE

JOHN SALZONE

CHAPTER
ONE

That song was playing again.

It was the song you heard everywhere the day after Halloween and non-stop until Christmas Day.

Mariah Carey's 'All I Want for Christmas.'

Liam wanted to cover his ears, but there was no escaping it. No matter where he was or where he went, he heard it. At home. In stores. Walking down the street. In passing cars or on the subway or on a plane. Mariah was everywhere.

Of course, there were those other Christmas songs in constant rotation at this time of year, too. 'Rockin' Around the Christmas Tree' by Brenda Lee. 'Do They Know It's Christmas?' by Band-Aid. 'Rudolph the Red-Nosed Reindeer,' 'Chestnuts

Roasting on an Open Fire,' 'White Christmas,' and so many others.

But the song everyone heard 24/7 without any reprieve was Mariah's.

Last year, Cher released a Christmas single from her first-ever Christmas album. Her song, 'DJ Play a Christmas Song' had hit the charts and given her another number one single. But it was no 'All I Want for Christmas.' Then again, Mariah's song wasn't an instant hit when it was first released in 1994, so maybe in another twenty-five years Cher's song would be playing non-stop since, right now, he barely ever heard it. Of course, Cher wouldn't be around to enjoy that achievement, but one never knew. She was only seventy-eight and kept herself in great shape. Look at Louise Rainier, the actress from the 1930s. The two-time Oscar winner had been one hundred and four when she died in 2014.

Liam stared around the office he was sitting in. Even though it was November 15, the office was fully decorated for Christmas. There was a tiny decorated Christmas tree on the gray steel desk in front of him, images of Santa and his reindeer on the walls, colorful tinsel and garland draped on the book-shelves, which were also decorated with dangling candy canes, angels, wreaths and bells, as well as a huge MERRY CHRISTMAS banner with images of Snoopy and Charlie Brown hanging from the ceiling. This was the office of a serious Christmas lover. Which meant he needed to expound on the joy of the holiday season when it was time for his job interview, even though the last thing he wanted to do was celebrate Christmas or anything else.

This had not been his year, although eleven months ago on January 1 he had believed—mistakenly—that this was FINALLY going to be his year and he was going to have a career breakthrough with TV and movie offers coming his way. He'd been a working actor for the last ten years, and his career had been successful. Okay, reasonably successful. It wasn't like he wasn't always hustling for his next job, but the work kept coming his way. A lot of it had been theatre—Broadway shows that were on the road—as well as some modeling. The roles did keep getting bigger, but it was never like he was the star or thrust into the spotlight. He was always the solid, reliable supporting player, even though he knew he could be much more than that if he was only given a chance. He knew he had to be patient and pay his dues. And he was. But he was always waiting for that one big break. Year after year after year.

Until last year.

Finally, he thought his breakout opportunity had fallen into his lap when he was cast on the reality TV show, *The Gay Househusbands of NYC*. Like the *Housewives* franchise on Bravo, the *Househusbands* franchise was similar, but only in that the cast was all gay. There were versions set in NYC, San Francisco, Aspen, and West Hollywood. The shows aired on the Viva network and were the creation of Ollie Hanson, sort of a poor man's version of Andy Cohen, the creative genius at Bravo. If there was a show that was a ratings hit for Bravo, chances were Ollie would create a version for Viva.

Looking back, Liam realized he'd been a fool. Reality TV lived for hot mess moments when something went wrong and then instantly went viral.

He couldn't say he hadn't been warned. His best friend and former roommate, Sebastian, had questioned him when he told him about the opportunity to be on the show. "Are you really sure you want to do this? I mean, they manipulate people on those shows to create drama. And they always want to have a villain. What if they decide to make you this season's villain?"

"Me? A villain?" Liam had laughed in disbelief. "Everyone loves me."

Liam had gotten on the radar of the show's

producers when they were scouting out the gym where he worked out. After a number of interviews, they finally decided to add him to the mix, and Liam joined the cast as a single. There were three married couples on the show and two singles. The producers wanted a third single so they could attach a single to each couple and watch what happened. Sort of an us-versus-them dynamic where the singles were envious of the lives of the marrieds.

Liam had decided going into the show that he wasn't going to play that game. He might be envious of another actor's career, but he was never envious of someone else's relationship. He knew how hard it was to find the right person—Hello! Thirty-two years old and still single!—and he would never want to come between a couple. But the producers didn't need to know that. He'd follow the script they gave him, but within reason. He knew how to be coy and flirtatious and charming, but he never stepped over the line, even if someone thought he might. He was specifically thinking of Sebastian and his rocky road to marriage with his husband, Dominick. There had been so many roadblocks to those two getting together that Liam decided to help push things along by igniting Sebastian's jealousy by pretending to have an interest in Dom. Granted, it had backfired on Liam at one point, courtesy of a strawberry cupcake served to him by Sebastian (he was allergic to strawberries and he'd broken out in hives after one bite), but in the end, he liked to think he had helped Sebastian and Dominick get their happily ever after.

So, he was friendly with everyone on the show. He tried not to be catty or bitchy or backstabbing. And it seemed to work. Everyone on the show had loved him. Well, correction–the marrieds had. The singles hadn't exactly rolled out the welcome mat, seeing him as a threat to their limited appearances. And why wouldn't they? Liam knew he was hand-some, and he'd always gotten his fair share of atten-tion. If the husbands fawned all over him, why not enjoy it? It gave him airtime, right? He was the new, shiny toy that they all wanted to play with. And it was all about the airtime and being seen by the audience.

In his early days on the show, he'd tried to come up with a catch phrase–like the character Gretchen Wieners in the movie *Mean Girls,* trying to make the word *fetch* happen–and his attempts had amused the audience since nothing he suggested ever stuck.

The one couple that had taken an extra liking to him had been Mark and Jason. They were a fortysomething couple with a huge design empire.

Mark handled the business side of things while Jason did all the creative stuff. Throughout the entire season, Mark and Jason kept flirting with him, inviting him over to their NYC penthouse for cocktails or dinner or long weekends at their place in the Hamptons, where they would sit around and bitch about the other cast members. Liam always tried to stay neutral because he didn't want to burn any bridges. Often, he felt like he was back in high school, where one clique was scheming against another. For most of the season, everything seemed to be going well and Liam had a feeling he would be asked back for another season.

He had also started dating a sexy Latino dancer named Pablo. He was adorable, with caramel skin, a head of lush curls, and the cutest dimples. And then there was what he could do in bed! Since Pablo was a dancer, he knew the exact meaning of the word versatile, and those muscular legs of his were more lethal than a pair of scissors. Liam loved being locked in them. He thought maybe if their relationship became more serious, the show would consider adding Pablo to the cast, too. He'd popped up in a few scenes so far this season, usually right after he'd had a workout or a rehearsal, looking all delicious with a light coat of sweat enhancing his rippling muscles. Maybe they could be the show's next couple. Who didn't love seeing a courtship/engagement/marriage unfold on screen?

But then, there was the weekend when Mark went out of town on business and Jason invited Liam over to the penthouse for dinner. The wine had flowed, Jason confessed he and Mark weren't as intimate with each other as they used to be, and he feared Mark no longer found him attractive. Liam found this comment to be insane. On a scale of 1 to 10, Jason was a 12. Jason said he didn't know what to do. Liam had offered some words of advice, urging him to tell Mark how he felt. The wine kept flowing as Jason asked Liam if he found him attractive and would sleep with him if Mark wasn't in the picture. Naturally, Liam told him he did find him attractive—he wasn't blind! In his gut, he suspected Jason might try to make a move, and that was the last thing he wanted, especially since he knew there were cameras set up in the apartment recording 24/7 for the show. He always needed to be careful about what he did or said, otherwise it could wind up on TV. He wanted to leave the apartment, yet for some reason he felt powerless, rooted on the couch as Jason inched closer and closer to him...

The next thing Liam knew, it was morning and

he was naked under the sheets in Mark and Jason's bedroom with absolutely no memory of the night before. Hurriedly slipping back into his clothes, he tiptoed his way out of the empty penthouse, praying he had just had too much wine and Jason had tucked him in bed. Although, the question as to why he had tucked him in *their* bed and not a guest bedroom kept niggling at him.

The entire day, Liam kept expecting Jason to call him, but he didn't. So, he pushed it to the back of his mind. If something had happened between them, surely Jason would have said something, right? But as filming continued for the season, Jason didn't say anything, so Liam didn't, either.

That is, until the taping of the show's reunion episode. Ollie, playing host to the cast the same way that Andy Cohen did with his housewives, blind-sided Liam with a question, asking him how it felt to break up a marriage. Liam, sensing the morning he had woken up in Mark and Jason's bed was coming back to haunt him, told Ollie he had no idea what he was talking about.

"Really?" Ollie had asked with a knowing smirk. "How about we refresh your memory?"

And then, a big screen descended before them,

on which there was a video clip of a naked Liam lying in bed next to a naked Jason.

After that, all hell broke loose. As the other marrieds and singles gasped in shock, Mark jumped out of his seat, lunging for Liam and calling him a backstabber. Jason, playing the victim, told Mark that Liam had plied him with wine and taken advantage of him.

Liam was speechless. He had never ever taken advantage of anyone. Whenever he slept with someone, it was consensual, although he had no memory of sleeping with Jason. When the cameras turned to him and Ollie asked Liam if he had anything to say, the only words Liam could utter were, "Nothing happened."

Those were the wrong words. Instantly, the entire cast pounced on him, calling him a liar, saying the proof was in front of all their eyes and he needed to "man up" to what he had done. Tyrell, one of the singles, shouted that Liam had always been jealous of the other marrieds and he'd been looking for a chance to break up one of their marriages. Denny, the show's other single, exclaimed that Liam had confessed to him that he was going to bag a rich husband by the time the season ended, and that it didn't matter if one of the husbands was already married.

None of it was true. Tyrell and Denny were both looking for their moment in the spotlight, and if it meant throwing Liam under the bus with their lies, then so be it.

When the reunion episode aired–tidbits about the big reveal had already been leaked out to the press– the fans were primed for something juicy to be revealed. And when it was, they went full-on scorched earth on Liam, bombarding all his social media accounts with nothing but hate, hate, and more hate. Not since Elizabeth Taylor had come between Debbie Reynolds and Eddie Fisher in the 1960s–or Brad Pitt leaving Jennifer Aniston for Angelina Jolie–were fans so invested in saving a celebrity marriage. And make no mistake, they were invested in Mark and Jason. Sales for their homeware line spiked, and they were on all the talk shows, holding hands while talking about how this crisis had brought them closer together and made them realize how much they had almost lost due to the "viper" they had let into their home.

That became Liam's new online name. Viper. Memes and cartoons were created with Liam's head on a viper's body, a forked tongue sticking out of his mouth with a cartoon bubble over his head saying, "Nothing happened."

The reunion episode was a ratings bonanza for Viva. Foolishly, Liam thought the show would have him back. That they would allow him to redeem himself in some way. I mean, they were always looking for story arcs, right? But they didn't. He was informed he wouldn't be returning for the show's next season. It wasn't that he had cheated with Jason that was the problem. The problem was that he kept denying it, the producers told him. But it was true! He had no memory of sleeping with Jason, even though there was footage of them naked in bed together. Despite the "proof," he wasn't going to admit to something he couldn't remember. In the end, it was Jason's word versus his, and Jason kept saying they had slept together.

But why would Jason do that? Why would he want to damage his marriage that way? Liam couldn't figure it out.

Finally, Liam gave up. No one was on his side. Well, that wasn't entirely true. His friends, like Sebastian and Dom, believed him, and Sebastian thankfully didn't say 'I told you so' when Liam revealed he was America's favorite new reality TV villain in an online poll.

His relationship with Pablo also ended.

"I thought we had something special, but we didn't," Pablo informed him via text. Text! He couldn't even call and give Liam a chance to explain himself. Like everyone else, Pablo believed Liam was a villain. Last he heard, Ollie had signed Pablo onto the show, claiming he wanted a little diversity but also wanted to keep Liamgate still alive by depicting how Pablo was picking up the pieces of his own life after being "betrayed" by the man he loved.

That was rich! He and Pablo had never said 'I love you' to each other, and if Liam was being honest with himself, he never really thought Pablo was the "one."

But had there ever really been anything close to the "one" in his life? There had been a number of short-lived relationships over the years, but never anyone he wanted to stay with long-term. He didn't know why that was. Oh, he always had a reason. The timing wasn't right. He was on the road too much. His career had to come first. So, instead of looking for someone to build something with, he hopped onto Grindr or Scruff or one of the many hook-up apps and found someone when he wanted to have sex with no strings attached. Some of the guys he sometimes saw more than once, but Liam had never made the time for a relationship. He always believed once his career was established, then he could focus on having someone special in his life.

Well, he saw how that had worked out. His career was gone and he was alone. Maybe if he'd paid more attention to his personal life–tried to balance his career with a relationship–he wouldn't be going through this by himself.

Everyone came out on top of the scandal except him. Liam connected the dots when his agent stopped calling with auditions. When he asked Jerry what was going on, Jerry informed him that he was toxic and no one wanted to see him. Not for theatre. Not for commercials. Not for modeling. Liam knew things were bad when he couldn't even get hired as a singing and dancing waiter. There was a diner in Times Square where the staff performed for the customers in between serving food. It was a huge tourist attraction with lines around the block, but despite his resume and experience, they didn't want him, either. And this was a place where one started their career to get where Liam's career had once been, so it would have been a step back for him. He was stunned. It was like his one season on the show had erased all his years of hard work.

Everyone kept telling him to be patient. That

eventually it would all blow over. But so far, it hadn't. It had been eleven months since the reunion episode aired, and he hadn't had a job since. What was he supposed to do with the rest of his life?

Sebastian had been good to him, throwing him some work by letting him drive the truck for the Bakequeery, his traveling bake shop that went from borough to borough, as well as letting him frost cakes and cupcakes in the kitchen of his newly opened store on Tenth Avenue. But minimum wage wasn't going to keep him living in New York City. Thankfully, he'd always been a saver, so he had money in the bank, but that money wasn't going to last forever. Which meant he needed a job, any job.

So, now he sat in the little town of Bramford Hills in upstate New York, three hours outside of New York City, where he used to have a life, waiting to be interviewed for a job. But not an acting job. No, those days were over, at least for now. He was hoping it was only a temporary freeze. He knew people loved to hate a villain, but he kept reminding himself they also liked to see villains be redeemed. And even though he had been labelled a villain after his first– and only–season on *Real Gay Househusbands*, he wasn't.

He was jarred out of his thoughts when he heard footsteps behind him.

"Sorry to keep you waiting," a fortysomething woman with shoulder-length brown hair and a smoker's rasp apologized as she sat down behind her desk. "It's our busiest time of the year. Lots of temporary help is being hired for the holiday rush. I'm Eloise Morton." She held out her hand for Liam to shake—he took note of her long, red fingernails decorated with silver bells—and then flipped through a stack of papers on her desk. "Now, let's see if I can find your resume. Aha!" She waved a piece of paper in the air. "Here it is!" She lifted the oversized pink eyeglasses hanging on a chain around her neck and slid them over her blue eyes. She started reading. "So, Mr. Liam West from New York City, what brings you to Bramford Hills? Aren't you far from your home base?"

"I've relocated," he explained. "For a couple of weeks."

"How come?" She gazed at him over the top of her glasses, her eyes traveling up and down his body. "You don't look like a small-town guy. You've got that big city shine on you."

Big city shine? What did that mean? Was that good? Bad? Liam chose to take it as a compliment and gave her a smile. "My sister Penelope and brother-in-law Steve are going to be house-hunting in California. They leave the day after Thanksgiving. He's a lawyer starting a new job in Silicon Valley in January. They don't know how long it's going to take to find a new house, and they don't want to take my eight-year-old niece, Sarah, out of school, so it's Uncle Liam to the rescue."

The phone call from his sister had been the escape he'd been looking for. Penelope knew he was just sitting at home feeling sorry for himself, so when the offer to look after Sarah was presented, he jumped on it.

"You're an actor?" Eloise's voice cut into his thoughts.

"Yes, I am," he proudly stated. And he would be again, he silently vowed.

She tapped on his resume with her pen. "I see you have lots of jobs and then a dry spell. You haven't worked in more than a year. Is there something you're not telling me? Something I should maybe know about?"

Did he tell her or not? Obviously, she wasn't a watcher of reality TV or she would have instantly recognized him. Maybe that was good? He had sometimes been recognized while walking down the streets of New York City. On those occasions, he'd been hissed at or called Viper. Eloise didn't seem like the show's demographic, but then look what had happened with *RuPaul's Drag Race*. A show that had been created for gay men in 2009 was now huge with teenage girls and twentysomething women. He didn't want to lie, but if he mentioned *Gay House-husbands of NYC* and Eloise decided to Google him, the jig would be up. There was no way he'd be hired. He didn't want to lie, but what did he say?

He was saved from answering when Eloise announced, "You impress me. This town could use some big city shine." She stared intently at Liam. "I've got something in mind for you. The perfect job."

"You do?" Liam asked in shock.

Eloise confidently nodded. "Mmhmm."

When he'd come to Bailey's, it had been with the hopes of getting some sort of seasonal job. Department stores were always looking for part-time help at this time of year, and what was he going to do with himself all day when Sarah was in school? Watch game shows, followed by *The Young and the Restless* and *The Bold and the Beautiful*? He'd been expecting a job in the stock room or maybe even gift wrapping. But Eloise said she had something special in mind for him. He started getting excited, like he used to when he'd have an audition and left feeling confident he'd gotten the job.

"I do," Eloise confirmed with a smile. "How'd you like to work in Santaland?"

"Like it? I'd love it!" he exclaimed. This was even better than he'd expected. She was hiring him to play Santa. "How's this?" he asked, standing up and taking a deep breath before releasing a, "Ho-ho-ho! Merry Christmas!"

Eloise shook her head, crinkling her nose and squinting her eyes. "No, no, no. I'm not seeing you as Santa."

Liam collapsed back into his chair, flooded with disappointment. "You're not?"

"No, I'm not."

"How come?"

"Have you taken a good look at yourself in the mirror?" Eloise asked with a raised eyebrow. "You don't give off Santa vibes. I need someone older."

"But I'd be wearing a costume. And I'd have a belly. And a beard."

Eloise shook her head. "Sweetie, when I said you have a big city shine, I meant it as a compliment. You've got star quality. And no matter what you're wearing or how you're disguised, it's gonna come through."We're an old-fashioned store and we need an old-fashioned Santa. That's not you."

Liam's disappointment instantly faded away. Oh. Well. When Eloise put it that way…

"What did you have me in mind for?" he asked, feeling excited again.

"An elf!" Eloise announced.

"Did you say *elf?*" Liam asked, trying not to sound shocked but failing.

"Uh huh. You know what an elf is, right? One of Santa's helpers. They make the toys."

"Yes…" Liam slowly answered as images of Will Ferrell suddenly filled his mind.

Eloise's eyes narrowed. "You got a problem with being a Christmas elf? Because if you do, I've got plenty of other applicants I can choose from."

"No! No problem at all," Liam said with his biggest smile. The last thing he wanted to do was piss off Eloise. "But don't elves need to be a little smaller? Shorter? More compact?"

"We're an equal opportunity employer, and right now we need elves of all shapes, sizes, and ethnicities. Are you interested or not?" Eloise was all business.

"I'm interested."

Eloise nodded with satisfaction. "Good."

"What's the job entail?"

"You stand by Santa's side, help the kiddies get on and off Santa's lap, hand them a candy cane, and then move on to the next one."

"Sounds easy enough."

Eloise shook her head. "It isn't. You've also got to control the parents. They try to sneak in line with their own cameras and take pictures of their little ones on Santa's lap. That's a big no-no at Bailey's. If they want a picture of their little angel on Santa's lap, then they have to buy the authorized photo taken by the store."

"What happens if they take a photo?"

"You delete it."

"How do I delete it?"

"First, you ask them politely," Eloise explained. "If they refuse, then you call over someone from store security and they'll take over."

"Sounds messy." Liam suddenly had visions of himself tangling with entitled Karens who were going nuclear on him. Plenty of those videos showed up on his Instagram and X feed on a daily basis.

"There are signs posted all over Santaland that say there are no personal photos allowed. If they break the rules, we're allowed to do whatever it is we need to do. Got it?"

Liam gulped. "Got it."

Eloise uncapped her pen. "How soon can you start?"

"As soon as you want me."

"The holiday season goes into full swing next Friday, the week before Thanksgiving. No better time to get started. Welcome to Santaland!"

After filling out a number of forms, Liam left Eloise's office with instructions to report back the next day when he'd be measured for his elf costume. He kept reminding himself that he needed a job, and for the next six weeks he'd be earning a paycheck. Besides, he wouldn't be the world's first gay elf. That honor went to Hermey, the gay elf and BFF of Rudolph the red-nosed reindeer, who wanted to be a dentist. He would be in esteemed company.

He could do this, he kept telling himself. He could get through the next six weeks and be an elf. He should be thankful. Happy. Grateful. He was finally working again. How bad could being an elf be? It couldn't possibly be the worst job in the world, could it?

CHAPTER
TWO
TWO WEEKS LATER...

"I hate Christmas!" Liam exclaimed.

At the sound of a gasp, he whirled around. Standing in his bedroom doorway, an expression of absolute horror on her face, was his eight-year-old niece, Sarah.

"Take it back, Uncle Liam," she begged, rushing into his room and wrapping her arms around his waist, gazing up at him with pleading blue eyes. "Take it back or Santa won't bring you any presents."

"Okay, okay, I take it back," Liam said, seeing that Sarah was upset and wanting to calm her down. He needed to be more careful about what he said around her. As much as he was hating the holiday season this year, he didn't want to spoil it for her. He gave her a hug and a kiss on the top of her blonde head. "Satisfied?"

"Yes," she answered, a big smile on her face. "Now you won't be on Santa's naughty list." She stepped away from Liam and sat on his bed, clutching a pillow. "Are you going to work?"

He twirled around in a circle. "Why else would I be dressed like this?"

Liam turned to see his image in the bedroom mirror, cringing at what he saw. He was wearing green tights, green shorts, and a striped green and white turtleneck. On his head was a pointy red felt hat, and on his feet were curled red slippers with bells around the ankles. He looked like the latest villain from a *Batman* movie.

It was the worst job in the world.

Over the years, Liam had had jobs that he'd hated, but this one took the cake. He was in hell, only it was a hell decorated for Christmas. He'd only been on the job for two weeks, but he was ready to quit. Four hours a day, three days a week, and all day on either Saturday or Sunday, he stood on his feet in Santaland, trying to look merry. It wasn't easy. Most of the kids were afraid to sit on Santa's lap and turned into little devils, kicking and screaming—even biting!—as he tried to lead them to Santa. You would think that a child waiting in line to see Santa and tell him what they wanted for Christmas would at least try to portray angelic behavior, but no. Still, it was his job, as an elf, to keep the line moving, to help the little ones hop onto Santa's lap, to allow them time to tell Santa what they wanted and then move them along so the next waiting child could take center stage.

But some of these kids didn't want to move. They wanted more than their allotted time with Santa. And their Christmas lists! It boggled his mind. Did they really think they were going to get everything they asked for? And their parents were no help. They allowed the bad behavior, begging and pleading for "just one more minute" with Santa. In the beginning, he tried to be accommodating, but when he saw how those extra minutes added up and resulted in the line becoming backed up, he put an end to it. He kept moving the kids along like the speedy conveyor belt of chocolate on that episode of *I Love Lucy.*

And then there were the pictures. As Eloise had warned him, despite all the NO PERSONAL PHOTOS signs plastered everywhere in Santaland, a number of parents sneakily tried to take their own. Some days, Liam looked the other way when it came to the sneaky photos. But when a parent blatantly ignored the sign and started directing their child to look into the camera, that was where he drew the line. First, he told them to stop taking photos. Most of the time, they listened. But the stubborn ones who refused? Well, as expected, they became nasty/entitled/arrogant—take your pick of obnoxious adjectives—and Liam had to call Security to escort them out of Santaland and watch as they deleted the photos while listening to a barrage of insults. Fun times, for sure.

Liam grabbed his wallet and stuck it in his back pocket. Then, he sorted through the change on top of his dresser, making sure he had enough for the bus. He hated wearing this outfit in public, but he had no choice. The employee locker room at Bailey's was under construction and wouldn't be ready until next week, so he had to get dressed at home. And he couldn't drive to Bailey's because his sister Penelope's car was getting a new engine and he was waiting for the garage to call when it was ready to be picked up. He'd already gotten his fair share of curious stares when he was on the bus. His parka covered the top part of his costume but not the bottom, revealing his green tights and the pointy red slippers with curled toes and bells around his ankles.

He was so over it. When was his life going to get back to normal?

Smothering a sigh, Liam headed downstairs to the first floor and pulled his blue parka out of the hall closet. As he wrapped a scarf around his neck, Sarah came downstairs in her own bright pink parka, holding a letter in her mittened hand.

"Whatcha got there?" he asked, pointing to the letter. "Don't you have..." Liam closed his eyes, trying to remember what class Sarah had that afternoon, "...ballet with your friend, Janie?"

Penelope and her husband had been gone for a week. Before leaving, Penelope had given Liam a copy of Sarah's after-school schedule. As he read it, his eyes had bugged out. Every hour of Sarah's day was jam-packed with extracurricular activities. When she wasn't in school, she had some sort of class. Ballet, gymnastics, ice skating, basketball. It was insane! What happened to the days when a kid came home from school, grabbed a snack from the fridge, watched some cartoons, and then ran outside to play with the other neighborhood kids?

Sarah rolled her blue eyes in exasperation. "I hate ballet class."

"If you hate it, why do you go?" Liam asked, genuinely curious.

"Because Mommy signed me up."

Liam bit back a sigh. His sister Penelope could be president of the Tiger Mom club. She was so focused on making sure Sarah had every advantage that she didn't think to ask what her daughter might want to do with her free time.

Liam had been in charge of Sarah since Penelope and Steve left for California the day after Thanksgiving. Since then, it had been just the two of them. When he had to work, Penelope's next-door neighbor, Babs Morris, who reminded Liam of Annie Potts as Meemaw from *Young Sheldon*, came over to watch Sarah, delivered her to her after school activities when she had them, or brought her over to her house when her grandchildren were visiting. On those days, when she just got to hang out with Babs' grandkids, the smile on Sarah's face was always brighter and happier when he came home from work and picked her up. Maybe it was because she was just being a kid and enjoying herself, with no pressure to learn something or become better at it. The first time he saw that smile, he decided that for the next few weeks he was going to let Sarah do whatever she wanted to do. Within reason. He wasn't going to disregard his sister's instructions–he'd keep Sarah to her schedule—but that didn't mean he wouldn't try to sneak in some Uncle Liam fun time.

"I'll tell you what. How about, as a reward for going to ballet class, we go to a movie this weekend? Anything you want to see."

"Even an R-rated movie?"

"How do you know about R-rated movies?"

"Janie's older sister, Michelle, goes to them all the time. She says only babies go to G-rated movies."

"No R-rated movies," Liam said. "But how does a PG-13 movie sound?" He was sure he could find a mild PG-13 comedy.

"Okay, but it's our secret, right? If Mommy asks, we went to see the new Minions movie. Deal?"

Liam crossed his heart and held out his hand for Sarah to shake. "Deal."

"Deal!" Sarah confirmed, crossing her own heart and shaking her uncle's hand.

"And if you really hate ballet class," Liam continued, "I'll talk to your mom when she gets back. Maybe there's some other class you could take instead."

Sarah's whole face lit up with a smile. "Really, Uncle Liam?"

He nodded. "Really."

"Yay!" She threw her arms up in the air. "You're the best!"

"Ready to go to Janie's?"

She shook her head. "Not yet. I have to do something first."

"What?"

She waved the letter she was holding in front of his face. "I have to mail this."

"Who are you sending it to?" he asked, reaching for the letter, curious.

She snatched her hand away so he couldn't grab it. "Santa Claus."

Liam nodded slowly. "Of course. Santa Claus. I should have known. It is that time of year."

"It is," Sarah confirmed, her voice serious.

"I could mail it for you," Liam offered.

Sarah stubbornly shook her head as she carefully put the letter in her parka pocket. "No. I want to do it myself. I have to make sure it gets to him."

"Okay, then let's hit the road. First stop, the mailbox, then Janie's house."

Liam held his hand out to Sarah, who grasped it, and together they left the house and walked to the mailbox down the street. Sarah wasn't tall enough to reach the top of the box, so Liam lifted her up and used one hand to open the mail slot. Sarah instantly slipped her letter inside and Liam closed the lid, then opened it again so Sarah could see it had gone down inside.

"How long do you think it will take to get to Santa?" she asked, once Liam put her back down on the sidewalk.

Liam shrugged. "I don't know. The North Pole is pretty far away. Maybe a couple of days?"

Sarah thought about that. "Christmas is still a long way away. But he'll have enough time to read my letter and then answer it."

"What did you ask Santa for?"

Sarah gasped. "I can't tell you!"

"Why not?"

"Because if I do," Sarah patiently explained, "Santa won't make it happen. It's a secret between Santa and me."

"Can you give me a hint?" Liam pinched two fingers together. "Just a little one?"

Sarah shook her head. "Nope. If I tell you, it won't happen." Sarah tugged on Liam's arm. "Come on. We have to get to Janie's."

He would have thought Sarah and Janie hadn't seen each other in months, rather than just a few hours earlier at school, they were so excited. As they raced up to Janie's bedroom to change into their ballet outfits, he had a short conversation with Janie's mom, Lynda, who was taking the girls to class and then dinner afterward. The mention of dinner reminded Liam that he needed to go grocery shopping. In terms of meals, there had been plenty of Thanksgiving leftovers–his sister always overcooked–but those were just about gone. He was going to have to start planning future meals and making sure the refrigerator was fully stocked.

After confirming the time he would pick Sarah up, Liam said his goodbyes and headed to the bus stop, still wondering what Sarah had asked Santa for. He'd try quizzing her again tonight when he tucked her into bed so he could pass along anything he learned to her parents. Although, knowing his sister, she'd probably gotten nothing but educational toys for his niece. He sighed. Penelope, who worked in finance and made gobs of money, was determined to mold Sarah in her image, but he had the sense that Sarah wasn't like his sister.

Dare he admit that maybe she had a little bit of her Uncle Liam in her? Well, if she did, he hoped she had more common sense than he had and when she was grown up, she wouldn't make a mess of her life the way he had.

The year would be over soon, he reminded

himself. And when a new year started, he would focus on getting his life back on track, both personally and professionally. For now, as hard as it was, he just had to get through the holiday season.

It started to snow while Liam waited for the bus. Soon, his teeth began chattering, and he shoved his gloved hands deep into his pockets. Where was the bus? It was already ten minutes late.

Liam stepped off the sidewalk and looked down the street. He tried to watch where he was walking because it had rained the night before and there were deep puddles. At that moment, a car with a Christmas tree tied to its roof sped by. Knowing what was going to happen, Liam tried to jump back to the curb, but he was too slow and found himself splashed.

"I don't care what anyone says," Liam grumbled, wiping away the excess water on his parka and face. "Scrooge had the right idea. Christmas? Bah, humbug!"

CHAPTER
THREE

Charlie Fisher was a Christmas nut. He would be the first to admit it, and proudly, he thought to himself as he made his way to the town post office for one of his favorite holiday traditions.

When the fall season started in September, Charlie started counting down the days until he could pull out his Christmas decorations and put them up. The day after Halloween, all the spooky decorations came down, and all the Christmas stuff came out. And there was a *lot* of Christmas stuff.

There were the brightly colored Christmas lights hung on the front porch—solid colored bulbs, not twinkling bulbs. The sleigh with Santa and his reindeer positioned on top of the garage, Rudolph's red nose blinking on and off. His Dickens Christmas village was set up in the living room on top of the coffee table. The Christmas stuffies positioned in rooms around the house–Charlie Brown, Linus, Lucy, Sally, Snoopy, Frosty, Rudolph, Clarice, Hermie, Santa, the Grinch, and Max.

The Christmas music! Holiday albums from Michael Buble`, Harry Connick, Jr., Nat King Cole, Frank Sinatra, Dean Martin, Bette Midler, and others. A constant rotation of Christmas classics wafted through all the rooms of his house.

And then there were the Christmas movies and specials: *A Charlie Brown Christmas*, *The Year Without a Santa Claus*, *Rudolph the Red-Nosed Reindeer*, *How the Grinch Stole Christmas* (the animated version only!), *It's a Wonderful Life*, *Christmas in Connecticut*, *Remember the Night*, *A Christmas Carol* (the 1938 version with Alistair Cooke), and then the contemporary version, *Scrooged*, starring Bill Murray. Not to mention *Elf*, *A Christmas Story*, *Home for the Holidays*, and *Home Alone*.

Finally, there were the trees. Yes, trees, plural. His main Christmas tree–always real–was purchased on the first day of December and set up in the position of honor in the front window of his house. It would be decorated only with his most favorite ornaments—the ones he had made in his childhood with colored tissue paper, pipe cleaners, and Styrofoam cups, as well as fragile glass ornaments handed down to him from his grandparents—draped with strands of blinking white lights, tinsel, and candy canes. But until that day arrived, there were the artificial trees. The one he put in his dining room (a metallic silver tree—shades of the 1960s!), not to mention the one in his kitchen (an evergreen dusted with snow) and the petite Christmas tree he put on his bedroom dresser. Plus, there were the holiday pillows, the holiday welcome mats, the Nativity scene, and the snowglobes.

But the best part of the holiday season—the very best part—was when he went to the post office and answered a letter written to Santa. Over the years, every letter he answered had the writer asking Santa for a specific kind of toy, which Charlie was usually able to get and make the child's Christmas wish come true. So, here he was this morning, ready to receive this year's letter from a Bramford Hills postal worker. The letters that were addressed to Santa c/o Bramford Hills were kept by their post office and then shared with those who wanted to make a child's Christmas happy.

The letter Charlie received wasn't what he

expected. It was different from letters he had read in the past. Very different. This little girl wasn't asking for a present for herself. No, she wanted Santa to do something for someone else. He read the letter more than once, and each time, he couldn't believe how sweet it was. Whoever this Uncle Liam was, his niece Sarah loved him very much and wanted to make his Christmas special.

He reread the letter for a fourth time.

Dear Santa,

All I want for Christmas this year is for my Uncle Liam to be happy. He used to have a boyfriend, but he doesn't anymore. That's when he really got sad. Could you help my uncle find a new boyfriend, Santa? If you do, I'll be very happy and you wouldn't have to bring me any presents. Well, I mean this year. Hopefully you'll bring me some next year because I always try to be good. Thank you.

Love,

Sarah Williams

There was another page attached to the letter, listing Liam's likes and dislikes, as well as where he worked. When he finished reading the second page, Charlie refolded the letter, slipped it into his back-pack, and left the post office.

As he walked home, thinking about the letter

he'd write back to Sarah, Charlie admired the houses in his neighborhood that were starting to be decorated. Brightly colored Christmas lights were strung along porches and around windows, while other houses avoided colored bulbs and went only with white lights. Plastic snowmen, Christmas angels, reindeer, and Santa Clauses stood on front lawns, and wreaths heavy with ornaments and bows hung from front doors and windows. It was all so merry!

When he got home, Charlie kicked off his boots and hung his leather jacket up on the coat rack. His black cat, Shadow, came running when he heard the front door open, and Charlie spent the required five minutes petting and cooing over him. Then, to warm himself up, he went into the kitchen to fix himself a cup of hot chocolate with marshmallows, Shadow following after him.

When the hot chocolate was ready, Charlie brought it into the living room, settling down on the couch while Shadow nestled by his side. As he sipped his hot chocolate, Charlie admired the decorated room. The tree was in the front window, red stockings trimmed with white hung over the fireplace, and his first Christmas cards were positioned on the mantel. There were no presents under the tree yet, but that would be fixed soon.

And speaking of fixing things...

Charlie unzipped his backpack and found Sarah's letter. He read it one more time and then got a pen and paper, writing a letter back to her from Santa. He kept the letter short, telling Sarah not to worry. He would use all the Christmas magic he could muster to make her wish come true. He'd try his best to make it happen by Christmas, but he couldn't promise that it would. It could take a little more time. And if it did, she should tell her Uncle Liam about her letter since he would still be happy knowing how much Sarah loved him. Because telling someone you loved them was always nice to hear. When he finished the letter, Charlie folded it up and stuck it in the self-addressed stamped envelope Sarah had enclosed. Then, he put his boots and jacket back on and headed for the nearest mailbox. Only after he mailed the letter did Charlie realize there was one small problem.

He didn't have a clue as to how he would make Sarah's Christmas wish come true.

———

After spending all night giving it some thought, Charlie finally figured out the solution to his problem. That wasn't to say he hadn't panicked at first. After all, other than Sarah's letter, he knew absolutely nothing about Uncle Liam. But after calming himself down, he realized the best way to solve his problem was to see the problem firsthand. Liam West needed a boyfriend, but before Charlie could find him one, he needed to see him. Seeing him in person would give Charlie a sense of the type of man Liam was. Maybe he'd even talk to him. He hadn't figured out a strategy yet, but he would. He had to. Otherwise, Sarah was going to be a very disappointed little girl on Christmas morning.

The first step in finding Uncle Liam a boyfriend would be to go to Bailey's. Sarah's letter said her uncle worked in Santaland as an elf, so that's where he'd start. Even though he hadn't met Liam yet, he liked him. How could he not? After all, he had to love Christmas as much as he did, otherwise he wouldn't be working in Santaland.

When Charlie arrived at Bailey's, he headed to the tenth floor, expecting to find a line of little ones and their parents waiting to meet Santa. Yet, when he arrived, Santaland was deserted. No Santa. No elves. A sign in front of Santa's throne said Santa would be back in an hour. Charlie decided he would do some Christmas shopping and come back.

An hour later, Charlie had found a beaded sweater for his mother and a Dr. Seuss Grinch tie for his father, as well as a few things for himself. Who could resist a Christmas discount? Checking his phone, he decided to head back to Santaland. Hopefully, Liam would be there.

The elevator was empty when Charlie stepped into it. He pressed the button for the tenth floor and waited for the doors to close. As they did, a hand reached out to shove the doors open. A man in his early thirties, wearing jeans and a navy blue parka, stepped into the elevator.

Charlie usually wasn't speechless around handsome guys, but this one was gorgeous. Movie star handsome. He was over six feet tall, muscular, with a face that rivaled Brad Pitt's and the most amazing green eyes.

Maybe in addition to finding Uncle Liam a boyfriend, Charlie might find one for himself, too. He hadn't been dating anyone since February, when his last relationship had ended. Oh, wouldn't that be a story to tell his friends? While playing Cupid for Uncle Liam, he found his own Mr. Right.

Charlie firmly believed in true love and happily ever afters. Even though he hadn't found someone special yet, he knew the man of his dreams was somewhere out there. They just hadn't crossed paths yet. But he couldn't worry about that now. Right now, he had to help Liam find the man of *his* dreams.

He started to smile at the guy–how could he not?–until he noticed the glare on his face. No, not a glare. More like a snarl. And it was aimed directly at him.

"Are you deaf?" the man harshly demanded. "I called out and asked you to hold the elevator."

His surly tone stunned Charlie. Then, he found his voice. "I didn't hear you," he explained. "Sorry."

"Yeah, right," he grumbled, pressing the same button Charlie had already pushed.

If there was one thing Charlie hated, it was being called a liar. "I didn't hear you," he insisted.

"You could have checked to see if anyone was coming," the man said.

Ordinarily, Charlie would just hold his tongue. But this guy was starting to get on his nerves. "Do I look like an elevator operator?" Charlie snipped, injecting a bit of edgy tone into his voice. Two could play at this game.

"Ever hear of common courtesy?"

"Ever hear of cutting someone some slack?" Charlie shot back. What was this jerk's problem? He had apologized to him, but this guy didn't want to let it go. It was like he was looking for a fight. What more did he want? "Do I look like I have eyes in the back of my head?" he couldn't resist adding. "I didn't see you. I said I was sorry. Let's move on."

The man covered his ears. "This Christmas music is driving me crazy."

'All I Want for Christmas' was being piped into the elevator through the department store's sound system. Charlie started humming along with the song. "Who doesn't love Diva Mariah's 'All I Want For Christmas'? It's my favorite song during my favorite time of the year."

"It's not my favorite time of the year," the guy complained.

Charlie stared at him in shock. "Why not?"

"Because I hate Christmas!" he exclaimed. "I hate everything about it." He began counting on his fingers. "The tree. The carols. The gifts. The cards. I can't wait until the holiday season is over."

He hated Christmas? Charlie was horrified. How could anyone hate Christmas? It was the most wonderful time of the year. He knew it would sound cliché, but it was like magic was in the air during the month of December. And this guy hated it?

He moved to one side of the elevator. He couldn't wait to get away from this guy. He checked the panel above the elevator doors as they ascended toward the tenth floor. Two. Three. Five. Just a few more seconds.

But then, the elevator came to a halt. Charlie waited for it to start moving again, but it didn't. He pressed a few of the floor buttons on the panel, but nothing happened. He did it again and again and again, but the elevator still didn't move.

He turned to the man, panic in his voice. "We're stuck!"

———

Liam sighed.

Stuck. He was stuck in an elevator. Why didn't that surprise him with the way his day had been going?

There had been no hot water at the house this morning, so he'd had to take a shower so cold that his teeth had been chattering. After the plumber came and fixed the water heater, Bailey's called and asked him to come in at four o'clock instead of six because someone was sick. The extra hours meant more money, but still, he hated wearing that elf costume. At least the dressing room was finally finished, so he hadn't had to wear his costume in public.

But now, he was stuck in an elevator with Mr. Christmas.

"What are we going to do?" the guy asked, his voice rising with panic.

"Calm down," Liam said. With his luck, the guy was probably claustrophobic. At any second, he expected him to start climbing the elevator walls, screaming to be let out. He chuckled, thinking of the 1964 horror movie, *Lady In A Cage*, starring Olivia de Havilland. For the entire movie, she had been trapped in a tiny elevator in her home while a band of juvenile delinquents broke into her house and terrorized her. It seemed like she was constantly screaming, "I'm a lady trapped in a cage!"

"Is something funny?" Mr. Christmas snapped. "Because I'm not amused by this situation!"

"Calm down, Kris Kringle," Liam said, reaching for the emergency phone and calling the maintenance department. "Someone will get us moving again."

"Will it take long?"

Liam hung up the phone and shrugged. "Depends on what the problem is. We could be here for five minutes or five hours." He sat down on the floor, hoping it would take a while before the elevator started moving again. The longer he was stuck, the less time he had to wear his elf costume. In the meantime, he might as well make the best of it.

"Why don't you sit down?" he suggested. "You're going to get tired of standing up."

At first, he thought the guy was going to disagree with him, but then he nodded and slumped down on the floor.

"Looks like you've been Christmas shopping," Liam said, pointing to all his bags.

"Do you have a problem with Christmas shopping?" the guy asked, his voice dripping with acid.

"Hey, I'm just trying to make conversation."

Mr. Christmas reached into his jacket and pulled out a pair of earbuds. "I'll listen to a podcast, thank you very much."

Twenty minutes later, the elevator started moving again, much to Liam's relief. He and Mr. Christmas hadn't spoken at all, ignoring each other while glued to their phones. Every so often, he found the man staring at him like he was some sort of freak. Okay, he'd been rude by biting his head off the way he had, but everyone was entitled to a bad day. Or was the guy recognizing him from *The Gay Househusbands*? That didn't happen as often as it used to, but it still happened on occasion. And when it did, it wasn't a pleasant experience. So far, no one in Bramford Hills had recognized him.

He thought about apologizing to him, but when the elevator doors opened, the guy raced out without even saying goodbye.

Liam shrugged. Oh, well. He'd probably never see him again.

After changing into his elf costume, Liam headed to Santaland. He could see a line of kids already waiting, and Santa was sitting on his throne. As he walked past the elevators, one of the maintenance men called out to him.

"Hey, Liam, you'll do anything to get out of working in Santaland, won't you?"

Liam laughed at the older man's words. "I didn't have anything to do with that elevator getting stuck, Evan."

"I'll bet," Evan said, closing up his toolbox.

Liam reached Santaland and walked down a snow-covered path. Both sides of the path were decorated with huge candy canes. As he walked, Liam smiled at the waiting kids. He was supposed to be happy and jolly because he was one of Santa's elves. But it was hard when he really didn't have any Christmas spirit left.

———

Hiding behind a Christmas tree so he wouldn't be spotted, Charlie watched as Liam walked into Santaland.

He couldn't believe what he'd just heard.

This was Sarah Williams' uncle? This was the guy he had to find a boyfriend for?

This...this Scrooge?!

Forget it.

CHAPTER
FOUR

But he couldn't forget it.

There was the letter. Sarah's letter. Which he had already answered and mailed back to her. Santa had said he would try to find a new boyfriend for her Uncle Liam. He had to make an effort even though he thought her uncle was a jerk. Correction, a huge jerk.

The only question was how he was going to do it. He couldn't possibly find Liam a new boyfriend.

Or could he?

He had to at least try to make Sarah's Christmas wish come true. She wanted a new boyfriend for her uncle. He had to find that boyfriend. But how? By finding another Christmas Scrooge?

Charlie sighed and took a deep breath. He could

do this. He had to do this. He had to put his personal feelings to one side. He and Liam hadn't gotten along. Fine. It didn't mean Liam wouldn't get along with somebody else. He just had to find that somebody else. But how? He gave it some thought and realized he needed to approach the situation logically. Before Liam could have a boyfriend, he needed to meet someone. And how did people meet other people? The light bulb went on over Charlie's head. On a date. That was it! He would set Liam up on a couple of dates, and hopefully he would click with one of the guys he went out with.

So, next question. How did he find these dates?

Charlie's phone buzzed with a text, and as he pulled it out of his back pocket, he realized he was holding the answer in his hand. He had friends. Lots of single friends. All he had to do was set one up on a date with Liam. He just needed to decide which one.

Charlie started scrolling through his contacts until his eyes fell on the name of his best friend, J.P., who was currently single. Well, eternally single by choice after having his heart broken by his college sweetheart, but he wasn't going to go there today. He pressed on J.P.'s name and listened to the phone ring before it was answered.

"J.P.!" he exclaimed.

"Charlie, what's up?"

"What are you doing?"

"Babysitting my niece, Nora."

"Perfect!" Charlie knew Nora was six years old. And what six-year-old didn't want to visit Santa? "Come down to Bailey's and bring Nora with you. I'm at Santaland on the tenth floor."

"Why?"

"I'll explain everything once you get here. Just trust me."

Thirty minutes later, J.P. arrived at Bailey's, along with his niece, whom Charlie always felt was the living, breathing version of Ramona Geraldine Quimby from Beverly Cleary's beloved children's classic. She had the same dark pixie cut with bangs and the same amount of spunk and sass.

She was tugging on her uncle's arm with one hand as he tried to steer her toward Charlie, but she was determined to check out a display of gingerbread houses. In her other hand, she held a hot dog bursting with sauerkraut and mustard, taking huge bites and talking with her mouth full. Finally, J.P. let go of her hand. "You can look at the gingerbread houses, but stay where I can see you, okay?"

She nodded before dashing off.

"That kid has more energy than the Tasmanian

devil," J.P. said as they kept an eye on her. "Plus, she's been a munch-mouth all day, eating non-stop. Give me some of her metabolism." J.P. patted his flat stomach. "I'm already starting to put on the holiday weight."

"Stop it!" Charlie scolded. "You look great. You always do."

And he did. J.P., short for John Peter, was one of Charlie's oldest friends. With his blond hair and piercing blue eyes, he looked like he belonged on a California beach with a surfboard under his arm. They had met when they were freshmen attending an all-boys Catholic high school. That first year, they had been in all of the same classes and learned to navigate the scary world of high school together, instantly bonding over so many of the same interests: old movies, daytime soaps, nighttime soaps, comic books, and a love of horror novels. Then, too, there was their shared interest in guys, which they never openly admitted to. Instead, they always danced around it when they would talk about which TV actors or movie stars or musicians they liked. When they were in high school, Charlie always suspected J.P. was gay, and wanted to tell him he was also gay, but in the late 2000s, being a gay teenager still wasn't something that was easy to talk about the way it was today. When they graduated from high school, Charlie couldn't keep his secret any longer and worked up his courage on the last day of summer before they went off to college, confessing all to J.P., who made a confession of his own: he was gay, too. It solidified their friendship even more.

"How goes the writing?" Charlie asked, knowing J.P. had started a new play. Over the years, J.P. had had a number of off-Broadway plays produced. He hadn't had a breakout success yet, but it was going to eventually happen. With each show, the reviews kept getting better and the runs kept getting longer. But to supplement his income as a struggling play-wright, J.P. also taught English at the local high school.

J.P. ignored the question. "I know I shouldn't gloat, but listen to this," he announced. "Guess who's doing dinner theatre in Henderson?"

Henderson was one town over from Bramford Hills, around an hour away.

Before Charlie could take a guess, J.P. gleefully blurted out, "Sam!"

Charlie groaned. Sam was the name that was never to be spoken, except by J.P. when he brought it up. Which he never did, unless, of course, he was on a rant about how horrible Sam was.

Sam had been J.P.'s college sweetheart. They met while working on one of J.P.'s one-act plays during their sophomore year–J.P. was in their college's writing program, studying to be a playwright, while Sam was in their acting program–and it had been love at first sight. After that, they were joined at the hip, making plans for their future and the careers they were going to have. That is, until a talent showcase during their senior year landed Sam a Hollywood agent who got him a supporting role in a sitcom. At the first whiff of success, Sam dumped J.P. and hightailed it to the West Coast.

J.P., naturally, had been devastated. There had been no discussion, no conversation, just a farewell note from Sam that he found in his dorm room, telling J.P. that he needed to focus on his career and he didn't have time for love and romance. After that, it was like J.P.'s heart had hardened. Every so often, there was a random boyfriend, but nothing long-term. They'd be around for a few weeks and then would be gone. It was almost as if J.P. was afraid of getting too close and having his heart broken again. Instead, his main focus was always on his playwriting.

Meanwhile, Sam's sitcom lasted a few years, but it was never really a show that took off in the ratings.

After it was cancelled, he did some other TV shows, but never made the leap to movies. Whatever his last TV show was–Charlie thought maybe it had been a crime procedural–it was cancelled two years ago. The work must have really dried up if Sam was now doing dinner theatre.

"He's doing *A Christmas Carol*, playing Scrooge. Talk about perfect casting. Scrooge didn't know how to love, and neither did Sam!"

Charlie knew he was going to need to bring this down quickly before J.P. went into a Sam-bashing spiral. Not that he blamed him. "Are we planning to get tickets to this show?"

"Of course not!" J.P. exclaimed. "But that's not going to stop me from leaving some anonymous reviews online, tearing his performance to shreds."

Charlie groaned. "Do you really want to do that?"

"Why not? He deserves it. He broke my heart."

"Yes. Ten years ago!" Charlie proceeded with caution. He didn't want J.P. to think he was disregarding his feelings, because he wasn't. "Don't you want to put the past behind you and move on? Why give him any more of your time and energy?"

"Because I gave him my heart and he stomped it to pieces, that's why! The lure of Hollywood and a

TV show was too much for him to resist, and I was collateral damage."

Charlie had liked Sam and had been hurt over the way he had betrayed his friend. He really thought they'd had something special. Charlie would never say this to J.P., but sometimes he wondered if some of J.P.'s anger had to do with the fact that Sam had made his dream of becoming an actor come true, while J.P. was still struggling with his.

"But don't you want more? Don't you want what you and Sam used to have, only with someone else?"

"Oh, Charlie, you're such a romantic. And that's one of the things I love about you. But we can't have everything we want. Sometimes you have to settle for less."

"Then, how about settling for that?" Charlie asked, taking J.P. by the shoulders, turning him around and pointing his finger toward Liam. "That should take your mind off Sam, don't you think?"

J.P.'s eyes lit up. "Yum! What do you know about him?"

"I know he's single." Charlie deliberately omitted Liam's lack of Christmas cheer and bouts of grouchiness. If there was one guy who could put a smile on someone's face and make their day brighter, it was

J.P. Hollis. Maybe Liam needed someone like him in his life.

"How do you know that?"

Charlie filled J.P. in on Sarah's Christmas letter. "How about helping me make a little girl's Christmas wish come true? While you're waiting for Nora to have her picture taken with Santa, you can chat him up."

"Good plan," J.P. said. "I like it. Nice and natural. All we need now is Nora."

In the few seconds they had shifted their gaze from Nora to Liam, Nora had taken it upon herself to rip the chimney off a gingerbread house and was gnawing on it.

"Nora!" J.P. wailed, storming over to her. "What are you doing?"

"Having dessert," she explained. She held out the white frosted chimney. "Want a bite?"

J.P. gazed at the price tag on the gingerbread house and his eyes bugged out. "You're having a seventy-five-dollar dessert!"

Charlie took the gingerbread house off the shelf. "I'll go pay for this. You two wait in line for Santa."

J.P. took Nora by her sticky hand. "Come on."

Charlie watched the two head off to Santaland, feeling quite proud of himself. Operation

Boyfriend was underway. By the time Nora had her picture taken, J.P. and Liam would have chatted and maybe even exchanged phone numbers.

He watched as J.P. and Nora joined the line, moving closer to Liam and Santa. But then something went wrong when they reached Liam. As he reached out to Nora to place her on Santa's lap, she clutched her stomach as her face turned a light shade of green.

"Oh, no," Charlie whispered. "No..."

Charlie knew what that stomach clutch meant.

And so did Liam, for he instantly held Nora far away from his body.

But it was too late.

"I don't feel so good," Nora wailed. "I'm gonna be sick."

And then, Nora barfed.

Everywhere.

Seconds later, chaos broke out. Little boys and girls started shrieking, but it wasn't only that. It was like Nora's barfing set off a chain reaction. Another little girl clutched her stomach, then a little boy, followed by another and another, and soon the line in Santaland was filled with retching children emptying out their stomachs.

Everyone scrambled to get away, and within seconds, Santaland was cleared out.

"I'll talk to you later," J.P. said to Charlie as he hurried past him with a wailing Nora in his arms. "It's okay, honey," he cooed. "You're going to be fine. You just have an upset tummy. When we get home, I'll give you some Pepto-Bismol and ginger ale."

Charlie watched J.P. and Nora disappear into an empty elevator. Then, he heard a voice behind him.

"I guess I should thank your friend's little girl," Liam said. "She's closed Santaland until the janitors can get here and clean up the mess."

"She's his niece." Charlie turned around. "And you look relieved," he observed. "Had your fill of kiddies today?" A thought suddenly occurred to him. If Liam hated Christmas so much, what was he doing working in Santaland? "Don't you like your job?" he blurted out before he could stop himself.

Liam shrugged. "It's a job."

"But a great job, right? You're spreading the magic of Christmas."

"It's not as easy as it looks. Trust me. And have you seen the outfit I'm wearing?"

"You wear it well."

And Charlie meant it. He didn't know what sort of fabric Liam's costume was made of, but it was tight and stretchy and clung in all the right places, bringing attention to his very fit body. Finding a boyfriend for Liam should be a slam dunk. If things didn't click with J.P., all he had to do was show a picture of Liam in this outfit, and it would be a very sexy Christmas for one of his lucky friends.

"Thanks. It's only for six weeks until I head back to New York City."

"You don't live here?" Sarah hadn't mentioned that in her letter.

"I'm taking care of my niece for a few weeks while her parents are out of town. And I absolutely love and adore her. But let's just say between Sarah and the munchkins I deal with every day, I've had my fill of kids."

"But kids are great!" Charlie exclaimed.

"Says the man who doesn't have any, am I right?"

"Well, yes," Charlie admitted. "I'd like to have kids someday, but first I need to find a boyfriend. And it needs to be a boyfriend who wants a family, too. Not so easy to find."

Why was he telling all of this to Liam? It was like he had lost control of his mouth. He was supposed to find him a boyfriend, not talk about himself. This conversation needed to shift immediately.

"I saw you chatting with my friend, J.P.," Charlie said.

"The guy I should be indebted to for this mini-break?"

Charlie nodded. "He's single."

"Uh huh."

Not the reaction Charlie was expecting. Why wasn't Liam bombarding him with questions, wanting to know more? "Aren't you single?"

"How would you know that?" Liam gave Charlie a suspicious look. "And if I am, how would you know I'm interested in dating guys?"

Charlie couldn't let Liam know about Sarah's letter. It would spoil the surprise. He was sure once Liam had a boyfriend, Sarah would happily tell her uncle that was what she'd asked Santa for this year.

"You mentioned taking care of your niece. You didn't mention anyone helping you, so I assumed you were single. As for being gay, well, I do have very good gaydar. And you just said you were interested in dating guys, didn't you?"

It was the best Charlie could come up with. Luckily, it got a laugh out of Liam.

"Well, your gaydar is working."

"What did you think of J.P.? As his best friend, I

can tell you he's a great guy. Did you exchange phone numbers?"

"No," Liam said, raising an eyebrow. "We got a little distracted by his niece, if you recall."

"I could give you his number," Charlie offered. "Or you could give me yours, and I could give it to him."

"How do I know you'll do that?"

Liam's question caught Charlie off guard. "Excuse me?"

"Maybe you're asking for yourself."

Charlie blushed. "I would never do that!"

"Do what?" Liam asked. "Steal a guy from a friend?"

Charlie gave a ferocious nod. "Yes. Besides, J.P. saw you first."

"But he rushed right out of here," Liam stated, folding his arms across his chest. "You guys didn't have much of a conversation. How would you know he was interested in dating me? And he didn't see me first, you did. Remember earlier? In the elevator?"

Charlie's mind went blank again. What was it with Liam and all these questions? It was like he was looking for an ulterior motive. Did he have trust issues?

Liam saved him from answering. "Your friend

seemed nice, but I'm not really into dating at the moment."

"You're not?" Charlie instantly felt sick, like Nora had a few minutes ago. If Liam didn't want to date, then making Sarah's Christmas wish come true was going to prove to be a challenge.

Liam shook his head. "I'm not going to be here very long."

"New York City isn't that far away. Only three hours."

"Six hours both ways," Liam pointed out.

"If you're into someone, you find a way to make it work."

"Have you done the long-distance thing?" Liam asked.

Charlie hadn't. Maybe if he did, he'd have more success in his own love life, because the short-distance thing hadn't produced any results. When it came to love and romance, Charlie's track record wasn't the best. Sure, there had been boyfriends over the years, but nothing long-term. He wasn't sure what had been missing from those relationships. Everything was always chugging along nicely, but then there was a sudden problem or issue that brought an end to things. Like his most recent boyfriend, Luke. They had been dating for over a year, and when Charlie brought up the possibility of moving in together this past Valentine's Day–I mean, how romantic was that?–Luke dodged the question and ghosted him the following day. No reason. No explanation. He just stopped answering Charlie's emails and texts and didn't return any of his phone calls.

"No, Liam," Charlie admitted. "I haven't."

"How do you know my real name?" Liam asked, his voice suddenly filled with suspicion as his body tensed up. He pointed to the tag pinned to his chest. "Because this says I'm Peppermint Elf."

Charlie's mind scrambled for an answer. He only knew Liam's name because of Sarah's letter. And then, he remembered earlier. With the maintenance man. "The elevator repairman called you Liam."

Liam's body relaxed. "Everyone at Bailey's knows who I am," he admitted.

"Because you hate your job so much?"

"Something like that." Liam noticed the janitors finishing up their mopping. "Duty calls. Time to get back to Santaland. I've got candy canes to give out." He started walking away.

"Hey! Wait!" Charlie called out.

Liam turned around, stopping at the entrance to Santaland.

"I know your name, but you don't know mine. It's Charlie. Charlie Fisher."

Charlie didn't know why it was so important for Liam to know his name, but he wanted him to. He watched as Liam gazed down at his curled booties before looking back up, a sheepish expression on his face. "I owe you an apology, Charlie."

"For what?"

"When we were in the elevator. I was having one of those days." Liam sighed. "Well, if I'm going to be honest, it's been one of those years. And I took it out on you."

Liam looked so sad and dejected. Charlie wanted to ask what was wrong and if he could help, but the words wouldn't slip out of his mouth. After all, he barely knew Liam. Instead, he said, "Christmas doesn't last forever. It'll be over soon."

"Not soon enough," Liam said before going back to work. "See you around."

———

The rest of the day, Liam tried to focus on his job, but his thoughts kept circling back to Charlie. Why had Charlie told him he didn't have a boyfriend? Was he interested? He hadn't gotten any sort of dating vibes out of Charlie, and he didn't think he was coming on to him. He seemed like a genuinely nice guy. Most importantly, he hadn't recognized him from *Gay Househusbands*.

After the *Househusbands* debacle, it was going to take him a while to learn how to trust anyone again. That's why he had been so suspicious with Charlie. Part of him had been wondering if he was a reporter looking to do a hit piece on him. There had been plenty of those, so why not one more to close out the year? But Charlie had had answers to his questions that made sense, and Liam had slowly lowered his guard.

He wasn't sure what to make of him.

Well, it didn't matter. He was busy with his job and Sarah. He probably wouldn't cross paths with Charlie Fisher again.

———

It was time to come up with Plan B.

Thanks to Nora's upset stomach, Charlie's plan to get J.P. and Liam together hadn't worked. He'd just have to come up with another situation to bring the two of them together.

What could he do?

He gave it some thought as he walked home from Bailey's, stopping along the way to buy some Christmas wrapping paper and bows. He didn't think Liam was going to agree to meet with J.P. alone. That meant he had to come up with a scenario that involved other people. A Christmas party would be too big, but maybe something smaller and more intimate. Like a dinner party! Yes! That would be it. Charlie would throw a small dinner party, and he'd invite Liam. Good food, good wine, good conversation. It would be a recipe for success and an opportunity for Liam and J.P. to get to know each other without it feeling like an official date.

Charlie started walking faster. He couldn't wait to get home and start planning the menu!

CHAPTER
FIVE

Liam was dreaming, and it was a wonderful dream. He'd been nominated for an Oscar for Best Actor and was attending the Academy Awards. Meryl Streep was reading the names of the nominees, and his name was the last to be announced. Meryl paused, smiling out at the audience before opening the envelope in her hands and removing the card inside. She looked down at it. And then came those four magic words. "And the winner is..."

But before Liam could hear his name from Meryl's lips, he was awakened by a loud screech in his ear.

"Uncle Liam!"

He ignored the screech, trying to hang on to the dream, but it quickly faded away before he could hear his name called. There was a bounce on his bed, followed by another screech into his ear.

"Uncle Liam!" Sarah gave him a shake. "Uncle Liam!"

Liam groaned, wrapping the sheets around himself as he burrowed deeper into his bed, pulling a pillow over his head. It was Saturday morning, and he wanted to sleep late. But it seemed like his niece had other ideas.

"What?" he croaked in a sleepy voice.

"It's time to wake up."

Liam opened one eye, peering at the clock on his nightstand. "It's eight o'clock. Give me another three hours."

Sarah did the math on her fingers. "But that would be eleven o'clock. No one sleeps that late."

"Tell me that in five years when you're a teenager," he said, pulling the bedspread over his head.

Sarah gave him a shake. "Wake up! I'm hungry."

Liam gave up, tossing back the bedspread. There was no winning this battle. "You know who else is hungry?" he whispered, opening both eyes and gazing around the bedroom, as if searching for someone.

"Who?" Sarah whispered back.

"The tickle monster!" he exclaimed, reaching out to grab Sarah and promptly tickling her.

"Stop, Uncle Liam! Stop!" she exclaimed between shrieks and giggles.

"But the tickle monster wants to hear you laugh! He's hungry for laughs."

"Then you need to laugh, too," Sarah declared, reaching out and tickling Liam, who stopped tickling his niece as he tried to fend her off between his own shrieks and giggles.

"Okay, I surrender," Liam said, waving his hands in the air. "Truce?"

"Truce," Sarah agreed.

Liam hugged her to his side, placing a kiss on the top of her head. Then, he got out of bed, pulling on his robe. "What do you want for breakfast?" he asked.

Sarah hopped out of bed, looking up at him. "Scrambled eggs and bacon?"

"Uncle Liam doesn't know how to make scrambled eggs and bacon." Sarah had breakfast at school during the week, and the last couple of weekends he'd been taking her to a local diner in the mornings. Today would be his first attempt at making breakfast.

They started walking down the hall toward the stairs to the first floor.

"Pancakes and sausage?"

"Try again," Liam called over his shoulder as they descended the stairs.

Sarah gave it some thought. "Waffles?"

Liam could do waffles. "Let's go check the freezer and see if we have any."

"We don't," Sarah said. "Mommy doesn't buy frozen ones. She makes them from scratch with the waffle iron."

"Of course she does," Liam muttered under his breath. "Because my sister is perfect."

"What did you say, Uncle Liam?"

"Nothing, sweetie. How about some cereal?"

Sarah perked up. "Oatmeal? With brown sugar and raisins?"

He'd meant dry cereal. Opening a box and shaking some flakes into a bowl. Maybe slicing up a banana. But he could handle oatmeal.

"Sure. If that's what you want," he said as they entered the kitchen.

Liam opened the cabinet next to the stainless steel refrigerator, searching for a box of Quaker Instant Oatmeal. The kind that came with the individual packets in different flavors. He didn't find it. Instead, he found a canister of steel rolled oats. Naturally. How much free time did his sister have in the mornings? This stuff took forever to cook. It wasn't even the quick-cooking kind!

"Let's save oatmeal for another day," Liam said, mentally making a shopping list and putting a box of Quaker Instant Oatmeal variety packets at the top of the list. "How about some regular cereal?"

"Okay," Sarah agreed, as she pulled a chair out from the kitchen table and sat down.

Liam opened another cabinet and was horrified to discover his choices were Corn Flakes, Raisin Bran, and Shredded Wheat. Boring adult cereals! He slammed the cabinet door shut. "Okay, that's it, we're going to the supermarket."

"We are? What for?"

"To buy groceries."

Sarah looked confused. "But don't we already have groceries?"

"Not the kind that we need." Liam held his hand out. "Come on, let's go get dressed. You, my darling, are about to experience the joy of opening a box of cereal and finding a toy surprise inside!"

———

At first, Charlie didn't hear the voice. He was too busy focusing on the menu for his dinner party as he walked to the supermarket. But then, it cut straight into his thoughts.

"Charles!"

Charlie groaned. He knew the person it belonged to. He ignored it. But the voice called out again. Louder.

"Charles!"

Charlie kept walking. He was not going to turn around. He was not.

"Charles!"

He picked up his pace, but the person calling his name did the same until finally the caller caught up with him and positioned themselves in front of Charlie, blocking his path.

"Charles! I've been calling your name for blocks. Why didn't you turn around?"

Standing before Charlie was his nemesis from high school, Claude Jenkins. Whenever Charlie looked at him, he thought of the actor Adrien Brody. They were both thin and lanky, and Claude kept his chestnut brown hair shoulder-length. With regard to Claude's wardrobe, everything he wore looked like it had just come off the men's fashion runway. Today, he was wearing an oversized wool overcoat in a purple and white plaid with a black silk scarf tossed around his neck and bright purple leather gloves.

Like Charlie, Claude was also gay. Even with that in common, Charlie and Claude never really clicked as friends, at least on Charlie's part. Claude seemed to think they were friends, but Charlie didn't. Maybe it was because Claude always thought he was better than everyone else, and that gave him a sense of entitlement. He'd been part of the in-crowd in high school, and coming from a rich family, he was always throwing parties, not to mention showing off his toys–the latest electronic gadgets, a new car, a speedboat, tickets to concerts (always on the floor), trips to Europe and the Caribbean. Whatever Claude wanted, Claude got.

That had especially been true when they'd been in drama club together. Claude always wanted the starring role in whatever show they were doing. Thankfully, Mr. Orson, who had been in charge of drama, played fair, but Claude would always throw a hissy fit whenever he didn't get the role he wanted. It always used to piss Charlie off, and so he would avoid Claude whenever he could. They'd gone to different colleges and been out of each other's orbits until Charlie had moved back to Bramford Hills, where Claude and his husband, Devon, had settled down as the picture-perfect couple.

"My name might be Charles, but it isn't the

name I go by," Charlie patiently explained. "It's Charlie. It's always been Charlie. No one ever calls me Charles. That's why I didn't turn around."

Okay, he was lying. But conversations with Claude were never pleasant, so he tried to avoid them whenever possible. However, living in a small town meant crossing paths with people one might not necessarily like and being cordial, even when they didn't want to be.

"But Charles sounds more sophisticated and grown-up," Claude pointed out.

"My name is Charlie," Charlie said between gritted teeth.

Claude closed his eyes and rubbed two fingers on the sides of his forehead. "I'm burning it into my memory. Charlie. Charlie. Charlie." Claude snapped his fingers. "I know! I'll make a connection. Whenever I think of you, I'll think of Starkist Tuna."

Charlie remembered the old TV commercial. Starkist didn't want Charlie the Tuna because they wanted tunas with good taste. And the unspoken message of the commercial was that Charlie the Tuna didn't have any. Thus, by association, neither did Charlie.

"What do you want, Claude? I'm in a hurry. I've got errands."

"I just wanted to remind you that it's that time of year again."

"Time of year?" Charlie had no idea what he was talking about.

Claude whipped out a stack of tickets from his Louis Vuitton shoulder bag. "For the yearly Christmas show!"

Charlie bit back a groan. Thanks to his money and connections, Claude ran the local community theatre and always put together the yearly Christmas show. Claude fancied himself a theatre genius, so the shows were always written, produced, cast, and directed by him. And always a train wreck. Charlie wished the town council would put their foot down and give someone else a chance–someone like J.P., who had talent–but they didn't want to risk losing the hefty donations Claude and Devon made to the town each year. And so everyone suffered through a bad Christmas show.

"This year's show is going to be brilliant, if I do say so myself," Claude confided.

"Is it?" Charlie asked, trying to sound interested.

"We're doing a musical version of *It's a Wonderful Life* called *Wonderful!*"

"Does that show even exist?"

"It does now! I've written all the songs."

Charlie suddenly recalled an episode of *The Simpsons* where the family went to see a musical version of *Planet of the Apes* in New York City. He tried not to shudder.

"How many tickets would you like to buy?"

"Now's not a good time," Charlie said. "I don't have my calendar in front of me." He started to walk around Claude. "If you'll excuse me, I've got to go."

"Where are you off to in such a hurry?"

The other thing Charlie had never liked about Claude was his desire to know everyone's business and then spread it around. Gossip much? When it came to Claude, yes! There was no way Charlie was going to mention the dinner party he was throwing. Knowing Claude, he'd try to finagle an invite for himself and Devon.

"The supermarket."

"For your little business? Catering, right?"

Charlie made his living as a graphic designer, working for a New York City publishing house doing all their print and online ads, not to mention their banners for trade shows and any other promotional materials that were needed. The job was full-time, remote, and he basically worked nine to five. In his spare time, he did some catering on the side. Nothing too crazy, just a few small parties for friends. Most of his clients were by word of mouth, and the extra money was nice. Charlie had always loved cooking, and his catering business was another way that he got to be creative.

Before Charlie could answer, Claude said, "Devon and I will be throwing a Christmas party later this month. Shoot me an email with your rates and menus. Maybe we'll hire you."

Maybe? Typical Claude. Not that he would ever consider working for him. He had no doubt Claude would be an impossibly demanding client.

"Thanks, but I'm already booked solid."

Claude shrugged, putting his tickets away. "Maybe next year."

Charlie nodded before walking away. *Or maybe when hell freezes over*, he thought.

———

Sarah's eyes bugged out as she stared at the brightly colored cereal aisle.

"Well, go ahead," Liam urged. "Take your pick. Whatever you want."

"Mommy never lets me eat this kind of cereal," Sarah slowly said, staring at a box of Fruity Pebbles.

"Well, Mommy isn't here. Uncle Liam is, and I say you can have whatever cereal you want."

"Are you sure? What if Mommy finds out?" Sarah chewed on her lower lip. "She's not going to get mad, is she?"

Liam crouched down so he was eye level with his niece. "If Mommy asks where the cereal came from, I'll tell her I bought it for me. Go ahead," he urged. "Pick! Pick more than one!"

That was all the encouragement Sarah needed. She threw a box of Fruity Pebbles into the cart, followed by a box of Coco-Puffs and Trix.

"What else do you want to buy?"

"Cookies?" Sarah hesitantly asked.

"Cookies, it is!" Liam said as he zoomed their cart in the direction of the snack aisle. "Follow me!"

Forty-five minutes later, their cart was filled with every kind of sweet treat known to man. Not to mention a stack of frozen pizzas, chicken pot pies, a variety of Lunchables, tater tots, chicken fingers, string cheese, potato chips, pretzels, crackers, Cheez Doodles, and three different kinds of cookies. There was also a container of chocolate milk and a pack of Hawaiian Punch.

Sarah stared at the bulging cart in disbelief. "We're really buying all that stuff?"

"Yes, we are. And we're going to start eating it as soon as we get home!"

As they headed toward the cash register, Liam's shopping cart was bumped by another cart as he turned a corner.

"I'm so sorry," the man pushing the cart said. "I wasn't paying attention."

Liam knew that voice. He looked across at him. It was the man from the department store. What was his name again? It popped into his head. Charlie.

Charlie's face lit up at the sight of Liam. "Now, this is a coincidence."

"It is?" Liam asked.

"I was just thinking about you."

"Why?"

Charlie didn't answer the question. Instead, he focused his attention on Sarah, who was shyly peeking out at Charlie from behind Liam.

"Who's this little miss?"

"My niece, Sarah."

Charlie gave a wave. "Nice to meet you, Sarah. I'm Charlie. I'm a friend of your Uncle Liam."

"We're friends?" Liam skeptically asked. They barely knew each other.

"Yes, we are," Charlie confirmed. "Or we're going to be. You're new in town, right? Between spending time with your niece and spending time with the kiddies at Bailey's, I would think you'd be starving for a little bit of adult conversation, no?"

"Maybe," Liam reluctantly admitted.

"I'm throwing a small dinner party tonight. Just a few friends. It would be great if you could join us."

Liam raised an eyebrow. "Is your friend J.P. going to be at this dinner?"

"If I say yes, does that mean you'll come?" Charlie eagerly asked. "Or does it mean you won't?"

"I'm not a fan of fix-ups," Liam stated. "I meant what I said yesterday. I'm not interested in dating."

"Who said anything about dating? It'll be a night of good food and good conversation. What do you have to lose?"

Liam gave it some thought. He'd pretty much been a hermit the last couple of months, barely leaving his apartment. Plus, Sarah was going to a sleepover, so his whole evening was free. It would be nice to have a night out.

"Okay, I'll come," he said, hoping he wasn't going to regret it.

Charlie gave Liam a huge smile. "Great! Let me give you my cell number." He rattled off a bunch of numbers, which Liam plugged into his phone. "Shoot me a text later and I'll send you my address and all the other deets." Charlie peeked at Liam's shopping cart. "That's a lot of processed food."

"I'm shopping for my niece. We went a little crazy."

"That's me!" Sarah reminded Charlie with a smile. "Uncle Liam said I could buy whatever I wanted."

"This is what you're feeding her?" Charlie whispered, a note of horror in his voice.

"It's kiddie food," Liam explained.

"You might as well give her a spoon and a bag full of sugar. She's going to be bouncing off the walls once she starts eating this stuff."

"Don't you think you're exaggerating?"

"I don't see any fresh fruits or vegetables," Charlie said.

"I like apples," Sarah offered. "And bananas."

The produce aisle was right across from them. "Why don't you go get a bag of McIntosh apples," Liam told Sarah. "You know which ones those are, right?"

Sarah nodded as she went off to do the errand, Liam keeping his eyes on her. "Look, enough with the guilt trip. By the time I get home from work, I'm exhausted and it's too late for me to make Sarah something from scratch. Not only that, but I'm not exactly a whiz in the kitchen. Rather than have her starve, this is the best that I can do. Once my sister gets back from California, Sarah's every meal will once again be organic."

"Can I offer a solution?" Charlie asked.

Liam sighed. "What?"

"I'm a part-time caterer, and we're going into my busiest time of the year. Usually, I have a lot of leftovers. I would be more than happy to bring a few meals over to you and Sarah."

"Why would you want to do that?"

Charlie shrugged. "Why not? 'Tis the season of brotherly love."

"As long as that's all it is," Liam grumbled as Sarah returned with the bag of apples, dumping them into the cart.

"So, that's a yes?" Charlie asked.

Liam stared at his niece, who was gazing at him with adoration. She was his everything, and if Charlie was offering to make her healthy meals, how could he say no?

"Yes. That would be great. Thank you. It's very thoughtful," Liam said before turning his attention back to Sarah. "Ready to pay for everything, Squirt?"

She nodded, and Liam steered their cart in the direction of the cash registers.

"Bye, Charlie!" Sarah called out, giving him a wave.

Charlie waved back. "Bye, Sarah! Bye, Liam!"

Liam waved a hand in the air.

"I like him," Sarah told her uncle. "Don't you?"

"He's okay," Liam reluctantly admitted, turning around and watching as Charlie headed down the meat aisle with his shopping cart.

CHAPTER
SIX

Charlie loved throwing dinner parties. The menu planning, the table setting, the flowers, the music—he enjoyed it all. And then, the best part was watching his guests come together, spending the evening sharing good food, conversation, and laughter. It was always the best time.

For tonight, since it was the holiday season, he'd gone with a Christmas theme. A red tablecloth decorated with a border of green holly. Gold cloth napkins rolled up with metallic reindeer napkin holders. His best crystal, china, and silverware would be used, and there was a bouquet of white roses in the center of the table.

The menu was simple. They were going to start with tomato soup, followed by a garlic-crusted roast beef, mashed potatoes, green beans, and dinner rolls. For dessert, an apple crumb pie with homemade vanilla ice cream.

The guest list was small. In addition to Liam and J.P., Charlie had also invited his friends Christopher and Gregory, an engaged couple. Christopher had also gone to high school with Charlie and J.P., and while they'd been friends, he'd been more of a loner, quiet and introspective, keeping to himself, his nose always buried in a book. It was only in college–they'd both gone to NYU– that Charlie and Christopher became closer friends when they found themselves at the same gay bar one night during their freshman year. Their fake IDs hadn't gotten them any beers, so they'd left the bar and gone to an Alfred Hitchcock revival at Film Forum, opening up to each other as they walked to the theatre.

Gregory was the complete opposite of Christopher. He was Mr. Personality, always up on the latest gossip, pop culture, and trends. The two had met three summers ago while vacationing in Provincetown during Solid Gold Tea Dance on a Thursday afternoon at the Boatslip Resort. This past summer, while once again vacationing in PTown, Christopher had proposed on Herring Cove Beach during a sunset, and Gregory had said yes. Now, they were busy planning a wedding for next July.

Even though he'd told Liam this was a casual dinner party, he was hoping sparks would fly between him and J.P. It had been too long since J.P. had had someone special in his life, and Charlie had a gut feeling about Liam. Despite his Scrooginess, someone who adored their niece as much as Liam had to be a good guy, and good guys always deserved to find someone special.

How did he dress for a casual dinner party?

Liam didn't want to make it look like he was making an effort. He wanted to look good, but not too good. His dressy clothes were in New York City, and all he'd packed was winter wear: sweaters, long-sleeved shirts, turtlenecks, and jeans.

In the end, he decided one could never go wrong with the basics. He went with a white shirt and a V-neck navy blue sweater. Black jeans and white sneakers. Simple. Casual. He didn't want to send J.P. any signals because he wasn't looking to date. Or hook up. He was still keeping people at a distance. Distance was better. After all, he'd thought he could trust his castmates on *Gay Househusbands* and every single one had turned on him. Okay, he should have expected it, then, but did fame matter so much to them? Liam shook his head in disgust. Stupid question. Obviously, it did.

Sarah was already at her friend Janie's for her sleepover. He'd be picking her up the next morning at ten o'clock. He hoped Sarah wasn't going to have to reciprocate with a sleepover at her house next weekend. He could handle one eight-year-old little girl, but six of them? Yikes!

Liam gave himself a spritz of cologne while working up his courage. Why was he so nervous? It was only a dinner party. It probably wouldn't last more than three hours and then he would be back home, just in time for the start of *Saturday Night Live.*

———

Charlie was taking the dinner rolls out of the oven when the doorbell rang. He left the baking sheet on the counter, scooted Shadow out of the kitchen, and hurried to open the front door, where he found Liam waiting on his doorstep.

"Welcome!" Charlie held the front door open. "You're the first to arrive."

Liam handed Charlie a bottle of wine as he walked inside. "I wasn't sure what you were serving, so I got a red."

"Red will go perfectly," Charlie said as he accepted the bottle and led Liam into the living room. "Let me take your coat."

Liam handed Charlie his parka as he surveyed the room. "Wow! It looks like Christmas exploded in here."

Charlie gazed at his decorations with pride. "It's my favorite holiday. You can never have too much Christmas. 'Tis the season. How about you?"

"How about what?" Liam asked, confusion in his voice.

"Have you decorated yet?"

Liam shook his head. "No."

"Why not?"

Liam shrugged. "I assume my sister will do it once she gets back."

"When will that be?"

Liam gave it some thought. "December twenty-third."

Charlie gasped. "The day before Christmas Eve?

No, no, no. You can't let that adorable little munchkin have a Christmas-free house. You have to decorate it immediately from top to bottom. If you need a little help–"

The doorbell rang, and Charlie left his offer unfinished as he went to answer the front door. When he returned, J.P. was in tow, who looked surprised to see Liam sitting on the couch.

"Oh!" J.P. exclaimed. "I didn't expect to see you here."

Charlie wasn't sure what to make of J.P.'s tone. He would have thought he'd be thrilled to see Liam again; he'd been so enthusiastic when he laid eyes on him for the first time yesterday.

"Liam is new in town," Charlie explained. "I thought he'd like to make some friends."

J.P. added his leather jacket to the parka Charlie was holding before joining Liam on the couch. Charlie took that as a good sign. It wasn't like J.P. was sitting across the room. Liam, on the other hand, looked distinctly uncomfortable and scooted over a bit while shooting Charlie an irritated stare.

"Let me hang these up," Charlie said, lifting his arms and ignoring Liam. "I'll be right back."

After hanging the coats, Charlie dashed into the

kitchen, returning with a platter of appetizers. "These are blue cheese pear tartlets," Charlie pointed out. "These are mini mushroom and goat cheese tarts, and these are sausage balls, but made with ground turkey instead of pork."

"Charlie gives the best dinner parties," J.P. said as he speared a sausage ball with a toothpick. "Everything is always delicious."

"You're going to give me a swollen head," Charlie said before holding the platter out to Liam, hoping that a possible romance was also going to be on the menu tonight.

———

Liam admired the appetizers. They looked like they could be photographed for a food magazine, they were so perfect. He reached for a tartlet just as the doorbell rang again. Charlie left the platter on the coffee table before hurrying off.

"How do you know Charlie?" Liam asked. He didn't want to come across as rude, which was what he would have been if they'd sat there in silence, but at the same time, he didn't want J.P. to think something might happen between them. Right now, getting his career back on track came first. Nothing else mattered, especially men.

"Charlie and I go all the way back to high school," J.P. said, popping another sausage ball into his mouth. "We grew up here. How about you? What brings you to town?"

"I'm taking a break from my acting career," Liam said, and as the words came out of his mouth, he felt like a huge load had been lifted off his shoulders. There. He'd finally said it out loud for the first time.

J.P. coughed mid-bite on his sausage ball. "You're an *actor?*"

"Yes, I'm an actor." J.P. was staring at him as if he was a vampire and he'd forgotten his cross, garlic, and Holy water. Before he could say anything else, Liam heard what could only be described as a gay voice–and there was nothing wrong with a distinctive gay voice–coming closer.

"You would *not* believe the day we've had. We had to go to a wedding cake tasting and I've eaten so much cake, I'm ready to burst. If I hear the words buttercream, fondant, or rosettes one more time, I'm going to scream. Small portions for me tonight, Charlie."

Charlie walked back into the living room with two men following after him. The taller of the two wore black horn-rimmed glasses, had brown hair with a sharp side part, and was dressed very preppy in khakis, boat shoes, and an argyle sweater vest. His companion was the complete opposite, bursting with color, from his dyed white blonde hair to his purple jeans, unbuttoned black shirt sexily revealing a bit of chest hair, and pointy red boots. A number of silver rings adorned his fingers, not to mention beaded bracelets on his wrists and gold chains around his neck.

At the sight of Liam, the guy with white blonde hair dropped the cake box he was holding, clasping both hands to the side of his face. "Oh my God! It's him! It's you! Here in the flesh."

"Who?" Charlie asked as he picked the cake box off the floor, wondering why Gregory was so excited.

"The Viper!" a wide-eyed Gregory exclaimed.

"The Viper?" Charlie repeated. "I don't know what you're talking about."

Gregory rushed over to Liam. "I'm a huge fan. You don't know how much of a fan I am. I was ready to give up on *Gay Househusbands of NYC*, but then they added you to the cast and I was glued to my TV."

"*Gay Househusbands of NYC?*" Charlie repeated.

Gregory rolled his eyes at Liam. "Naturally, Mr. PBS over there has no clue what I'm talking about. All he watches are those British imports on Sunday nights." Gregory turned around. "Charlie, angel, we have a real-life reality TV star in our midst."

"I wouldn't exactly say I'm a star," Liam muttered, suddenly wishing he could disappear as they all stared at him.

His past had caught up with him. For weeks, he had deluded himself into believing that maybe, just maybe, the mess with *Househusbands* was behind him.

And now, it wasn't.

"I think I should leave," Liam announced.

"Why?" Charlie asked, a note of panic in his voice.

Why is he so upset? Liam wondered. It was just a dinner party.

"I'm sorry!" Gregory exclaimed. "Don't go. Please. I didn't mean to call you the Viper or make you uncomfortable. It just slipped out. I'm Team Liam all the way." He gave Liam a conspirative look. "Don't you find it suspicious that there was never any footage of you and Jason doing the nasty? If they had it, wouldn't you think they would have shown it? All they had to do was blur out the naughty bits."

Gregory slipped his arm through Liam's, clinging to it possessively and leading him in the direction of the dining room. "You're not leaving," he insisted. "You're staying. You're going to sit next to me at dinner, and you're going to tell me all about yourself. I want to hear everything. And I promise not to bring up *Gay Househusbands* again."

Liam gazed over his shoulder at Charlie, searching for help, but Charlie just shrugged and announced, "Everyone, find a seat at the table. Dinner is about to be served."

Liam sighed. It looked like he was staying.

After Gregory's bombshell—and Charlie still wasn't exactly sure what Gregory was talking about—he worried the dinner might turn out to be a disaster. Or Liam would still leave without giving Charlie a chance to match him with J.P. But disaster had been averted, and as promised, Gregory didn't bring up the reality show Liam had been on. Although, now, Charlie was curious and planned to do some Internet sleuthing later that night after everyone had gone home.

The tomato soup with homemade croutons had

been the perfect starter for a cold wintry night. Now, as Charlie sliced the roast beef, passing around plates, he stared around the table at his friends, feeling grateful for having them in his life. It was clear Gregory liked Liam from the way he was monopolizing all his attention. Deciding that Liam deserved a break from Gregory, in the hopes that J.P. might have a chance to talk with him, Charlie asked Gregory about the wedding plans.

"Let me fortify myself," Gregory said, lifting his wine glass and taking a hearty sip. "You would not believe the amount of money a wedding costs," he exclaimed. "And we're trying to keep everything low key."

J.P. added a spoonful of mashed potatoes to his plate and then passed the bowl to Liam, who was sitting next to him. "Low key is not what comes to mind when I think of you, Gregory."

Gregory stuck his tongue out in response.

"Maybe you should elope," Charlie suggested.

"And miss out on everyone seeing me in a fabulous tuxedo? Not to mention the huge party afterward? Never!"

"He's just marrying me for the gifts," Christopher deadpanned.

"Silly man," Gregory said softly, blowing him a

kiss while reaching across the table and squeezing his hand.

Charlie gave a contented sigh. One day, he hoped to have what Christopher and Gregory had. They were complete opposites, and yet they were the perfect couple, balancing each other out and always in sync. Well, his search for Mr. Right would have to wait for the new year. He had to find a Mr. Right for Liam before Christmas Day. Hopefully, he was sitting right next to him.

"How's your holiday season going so far?" Christopher asked Liam.

"Liam's taking care of his niece, Sarah, while her parents are in California looking for a new house," Charlie explained. "He and J.P. met yesterday when J.P. brought Nora over to Bailey's to meet Santa."

"Ooooh," Gregory cooed, batting his eyes at Liam. "Are you Santa? Can I sit on your lap and tell you what I want for Christmas? Although, I have to warn you, I'm *very* naughty."

"Sorry to disappoint you, but I'm not Santa," Liam said while buttering a dinner roll. "I'm one of his elves. Peppermint."

"I bet a lot of gay daddies would love to suck on your candy cane," Gregory purred.

Christopher swatted him across the table with his napkin. "Behave!"

"You should see the size of Nora's list," J.P. groaned. "She wants practically everything. If she sees a commercial for something on Disney or Nickelodeon, it goes on her list."

"I wish I knew what Sarah wanted for Christmas," Liam said.

"She hasn't told you?" J.P. asked.

Liam shook his head. "The only person she's told is Santa Claus. She wrote him a letter last week telling him what she wants for Christmas and he wrote back. The letter came today and she was practically bouncing off the walls after she read it. I wish I knew what it said, but she refuses to tell me. I don't have a clue."

"Any idea why she's being so secretive?" Christopher asked.

"Maybe it's because she believes in the magic of Christmas," Charlie said.

"I guess I could look around in her room and see if I can find the letter," Liam mused. "That might be helpful."

Charlie panicked. If Liam found the letter, it would spoil everything. "No! You can't do that."

Liam looked at Charlie in surprise. "Why not?"

"It would be an invasion of her privacy."

"She's eight years old. What could she possibly have asked Santa for that she doesn't want me to know about? Besides, how else am I going to get her what she wants if she doesn't tell me?"

"She's a little girl," Charlie patiently explained. "Little girls like their secrets. Give her some time. I'm sure she'll eventually tell you."

Liam shrugged as he poured some gravy over his slices of roast beef. "I guess you're right."

"Maybe you could arrange a play date with Sarah and Nora," Charlie suggested, thinking that would be the perfect way to get Liam and J.P. together.

"I can give you my sister's phone number," J.P. offered.

"No!' Charlie practically shouted. How could a romance between J.P. and Liam develop if they didn't spend any time together? "Don't you think your sister deserves a break, J.P.? After all, she just had a baby, and I'm sure she'd like a little downtime. You should give Liam your number. What could be more fun than two guncles spending time with their nieces?"

"I'll have to look at Sarah's schedule and see what days she has free," Liam said.

"Schedule?" Gregory asked in horror. "Your niece has a schedule?"

"Nora does, too," J.P. added.

"What happened to the days when kids were free to be kids?" Gregory demanded. "Do they have to have schedules like adults?"

"Speaking of kids, what are you two thinking?" J.P. asked. "First comes love, then comes marriage. Are we going to see Gregory and Christopher with a baby carriage at some point?"

Gregory rolled his eyes, pointing his knife at Christopher. "I can't get this one to commit to getting a dog. You think I'm going to convince him we should have a baby?"

"If we got a dog, who would be the one taking care of it? Walking it? Disciplining it? Cleaning up its messes? Not you. Me! And while you would be ignoring our fur baby once the novelty of it wore off and I did all the work, it would probably give you all its love and attention. If you can't take care of a dog, you certainly can't take care of a baby."

"It's not the same thing!" Gregory huffed.

Christopher lifted his wine glass, gazing at Gregory over the rim. "Isn't it?"

"I can't believe you would think I'd ignore our child!"

Christopher took a sip of wine. "I would like to think you wouldn't." He shrugged. "But you never know."

Charlie loved when Gregory and Christopher bickered. It gave him a window into the ups and downs of a relationship. Not that he hadn't witnessed the same thing with his parents and grandparents when he was growing up, but it was different when it was a gay couple. The dynamic of two men trying to make their relationship work was easier to identify with, although love was still love.

"I resent you thinking I would treat our child the same way I would treat an animal!"

"Okay, change of subject," Charlie announced after gazing around the table to make sure everyone had what they needed. Only then did he sit down and focus on his own dinner plate. "Guess who I ran into today on my way to the supermarket?"

"From the way your lip is curling, I would have to say Claude Jenkins," Gregory guessed.

"Who's Claude Jenkins?" Liam asked.

"My nemesis from high school," J.P. explained.

"Ours, too," Charlie clarified, pointing to himself and Christopher with his fork. "We all met in high school when we joined the drama club. Because where else were closeted gay boys supposed to go?"

"Claude's been my nemesis since I moved to town," Gregory added.

"What's he done that's so awful?" Liam asked.

"Where do we begin?" Gregory sniffed. "Claude struts around Bramford Hills like he's its king and we're all the peasants living under him."

"I wouldn't go that far," Charlie said while dipping a forkful of roast beef into a bit of gravy.

"I would," Gregory stubbornly stated. "He thinks he rules this town, and all of you let him get away with it. I don't know why you just don't put him in his place."

"It's not that we let him get away with it," Christopher said. "He just has deeper pockets than the rest of us. Money talks."

Gregory rolled his eyes. "If he has deep pockets, it's because he married a sugar daddy."

Charlie waved his fork in the air while chewing, then swallowed. "We don't know if that's true."

Gregory rolled his eyes. "Reality check! Devon is twenty years older than Claude and looks like Boss Hogg from that old TV show from the seventies, *The Dukes of Hazzard*."

"Maybe they're in love," Charlie insisted.

"Claude's in love all right–with the almighty dollar!" Gregory exclaimed.

"What's wrong with having a sugar daddy?" Liam asked.

All conversation stopped as four sets of eyes turned in Liam's direction, waiting to hear more.

———

The dinner wasn't as bad as Liam thought it was going to be, especially after the *Gay Househusbands* bombshell had come out. In fact, it was kind of nice. But had he suddenly ruined it with what he'd just uttered?

"You sound like you're talking from experience," Gregory said, eyes alight with excitement.

Liam squirmed in his seat, wishing he could take back the words. "Maybe I am."

"Ooooh!" Gregory happily squealed, clapping his hands together. "Do tell!"

"Gregory!" Christopher snapped.

"He brought it up," Gregory said defensively. "I didn't."

Liam didn't know why he had said it. Maybe it was because the wine had loosened his tongue. Or maybe it was just because it felt like he could be honest. These were nice guys and, with the exception of Sebastian and Dominick, he hadn't felt this comfortable with a bunch of gay guys in a long time.

"No, it's fine," Liam said, taking a sip of water to moisten his suddenly dry mouth. "I've had a sugar daddy."

"Of course you have, darling," Gregory purred. "Was there ever any doubt? You're gorgeous."

"It's not something I'm embarrassed about. And I wasn't intentionally looking to have one. It sort of just happened."

"What do you mean?" Gregory asked, a note of intrigue in his voice.

"This guy and I met, we dated for a while, and I don't know." Liam shrugged. "He always offered to pay for everything. At the time, I was a struggling actor not making much money, so I appreciated when he would pick up the bills."

"He didn't keep you in an apartment, did he?" Gregory asked, suggestively raising an eyebrow. "A little love nest?"

J.P. threw a dinner roll across the table at Gregory. "This isn't some Joan Crawford melodrama from the forties!"

"Ouch!" Gregory squealed, acting as if J.P. had lobbed a brick at him.

"Don't you dare throw that back," Charlie

warned as Gregory picked up the roll. "No food fights in my house."

Gregory glared at J.P. before taking a dainty bite of the roll.

"No, I had my own place," Liam answered. "Although, it was nowhere as nice as his."

"You got lucky and he fell into your lap." Gregory took a sip of his wine, waving a hand in the air. "Nothing wrong with that. I'm sure it was the complete opposite with Claude."

"We don't know that," Charlie insisted.

Gregory sighed. "You're always such a romantic."

"Let's stop talking about Claude," Charlie said.

"Fine with me," Gregory agreed.

"In a minute," J.P. said. "Did he tell you what he's putting on for this year's Christmas show?"

"A musical."

"*White Christmas? Holiday Inn?*"

"No..."

"*Elf? The Best Christmas Pageant Ever?*"

"No."

Liam thought Charlie seemed reluctant to tell J.P. about the show. He wondered why.

"Don't keep me in suspense," J.P. said. "Tell me!"

"It's something new. *Wonderful!*"

"How can it be wonderful when it hasn't opened yet?" Gregory asked.

"No, it's called *Wonderful!*" Charlie clarified. "It's a musical version of *It's a Wonderful Life.*"

Gregory began laughing hysterically. "You've got to be kidding! Since when did Claude become a lyricist?" He stared at J.P. "This is all your fault. Why do you let him get away with this every year?"

"Get away with what?"

"You know what," Gregory stated in exasperation. "Running the Christmas show! Aren't you the one with the off-Broadway hits? You're so talented. You should be the one putting on the show, not him. We'd sell a hell of a lot more tickets, that's for sure. Don't you remember all those empty seats last year?"

"Claude has the city council in his back pocket, so for as long as he wants to run the Christmas show, he's going to run it," J.P. reminded Gregory.

"Because of that, we're going to be subjected to more bad theatre courtesy of Claude Jenkins?" Gregory huffed.

Liam's gaze kept ping-ponging back and forth between Gregory and J.P. as they continued arguing. Finally, he asked, "Have you ever thought of putting on a competing show?"

Gregory gasped. "Good looks and brains. Why am I not surprised? It's genius!"

"I don't know," J.P. reluctantly stated. "It would be a lot of work."

"You wouldn't have to create something original," Liam pointed out. "You could license a show. It's not that expensive."

"Couldn't hurt to give it some thought," J.P. reluctantly agreed.

"I'd be happy to help," Liam offered. "When I could. Between my job and taking care of Sarah, I don't have a lot of free time."

"I'll help, too," Gregory offered. "Anything to knock Claude off his perch!"

"Okay, no more theatre talk," Charlie said, rising from his seat and starting to clear the table. "Who's ready for some dessert?"

———

Charlie was in the kitchen making a pot of coffee to go with the pie and ice cream when J.P. came in with a stack of dishes.

"What do you think?" Charlie eagerly asked, rushing to his side. His dinner was a success! Liam and J.P. were going to be spending more time together, especially if they mounted a Christmas show.

J.P. stared at Charlie with caution. "About?"

"Liam!"

J.P. opened the door of the dishwasher and began filling it. "Not a chance."

Charlie couldn't believe what he was hearing. "Why not? You liked him yesterday."

"And I like him even more today." J.P. began filling the silverware caddy with knives and forks. "He's a nice guy."

"Then, what's the problem?" Charlie asked, totally confused. "Please explain it to me."

"He's an actor, which I didn't know yesterday," J.P. stated, closing the door of the dishwasher and leaning against the counter. "Now, I know. And I'm done with actors. I'm not going down that road again."

"It's not the same," Charlie pointed out, grabbing a dish towel and wiping down the counters. "You can't compare Liam to Sam."

"Oh yes, I can." J.P. began counting off on his fingers. "All actors are egotistical, self-centered, vain, petty, manipulative..." He held up his other hand. "Want me to go on?"

"You're not being fair to Liam."

"He had a sugar daddy," J.P. added. "Obviously, he's used to someone providing him with the finer things in life. That's not me. Not on my salary."

"But he doesn't have a sugar daddy anymore," Charlie reminded J.P. "If he did, why would he be working at Bailey's?"

J.P. shrugged. "Don't know, don't care. I'm happy to have Liam as a friend, but that's as far as it's going to go."

"But—"

J.P. held up a hand, cutting Charlie off. "Sorry, I've made up my mind. You'll have to find someone else to be Liam's Christmas boyfriend."

If there was one thing that Charlie never ran away from, it was a challenge. He folded his arms across his chest and gave J.P. a determined look. "Don't worry, I will."

Charlie waved good night from his front porch as everyone walked away from his house, the streets and sidewalks glowing from his neighbors' brightly colored Christmas lights and decorations. Once they were all out of sight, he went back inside with a sense of satisfaction. His dinner party had been a success.

It had been fun catching up with everyone, and it looked like Liam had made some new friends since they all exchanged cell numbers. Okay, his first attempt at matchmaking had been foiled, but he wasn't giving up.

After Charlie cleaned up the last of the mess in the kitchen and restored order in the dining room, he made his way up to bed with his laptop, Shadow trailing behind him. As Gregory pointed out, he wasn't much of a fan of reality TV. British mysteries and dramas on PBS and Britbox were what he enjoyed. But he was curious about *The Gay House-husbands of NYC...*

After Googling the show, its website came up and he started streaming an episode.

One episode became two, and then two became three.

Charlie had to be honest, he did not like the men on the show at all. They were all silly and vapid and petty. Why would people waste their free time watching these people spend crazy amounts of money and then cry about their lives between petty squabbles with so-called friends? Did it make them feel better about themselves? Did it give them something to aspire to? He didn't get it.

But there was something he did like about the show.

Liam.

Unlike the others, he seemed real and genuine.

There were also a lot of gratuitous shots of Liam wearing barely anything.

Was that what he looked like underneath all those clothes? Charlie wondered, watching as Liam went on a swimsuit shopping spree with one of the other singles and modeled one swimsuit after another in the search for the perfect fit.

Charlie didn't know how it began, but suddenly, as he kept watching Liam on the screen, he started having thoughts of a naked Liam, wondering what it would be like to kiss and touch him and have Liam do the same. His body was extremely well-defined, and he wondered how many hours Liam spent in the gym to get such results. He was so finely chiseled, he may as well have been a work of art. Soon, he found himself becoming aroused, and within seconds, his erection was throbbing against the sheets.

Charlie slammed his laptop shut.

What was happening? Was he really getting turned on by Liam? If he was, it was only because he'd been in a dating dry spell. He couldn't even remember the last time he'd been out with a guy.

Spring? Summer? Obviously, it hadn't been memorable if he couldn't remember.

He took a deep breath, calming himself down.

Okay, this was a plus. Liam had a hot body. A very hot body that was capable of turning men on. Case in point. He could use that to his advantage when trying to set him up on a blind date.

The only question was, who did he set Liam up with next?

CHAPTER
SEVEN

The following morning, Liam thought of Charlie's words from the night before. Was Sarah missing out by not having the Christmas decorations up?

Liam remembered when he was a kid, how excited he used to get when he and Penelope would help their dad carry in the boxes of Christmas decorations from the garage. Opening each one and unpacking the decorations, rediscovering them one by one before they were hung on the tree–it was just as much fun as opening presents on Christmas morning.

"Hey, Squirt," he called up the stairs.

Sarah stuck her head over the banister, her long blonde hair falling down in a silky sheet. "Yes, Uncle Liam?"

"What would you say about doing some decorating?"

"You mean putting up the Christmas tree? Oh boy, oh boy, oh boy. Yes!" Sarah ran down the stairs and started dancing around Liam. "I love when the Christmas tree goes up."

"Because of all the presents?" Liam casually asked, thinking this might be a way to get Sarah to reveal what she wanted from Santa this year.

"No! I like how pretty everything is when it's decorated. And the presents don't come until Christmas Day, silly."

"Speaking of presents, want to give me a hint about what Santa is bringing you?"

Sarah shook her head and mimed locking a key over her lips.

This kid was stubborn! Just like her uncle. "But what if Santa can't find what you asked for? Maybe I could help him find it," Liam suggested.

"Santa doesn't need any help," Sarah patiently explained. "He's Santa!"

Liam sighed. "Right. He's Santa."

"The Christmas tree is up in the attic," Sarah said, taking Liam by the hand and pulling him in that direction.

"Up in the attic?"

Sarah nodded.

"You mean you have a *fake* Christmas tree?" Liam asked, trying hard not to sound horrified but failing.

Growing up, they had always had a real tree. They would go to the Christmas tree farm and take their time wandering around, trying to find the perfect one.

"Mommy says a real tree makes too much of a mess," Sarah explained.

"How hard is it to pull out the vacuum every couple of days and suck up some stray pine needles?" Liam muttered under his breath.

"What?" Sarah asked.

"Nothing, sweetie. Uncle Liam is talking to himself." He clapped his hands together. "We're going to do things differently this year."

"We are?"

Liam nodded with determination. "This year you're going to have a real Christmas tree. One that we're going to pick out and cut down ourselves."

Sarah gasped. "You mean like a Charlie Brown Christmas tree?"

"If that's what you want," Liam agreed, "then that's what you're going to have."

"I can pick any tree I want?" Sarah asked as if

she wasn't sure whether she should believe him or not.

"Any tree. Now, go upstairs and finish getting dressed." Sarah was still in her pajamas, and he needed to do something with her hair. The last thing he wanted was tangles. He'd made that mistake the first week he was here, letting her keep her hair long and loose, and when she'd wanted pigtails, it had been impossible to get a brush through her hair. There had been lots of tears and crying from both Sarah and Liam.

Sarah had just dashed back upstairs when the doorbell rang. Liam answered it and found Charlie waiting on the front porch with an armful of Tupperware.

"It's Connie Casserole," he sang out.

"Did someone recently watch *The Boys in the Band*?" Liam asked, recognizing the character Emory's line.

"It was on TCM the other night. I always try to watch it. Such an important movie. One of the first mainstream gay pictures. And, of course, it was a hit play first. Groundbreaking."

"I've performed it," Liam said.

"You have? Wait, don't tell me. Let me guess who

you played." Charlie closed his eyes and then opened one eye. "The cowboy?"

Liam sighed. "Is it that obvious?"

Charlie shrugged. "Well, it was either that or Larry. Both were beefcake roles. And look at you. You have a body that men would pay for."

"Thank you?"

Charlie blushed. "You know what I mean." He held out his arms. "I come bearing gifts. Or in this case, a week's worth of meals for you and Sarah."

"You didn't have to do that," Liam said, touched by Charlie's thoughtfulness. "I know you mentioned it at the supermarket, but I didn't expect you to actually do it. This is so nice of you."

Charlie shrugged. "No need to thank me. A lot of it is leftovers from last night. As usual, I made too much food, but I always worry I'm not going to have enough. It's the Italian in me. But it should tide you over. And why would you think I wouldn't do it?"

"I guess I'm used to people making promises and then not coming through. An actor's life. Thank you." Liam took the Tupperware from Charlie's arms. "Come in."

Sarah came running down the stairs, holding a hairbrush. "Hi, Charlie," she greeted, giving him a smile. "What are you doing here?"

"I was bringing over some food for you and your uncle. What are you two up to today?"

"We're going to a Christmas tree farm," Sarah announced, her voice filled with excitement.

"You are?" Charlie stared at Liam in surprise. "Really?"

"Uh huh. We're going to get a tree. Any tree I want! Uncle Liam said so."

"He did, did he?" Charlie asked, giving Liam a sly smile.

"I was thinking of what you said last night," Liam explained. "Sarah and I are going to spend today decorating for Christmas."

"Need any help?" Charlie offered.

Liam hadn't ventured up to the attic yet, but knowing his sister, he was sure there were lots of boxes to carry down and unpack. An extra set of hands would make the decorating go faster.

"Are you sure?"

"Sure, I'm sure. Plus, I'll take you to where you can find the best Christmas trees in town. It's a family farm I've been going to since I was a little kid." He held his hand up in the air, measuring against Sarah's head. "When I was just as big as you. They have the best trees. Plus, they give you free hot chocolate. Do you like hot chocolate, Sarah?"

"Does it come with marshmallows?"

Charlie gave it some thought. "I think so."

"Sounds good to me." Sarah then tugged on her uncle's arm, holding out the hairbrush. "I want a ponytail today, Uncle Liam."

"I'll do the ponytail," Charlie offered, "while your Uncle Liam puts all that food away. If that's okay with you, Miss Sarah?"

"Sure," Sarah agreed, taking Charlie by the hand and leading him to the couch in the living room, handing him her hairbrush and a red ribbon while her uncle disappeared into the kitchen with the leftovers. Charlie positioned himself behind her and started running the brush through her hair.

"Are you counting down the days until Christmas?" Charlie asked.

Sarah nodded.

"I bet you're going to get lots of presents."

"I don't want any presents. Well, I did ask Santa for something," she confessed. "But it's not for me."

"What do you mean?" Charlie innocently asked, knowing what Sarah was going to tell him.

"I can't tell you."

"Why not?"

Sarah peeked in the direction of the kitchen, as if

making sure Liam couldn't hear them. "Can I ask you a question, Charlie?"

"Anything you like."

"How do I know if Santa will make my Christmas wish come true?"

"You wrote him a letter, right? And didn't he answer it?"

Sarah gasped. "How do you know that?"

"Didn't you know Santa has helpers?" Charlie asked as he finished brushing Sarah's hair into a high ponytail and wrapped the red ribbon around it.

"He does?"

Charlie nodded. "Uh huh. Because he can't do everything by himself. Can you keep a secret?"

Sarah nodded solemnly.

"I'm one of his helpers."

"You're helping Santa?" Sarah looked at Charlie skeptically. "Prove it."

"You wrote a letter to Santa asking him to find a boyfriend for Uncle Liam."

Sarah's blue eyes widened with shock. "That's right. But how do I know if Santa will bring Uncle Liam a boyfriend?" She bit her lower lip. "I don't know if he's been good this year."

"Why would you say that? Isn't he here taking care of you while your parents are away?"

Sarah peeked down the hall toward the kitchen again and lowered her voice, as if afraid of being overheard. "Mommy says Uncle Liam makes bad decisions," she whispered. "Like being on that TV show. I heard her tell Daddy."

"Making a bad decision doesn't mean you're a bad person," Charlie patiently explained. "It just means you made a mistake. And people learn from their mistakes so that they don't make them again. Your Uncle Liam is a good guy. I'm pretty sure Santa is going to try his absolute hardest to find him a new boyfriend by Christmas. And you want to know why?"

"Why?"

"Because *you* wrote him a letter asking, and I have no doubt you've been a very good girl this year."

"I've tried," Sarah shyly admitted. "Sometimes, it's hard."

"Of course it is," Charlie agreed. "But don't you worry. I'm helping Santa with your Christmas wish."

Sarah happily clapped her hands. "Yay!"

"What are you two whispering about?" Liam asked as he came back into the living room, eyes darting back and forth between the two of them.

"Nothing," Charlie said, giving Liam an innocent smile. "Absolutely nothing."

"Are you sure?" Liam studied them intently. "You're not keeping a secret, are you?"

"Maybe we are." Charlie winked at Sarah. "But that's what Christmas is all about!"

———

When they arrived at the Christmas tree farm, Sarah went running off in search of the perfect tree while Charlie and Liam trailed behind, sipping from paper cups of hot chocolate.

"Did you have a nice time last night?" Charlie asked, crossing his fingers that Liam wasn't going to say he wanted to go out with J.P. After Liam insisted he didn't want to date, it wouldn't surprise Charlie if he had changed his mind after spending time with J.P. last night. But now, there was the issue of J.P. not being interested.

Liam gave it some thought before answering. "Other than when I was called the Viper and then admitted to having had a sugar daddy, I would say the evening was a success."

Charlie groaned. "Leave it to Gregory to liven up a dinner party."

"As the host, how did you view the evening? Success? Failure?"

"Failure? My dinner parties are never a failure!"

Liam poked Charlie in the chest. "Admit it, you were playing matchmaker between me and J.P., and you didn't get the results you wanted."

"Maybe I was," Charlie confessed. "Do you want to go out with him?"

Liam shook his head. "No."

Charlie let out the breath he'd been holding. "Okay."

"Why do you sound so relieved?"

"I'm not relieved," Charlie quickly explained. "I thought you two were hitting it off, but when I talked with J.P. later in the kitchen, he said he liked you. But only as a friend."

"Was this before or after the sugar daddy bombshell?"

"After," Charlie admitted. "But that had nothing to do with it. Honest! J.P. hasn't dated in years. He had a very bad breakup when he was in college. He really loved the guy, and Sam broke his heart." Charlie paused. "Sam was an actor. Now, whenever J.P. hears that word, his defenses go up."

"No wonder he looked at me like he wanted to drive a stake through my heart when I told him I was an actor."

"So, what's your type, Liam? Give me a little help here."

"I don't have a type. I'll go out with anybody." *And that's been the problem,* Liam thought. *I haven't been particular in my choices. I've gone out with everyone and everybody, never really searching for that one special person.*

He had been so focused on his career, on becoming a success, that he had put relationships on the back burner. Sure, he liked sex. And over the years, he'd had a lot of it. Plenty of times with strangers he'd met for the first time. There was always that pull, that thrill, that excitement of hooking up. Of meeting a guy and locking eyes and knowing they both wanted to have sex with each other and wasting no time getting to it. Hand jobs. Blow jobs. Anal. Sex in planes. In parks. In theatres. The list of places where Liam had had sex could go on and on. It was always a good time. But that's all it was. Short. Fast. Fleeting. Somewhere along the way, he'd forgotten sex was supposed to be a special act between two people. An expression of love and desire and longing. He couldn't remember the last time he'd had that. Or if he ever would again.

But had he ever?

There had really never been that one special

someone in his life. Sure, there had been boyfriends–
so many boyfriends over the years–but no one who
took his breath away or who he thought about 24/7.
Maybe something could have happened with Pablo
if there hadn't been that mess with *Gay Househusbands*. He hadn't thought Pablo was the "one," but
that could have changed over time.

"How about your sugar daddy?" Charlie asked,
breaking into his thoughts. "You don't mind talking
about him, do you?"

Liam shrugged. "We did last night. He was
older. Dark five o'clock shadow that contrasted beautifully with his gray hair. Icy blue eyes. I used to call
him the Silver Fox. There's been nothing going on
between us for a couple of years. We're still friends.
And he was good to me during the *Househusbands*
debacle."

Liam remembered all the times the Silver Fox
had called. Another true friend. He'd offered some
financial assistance, too, but Liam had gently turned
him down. This was his mess, and he was going to
get himself out of it on his own.

"Want to talk about it?" Charlie gently asked.

"The *Househusbands*?" Liam scowled as he
thought of how he had been done wrong by the
show. "Not really."

"Then, time for a change of subject!" Charlie announced. "Listen, I know you said you weren't dating, but how would you feel about something low-key and casual?"

"Like what?" Liam asked, his voice heavy with suspicion.

Before Charlie could answer, they heard an excited shriek from Sarah.

"I found it! I found it!"

Liam and Charlie hurried in the direction of her voice, where they found Sarah standing in front of a six-foot Fraser fir.

"Isn't it the most beautiful tree you've ever seen?" she asked.

With its upward-turned branches and blue-green needles, Charlie had to agree that it was a magnificent tree. "Looks like you've found your Christmas tree," he said. "Let's get someone to cut it down so you can get it home and start decorating."

―――――

Back at the house, Liam left Charlie and Sarah in charge of finding a spot for the tree while he went up to the attic and started carrying down boxes. When he returned to the living room, he found Charlie had positioned the tree in front of the room's main window.

"You should probably turn off the radiators or at least lower the heat," Charlie said. "It will keep the tree from drying out. And don't forget to water it daily."

"We have to keep the tree alive until Christmas," Sarah explained to her uncle as she opened one of the boxes he put down.

"You can be in charge of the watering," Liam said as Sarah began removing tissue paper and unpacking the ornaments.

"We never finished our conversation at the Christmas tree farm," Charlie said as he untangled a strand of Christmas tree lights.

"What conversation was that?"

"The dating conversation."

Liam sighed. "You're not going to give up, are you?"

"Just hear me out. I'm thinking of a coffee date. I've got this friend named Stuart. He owns the town bookstore. Smart. Intelligent. Cute."

"If Stuart is smart, intelligent, and cute, why is he single?"

"Why are you single?" Charlie lobbed back.

"It's a choice."

"Maybe it's a choice for Stuart, too."

"And how about you, Mr. Fisher? You're playing matchmaker with everyone else's love life. What about yours?"

"It's Christmas!" Charlie waved a hand dismissively. "I don't have time for romance. I've got too much to do! Maybe in the new year."

Liam raised an eyebrow. "In the new year?" he skeptically asked.

"Honest. I don't want to be single forever. I want to find someone to share my life with. But enough about me. Let's get back to you. How about it? Coffee date with Stuart? Last night wasn't so bad, and you had a good time, right?"

"Yes, I did," Liam honestly admitted.

"You have to put yourself back out there," Charlie urged. "My friends didn't judge you last night, did they?"

"No, they didn't," Liam admitted, which was a nice change of pace. They had gotten to know him and hadn't made any snap decisions based on what they had seen on TV or read online.

"Think of it as a mini dinner party. With a guest list of two. You and Stuart. And it's just the dessert part."

"I'm not really a dessert person."

"Then, think of it as an opportunity to make a new friend."

"Didn't I make three new friends last night?"

"You can never have enough friends," Charlie proclaimed.

Liam could see this meant a lot to Charlie. And he had come over with those meals. Plus, he was helping with the Christmas decorating. "Make a new friend?"

Charlie nodded. "Uh huh."

Against his better judgment, Liam caved. "I'll probably regret this, but why not? I like coffee. I like conversation. How bad could it be?"

CHAPTER
EIGHT

It was bad. Very bad.

But it hadn't started that way.

Liam had gone to Stuart's shop, The Book Nook, and was surprised to discover it was the bookstore where he often brought Sarah on the weekends when she wanted to buy a book. The whole atmosphere of the shop was warm and cozy, with armchairs hidden in nooks and couches covered with pillows and afghans. It felt more like a community space than a place of business, but a place of business it was. If there was a type of book you were interested in, there was a section to find it. Romance, mystery, fiction, film, memoir, sci-fi, gardening, cooking–on and on it went. The store was like a maze, on two floors, and took up half a city block. It was the perfect place to be if you loved books, especially on a cold December afternoon, as evidenced by the seated and wandering customers.

Since the store was so inviting, Liam had credited that as a reflection of Stuart's own personality.

He couldn't have been more wrong.

They had agreed to meet in the store's café. Liam had forgotten to wear his gloves, so he was rubbing his hands together as he searched the café for Stuart. He saw a lone man with curly brown hair and wire-rimmed glasses sitting at a table nursing a cup of coffee while flipping through the latest issue of *Out* and went over to say hello.

"Stuart?"

The guy's brown eyes lit up. "Hi!"

Liam internally groaned. He knew that look. It was the hook-up look.

Liam took the seat opposite him, taking off his parka. "Sorry I'm late. I had to drop my niece off at an ice skating lesson."

"So, there's no one at your place?"

There was no mistaking the unspoken suggestion. "The cleaning woman is there," Liam lied, trying to figure out how soon he could make his escape. Before he could say anything else, he heard someone clearing their throat behind him. Loudly.

Liam turned around in his seat. Standing behind him was a bald man with a handlebar mustache, looking none too happy.

"Are you Liam?" the man asked.

"Yes."

"I'm Stuart," he said in a glacial tone.

Liam turned back to the guy sitting across from him. "I thought you were Stuart."

He shook his head and gave Liam a coy smile. "I'm anyone you want me to be."

Liam grabbed his coat and left the table, turning to Stuart. "Sorry about that. I asked if he was Stuart, and he didn't correct me."

"Did you?" The icy tone was still there, and it was icier, if that was even possible.

"I made a mistake." Jeez, what did this guy want? Why was he acting so huffy? "Do-over?"

Stuart gave a dramatic sigh. "Grab a table and I'll be back with two coffees."

Liam found a table far away from the guy with the magazine, who kept sending him flirtatious looks. Liam ignored him. Stuart returned to the table, putting down two mugs, along with a small pitcher of milk and some packets of sugar.

"Black is fine with me," Liam said, taking a sip of

the coffee. "You have a lovely store. I bring my niece here all the time."

"Thank you." Stuart gazed around the store proudly. "I've worked hard to make it a place where people want to come. How old is your niece?"

"Eight."

"What does she like to read?"

"Right now, she's into Beverly Cleary. She can't get enough of her books. We read them out loud every night before she goes to sleep. I'm going to miss it when I go back home."

Stuart gave him a confused look. "I thought you lived here? In town."

Liam shook his head as he took another sip of coffee. "No. I live in New York City. I'm watching my niece for the next few weeks while her parents are out of town."

At the mention of New York City, Stuart's face turned to stone and he slammed down his mug, sloshing coffee onto the table. "I don't do long-distance relationships. The last relationship I had was a long-distance relationship, and it turned out to be a disaster." Stuart's voice started to rise. "I thought we meant something to each other, but it turns out every time I left New York City to come back here, he was hooking up with his personal trainer, who kept trying to gaslight me."

"Gaslight you?" Seriously? Or was Stuart perhaps exaggerating?

"Whenever I went back to New York City, I would find my stuff in our apartment moved around. Clothes weren't where I had left them in the closet, shoes I left in one spot were in a different spot. It was little things, but it was all a message to let me know."

"Let you know what?" Liam carefully asked.

"That he was in my space," a seething Stuart stated. "Our bed. That he was stealing my man!" Stuart gave Liam a crafty look. "They thought they were so smart, but I caught them in the act when I arrived at the apartment early one weekend. They were doing it in the shower. You should have seen the expression on their faces when I lunged at them with a knife."

Liam blinked at Stuart in disbelief. "You *lunged* at them...with...a...knife."

"I wasn't going to use it," Stuart casually explained. "I only wanted to scare them. It was for effect."

Liam didn't know what to say. Obviously, Stuart's boyfriend's betrayal still ran deep. Too deep, actually. And Liam's life was already complicated. He didn't need any more drama in it. No, thank you.

Liam scalded his tongue finishing his coffee and threw some bills on the table, not wanting Stuart to think he owed him anything. Their date was officially over.

"This was nice, but I've got to run. Merry Christmas!"

———

Once outside the bookstore, Liam wasted no time calling Charlie on his cell, planning to give him an earful. He wanted to tell him all about his horrible date while the details were still fresh in his mind.

"Is your coffee date over already?" Charlie asked. Liam could hear a tone of worry in Charlie's voice. Good. He had a reason to be worried, and he was about to find out why.

"More like a coffee therapy session."

"How so?"

"I thought you said you were friends with Stuart."

"Well, not exactly friends like I am with J.P. and Christopher and Gregory," Charlie slowly answered.

"Then what?"

"Acquaintances?"

"Passing acquaintances?" Liam clarified.

"He's always been pleasant when I've been in the store," Charlie said, sounding defensive. "And the last time I saw him, he mentioned he was dating again."

"You didn't think to ask him why he was dating *again*?" Liam pointed out. "That should have been a red flag."

"What happened? What went wrong?"

"Have you heard the expression, 'don't judge a book by its cover'? Well, Stuart may seem perfect on the outside, but he's not on the inside." Liam proceeded to fill Charlie in on the antics of his date.

"Ouch!" Charlie exclaimed. "I had no idea he had so much baggage. He's always been so calm and friendly when I've talked with him in the bookstore. When I suggested meeting you, he seemed into it."

"I don't know why. The guy clearly has trust issues."

"It won't happen again," Charlie promised. "Next time—"

Liam cut him off. "There won't be a next time. No more fix-ups."

"It was one date. Granted, a bad one, but you can't throw in the towel."

"I can and I will. No more dates, Charlie," Liam said, a steely tone in his voice. With those final words, he disconnected the call.

———

"Liam? Liam? Hello? Are you there?"

The line was dead.

Charlie sighed. Okay, Stuart had been a mistake. Lesson learned. In the future, he'd have to do his research so the next date went much more smoothly.

Because there *would* be a next date. There had to be. Because Santa had to find Liam a boyfriend.

And there were only twenty more days until Christmas.

CHAPTER
NINE

The best part of Liam's day was walking Sarah to school. They would talk about what she thought she was going to learn that day, her teacher, her friends, her after-school plans, and what they were going to do for fun that night.

"Sarah!" Liam called up the stairs. "Come on! Speed it up. You're going to be late."

Sarah rushed down the stairs, tossing her Snoopy backpack over one shoulder. Liam handed her a brown paper bag with her lunch inside. "Chop, chop. We need to get going. I shouldn't have let you stay up so late watching that movie. Not on a school night."

Liam hustled Sarah out the front door, and as they started walking down the street, she slipped her hand into Liam's, something she did every morning.

She smiled up at him. "I like walking to school with you, Uncle Liam."

Liam's heart melted, not only at the words but at having Sarah's tiny hand nestled within his own. He loved this kid so much. She was always so bright and sunny and happy. Nothing ever seemed to get her down.

"I like walking to school with you, too."

"You're more fun than walking with Mommy."

"What do you mean? Don't you like walking to school with her?"

Sarah shrugged. "Yeah, but Mommy is always too busy to talk to me. She always says, 'give me a minute' or 'wait just one second'. She's always on her phone answering emails or texts."

Liam knew Penelope was a workaholic, and obviously, Sarah did, too. "You know your mommy loves you, right? She has a very important job and she's very busy."

"I know, but sometimes I wish she'd just be a mommy."

"What do you mean?"

"Janie's mommy stays home all day. She's waiting when Janie gets home from school to hear all about her day."

"But your mommy listens to your day, doesn't she?"

"When she gets home from work," Sarah explained. "But sometimes she's too tired to listen to me and asks if we can talk after dinner."

Liam fumed. The next time he was on the phone with his sister, he was going to have a serious conversation with her. He knew Penelope and his brother-in-law adored their daughter, and they worked as hard as they did to give her the best of everything, but they needed to be reminded that material things weren't everything. Sometimes, a few minutes of attention meant the world to a small child.

When they reached the school, Liam bent down on his knees so Sarah could give him a hug and a kiss on the cheek. "Love you," he said.

"Love you more!" she said back, as she did every morning.

Liam watched Sarah walk into the school with a friend. As he did, he saw a group of moms standing across the street. It was always the same four women, with the queen bee of their group standing in the middle, surveying everyone around her. He knew she was the queen bee from the way the other women always deferred to her. It reminded him of the cliques back in high school, and it made him want to roll his eyes. Didn't anyone ever grow up?

On the opposite corner, there was always one woman who stood alone, a redhead looking fabulous in dark sunglasses and what he assumed was a real fur coat, it was so thick and lush, with a designer handbag slung over one shoulder. Every day, it was a different designer bag. Chanel. Gucci. Ferragamo. Burberry. In all the times he'd dropped Sarah off, he'd never seen any of the other moms talk to her. He wondered what her story was. Maybe one morning he'd strike up a conversation, but not today. He was running late and needed to get to Bailey's for his shift.

————

That night, Liam was exhausted. It had been another long day of being on his feet, wrangling children on and off Santa's lap. After giving Sarah dinner, all he wanted to do was collapse on the couch and veg out. He had just picked up the remote and was aiming it at the TV when Sarah came into the living room.

"Finished with all your homework?" he asked. She knew the rule, which was a Penelope rule. No TV until all her homework was done.

She nodded while handing him a piece of paper.

"What's this?" he asked.

"A reminder."

"For what?" He scanned the page.

"The Christmas cookies."

"What Christmas cookies?"

"The cookies Mommy said she would make for the Christmas bake sale."

"When is it?"

"Tomorrow."

"What?" Liam sighed. "How many cookies am I supposed to bake by tomorrow?"

Sarah shrugged. "I don't know. I think it's on the form."

Liam perused the paper Sarah had handed him. "It's not. It just says where I'm supposed to drop the cookies off."

"The other form," Sarah patiently explained. "On the refrigerator."

There was a mountain of papers attached to the refrigerator with magnets. Shouldn't his sister have given him a heads-up about important info like this? Liam got off the couch and returned to the kitchen, shuffling through the papers until he found the form he needed. He shrieked.

"Your mom promised to make eight dozen cookies?" he asked in disbelief.

Sarah started doing the math in her head. "Eight times twelve..."

"Ninety-six!" Liam exclaimed. "That's almost a hundred cookies. How am I supposed to bake a hundred cookies by tomorrow morning?"

"With the oven?"

"Let's see what's in the cabinets," Liam grumbled. So much for a *Girls5Eva* binge. By the time he finished baking all these cookies, it would be time for bed. "I'm sure your mom has some bags of chocolate chips."

"They have to be Christmas cookies."

"What does that mean?"

"They have to be decorated," Sarah patiently explained. "For Christmas."

Liam sighed again. He didn't know the first thing about baking, despite having had a roommate who was a baker. He knew even less about decorating cookies. He grabbed his iPad off the kitchen counter and Googled Christmas cookies. How hard could it be?

———

It was hard. Very hard.

"Why don't we just buy some cookies at the supermarket?" Liam suggested. "That would be so much easier." He didn't know what he was doing wrong, but his first two batches of cookies had been disasters. One batch was super soft–almost liquidy–while the second burned to a crisp.

Sarah gasped at her uncle in horror. "That would be cheating. Cheating is wrong."

Out of the mouth of babes, Liam thought. "Okay, we'll try again."

An hour later, Liam took two trays of cookies out of the oven.

"They look burned," Sarah announced.

"They're not burned. Not like they were the last time," Liam clarified. "They're a little bit crispy. Don't worry, once we frost them, they'll look great."

After he finished frosting the first batch, Sarah wrinkled her nose, pointing to the iPad propped up on the counter. "How come they don't look like the pictures?"

"Those cookies were professionally frosted. Of course they're going to look better than ours."

Sarah gave her uncle a dubious look. "Our cookies look scary."

Liam didn't want to admit it, but she was right.

In addition to not being a baker, he also wasn't an artist, and he didn't have a steady hand when it came to frosting. "They're not scary." Liam's mind scrambled. "They look like characters from *The Nightmare Before Christmas*."

"*The Nightmare Before Christmas*?"

"It's a spooky Halloween Christmas movie."

"A Halloween and Christmas movie?" Sarah stared at Liam in confusion. "What's that?"

Liam explained the movie to Sarah. "We'll watch it one night."

"I don't think I'm supposed to bring spooky Christmas cookies to the bake sale. I need to bring *pretty* Christmas cookies," Sarah stressed. "And those cookies are *not* pretty."

"It doesn't matter what the cookies look like," Liam assured his niece. "It's how they taste."

Liam grabbed one and took a bite. Sarah did the same. They both spit it out at the same time.

"Eww! Salty!" Sarah exclaimed, sticking her tongue out and scraping it against her teeth. "Yuck!"

Sarah was right. The cookies were salty and tasted like Play-Doh. Only ten times worse. He must have gotten confused when he was mixing the ingredients.

"What are we going to do, Uncle Liam?" Sarah implored, eyes filled with worry.

There was only one thing he could do. Call for help.

———

"I really appreciate you coming over on such short notice," Liam said to Charlie, holding open the front door.

"Not a problem," Charlie said, unwinding his scarf as he walked inside and followed after Liam. "I love making Christmas cookies."

Charlie stopped in his tracks as he walked into the kitchen. It was a disaster. It looked like Liam had used every bowl, baking sheet, and piece of cutlery. Cookie dough and frosting were splattered everywhere.

"We made a mess," Sarah announced from the stool she was sitting on. "Are you going to help Uncle Liam make some good cookies, Charlie?"

"Thanks a lot, Squirt," Liam grumbled.

"I'm going to try," Charlie said. He turned to Liam. "How about you tuck Miss Sarah into bed, and I'll start cleaning up down here? A clean kitchen makes for easier baking." Then, he gave Sarah a kiss on top of her head. "You go to sleep and have sweet dreams. When you wake up in the morning, your cookies will be waiting for you."

Sarah gave Charlie a hug. "Thank you!"

Three hours later, the cookies were done. Charlie had scooted Liam out of the kitchen, telling him to relax in the living room. When the last cookie was frosted, Charlie called him back into the kitchen.

"You baked these all yourself?" Liam asked, looking around in amazement. "You didn't have any Christmas elves helping you?"

"If I remember correctly, *you're* the elf and you didn't do such a great job in the baking department."

"These look too good to eat," Liam said as he admired the different platters of cookies on the kitchen counter and table.

"Try one," Charlie urged. He held one out in the shape of a Christmas tree decorated with green frosting and tiny red dots, bringing it to Liam's lips. Liam gave Charlie a smile before opening his mouth, allowing Charlie to slip part of the cookie inside. As he gently bit down, his lips closed around Charlie's finger, giving it a gentle suck as he broke off a piece of the cookie.

Charlie couldn't help but be aware of Liam's

lips. They were plump and firm and looked so kiss-able. He'd never noticed that before. Well, he'd never been so up close in Liam's personal space. That was probably why. Now that he'd taken the first bite, Charlie expected Liam to reach for the cookie himself, but instead, Liam's lips locked more firmly around his finger.

"Mmm. So good," Liam whispered.

Was he talking about the cookie or his finger? Charlie wondered, suddenly feeling lightheaded. Did Liam know what he was doing? It was almost as if he was tasting Charlie instead of the cookie. And that was sort of turning Charlie on.

"Fingers are off limits," Charlie scolded, snapping out of his daze and popping his finger out of Liam's mouth before his overactive imagination got carried away. Liam was *only* eating a cookie. Nothing more. It wasn't like he was coming on to him. He'd made it clear more than once that he wasn't looking for a boyfriend.

"Oops! Sorry." Liam blushed, popping the rest of the cookie in his mouth. "Guess I kind of lost myself. It was so tasty."

My finger or the cookie, Charlie wondered again as he wiped off his finger with a napkin, studying Liam as he finished chewing. Yes, he could see a guy falling for Liam. He was the whole package. He just had to figure out who to deliver him to.

"You don't know how much I appreciate this," Liam said, waving at the platters. "You've rescued me again."

"Anything for Sarah."

"I think she might have a little crush on you," Liam confessed. "When I told her you were coming over to help, her whole face lit up."

"What can I say? I'm crushable." Charlie decided it was time to get Operation Christmas Boyfriend back on track. "How about you, Mr. West? Are you crushable material?"

"I'm solo material," Liam reminded him.

Charlie huffed in exasperation. "You can't expect to be alone the rest of your life."

"Who said anything about the rest of my life? For now, I'm happy with just me."

But Sarah isn't, Charlie reminded himself.

Liam gazed at the clock on the kitchen wall. "It's almost midnight. I'm sorry this took so long. You should get home."

"After I clean up."

"I'll do the cleaning up," Liam firmly stated, taking Charlie by the shoulders and marching him in the direction of the front door. "It's the least I can do.

You've already done more than enough, and I'm extremely grateful. I owe you one. A big one."

Charlie turned his head around, a wicked grin on his face. "Say that again."

Liam groaned. "You heard me the first time."

"I certainly did. And you'll be hearing from me once I figure out who to set you up on a date with next!"

CHAPTER
TEN

"Wow!" The following morning, Sarah stared at the platters of cookies with shock and awe, rubbing away the last bits of sleep from her eyes. "They're so pretty. Charlie made all of these?"

Liam nodded. "Uh huh. I wanted you to see them before I boxed them all up. And they taste really good, too. I sampled a couple. Want one?"

"Cookies for breakfast?" Sarah stared at her uncle dubiously.

"I won't tell if you won't," Liam promised as he held a platter out to his niece. She selected a snowman cookie decorated with mini gumdrops, and he watched as she took a bite.

"It's not salty!" Sarah proclaimed with a smile. "It's delicious."

Liam pretended to be hurt. "I didn't mean for my cookies to be salty."

Sarah pressed her head against Liam's side as she munched on her cookie. "I know you tried your best, Uncle Liam." She gave him a few consoling pats on the back. "But Charlie is a better baker."

"I agree," Liam said as he began transferring the cookies into Tupperware containers while nibbling on a gingerbread man.

"And he's a really good decorator," she continued. "He helped a lot with the Christmas tree."

"He did," Liam agreed.

"And he's cute."

Liam laughed. "Yes, he's cute."

"So, how come you don't go out with him?"

Liam choked on the bit of gingerbread man he was chewing on. "Go out with Charlie?" he gasped while trying to suck in a breath.

Sarah eagerly nodded.

"Why would I want to go out with Charlie?"

"Because he's nice," Sarah patiently explained. "And he does nice things for us."

"Well, yes. Sure."

"Don't you like him?"

"Of course I like him. But I don't *like him* like him."

Sarah looked perplexed. "Why not?"

Good question, Liam thought to himself. "Charlie is my friend," he explained. "Friends and dating don't mix. If you go out with a friend and things don't work out, well, there's a chance you might lose that friend. I like having Charlie as a friend."

And as he said the words, Liam realized they were true. Since coming to Bramford Hills, he'd made a friend in Charlie. Someone who saw him for who he was and didn't have any sort of agenda. Who didn't want anything from him other than to be there for him.

"Monica and Chandler were friends on *Friends,* and then they got married," Sarah pointed out.

"That's a TV show," Liam patiently stated. "TV shows are make-believe. They're not like real life. Uncle Liam doesn't have time for dating—" *Even though he keeps getting roped into blind dates courtesy of Charlie,* Liam added silently, "—and he's too busy taking care of you and working at Bailey's. Now, let's get going. You run up and get dressed, and I'll finish boxing up these cookies so we can head off to school."

"You should go out with Charlie," Sarah decreed

before leaving the kitchen. "He would be the perfect boyfriend."

"For somebody else," Liam shouted after his niece. "But not for me."

The last thing Liam needed in his life was a boyfriend...even one who would be as perfect as Charlie.

———

After dropping Sarah off at her classroom, Liam headed to the school cafeteria with his cookies. He couldn't wait to unbox them and put them on display. Even though they were homemade, they looked professional. He was sure they were going to sell like crazy.

When he arrived, he found the Queen Bee, who was always outside the school, sitting at a table at the cafeteria entrance. Flanking her on both sides was her mom posse.

"Good morning!" Liam greeted them with a smile. "I'm reporting for cookie delivery!"

Queen Bee stared at Liam with disdain, which shocked him. Why would she give him such a dirty look?

"What...are...those?" she asked, almost hissing,

staring at his stacked Tupperware with something akin to horror.

"Cookies," he slowly said. "Christmas cookies."

"We have more than enough Christmas cookies. Thank you. We don't need yours." She gave him a little shooing motion, as if indicating he should leave.

He was not leaving. He knew when Sarah came down to the cafeteria later today for lunch, she'd be looking for Charlie's cookies. He dropped the cookies on the table. "My sister committed to making these cookies for my niece's class. Sarah Williams. She's in third grade. The cookies are for the bake sale happening later this afternoon." His tone of voice turned hard. He meant business and wasn't playing games. "Now, tell me where I should leave them, or do I have to go to the principal's office?"

The woman sighed and barely stopped herself from rolling her eyes. "Over there," she instructed, pointing with a French-tipped fingernail to a table in a dark corner.

"But there's all this open space," Liam said, pointing to the tables in front of them under bright lights. "Why there and not here?"

"This space is reserved," Queen Bee explained.

"That's right. Reserved," one of the moms repeated.

"Yes, reserved," a second mom echoed.

"Who reserves space for Christmas cookies?" he asked in disbelief. Was there some PTA rule he was unaware of? Did cookie space need to be earned based on how many meetings one attended?

"I'll show you where to put them," a low, throaty voice from behind him said.

Liam turned around, finding himself face-to-face with the Fabulous Redhead. She slipped her fur-draped arm through his and gently walked him away from the table once he had collected his cookies.

"What the hell is going on?" Liam whispered as they headed to the corner table.

"Welcome to the club."

"Club?"

"The Banished Moms Club. Courtesy of Delia and her goons. I'm Bibi Longacre. My daughter and your niece are in the same class."

"Liam West. And we're banished? Why?"

"Because we're a problem."

"Problem?"

Bibi sighed. "Are you going to repeat everything I say, sweetie? If you do, we're going to be here all day, so listen and listen closely. The woman you just spoke to is Delia Danvers. She's the head of the mean moms. They rule Bramford Hills Elementary. What they say goes, and according to them, we don't make the cut."

"Why not?"

Bibi folded her arms across her chest and bobbed her head from side to side, her gold tassel earrings swinging. "In your instance, they *know*."

"Know what?" Liam asked, a feeling of unease starting to stir in his stomach.

Bibi bit her upper lip in indecision before making a hissing sound. That's all she needed to do, and Liam instantly knew. The Viper. *Gay Househusbands*. His secret was out. But how? It had been almost a year, and Delia and her posse weren't exactly the show's target demographic.

As if reading his mind, Bibi said, "Last night, there was a repeat of Ollie's late-night show." Ollie, once again trying to rip off Andy Cohen, had a daily late-night talk show on Viva called *Let's Dish!* "It was the episode rehashing when everything came out about you and Mark and Jason."

Liam closed his eyes in defeat. Was that show going to haunt him for the rest of his life? "Okay, so we know why they don't like me. I guess I'm what? Low rent? Trashy?"

"All of the above. Plus, scandalous!" Bibi

explained, leaning in closely. "They don't do scandalous in Bramford Hills."

"Why don't they like you?" Liam asked.

Bibi threw her hands up in the air in exasperation. She was wearing all sorts of glittery jeweled rings, he noticed, except the one ring that mattered most in the suburbs: a wedding band. "I'm divorced and they all think that because I'm single, I'd want to steal their husbands."

Liam arched an eyebrow. "Do you?"

"I could if I wanted to." Bibi struck a pose, pulling back her full-length mink coat and showing off her sleek and trim body in a lavender bodysuit and thigh-high black boots. "I had a husband. Once was enough. Besides, have you seen what their husbands look like?" She didn't wait for an answer. "Count yourself lucky, although I will admit that I'm tempted to screw around with their men just to get back at them. And don't think I wouldn't succeed!"

Liam cracked a smile. "There was never a doubt in my mind."

"They probably think you're after their husbands, too. It wouldn't surprise me." Bibi placed a hand on Liam's arm. "Don't let it bother you, honey. These women are bored with their lives. They have nothing better to do with their time than to make our lives miserable because they're so miserable in their own."

"Fine," Liam said. "I can live with that. But they don't take it out on our kids, do they?"

Bibi gave it some thought. "Not obviously, but they do it in subtle ways."

Liam's rage instantly ignited. "How subtle?"

"Being left out of a group trip to a movie. Not having an extra ticket to a concert. No invite to a birthday party or slumber party. That happened to my daughter, Annie, last year, when Delia's daughter, Rose, turned seven. I had to do some fast scrambling to tell her why she didn't get an invitation. I told her it was because we were spending the weekend in the city and going to see *Wicked*, and I'd told Rose's mother she wouldn't be home for the party. Thankfully, Annie bought it."

Liam's rage was now bubbling. Of all the lowdown, mean things to do to a child. *No one* was going to hurt his niece.

"In all honesty, the kids are sort of oblivious to it," Bibi confided. "Delia and her cronies hang out with each other, which means their kids do, too, so there's no intermingling with the rest of the class."

"That doesn't piss you off?"

"Of course it does!" Bibi exclaimed, eyes bugging

out. "My daughter is just as good as their kids. I don't ever want her feeling less than. I've been trying for years to figure out a way to even the score with them, but nothing has come to mind." Bibi paused. "Until today." She started nibbling on a sparkly violet fingernail, staring intently at Liam. "I've suddenly gotten an idea, but I'm going to need your help to pull it off. Interested?"

Liam stared over at Delia and her posse, looking all smug as they cackled with each other. "If it means putting Delia in her place, then yes, I am. Count me in."

"Good!" Bibi took him by the hand. "Then, come with me!"

After leaving the school, Liam and Bibi headed to the nearest coffee shop. Once they ordered mocha lattes and found two plush armchairs to sit in, Bibi laid out her plan. "You know that the Christmas bake sale is also a competition, right?"

"It is?"

Bibi nodded as she took a sip of her latte. "The class that sells the most cookies wins a pizza party. Don't ask me why the kids get so excited about a pizza party. You'd think they never had a slice. All the money from the bake sale goes to the school's library fund. They want to build a new wing."

"Okay."

"Obviously, with Delia's cookies being front and center, they're going to sell right away and put Rose's class in the lead. We need a reason for people to come to our table as soon as they enter the cafeteria. For that to happen, we're going to offer more than cookies."

"We are?"

Bibi nodded, an excited look washing over her face. "Oh, yes. Our cookies are going to come with a little bonus."

"What kind of bonus?"

"Buy a cookie–which we will be up-pricing, of course–and get a photo with a sexy Santa." Bibi leaned forward in her armchair. "You, my friend, are going to be our sexy Santa."

Liam nearly spat out his latte. "Sexy Santa?"

Bibi waved a hand. "Don't be so modest. I've seen you in your elf get-up at Bailey's, but no one is going to be interested in a sexy elf. The pointy ears are a turn-off. However, a sexy Santa is always appealing. It's sort of taboo, you know?"

"Aren't I in enough hot water from my escapades on *Gay Househusbands*? Now, you want me to scandalize this town with sexy Santa photos?"

"Come on! Loosen up. It's for a good cause. Do

you know how many bored housewives there are in this town? Have you seen what some of their husbands look like? Trust me, a photo with you will be a thrill. They get to snuggle up next to all your hotness. Smell your delicious cologne. Maybe nibble on an ear or squeeze a muscle."

"Hey!" Liam held up a hand. "I might consider being a sexy Santa, but we're going to be in an elementary school. Let's keep this G-rated."

"Does that mean you'll do it?" Bibi asked, holding her breath.

He really didn't want to. But Bibi seemed confident this scheme was going to work. And he did want to put Delia in her place. But what if it backfired? What then? Well, he'd already hit rock bottom. How much lower could he go? It also meant Sarah's class would probably make the most money from the bake sale and win the pizza party. He couldn't deny her that. Liam caved. "Fine, I'll do it. But again, it has to be G-rated. No showing of skin. My Santa suit stays buttoned up. No showing of my chest or any other body parts. This is my niece's school. I don't want to embarrass her or her parents."

Bibi happily clapped her hands together. "Yay! Don't worry, it's only a little naughty fun."

"How naughty? Because I've had my fill of naughty for this year."

"It's going to be fun naughty, not scandalous naughty. Promise!" Bibi got out of her armchair, holding a hand out to Liam and pulling him up to his feet. "Come on, we haven't got much time. We need to find you a Santa suit!"

On their way out of the coffee shop, they ran into Gregory, who did a double-take seeing Liam with Bibi.

"My worlds are colliding!" he exclaimed, his head swiveling back and forth. "How do you two know each other?"

Bibi rolled her eyes. "Why am I not surprised you would know the hottest gay man in town?"

"Darling, I'm engaged to the hottest gay man in town," Gregory corrected her. "Get your facts straight."

"Sorry. I meant the second hottest."

"You're friends?" Liam asked.

"And next door neighbors," Bibi clarified.

"Bibi has the most darling little girl," Gregory gushed. "Annie. You should set up a play date with her and your niece."

"We will," Bibi said, looping her arm through

Liam's and trying to make her way around Gregory. "If you'll excuse us, we're in a rush."

Gregory blocked Bibi's path, his eyes narrowing. "What are you up to, Beebs?"

"Up to? Me?" she innocently asked while pressing a jeweled hand against her chest. "I don't know what you're talking about."

"Come on. 'Fess up. You look like the cat that ate the canary. Dish!"

Bibi turned to Liam. "Should we tell him?"

Liam gave a shrug. "Why not?"

Bibi quickly brought Gregory up to speed on their plan. "I love it!" he cackled when Bibi had finished. "It's about time you put those bitches in their place. Count me in."

"Count you in? For what?" Bibi asked.

"To spread the word!" Gregory whipped out his cellphone and snapped a few photos of Liam. "All I have to do is send out a few photos on my social media accounts with some suggestive captions, and all the gays in Bramford Hills will come flocking to our little schoolhouse. We'll have a line out the door and around the block."

"For a picture with me?" Liam skeptically asked. "I think you're overestimating my appeal."

"Have you taken a look in the mirror lately?"

Gregory asked. "You're hot! One of the hottest guys to come through this town in a long time. With the exception of my Christopher, of course."

"I don't feel hot," Liam admitted. "If you want to know the truth, I feel dirty. Sleazy."

Gregory gasped. "Why would you say such a thing?"

"I know why," Bibi said, gently placing a comforting hand on Liam's arm. "There was a repeat of *Let's Dish!* last night and a certain episode of *Gay Househusbands* was rehashed."

"Let's call it what it is," Liam said. "The cheating episode. Although I have no memory of cheating on Mark with Jason."

"Look, I know talking about *Gay Househusbands* was taboo on Saturday night, but we're going to talk about it now," Gregory said, a commanding tone in his voice. "Whether or not you did or didn't sleep with Jason–and I don't believe you did!–you shouldn't be the one shouldering all the blame. If you did sleep with Jason, and that's a very big if, then you made a mistake. Whatever happened was in the past. It's over. Done with. Time to move on."

"Easier said than done when it's constantly thrown back in my face," Liam said, trying not to sound bitter but failing. "And damaging my career."

"Then, do something about it!" Gregory exclaimed. "Fight back. Don't run away and hide. Own your past. Look, I'm not saying you have to do a redemption tour–if this were *Ru Paul's Drag Race,* we'd call it a Ru-demption tour–but you need to take control of your narrative and show those gay house-husbands you're not going to roll over and play dead."

Is Gregory right? Liam wondered. Had he been running away and taking the easy way out instead of dealing with his problem head-on? It had just been so overwhelming when his entire world came crashing down around him. And he really hadn't had anyone close to lean on, like a boyfriend or partner, since Pablo had abandoned him at the first sign of his own opportunities, leaving him all alone.

Gregory pressed a few buttons on his phone while making a shooing motion. "Run along and get your Santa suit while I get the word out."

Bibi and Liam went to a local costume store, which was fully stocked with Santa suits. After finding one that fit, Bibi bought the costume and then told Liam they were taking it to her seamstress.

"What for?"

"Darling, if you're going to buy off the rack, then

you need to do a little creative tailoring. A nip here. A tuck there. We want to show off the goods!"

"As long as I'm a G-rated Santa!" Liam reminded Bibi. "We can leave what's under the wrapping to everyone's imagination. Besides, it's more fun wondering what's hidden under the packaging than showing it off."

After seeing Liam in his Santa suit, Bibi's seamstress, an elderly Italian woman who barely spoke any English, knew exactly what to do. When Liam gazed at himself in the mirror a second time, he saw that the Santa suit fit him like a glove, clinging to his muscles in all the right places.

"Oooh, honey," Bibi exclaimed, happily clapping her hands, "they are so going to want to unwrap you!"

When they got back to the school, Liam was shocked to see there was a line out the door and winding around the block.

"Looks like Gregory delivered as promised," Bibi gleefully stated. "Ready to take some photos?"

Liam gazed at the line of men and women waiting for him. They had all come here for him. Okay, maybe some of them were here because they wanted to see the evil Viper in person, but that couldn't be the case with everyone, could it?

There was only one way to find out.

Because Liam was done with running away.

He waved to everyone as he headed to the front of the line and walked into Bramford Hills Elementary. "Who wants a photo with a disgraced reality star?" he announced.

———

Charlie was supposed to be designing an advertisement. One of his company's *New York Times* bestselling romance authors had a new novel coming out, and they were running a full-page ad in *People* and *Us Weekly*. This was his fourth attempt at the ad. His boss kept kicking it back to him, telling him it needed to be bigger and bolder.

Charlie's phone buzzed. He ignored it, keeping his attention on his computer screen. But then, it buzzed again. And again. Someone wanted him. Picking up his cell, he saw there were a number of texts from Gregory, followed by some photos. When he clicked on the photos, his mouth dropped open.

It was Liam. Santa Liam.

A sexy Santa Liam. Like he'd never seen him before.

Charlie knew Liam was handsome. Okay, very

handsome. He'd have to be blind not to notice. But handsome guys were everywhere. Except in these photos, there was a little something *extra*. A naughty twinkle in Liam's eye. A seductive smile. A look that promised something intimate, only to be discovered behind a closed bedroom door.

In a word, Liam was hot. No, very hot. Like, 'want to rip his clothes off and get naked with him' hot and 'have him do all sorts of wild and fun things with you' hot.

Charlie felt himself starting to get hard. Again. Just like the other night when he'd been Googling Liam online.

Enough!

Charlie shut down his carnal thoughts and scrolled through Gregory's texts, discovering that Liam was posing for photos at Bramford Hills Elementary to help raise money for the school's library fund.

Suddenly, Charlie had the urge to read a book.

He abandoned his computer, deciding it was time for a late lunch and a visit to Bramford Hills Elementary. If Liam was posing for photos, then he was going to get one for himself as proof that he knew Liam. It would be the perfect bait to use as he searched for a new guy to set Liam up with.

Minutes after locking his front door and walking down the street, Charlie heard Claude's voice calling out to him.

"Chuck! Chuckster! Chuckeeeeee!"

Charlie ground his teeth. Whether intentional or not, Claude was calling him by the wrong name again. He turned around impatiently, deciding he wasn't going to say anything this time.

"What is it?" he snapped as Claude caught up with him, laden with shopping bags filled with wrapped Christmas presents. It came out harsher than he wanted, but Claude always pushed his buttons. Plus, the only time he heard from him was when he wanted something.

"You're sounding a bit testy," Claude sniffed. "Does it have anything to do with the man I saw you with on Sunday?"

"Man?" Charlie's guard was instantly up. It was never good when Claude wanted personal info because he never knew what he was going to do with it. "What man?"

"Tall, dark, and handsome," Claude supplied. "You were with him at the Christmas tree farm."

"Oh! Liam!" Darn! That slipped out.

Claude pounced, his eyes lighting up. "Who's Liam?"

Charlie debated on giving Claude an answer. He could just keep him in the dark. But Claude did have a pool of gay friends. Maybe one of them would be interested in Liam. But did he really want to do that? They were probably just as horrible as Claude. Okay, that was mean. Claude wasn't horrible. Just irritating. He always had been and always would be. Plus, he reminded himself as he always did when dealing with Claude, living in a small town meant being polite and courteous, even when he didn't want to be. "Just a friend."

"Friend..." Claude paused and then said suggestively, "...or boyfriend?"

"Friend," Charlie said in a firm voice, making it clear the topic wasn't open to further conversation.

"But maybe hoping to be more?"

Charlie ignored the question. "I don't mean to be rude, but I'm running late."

"Where are you off to?"

"Christmas errands," Charlie lied.

"I won't keep you," Claude said. "I just wanted to personally invite you to our Christmas party. The invite's in the mail, but I wanted to mention it so you could mark your calendar. I hope you don't mind that we didn't hire you to do the catering. We wanted to go with someone a little more high-end."

You wanted to overpay someone you read about in a magazine and then brag to everyone at the party about how much you spent on the catering, Charlie thought to himself. *And you wanted to tell me to my face that you weren't hiring me for whatever sense of satisfaction that gave you.* But fine. It was Claude's money. He could do whatever he wanted with it.

Charlie pretended to look excited. "It was so thoughtful of you to include me on your guest list. And I'm so glad you found a caterer. I'm so booked up, I would have had to turn you down. I'll look for the invite and let you know if I can make it."

"Bring your friend, if you want," Claude said. "The more the merrier. Devon and I always love meeting new people."

"How thoughtful of you," Charlie said before peeking at his watch. "I really have to run." He turned his back on Claude and hurried down the street. "Bye!"

CHAPTER
ELEVEN

It wasn't as bad as he thought.

In fact, it was kind of fun. Everyone was being so nice to Liam, and they all seemed genuinely excited to meet him and have their photo taken with him.

Well, not everyone.

Liam thought Delia was going to lose her shit when she saw him and Bibi return to the cafeteria and take center stage in the room, pulling the table with their cookies from out of the dark corner.

"What do you think you're doing?" she demanded, marching up to them and getting in Bibi's face.

"Step back," Bibi ordered, putting out a hand and gently pushing Delia away from her. "In case it's not obvious, we're working at the Christmas bake sale."

Delia pointed her thumb at Liam. "And what's he doing here in that outfit?"

Bibi tossed her red tresses back as she began opening the boxes of cookies. "Didn't we tell you, sweetie? We're going to be offering something besides just cookies. Pictures with Santa!"

"That's not allowed!"

"Says who?" Bibi threw back. "You might be president of the PTA, honey, but there aren't any rules as to what can and can't be sold here today. Plus, it's for a good cause." Bibi gave Delia a saccharine sweet smile. "You can't be against that, can you? Or should we start calling you Lady Scrooge?"

People in line started hissing at Delia. "You're holding things up."

"Move it, lady! We haven't got all day."

"Get to the back of the line!"

Bibi made a shooing motion at Delia with her hands. "If you don't mind moving it along? We've got cookies to sell and pictures to take."

Realizing she had lost the battle, Delia sulked off as Liam took his place behind the table with their cookies.

"Come right up and meet Santa *Cause*," Bibi

announced. "This Santa is raising money for a good cause. Cold, hard cash for a new school library. Dip into your pockets. Only twenty-five dollars for a cookie and a photo with Santa Liam!"

"Twenty-five dollars?" Liam whispered in Bibi's ear. "Are you nuts?"

"Am I?" Bibi asked with satisfaction. "I don't think so. Just look at them all reaching into their wallets and purses."

Liam was dumbstruck. Bibi was right. No one was questioning the price. "Let's raise some money!" she announced to everyone in the room.

Bibi was the perfect photographer. She knew exactly how to position people with Liam and take a photo with her phone within seconds, showing it to the person before texting it off to them. Liam made time for everyone, asking their name and giving his undivided attention as he made small talk before posing and sending them off with a cookie.

"Who's next?" Liam asked, shocked when Eloise from Human Resources at Bailey's sidled up to him.

"This is how you spend your day off?" Eloise asked as she handed Liam her twenty-five dollars and plopped down on his lap. She draped an arm around his shoulder as she snuggled against his chest, toying with the buttons of his jacket. "I think I might have made a mistake casting you as an elf."

"You said you didn't want me as Santa," Liam reminded her. "Besides, this is a different demographic."

"I was wrong," Eloise said. "I can admit when I'm wrong."

"Say cheese!" Bibi called out.

"I've got an idea," Eloise said as they smiled for the camera. "Tell me if you like it."

"Shoot."

"How would you feel about Santa after Dark? The bigwigs at Bailey's are always looking for new ways to get more customers into the store. We could offer cocktails and photos with Santa for adults after the store closes at night. Maybe do it one or two nights a week so it feels kind of special."

"And you'd want me to be your Santa?"

"Have you taken a look at this line?" Eloise asked. "Of course! Give the people what they want. And honey, they want you!"

Bibi sidled up to Eloise. "You do realize that Liam would have to be paid extra. Not his usual hourly rate."

Eloise jerked a thumb at Bibi. "Who's this? Your agent?"

Considering he hadn't heard from his agent in months and Bibi was currently negotiating on his behalf, the answer was yes. "Ms. Longacre is the one to talk to about my going rate."

Eloise sighed as she got off Liam's lap. "I'm sure I can swing a few extra bucks."

"We'll talk," Bibi told Eloise as she texted her a photo. Then, she turned back to the line with her camera. "Next!"

———

It was Charlie's turn to take a photo.

Waiting in line, watching Liam as Santa, had been a revelation. This was a man who was a natural-born performer. There was a spark and energy to Liam that was missing when he was working as an elf at Bailey's. Here, the spotlight was all on him and he was shining. Maybe it was because it was for a good cause, or maybe it was because this was what Liam was meant to do.

"Next!" the woman taking the photos called out again, snapping her fingers in Charlie's face. "Let's get moving! We haven't got all day."

Charlie stepped up to Liam, who was shocked to see him.

"What are you doing here?"

"Nothing in this town ever stays quiet," Charlie explained, waving his phone in the air. "Gregory looped me in."

"He bought a hundred dollars' worth of cookies," Liam said.

"My pockets aren't as deep as Gregory's. I'm afraid I can only afford one cookie. That entitles me to one photo, right?"

Liam patted his knee. "Hop on board and tell Santa what you want for Christmas. Have you been a good boy this year?"

Charlie nestled himself on Liam's knee. "I don't know. You're Santa. You tell me."

Liam gazed into Charlie's eyes. "I think you've been very good."

"Have I?" Charlie asked, locking eyes with him.

Liam nodded. "You've been a very good friend. If you hadn't baked those cookies last night, I wouldn't be sitting here right now, realizing how much I miss being an actor. You've also helped me with Sarah by decorating for Christmas and making us meals. You've introduced me to your friends, so I'm not home alone feeling sorry for myself. So, thank you again."

Charlie didn't know how it happened, but he slid off Liam's knee and into his lap, putting his butt into direct contact with Liam's package. And it was quite a package.

Maybe it was because of the sudden extra weight, but Liam shifted in his seat. As he did, he rubbed himself against Charlie's butt.

Charlie couldn't help himself. He inadvertently rubbed up against Liam's crotch, more than once, as he tried to resettle himself. And then, he felt something. Something hard. Pressing against him. Was it his imagination, or did Liam have an erection?

"Sorry about that," Liam apologized with a blush on his cheeks, shifting Charlie back to his knee. "Sometimes, it has a mind of its own." He turned back to the woman taking photos. "Bibi, we're ready."

"You two look so good together," Bibi gushed. Their heads were tilted and pressed against each other as Liam drew Charlie closer to him. "If we were running an ad, I'd go with this photo of the two of you," she said, aiming her phone. "Sweet and sexy."

"We can guess who the sexy one is," Charlie said with a raised eyebrow.

"And we know who the sweet one is," Liam lobbed back. "Although, I don't know." He took a closer look at Charlie. "In the right light, you've got a sexy thing going on."

Charlie's heart fluttered, and he didn't know why. "Sweet talker." His phone pinged as Bibi texted him the photo.

"It's a great picture," Charlie said, showing it to Liam.

"Going to crop me out so you can use it as a profile pic on Grindr or Scruff?" Liam teased.

"Close," Charlie said. "I'm going to crop myself out and use it as bait to find you a man. You owe me a blind date, remember?"

Liam groaned. "I was hoping you'd forgotten."

"Although you really don't need my help finding a date." Charlie pointed to the line. "You can have your pick of any guy here."

"Why are you so determined to fix me up with someone?" Liam asked.

"You're putting your life back together, right? You used to have a boyfriend. Don't you want to have one again?"

"I guess." Liam shrugged. "At some point."

"Some point might never happen unless you put yourself back out there."

"I suppose..." Liam reluctantly admitted.

"Okay, no more talk of boyfriends and dating," Charlie said. "Are you doing anything tonight?"

"No plans. Just me and Sarah at home."

"Think you can find a babysitter?"

"Sure. Why?"

Charlie waved a hand in the air. "It's obvious that you're meant to perform and have an audience. Feel like having one tonight?"

There was no missing the excitement that flickered in Liam's eyes. It gave Charlie a warm feeling inside for two reasons. First, Liam was happy. Second, he was the one making him happy.

"How?"

"That's for me to know and you to find out," Charlie mysteriously stated. "I'll explain when you swing by my house tonight. Come at seven."

And with those final words, Charlie left Liam's lap and disappeared back into the school.

———

"Uncle Liam, why were you dressed as Santa?"

It was six o'clock, and Liam was trying to hustle Sarah out of Bramford Hills Elementary. He'd spent the entire afternoon posing for photos while Sarah was in the gym playing basketball in the after-school league. Now, she was taking her sweet time as she loaded up her backpack with textbooks and notebooks from her locker. She should have done it when her game was over, but instead she had gone to the school library to start on her homework while Liam finished up.

"I was helping out the real Santa."

"Like Charlie?"

"What do you mean?"

Sarah slapped a hand over her mouth, like she had let a secret slip out. Before he could question her some more, he heard a voice behind them.

"Liam! It is Liam, isn't it?'

Liam turned around to find a stranger staring at him. Tall, lanky, with defined features and feathery brown hair. Like a male model found on a European runway. He was dressed all in green–forest green wool pants, green suede loafers, green turtleneck, and green overcoat with a light green scarf tossed around his neck and matching leather gloves. Although he didn't know who the man was, the man seemed to know him. Liam silently groaned. He hoped this wasn't a *Househusbands* groupie.

"Yes..." Liam hesitantly answered. "I'm sorry, but

have we met? You seem to know me, but I don't know you."

"Indirectly. We have a friend in common. Charlie Fisher. I glimpsed you with him at the Christmas tree farm on Sunday."

"Okay," Liam said, still not having a clue.

"I'm sure he's mentioned me. I'm Claude." He held out a hand. "Claude Jenkins."

Liam took his hand, wondering why the name was ringing a bell. And then, he remembered. This was the guy who'd gone to high school with Charlie and J.P. and Christopher. The guy none of them had liked.

Liam wasn't one to instantly judge someone, but something about Claude made him put his guard up, and he quickly dropped Claude's clammy hand from his after giving it a quick shake. There had been something a little too possessive in Claude's grip for Liam's liking.

"Who's this adorable little creature?" Claude purred, getting a glimpse of Sarah, who was hiding behind Liam.

Sarah popped her head out from behind her uncle's waist. "I'm not a creature," she almost shouted. "I'm a little girl!"

"This is my niece, Sarah," Liam introduced. "Sarah, this is Mr. Jenkins. He's a friend of Charlie's."

"Please, call me Claude."

Liam wasn't sure if he was talking to him or Sarah. Maybe both of them. "Claude," Liam repeated.

Sarah stared at Claude suspiciously, gazing at him from head to toe. "Is your heart two sizes too small?"

Claude stared at her in confusion. "What?"

"Are your shoes too tight?"

"I beg your pardon?" Claude asked, sounding dumbfounded.

"Do you have a dog? And if you do, is his name Max?"

Liam tried not to laugh, but a guffaw slipped out, then another as he saw Claude realize what Sarah was asking.

"Little girl, I am not the Grinch!" he huffed, looking offended.

"You can't blame her for coming to that conclusion," Liam chuckled. "You are dressed all in green." *And you sort of have a grinchy sourpuss look on your face right now*, Liam thought.

"I am not the Grinch," Claude stated for a

second time. "In fact, I'm filled with the spirit of the holiday season. My husband, Devon, and I are having a little Christmas gathering next week, and I wanted to invite you."

"Why?" The question slipped out before Liam could stop himself.

Claude looked at him in confusion, as if unable to comprehend someone turning down a party invitation from him. "Why not? You're new in town, and I assume you're getting to know people. Devon and I can introduce you to all the right people in Bramford Hills." Claude gave a disdainful sniff. "Not like Charlie and that group of friends he still runs around with from high school."

Liam's hackles rose. "What's wrong with having old friends?"

"Nothing," Claude said, realizing he'd made a mistake as his voice took on a calming tone. "Don't take what I said the wrong way. I only meant sometimes old friends hold you back. They can't take you to the next level. That's why it's so wonderful to meet new people. You never know what they might be able to do for you."

There was a next level in Bramford Hills? Liam wondered. *Who knew? And who wanted to get there other than Claude and his crew?*

"I think Charlie's doing okay with the friends he has. I met them last weekend and I liked them all."

Sarah, sensing that maybe Claude was being a bit grinchy toward Charlie, stuck up for him. "I like Charlie. A LOT!"

"I like Charlie, too," Liam agreed with his niece.

"I like Charlie," Claude soothed them both. "And he's been invited to the party. Now, as much as I'd love to keep chatting, I'm here to start rehearsals in the auditorium for the town Christmas pageant. I must be off." Claude headed down the hallway, waving a hand over his back. "See you next week. Ciao!"

Liam wasn't sure what had just happened. And it was a little presumptuous of Claude to assume he'd be going to his party.

Liam checked the time on his watch. Six-thirty. They were definitely running late. He needed to get Sarah home, feed her, get her started on her homework before Babs came over, and then make his way to Charlie's. He slammed Sarah's locker door shut. "Let's get going."

Sarah was staring down the hallway at a departing Claude, her cute little face scrunched up in a frown. "I don't like him, Uncle Liam. Even though he said he wasn't the Grinch, I don't believe him. I think he really is the Grinch. Or at least, related to him."

"Me too, Sarah," Liam agreed, holding out his hand to her as they walked toward the school exit. "Me too."

"Okay, what's the big surprise?" Liam asked when Charlie opened his front door for him. "You've got me intrigued."

"Come on in and I'll give you all the details," Charlie said, quickly closing the door so Shadow couldn't dash outside. He was an indoor kitty, but always determined to explore what was in the outside world.

"Is it my imagination, or did you decorate even more?" Liam asked as he took off his parka.

"I did add some tinsel and garland to the banister," Charlie said as he hung Liam's parka in the hall closet. "And I bought a bunch of poinsettias and a Christmas cactus."

There was a poinsettia positioned on the outside of each step leading up to the second floor, alternating between plants with white leaves and red leaves, and the Christmas cactus was blooming with pink flowers, having pride of place on the coffee table, along with a platter of cheese and crackers, a bottle of wine, and three glasses.

"Is someone else joining us?" Liam asked as he took a seat on the couch.

"We'll get to that in a bit," Charlie promised as he uncorked a bottle of merlot and poured Liam a glass.

"Thanks," Liam said, taking the glass as Charlie poured one for himself and sat in the armchair opposite him while Shadow prowled around the coffee table, hoping for a bit of cheese. "You mentioned something about an audience..."

Charlie nodded. "Yes! But one that's small. Yet intimate. I know you're an actor, and I know you like to sing. This would sort of be like singing for the public. Actually, you would be singing in public, too."

"How did you know I like to sing? I've never mentioned it."

"I might have done a little research on you after

learning about that reality show," Charlie confessed. "But only because I'd never heard of it!" he rushed to say. He didn't want Liam to think he was snooping into his past. "I was curious. I didn't know anything about your acting career."

Liam rolled his eyes. "Being on a reality show is not really acting. Well, maybe for some of the other cast members it is, but not me. I was trying to be my authentic self, but you can see how well that worked out for me." Liam took a sip of wine. "It was a hot mess."

"I didn't watch *that* episode," Charlie quickly said. He didn't know why he chose not to. After all, it was the most explosive episode of the season. But at the same time, it was vile and toxic. It had done so much damage to Liam's life–although some would say Liam had done the damage to himself–and Charlie didn't want to be a part of that in any way.

"I'm trying to forget it ever happened," Liam said. "Actually, all of it. I was such an idiot agreeing to do that show. My friend Sebastian warned me, but I didn't listen." Liam raised his wine glass. "A toast to my stupidity."

"Stop beating yourself up. You made a mistake. It's over. Time to move on."

"Gregory said something similar earlier today."

"Gregory is a smart guy. That's why I like him."

"He's also engaged to your best friend. You have to like him."

"Christopher hit the jackpot with Gregory. Some of his old boyfriends?" Charlie shuddered. "At least Christopher eventually broke up with them. Not that I ever said anything negative. You always have to walk a fine line when one of your best friends starts dating someone you know isn't right for them. But enough with talking about the past. Let's talk about tonight. How would you like to go Christmas caroling?" Charlie held his breath, waiting for Liam to burst out with excitement.

Except, he didn't.

"We're going to do all sorts of songs," Charlie continued. "*Silent Night, O Come All Ye Faithful, Joy to the World, Jingle Bells, Deck the Halls*, and a bunch more. We'll be singing in the town square."

"I don't know," Liam said, swirling the wine in his glass. "I'm not exactly feeling the Christmas spirit this year."

"How can you say that after spending hours today as Santa?"

"That was for Sarah. I'd do anything for her."

"And this is for you!" Charlie pointed out. "You

like singing, right? Why deny yourself the chance to do something you love?"

"I guess," Liam reluctantly agreed. "Maybe."

Charlie could see Liam's resistance was melting. And was that a slight glimmer of excitement in his eyes? He'd hit a nerve. He just had to keep hitting it until Liam agreed to come along.

Shadow, deciding he didn't like being ignored, chose that moment to jump up onto the couch and into Liam's lap...just as Liam was raising his wine glass. Within seconds, Liam's glass of merlot sloshed all over him. Shadow, not liking getting splashed by a few droplets, hissed before jumping back off the couch and racing down the hall to the kitchen.

"Bad kitty!" Charlie shouted before jumping to his feet and rushing over to Liam. "Your shirt's all wet. Quick, take it off and I'll toss it into the washer."

"It's no big deal," Liam said as he reached for some cocktail napkins and patted at the wet patches on his dark blue plaid flannel shirt. "You can't even see the stains."

"We're going to be outside for at least a couple of hours."

"Oh, we are, are we?" Liam asked.

"Yes, we are. You're coming caroling and I don't want to hear another word about it," Charlie firmly stated. "You know you want to go, so don't deny it. It's cold out there and you can't have a wet shirt clinging to your body. Take it off."

Liam removed his shirt, and it was all Charlie could do not to drool. He'd seen Liam shirtless on the episodes of *Househusbands* that he'd watched, but there wasn't any comparison. The real thing was so much better. Liam's chest was chiseled and furry with a lush blanket of dark chest hair. Suddenly, Charlie had an image of himself burying his face in all that fur, inhaling its musky scent, and then making his way down Liam's treasure trail before going even lower...

"Charlie?"

Charlie snapped out of his daze. "Sorry." He snatched the shirt out of Liam's hand. "Let me dash to the laundry room. I'll put some Shout on this and toss it into the wash. Then, I'll get you another shirt to wear."

Charlie disappeared to the laundry room, where he found the Shout and a scrub brush. He was working on removing the stains, his hands all wet and sudsy, when the doorbell rang.

"Do you mind getting that?" he called out to Liam.

"Sure."

Seconds later, Charlie remembered who was at the front door. Yikes! He threw the shirt into the washer, added some detergent before turning it on, and then ran back out to the living room, where a shirtless Liam and J.P.'s friend, Austin, were staring awkwardly at each other.

"Sorry, sorry, sorry," Charlie apologized. "This was not how the two of you were supposed to meet. Liam, this is Austin. Austin is a gym teacher at the high school where J.P. teaches. Austin, this is Liam." Charlie turned to Liam with a smile. "Austin is coming caroling with us."

"I think this is the first time a blind date has greeted me shirtless," Austin said. "Not that I mind."

"Give us a couple of minutes," Charlie told him, steering Liam in the direction of the stairs before he could say anything. "There was a little accident before you arrived, and we need to get Liam another shirt. Be right back!"

"I'm fine with the shirtless look," Austin called after them.

Charlie hustled Liam up to his bedroom, where he pulled open a drawer and found a black sweat-shirt. "This should fit you," he said, tossing it to Liam.

Liam caught the shirt but didn't put it on. "Mind explaining?"

"Explaining?" Charlie tried to sound innocent.

Liam pointed a finger down at the floor. "Austin?"

"Austin!" Charlie gave a smile. "Well, you did agree to another blind date."

"Yes," Liam said as he pulled the sweatshirt over his head. "But a heads-up would have been nice."

"I was going to tell you." Charlie couldn't help but notice how good his sweatshirt looked on Liam. When Charlie wore it, it was all loose and baggy. On Liam, it fit like a glove. "But I got distracted."

"Distracted? By what?"

You, Charlie thought. *Although, I don't know why! Maybe I need to jumpstart my own love life instead of yours. Because you keep inadvertently turning me on! Maybe I need a guy of my own to focus on.* "By the wine! I was just about to tell you about Austin when Shadow jumped on you."

"Well, he's here," Liam said. "So, I'm stuck."

"Don't think of it that way!" Charlie pleaded. "Think of it as a chance to meet someone new. J.P. says he's a nice guy."

"I guess I have no choice," Liam grumbled.

"He already likes you!" Charlie pointed out.

"He likes my chest," Liam tossed back.

"That's something, isn't it?" Charlie knew he was grasping at straws.

Liam rolled his eyes.

"You won't be alone," Charlie said. "I'll be there, too. And look at the bright side. You're going to be singing! You're looking forward to that, right?"

Liam shook his head and sighed. "Let's get this night over with."

Charlie watched as Liam left his bedroom and headed back downstairs. He'd wanted to do something nice with the caroling and blind date. How had it all gone so wrong?

———

Liam knew he was being a brat, but if there was one thing he didn't like, it was being blindsided, especially after what had happened on *Househusbands*. Since that infamous episode, his guard was always up.

They had walked to the town square, he and Austin side by side, with Charlie trailing behind. Liam assumed it was because Charlie wanted to give him and Austin some alone time. Austin wasn't a bad-looking guy–he had dirty blonde hair that was super shaggy, green eyes, and a crooked grin that went well with the dimple on the side of his mouth. He must have had acne as a teenager because his cheeks were pitted and craggy, but it worked for him, giving his face a rugged look. And for a gym teacher, he had the requisite body: built, built, and built. Muscles everywhere. Liam wondered if Austin spent all his free time working out in a gym or if he'd had a little steroid enhancement. Liam had never gone down that path, but he knew there were a number of guys, gay and straight, who did.

Austin kept trying to make conversation as they walked, but Liam kept giving him one-word answers. He knew Austin wasn't the one at fault, so why was he being such a prick toward him? He seemed normal. Outgoing and friendly. No red flags so far. Of course, the last guy Charlie had set him up with had seemed normal before he began channeling Alex Forrest from *Fatal Attraction*.

"Let's start over," Liam said when they reached the town square. "I didn't know our blind date was tonight, so I was caught by surprise. I was busy processing it as we walked. I'm Liam West, an out-of-work actor currently working at Bailey's department store as a Christmas elf. I'm in town for the next couple of weeks, taking care of my niece, Sarah. I like all kinds of sports, my favorite movies are film noirs, musicals, and anything starring Gena Rowlands. My favorite color is blue, my favorite food is pizza, and I don't know what I'm going to do for a career once this gig at Bailey's ends. What other opportunities are out there for out-of-work elves?"

"Maybe star in a porno? *The Elf Who Came for Christmas*," Austin threw out with a laugh. "*Jingle Balls. The Twelve Lays of Christmas.*"

Liam blinked at Austin. Had he heard him correctly?

"There's a whole subgenre of Christmas porn out there," Austin said, a tone of knowledge in his voice. "With your body, you'd find work." Austin leaned in. "Have you ever done it with someone while dressed as an elf?"

Liam couldn't tell if Austin was being serious or if he was joking. Fortunately, songbooks were being handed out as the carolers gathered on the square, and he chose not to answer.

The square was decorated like something out of a Dickens village. In the center of it, there was a fully lit and decorated Christmas tree that was at least forty feet tall with a shiny gold star on top. A nativity scene was positioned in front of the tree, with Mary, Joseph, the Three Wise Men, and assorted barn animals positioned around an empty cradle waiting for the arrival of Baby Jesus on Christmas Day. Red ribbons were wrapped around the lamp posts as well as double strands of white Christmas lights.

"Here you go," Charlie said, handing a songbook to Liam, a hopeful look on his face. "Hitting it off with Austin?" he whispered.

Liam snatched the songbook out of Charlie's hand. While he might have thawed out with Austin, he was still a bit miffed at Charlie. "The jury's still undecided."

As he turned to the first page of the songbook, Liam decided he would give Austin the benefit of the doubt. Perhaps, Austin was trying too hard to make a good first impression. For now, Liam just wanted to focus on singing.

After the first carol, *We Wish You a Merry Christmas*, was sung, Liam had to admit Charlie was right. As soon as that songbook was placed in his hands and he opened his mouth to sing, he felt like his old self. He could see the joy on the faces of the people listening to them, and it made him feel good inside. Like he used to feel on stage when he was giving a performance. As an actor, he fed off the energy of his audience, and he hadn't had an audience in such a long time.

This was what he was meant to do.

This was what he had missed doing for the last year.

The big question was, how did he get to do it again in the new year?

The group sang for an hour in the town square before deciding to go from house to house. As the group of carolers moved, Austin, who had been standing behind Liam, lagged behind.

"Psst!"

Liam turned around. Austin was tilting his head to the right, where there was a patch of trees. Liam walked over to him. "What's up?"

"Wanna do it in the woods?" Austin asked.

Liam's jaw nearly dropped open. This was the suburbs. This was the town where his niece lived! Not that he was going to say yes, but what if he did and they were caught? He couldn't scandalize Sarah or his sister that way.

"No, I don't want to do it in the woods!" Liam snapped, trying to keep his voice down so they weren't overheard. That's all he needed, rumors that the Viper was engaging in public sex. The old Liam would have agreed without a second's hesitation. But he wasn't the old Liam anymore. These last few weeks, taking care of Sarah, had made him realize there was more to life than just focusing on himself.

Austin nodded. "Yeah, I agree. It's kind of cold. We should do it inside. Are you a top or a bottom?"

"Excuse me?" While it was the requisite sex question between gay men, it still threw Liam for a loop.

"I'm not going to invest a lot of time in this relationship if we're not sexually compatible," Austin said matter-of-factly. "Why waste our time, right?"

Relationship? What relationship? They were on a first date! One that was quickly coming to an end if Liam had anything to say about it.

How much longer was he going to be on this sexual merry-go-round? he wondered. He was thirty-two years old. Everyone he knew was pairing up. And here he was, going on blind dates. Bad blind dates! There had been a time when he used to like to date. Okay, it had been a while. But why had that stopped? When had everything just turned to sex and scratching an itch? He couldn't even remember.

Well, if he was being honest with himself, he did remember. It was why he slept around so much. Because he didn't want to get close. On more than one occasion, when he was younger, he had thrown himself into his relationships, always hopeful they would become long-lasting. Because who didn't want to live happily ever after, right? But without fail, something always went wrong. There was David, the investment banker, who felt Liam wasn't on the same level as him professionally and didn't want to be stuck, in his words, with carrying the financial weight of their relationship in case things became serious. Then, there had been Stephen, a fellow actor, who had seemed like the perfect match until he became jealous of Liam's success and told him he couldn't be with someone who was, in his words, stealing opportunities away from him. After Stephen came Marco, Tim, Pete, Jude, and a handful of others. All those relationships had fizzled out after a certain amount of time until finally, one day, Liam had had enough. Why was he the one who was always getting walked out on? Why was he the one who kept putting his heart on the line? No more. From that day forward, he decided he would put himself first. He wouldn't grow attached, and he wouldn't think of the future. He would live in the moment.

Of course, everyone thought he was Mr. Love 'Em and Leave 'Em, but that wasn't true. If he left first, then he didn't risk getting his heart broken. It was a way of protecting himself.

"We gonna move this indoors or what?" Austin asked, cutting into Liam's thoughts as he grabbed his crotch and gave it a tug.

Ugh, Liam thought. Time to bring this evening to an end. Now.

"What are you?" Liam asked.

"Top."

Liam managed a crestfallen look on his face. "Sorry, I'm a top, too, and everyone knows two tops don't equal a relationship. Bye!" And with that, Liam turned his back on Austin and hurried to catch up with the other carolers.

"Where did you disappear off to?" Charlie asked as an out-of-breath Liam rejoined the group. "Where's Austin?" He looked around. "Did the two of you find some mistletoe and put it to good use?"

"No!" Liam snapped. "We didn't find any mistletoe. If only our evening had been that G-rated."

Confusion washed over Charlie's face. "Huh?"

Liam was steaming mad. He'd been mad for months, and his anger had been bubbling beneath the surface. Now, it was ready to come out, and Charlie was the one directly in the line of fire. "How many times do I have to tell you I don't want to date? Yet, you keep ignoring me. First, you set me up with a psycho. Now, a horndog! What's going to be behind door number three? Enough!"

"Things didn't work out with Austin?" Charlie meekly asked.

"He wanted to do it in the woods. Now!" Liam hissed in a low voice. "With Christmas carolers in the background. What the hell?"

"Oh."

"Is that all you have to say?"

"I guess you could say he's spontaneous?"

Liam rolled his eyes. "Don't try to put a positive spin on it. Then, he wanted to know if I was a top or a bottom because he was a top, and unless we were sexually compatible, he didn't want to waste time on a relationship."

"He's upfront about what he wants," Charlie stated. "What's wrong with that?"

Liam bit back a scream. Did Charlie always look for the positive in any situation? He was getting a little fed up with his goody-goody routine.

"Do me a favor, Charlie. No more blind dates. I'm done. In fact, I'm done with everything tonight."

"But we still have more caroling to do!"

As much as Liam wanted to stay and continue to sing, he was too angry. He wanted to be by himself.

"Why should I stay? So you can try to set me up with someone else?"

"I wouldn't–"

Liam cut him off. "Leave me alone, Charlie! Go play matchmaker for someone else. Or here's a suggestion. Why don't you find a man for yourself? Or have you already tried and no one is interested?" He shoved his songbook at Charlie. "Goodnight!"

"Liam! Wait!" Charlie called out.

But Liam didn't stop. He just kept walking.

CHAPTER
THIRTEEN

The following morning, Liam overslept.

And if he overslept, then that meant Sarah had overslept since he was usually the one who roused her out of bed in the mornings. If she had gotten up already, he'd have heard her puttering around, but the house was quiet.

He stared at the time on the clock radio on his nightstand with one open eye, then jumped out of bed. It was eight o'clock. Usually, he was out of bed and dressed by seven, giving him at least ninety minutes to get Sarah ready for her day. Today, he'd have only half that time.

"Rise and shine," he called out, walking into Sarah's bedroom and pulling away the sheets and blanket. "Time for school."

Sarah gave Liam a grumpy look. "I don't want to go to school today."

"Why not? Are you not feeling well? Do you have a tummy ache?" Liam asked, instantly going into protective uncle mode. He pressed a hand to her forehead. "You don't feel hot. Nice and cool."

Sarah swatted away Liam's hand before wrapping herself back up in the sheets and turning away from him.

"I know a warm bed is tempting on a cold winter morning, but we're running late. You get dressed while I go downstairs and make your lunch."

In the kitchen, Liam rummaged through the refrigerator, grabbing a jar of grape jelly and a loaf of bread. He found the peanut butter in the first cabinet he opened and set out to make a peanut butter and jelly sandwich.

"You're making it the wrong way."

Liam whirled around, startled by the sound of his niece's voice. "Why are you still in your pajamas?"

Sarah ignored his question. "I like my bread toasted. And you need to put the peanut butter on first, then the jelly. If you put the jelly on first, it makes the sandwich all soggy."

Was it his imagination, Liam wondered, or was there a little bit of tone in his niece's voice?

Having given her decree, Sarah then went over to a cabinet and found a box of cereal. She poured herself a bowl before going to the refrigerator for some milk and orange juice. She poured the milk, then poured herself a small glass of orange juice. She carried everything over to the kitchen table, sat down, and proceeded to eat her breakfast at a leisurely pace.

"Sarah, you didn't answer my question. Why aren't you dressed for school?"

"Breakfast is the most important meal of the day," she stated matter-of-factly, ignoring his question. "We learned that in health class."

"Well, hurry up. We're running late. You should have gotten dressed first." He couldn't scold her for eating breakfast since they were too late for breakfast at school.

Sarah slipped a spoonful of cereal into her mouth. "I don't have anything to wear."

"What do you mean?" Liam knew his niece had a closet full of clothes, so he wasn't sure what kind of game she was playing. "Finish up," he urged her. "Then, we'll look in your closet."

"I'm done," Sarah said, pushing the mostly full

bowl of cereal away from her, as well as the full glasses of milk and juice.

"You barely touched your breakfast," he pointed out. "Someone's eyes were bigger than their stomach," he said, using his grandmother's favorite expression.

"I don't have time for breakfast. You said we were running late, remember?"

Liam took a deep breath. He didn't know what had happened to his sweet, adorable niece, but she'd been replaced by this brat. He got the sense she was looking for a fight, but he wasn't going to give her one. "Please take your dishes to the sink."

Sarah did as she was told, but when she reached the sink, she turned to her uncle.

"There's no room."

"Huh?"

She sighed. "There's no room in the sink," she repeated. "Because somebody hasn't been doing the dishes."

Wondering if Sarah was sassing him, Liam took a peek at the sink and saw she was right. Okay, he'd gotten behind on the housework. The sink *was* filled with dirty dishes. As was the dishwasher, which he'd forgotten to run, which was why the sink was full. Rooms needed to be dusted. Sheets needed to be changed, beds needed to be made, rugs needed to be vacuumed. Running a house was a full-time job. When was he supposed to get it all done? With his hours at the department store, shuttling Sarah around, and trying to have something of a personal life, things were falling by the wayside.

"I'll take care of the dishes while you're at school," Liam said, taking his niece by the hand and leading her back to her bedroom. "Let's see what we can find for you to wear."

Peering into Sarah's closet, Liam could see she had been correct. There were slim pickings. He'd have to add laundry to his list of chores today. Both his clothes hamper and Sarah's were overflowing, but he'd kept ignoring them. He rummaged through the hangers and pulled out two. "Here, why don't you wear this?" he suggested, giving her a pink ballet tutu and a purple turtleneck.

"I'm not going to wear that," Sarah proclaimed, a look of horror on her face. "That's my tutu for ballet class."

"Why not? If it was good enough for Carrie Bradshaw, it's good enough for you."

Sarah's face scrunched up with confusion. "Who?"

"When you turn twenty-one, I'll take you out for

a cosmopolitan and then we'll binge-watch *Sex and the City* and you'll know who Carrie Bradshaw is and that what I'm suggesting you wear is a fashion statement."

Sarah folded her arms over her chest and gave Liam a glare. "I'm not going to school if I don't have something to wear."

"I gave you something to wear."

"It's not an outfit."

Liam turned back to the closet. This time, he pulled out a pair of jeans that had heart-shaped patches on them and a yellow T-shirt. "How about this?"

"They don't go together," Sarah said. "I'm not going to wear something that looks bad on me."

Liam couldn't believe what he was hearing. "You're eight years old! How can you have any sense of fashion?"

"I know what looks good on me, and those two outfits do *not* look good."

Liam silently counted to ten before smiling at his niece. "Sarah, I'm running out of patience. Those are your two choices. Pick one and let's get going."

"No."

"Sarah Denise Williams," Liam warned, using

her full name so she would know he meant business. "I'm not going to say this again. Get dressed."

Sarah stamped her foot. "No! I'm not putting those clothes on."

Why was she being so impossible? "When I tell you to do something, you do it, Missy," Liam ordered in his sternest tone of voice. "Understand?"

He had used the word, missy, knowing that when his sister used the word, it meant she was through with Sarah's games, and it was time to lay down the law. Although in calling her that, he suddenly felt like Faye Dunaway channeling Joan Crawford in *Mommie Dearest*. This was the first time his niece had rebelled against him since he'd been watching her, and he was completely unprepared.

"Sarah..."

She glared at him.

What was he going to do? They were at a standstill.

And then, the doorbell rang.

"Saved by the bell," he told his niece. "When I get back up here, I better find you dressed."

Liam hurried down to the first floor and flung open the front door, where he found Bibi waiting on the porch.

"What are you doing here?" he asked.

"I could ask you the same thing," Bibi said, shaking off her hot pink leather jacket as she walked into the house. She looked like a giant pink snowball. Her jeans were tucked into pink furry-heeled boots, and her sweater was a fluffy angora pink concoction. "Is Sarah sick? When I didn't see you at school this morning, I started to worry. I don't think anything is going around, but *you* look like something the cat dragged in." Bibi raised her eyebrows suggestively. "Wild night with one of your Santa fans?"

Liam shook his head. "I haven't had a chance to shower or make myself presentable. I just rolled out of bed, and I've been tangling with my niece. Usually, she's an angel, but this morning she's a she-devil."

Bibi waved a hand dismissively. "Consider yourself lucky. You've got Sarah on temporary loan. I've got the eighteen-year package with Annie. You ain't seen nothin' yet. The clock is ticking down to the teenage years. You think she's bad now? Wait until she hits thirteen. I'm so not looking forward to the day when Annie can criticize me, give me the silent treatment, borrow my clothes without asking, and lie to my face."

"How do you know she's going to do all that?"

"Like mother, like daughter. I was a hellion with my mother, so I'm sure it's in the genes. Annie is already giving me attitude. Brace yourself, it's only going to get worse as Sarah gets older."

"My sister will be the one dealing with that. Not me. Except for whatever's going on today."

"What do you think the problem is?"

Liam shrugged. "I have no idea. But she's giving a master class on how to be a brat."

"Let me see if there's anything I can do to help," Bibi offered. "Where is she?"

"Up in her bedroom."

Before heading up to the second floor, Bibi reached into her Marc Jacobs shoulder bag, handing Liam a bottle of champagne and orange juice.

"Do you always carry around the makings of mimosas with you?" Liam asked.

"Toss those in the fridge. Once I solve your Sarah problem, you and I are celebrating."

"What are we celebrating?"

"You'll find out!" Bibi stated mysteriously.

As Bibi went upstairs, Liam headed into the kitchen with the champagne and orange juice. After putting them in the refrigerator, he finished making Sarah's peanut butter and jelly sandwich (the correct way). He had just put it into a brown paper bag, along with a banana and a box of raisins, when Bibi and Sarah, now fully dressed in a red and green plaid skirt and red turtleneck, returned to the kitchen.

"How did I miss that outfit? You look very Christmasy," he complimented his niece, hoping she wasn't going to take offense.

"I'm going to drop Sarah off at school while you start cleaning up around here," Bibi said.

"Don't forget your lunch," Liam said, holding out the bag to Sarah.

"Thank you, Uncle Liam," she said in a small voice.

"You're welcome." He pointed to his cheek. "Can I get a little sugar before you go?"

He knelt down, and Sarah wrapped her arms around his neck, giving him a kiss and a tight hug.

"See you after school," he said, giving her a kiss back.

After they left, Liam ran the dishwasher and tackled the dishes in the sink, squirting everything with a burst of Dawn before running the hot water. When Bibi returned, she went straight to the refrigerator, popped open the bottle of champagne, poured each of them a half glass, and then added some orange juice.

"To us!" she exclaimed, handing Liam a glass and clinking hers against it.

"What's the occasion?" Liam asked, drying off his wet hands with a dish towel before taking a long sip of his mimosa. After the morning he'd had, he needed it.

"First, our coup over Delia. Between your cookies and mine, we made over five thousand dollars at the bake sale for the school library fund. I wish you could have been there this morning when I rubbed that news in her face."

"Haven't you ever heard of being a gracious winner?"

Bibi ignored the comment. "I'm surprised I didn't turn to stone after the look she gave me."

"Revenge is sweet." Liam saluted Bibi with his glass. "Bravo. It was all your idea."

"It gets even better!" Bibi gushed.

"It does?"

"You're never going to believe what I tell you next."

Liam leaned against the kitchen counter, taking another sip of his mimosa. "Try me."

"The other moms at school want me to run against Delia for PTA president this spring! Apparently, they've had enough of her dictatorship and they're ready for a change. And that change is me. They think I'm daring and innovative." Bibi clinked her glass against Liam's again. "We're going to have so much fun."

"We?"

"You. Me. Us!"

"Bibi, I'm only in town for a few weeks. Until my sister and brother-in-law return home. Then, I head back to New York City."

"Nooooo!" Bibi wailed. "You can't. You mustn't! You have to stay here. I can't do this without you. Who's going to be my campaign manager? You have to help me win."

"You just want to use my hot body again," Liam dryly stated.

"Of course!" Bibi brazenly admitted, finishing off her mimosa and making a second. "That goes without saying. But you can't be serious. Tell me, what's so important back in New York City?"

Liam gave it some thought. Other than his friends, Sebastian and Dominick, there really wasn't much waiting for him. But he couldn't stay here. First of all, he didn't have a job, and he had to make a living.

"What's going on in your mind?" Bibi demanded. "I can see all sorts of thoughts racing across your face. What's your plan? You're going to stick around, I hope?"

"How can I stick around? There's nothing for me here."

Bibi shook her head forcefully. "I would have to disagree. You have a lot." She started counting off on her fingers. "Family. Friends. Fans!" she reminded him. "How does it compare to your old life?"

It's like night and day, Liam thought. When he lived in New York City, it seemed like he was always hustling. Looking for that next job. Looking for the next guy to hook up with. There was never any downtime. As an actor, he always needed to be one step ahead because he was looking for that big break that would take him to the next level. It was exhausting. But at the same time, it was exhilarating. It was what fueled him. It gave him a purpose. If he didn't have his acting career, what would he have?

"Enough about me," Liam said. "What was going on with Sarah this morning? How did you change her back to her usual sweet self?"

"I got the whole story from her on the car drive to school."

"And?"

"She misses her mom and dad, but her mom more. She and Penelope were supposed to FaceTime last night, and Penelope had to cancel because of a last-minute business meeting. She's really upset about that. I think she figured if she acted up, you would have to call her mother, and then Penelope would have to make time for her and scold her for being such a little monster with you. She's a smart kid. You gotta give her credit for that."

"She takes after her uncle," Liam bragged, "in case you were wondering."

"She knows she's been bad with her Uncle Liam. She knows you love her and take good care of her, and now she thinks you're mad at her. She was very remorseful, by the way, almost to the point of tears. As much as she loves you, I think she's craving a feminine touch."

"Hey, I'm in touch with my feminine side," Liam said. "I let her paint my fingernails," Liam waved his purple fingernails in front of Bibi's face, "and put make-up on me when she wants to play beauty parlor."

"You know what I mean. Sometimes, a little girl just wants her mommy."

Liam sighed. "I know. I'll have a talk with my sister. She can be such a workaholic."

"We're all guilty of it. Once you become a parent, you lose your identity and it becomes enmeshed with your child's. Sometimes, you have to remind yourself that you're still your own person, not just Mommy or Daddy, and you go overboard in other parts of your life. Like working too many hours to validate yourself, thinking you'll make some free time to do the things you really want to do. Like spending time with your child."

"I'll go easy on Penelope," Liam promised. "Maybe I can surprise Sarah with a FaceTime this weekend."

Bibi put down her empty champagne glass. "Oh! I almost forgot the best part of my morning." She reached into the back pocket of her jeans, whipping out her cellphone and waving it in the air. "You're trending!"

"What?!" Liam declared in shock.

Bibi handed Liam her phone. "Here. Look! Just type in hot Santa, small town Santa, super sexy Santa, even Santa Viper, and you pop up! You're on people's radars!"

Liam started scrolling through Bibi's Instagram. She was right. Pictures of him kept popping up with all of yesterday's happy cookie buyers. Was this good or bad?

He didn't know. Only time would tell.

"Okay, darling, as much as I'd love to keep chatting with you and sipping mimosas, I've got to get on with my day." Bibi snatched back her phone. "What's on your agenda?"

"I've got the afternoon shift at Bailey's. But first, I have to apologize to someone."

Part of the reason he'd overslept this morning was because he hadn't slept well the night before. He kept tossing and turning, remembering how he'd stormed off on Charlie and the hateful words he'd said. Why had he said them? Yes, he had been pissed off over the situation with Austin, but that was no reason to take it out on Charlie. It hadn't been his fault. He'd probably ruined the rest of his night.

Of course guys would be interested in dating Charlie. Charlie had been nothing but sweet and kind and helpful to him and Sarah ever since the day they first met. He'd even gone out of his way to introduce him to his friends, and, despite Liam's best efforts, kept trying to set him up on dates because he felt Liam deserved a boyfriend.

A guy like that was a catch.

And a great friend.

But how did he repay him? By being an arrogant shit.

Liam sighed as he tried to figure out a way to make things up to Charlie, hoping he would forgive Liam for what he had said in the heat of the moment.

CHAPTER
FOURTEEN

Charlie couldn't stop thinking about what Liam had said the night before. The words kept bouncing around his mind.

Was he right? Was no one interested in dating him? It wasn't like Charlie was making much of an effort.

When he was younger, he remembered always being checked out. Cruised. Always having more than one choice. Of course he'd been living in a big city back then, and there were always opportunities to hook up with someone in real life if he didn't want to hop on an app and do some swiping. But Bramford Hills was different. How big was the town's gay dating pool? Not very. And there wasn't even a gay bar or community center. That's why he didn't have a boyfriend. There weren't enough options or places to meet. It wasn't because anyone wasn't interested.

Charlie tried to focus on the Christmas letter he was writing. He enclosed it with his holiday card each year, giving family and friends an update on his life. But he hadn't gotten very far. His mind kept going back to Liam's words. He knew he wasn't gorgeous like Liam was, but he was good-looking, and he'd had his fair share of boyfriends over the years. And he still would. Well, yes and no. He didn't want to keep searching and searching for the right guy. He wanted to find him and then be done with the search. Hopefully forever.

The sound of a soft meow pulled him from his thoughts. Charlie looked down at Shadow, who was gently pawing at his leg, wanting some attention. He picked the cat up and gave him a snuggle. "Thanks, buddy. It's nice to know someone loves me."

After a few more minutes of hugs, Shadow had enough and began wiggling to get free. Charlie was putting him back down on the floor when the doorbell rang. Opening the front door, he found himself staring at a large Christmas wreath made of pine and spruce. It was festooned with ruby red and white berries, pinecones, tiny glass ornaments, sprigs of holly, and a big red bow. From behind it came a voice.

"I come in Christmas." Liam lowered the wreath from his face. "And to apologize."

Charlie wasn't going to make this easy. He folded his arms over his chest and leaned against the door frame, giving Liam a look of fake confusion. "Apologize for what?"

"What I said when we were caroling."

"About no one being interested in dating me?"

"Yes," Liam whispered. "I feel awful about how last night ended. Can we pretend I didn't say those words?"

"But you did say them," Charlie reminded him. "And you can't take them back."

"I would if I could."

"Why did you say them in the first place?"

Liam shrugged. "I don't know. I was mad and lashing out. Not just at you. It was a build-up of my life over the past year. The unfairness of everything. The helplessness. I shouldn't have stormed off the way I did. And I shouldn't have taken things out on you. That wasn't cool. I was being a brat, sort of like Sarah was this morning."

"Sarah? A brat?" Charlie was shocked. "I don't believe it."

"Believe it. Full-on tantrum, but she eventually got over it. Just like I got over my tantrum." Liam handed Charlie the wreath. "Please accept this as part of my apology. I'm sorry. Really sorry. Of course someone would be interested in you. You're the real deal. Sweet, funny, thoughtful, a great cook, and handsome."

Charlie lifted a hand, waving it in a gesture to continue. "Don't stop. Let's hear some more."

"You're great, Charlie. Really great. If the spirit of Christmas were a person, it would be you."

Charlie held up the decorated wreath, admiring it. "Why did you buy me this?"

"It was the only Christmas decoration you didn't have yet."

"True." Charlie hung the wreath on a hook on the front door. "It'll look good here," he said, deciding to put Liam out of his misery. "Apology accepted. And I will admit that sometimes I can be a little overzealous."

Liam raised an eyebrow. "Sometimes?"

"Okay, all the time. But it's only because I care," Charlie said in his defense.

"I know. You care about everyone. It's what makes you one of a kind."

"If it makes you feel any better, when I got home

last night, I called J.P. and gave him an earful. He told me he didn't know about Austin's preference for outdoor activities."

"Everyone's got secrets. I bet you do, too."

Oh, I've got a secret. A big one. I have to find you a boyfriend by Christmas Day, and I'm running out of time.

"I wonder if Austin found the bottom he was looking for," Liam mused. "Contrary to what I told him about only being a top, I'm versatile. I can go either way. And you?"

"Me?" Charlie was caught by surprise. Why would Liam want to know if he was a top or a bottom?

"I showed my cards." Liam playfully poked Charlie in the chest with a finger. "Now, it's time for you to show yours."

"Bottom," Charlie admitted.

"Never wanted to be a top?"

"The guys I've been with have always wanted to call the shots. Not that I've minded."

"Ah! You're a power-bottom."

Charlie blushed. "I wouldn't say that."

Liam moved closer to Charlie. "You're everything a guy could want, Mr. Fisher. So, why are you still single?"

"This question keeps you up at night?"

"I'm serious. Why aren't you with someone? You should be."

Charlie shrugged. "I don't know. Don't think I haven't asked myself the same question on nights when I'm home alone. Or when I'm at a dinner party and everyone is paired up except me. Maybe I should be more proactive. Maybe I should join some clubs or go out on more dates. Or maybe I should have sex with no strings attached. Maybe I'll meet someone that way."

Liam shook his head. "You don't want to do that. Have meaningless sex, I mean."

"Why not?"

"Trust me. You'll never meet anyone that way."

"Sounds like you're talking from experience."

Liam rubbed a hand across the back of his neck, wincing. "I am. And I regret it. I wasted a lot of years jumping in and out of beds, hooking up with guys, and having those relationships go nowhere. You don't want that, Charlie. You're too good for that. Too special."

"Thanks," Charlie whispered, touched by Liam's words and the fact that he was revealing a part of himself that Charlie suspected he kept hidden, the part that made him so averse to dating.

"If you see a guy you're into, you should make a move," Liam encouraged. "Don't sit around waiting for him to do it. Go up to him and let him know you're interested. You'll definitely get his attention, and then you can get to know each other."

"Like you do?"

Liam nodded. "Like I used to do. Although, I was more interested in hooking up. But it's the same idea, so you should get results."

"How?"

"You could start by complimenting a guy on his appearance. Eyes are always a good place to start. Talk about the color or how mesmerizing they are. Or compliment him on something he's wearing. Like a shirt, a belt, or a piece of jewelry. Something to get a conversation started. Then, as you start talking, move in a little closer. Lean in as you're chatting. Compliment him on his cologne."

"What if he isn't wearing any cologne?"

Liam raised an eyebrow suggestively. "Then, tell him that intoxicating scent must be him, and it's driving you crazy. You could ask if that's how he smells all over. Keep your gaze focused on his eyes so he knows how into him you are. Then, slowly move your eyes down to his lips and back to his eyes, and give him a smile. That should get you at least one date."

"Is that what you would do?" Charlie asked.

"I'm a bit more daring."

"So, what would your next move be?"

"If we're talking about me, I would move in closer..."

"And?"

"Give him a kiss. It can be a short kiss or a long one, but definitely a kiss." Liam then closed the distance between himself and Charlie, pulled him into his arms, and kissed him.

Charlie figured it would only be a quick kiss, sort of showing him what to do, but then something happened. The kiss grew. And grew. It didn't end when it was supposed to. It kept going on and on as it became something more intimate. Less chaste and more sexual.

Charlie's mouth opened and Liam's tongue slipped inside, exploring its warmth as the kiss deepened, taking Charlie's breath away. Liam smelled of sandalwood and peppermint, and Charlie inhaled deeply, wanting the scents wafting off Liam to wrap around him like a warm, fuzzy blanket. No, he didn't want a blanket. He wanted Liam to wrap himself around him. He wanted to feel his hot, silky skin pressed against him right before Liam reached for his hard, throbbing cock, his fingers lightly caressing before tightening their grip around him and making him powerless to his touch. At the thought, Charlie suddenly felt lightheaded and his entire body tingled, his senses going into overdrive as Liam's lips and tongue meshed with his, becoming one.

What's going on here? Charlie wondered. What was happening? He didn't know, but the kiss was *amazing*. Unlike any other he'd ever had. If kisses were like fingerprints, then Liam's kisses were one of a kind. Totally unique. And unforgettable.

Before Charlie could explore more, before he could lose himself in the experience and the connection between the two of them, Liam pulled away, ending the intimate moment.

"Sorry about that," he said with a sheepish grin. "I got carried away. But I wanted to give you an example."

"Some example," Charlie whispered, tracing a finger over his lower lip.

"Sometimes, actions speak louder than words," Liam said. "For me, it never hurts to start with a kiss. Especially when it's good. But maybe you'd want to ease into things with some conversation and then a first date before moving on to that."

Did Liam think their kiss was good? Because it was better than good. It was great.

"It hints at the promise of more exciting stuff to come," Liam continued. "And it hooks a man. Intrigues him. Makes him wonder what might be next. Get it?"

Charlie slowly nodded because he agreed with everything Liam had just said. Because if one kiss with Liam was this good, what might another be like? And what might come after it? "Got it."

Liam glanced at his watch. "I'd love to stay and chat some more, but I've got to get to Bailey's. We're all good, yes? Still friends?"

Charlie nodded, his lips and body still reeling from Liam's unforgettable kiss as he watched him leave the porch and walk down the sidewalk.

———

It was all Liam could do not to glance back over his shoulder. Charlie had seemed like he was in a daze. And he knew why. The kiss had been unexpected and probably thrown Charlie for a loop.

Would he need to apologize again? Liam didn't know why he did it. Maybe it was because he still felt bad about what he had said to Charlie the night before. Maybe it was because he wanted to give Charlie a boost of confidence, or give him back his confidence. All he knew was that he wanted Charlie to know that he had been wrong. That he was hot. Desirable. Attractive.

The kiss went on longer than he thought it would. It hadn't been meant as a real kiss, but from the second Liam's lips touched Charlie's, everything else had faded away, and he'd been aware only of the sensation of Charlie's lips, mouth, and tongue before finally realizing he had gone farther than he'd planned and pulling away. He'd apologized and didn't think Charlie had taken offense, especially since Charlie now knew what to do in the future. All's well that ends well, right?

Maybe not.

Liam ran his tongue over his lips, the taste of Charlie still lingering. Sure, he'd kissed plenty of guys over the years, but he'd never felt the way he had while kissing Charlie. It was weird. That kiss had been electric. Maybe it had something to do with it being so cold outside? Some sort of body reaction? His cold lips joining with Charlie's warm ones? That had to be it.

Liam was so lost in his thoughts that he found himself bumping into someone as he turned a corner.

"If it isn't sexy Santa himself!" Gregory teased.

"Hey!" Liam greeted, giving him a smile. "What's up?"

Even in winter wear Gregory looked like he had stepped out of the pages of a men's fashion magazine. His entire ensemble, from mirrored sunglasses to a snow white leather trench coat with its upturned collar and red silk scarf, made him look like Mr. Fashion.

"Not much going on with me, but you must be basking in your glory. Not that I blame you. It's long overdue, and I was happy to be of assistance."

Liam had no idea what Gregory was talking about. "I'm afraid you've lost me. Basking in what glory?"

"Don't you know?" Gregory pulled out his cell-phone, waving it in Liam's face. "Thanks to me, you're trending!"

Liam gazed at the phone, then back to Gregory. "I thought I was trending because of Bibi."

"What?!" Gregory shrieked. "That she-devil! It's just like her to steal my thunder. Next time I see her, she's getting a piece of my mind. You're trending because of *moi*. Don't you remember? As soon as I knew you were posing for photos, I sent out a text to all my gays. Why do you think so many hot guys were waiting to buy Christmas cookies from you? It's the unofficial Viper club! We're all flooding our social media platforms with pictures of you, telling everyone of your good deed to raise money for the school library."

"The idea did start with Bibi," Liam gently reminded him, ever the peacekeeper. "But I owe my thanks to both of you."

"Of course, the timing could have been better."

"What do you mean?"

Gregory clasped a hand over his mouth in an *oops* gesture, shifting nervously.

"Spill it," Liam demanded. "Now."

"I hate to be the bearer of bad news, but commercials have started airing for the new season of *Gay Househusbands of NYC*."

"What does that have to do with me? I'm not on the show anymore."

"You might be gone, but the memory lingers." Gregory pulled up his phone and logged on to YouTube, playing a clip for Liam. A voiceover discussed the aftermath of Liam's betrayal and asked if everyone's lives would ever be the same again. Then, there were the voices of cast members saying things like, "We trusted him and he stabbed us in the back!" and "I don't feel sorry for him. He got what he deserved for betraying all of us."

Liam rolled his eyes. "Such bullshit!"

Gregory ended the clip. "Don't worry," he soothed. "It'll all die down. They can't fuel an entire season based on last season's scandal."

"Can't they?" Liam worriedly asked.

"No," Gregory firmly stated. "Trust me. You've got to put this out of your mind and focus on moving forward. Don't give that snake, Ollie, any more power. If anyone's a viper, it's him. I still believe something shady happened last season."

"I'll try," Liam sighed, trying to push all thoughts of *Gay Househusbands* out of his mind and failing.

"You need to do something fun, and I know just the thing!" Gregory exclaimed. "J.P. and I are driving to Henderson tomorrow to do some Christmas shopping. If you don't have to work, why don't you come along? They've got a great Christmas fair. A fun car ride, a little lunch, some shopping, and maybe even a Christmas cocktail or two. What do you say?"

It did sound like fun. And Liam could use a distraction. Even though he had a forty percent discount at Bailey's, it couldn't hurt to scope out the Christmas fair and see if he could find any gifts that were different and unique. Plus, he really needed to get started on his Christmas shopping, and this would be the perfect opportunity.

"Count me in. I don't have to work until tomorrow night."

"Yay!" Gregory clapped his hands together. "Road trip!"

———

That kiss. Charlie couldn't get it out of his mind.

It didn't mean anything. Of course it didn't. Liam said it himself. He was telling him what to do when he met a guy he was attracted to. That was all. They were just friends. Nothing more. Although, apparently, from the way Charlie's body had reacted to Liam's kiss, it had been a bit too long since he'd been with a man. He'd have to do something about that, but for now, Charlie needed to put his sudden desire for a boyfriend on the back burner and focus on finding Liam a boyfriend by Christmas.

His cellphone vibrated in his back pocket, and he pulled it out to see J.P. calling.

"What's up?" he asked.

"How are you doing with your Christmas shopping?"

Charlie gave it some thought. "Making progress.

Not as much as I would like, though. I need a day where I can try to get it all done. Why?"

"Gregory and I are driving to Henderson tomorrow to do some Christmas shopping. Want to tag along?"

Charlie didn't even hesitate. "I'd love it!" It would be the perfect distraction. He'd be far away from Bramford Hills, and he could put Liam far, far out of his mind.

CHAPTER
FIFTEEN

Well, this was awkward.

Liam and Charlie were squeezed into the back-seat of Gregory's car. Gregory, being Gregory, had gone for appearance rather than substance and decided to drive his cherry red Mercedes to Henderson. When Gregory arrived to pick him up, Charlie hadn't expected to find Liam sitting in the backseat, and from the look of surprise on Liam's face, he hadn't been expecting him, either. They'd given each other a smile and said good morning, but so far that was it.

Why was he feeling uncomfortable around Liam? Usually, they had an ease around each other, but today it was missing. Charlie sighed. He knew why, although he didn't want to admit it. It was because of that kiss.

Liam had kissed him. So what? It hadn't meant anything. He kept telling himself that, over and over. Then, why wasn't he able to get it out of his mind? Why wasn't he able to forget about it? Charlie had to snap out of this. He needed to focus, and his focus had to be on finding a boyfriend for Liam by Christmas.

"There are five of us in this car, Gregory," J.P. complained from the front seat. "We should rethink this. Let's go back to my place and get my SUV."

Gregory shuddered as they drove down the street. "Ugh. Such a butch car. So big and bulky."

"Not to mention roomy!" J.P. pointed out. "Where are we going to fit all our Christmas packages? Your trunk isn't that big."

"We'll have them shipped."

"It's Christmas!" J.P. wailed. "Do you know how long that will take?"

"Complain, complain, complain. Besides, we'd have more room if a certain diva hadn't decided to invite herself."

"I've got Christmas shopping, too," Bibi declared from the backseat, where she was sitting behind

Gregory. "I still can't believe you didn't ask me to come."

"Darling, you know I adore you and you liven up any event I invite you to," Gregory said, looking up at her through the rearview mirror, "but this was supposed to be a boys-only trip. To cheer up Liam."

"Then, it's a good thing he mentioned the trip to me this morning when we dropped the girls off at school, otherwise I wouldn't have known anything about it!"

"You need cheering up?" Charlie asked Liam, wondering what had happened since he'd last seen him. They were pressed together, side by side. Charlie was sitting behind J.P., against the window, while Liam was sandwiched in the middle between Charlie and Bibi. With all their bulky sweaters and coats and scarves—not to mention Bibi's oversized red alligator Chloe bag—there really wasn't a lot of room to move around. "What's wrong?"

"That horrible show is starting its new season," Gregory announced.

"And that date Liam had with Austin didn't help," J.P. added, turning around in his seat. "Sorry about that. I didn't know Austin was so...adventurous. He and I are more work friends than outside school friends."

"You should have come to me, Liam," Gregory said as he stopped at a red light. "I know so many great guys I could set you up with."

"Thanks, but no thanks."

"You guys are fixing Liam up?" Bibi elbowed Liam in the side. "Why wasn't I made aware of this?"

"No one is setting me up on blind dates," Liam said. "Not anymore." He gave a pointed look toward Charlie.

That's what you think, Charlie thought to himself. If he had to use his friends to set Liam up on future dates, then that's what he was going to do. So far, Liam had been on two bad dates. It didn't mean the next one was going to be bad.

"You should at least listen to Gregory," Charlie suggested.

"I'll pass," Liam told him. "But thank you, Gregory."

"Please, please, please let me set you up on a blind date," Bibi pleaded. "I've made so many great matches for my friends."

"No," Liam firmly answered. But Bibi was relentless. She kept begging until finally Liam caved.

"I know the perfect guy for you," Bibi raved. "He's a little eccentric but very, very nice."

"What do you mean by eccentric?" Liam asked, his voice heavy with suspicion.

"He's a collector."

"What does he collect? Not something weird and gross?"

"Nothing like that. He's into dolls. You know, Barbies."

"What's eccentric about that?"

"He's really into them. Half the rooms in his house are filled with dolls."

Liam stared at Bibi in disbelief. "And you think I'd be a good match with this guy because…"

"Just give him a chance!" Charlie encouraged, earning a glare from Liam. "Everyone needs a hobby."

"What have you got to lose?" Bibi asked.

"My sanity!"

"When this all works out and the two of you get engaged, I want a front row seat at your wedding," Bibi said.

"Aren't you jumping the gun a bit? Who said anything about getting married?" Liam asked.

"Isn't the point of dating to find someone you want to marry?" she asked.

"Look at me and Christopher," Gregory exclaimed, taking the hand with his engagement ring off the steering wheel and waving it in the direction of the backseat.

"It's a blind date, and it's going to be my last blind date," Liam announced. "Is everyone listening? This guy is it."

"Maybe he'll be the one," Charlie suggested.

"Yes, the *last* one," Liam shot back.

"Think positive!"

"I'm positive this is going to be another disaster," Liam said.

"And if I'm right and you're wrong?" Charlie asked.

"We'll figure out a way to settle up. Now, can we talk about something else other than my love life?"

"Just give me a minute," Bibi said, holding up a finger. "I'm texting Timothy right now." Seconds later, she happily squealed. "He's interested! Are you free tonight? He's suggesting drinks at his place."

"I've got work tonight, but I could swing by his place for a quick hello before I go in. Say around six?"

"Are you sure you want to go to his place?" Charlie quickly asked. "Isn't it better to meet somewhere neutral in case you want to make a fast getaway?"

"I thought you said he was going to be the one," Liam pointed out. "Why would I want to get away?"

"First dates can be awkward."

"If I survived the psycho and the horndog, I can survive the doll collector."

Bibi swatted at Liam. "Don't call him that."

"Ouch!" Liam rubbed his arm. "That hurt."

"Don't be such a baby. I barely touched you," she said, rummaging through her bag for her compact and lipstick. Once she found them, she began touching up her lips.

"I met the infamous Claude the other day," Liam announced to the car.

"What did you think?" Gregory eagerly asked as the light turned green. "Don't hold back. Spill, spill, spill!"

"It's the holiday season," Charlie said. "Can we please not turn this into a bitch session about Claude?"

Gregory looked up into the rearview mirror and stuck his tongue out at Charlie. "Poo! You're no fun."

"I can see why he's not your favorite person," Liam began. "He was certainly charming, but I didn't feel relaxed around him. I felt like he wanted something from me."

"He's a user," Gregory quipped. "Always putting himself first. He'll help himself before anyone else."

"Sarah didn't like him. She thought he was the Grinch. Claude wasn't amused."

Laughter broke out in the car.

"Always trust children and animals," J.P. chuckled. "Their instincts are never wrong."

"He was on his way to a rehearsal for the town Christmas play."

J.P. turned around in his seat. "I had to go over to the elementary school the other day to pick up some files for next year's incoming freshman class. Claude's rehearsal was going on. Call me a masochist, but I couldn't resist. I had to stick my head into the auditorium to get a peek."

"And?" Charlie asked.

J.P. sighed. "As expected, it was a disaster."

"Of course, it was! The man has no talent. This is why you need to give Claude some competition and mount a Christmas show of your own," Gregory insisted as he stopped for another red light. "There's more than enough people in this town to see two shows."

"It's too late to do something original," J.P. said.

"Who says it has to be original?" Charlie asked. "Why not license a Christmas show like Liam suggested at dinner? Anything else has got to be better than *Wonderful!*"

"Like?"

"How about *A Charlie Brown Christmas?*" Liam suggested. "It's pretty simple and straightforward."

J.P. shook his head. "That's a show for kids."

"*You're a Good Man, Charlie Brown* was written for and performed by adults," Liam pointed out. "And there are two versions of *A Charlie Brown Christmas* available. One for kids at thirty minutes, and one for adults at ninety minutes. It's really not that much of a stretch. And who doesn't love *A Charlie Brown Christmas?* Everyone grew up watching it. It has a nostalgic factor, which would definitely help sell tickets."

"Doesn't Claude's show have a nostalgic factor, too?" Bibi asked.

"It has a nausea factor," J.P. stated. "I can't imagine anyone sticking around for the second act."

"It wouldn't take much of a set," Liam continued. "And the cast would be small."

"Would you direct it?" Gregory asked Liam as the light changed, and he started driving again.

"Me?" Liam's voice was filled with shock. "I don't have time to direct a play. I can barely stay on top of my life right now. Plus, I've never directed a show before."

"But doesn't Eloise have you working after hours at Bailey's?" Bibi asked. "Courtesy of my negotiating skills."

"Yes…"

"So, your days would be free," Charlie pointed out. "You could squeeze in rehearsals then. This could be the way to get your foot back in the world of theatre."

"From a local production?" Liam skeptically asked.

"Don't forget the power of social media," Bibi said. "I got you trending."

"Don't you mean *I* got Liam trending, Bibi darling?" Gregory corrected. "You weren't the only one using their social media platform. It was my gays who spread the word."

"Let me think about it," Liam said.

"I want in on this, too!" Bibi exclaimed.

"You do? Why?" Liam asked.

"It would be a great way for me to get votes! If we give a cut of the ticket sales to the school's new library fund, I'd have an advantage over Delia. In fact, if you did a show every year, we could give some of the proceeds to them. Claude doesn't do that with his shows, does he?"

"I don't think so," J.P. said. "He's never told anyone where the profits go."

"Probably lining his own pockets," Gregory sniffed.

"Who's Delia?" Charlie asked.

"My nemesis at the elementary school. She's a mean mom I'm running against for PTA president in the spring." Bibi excitedly bounced up and down in her seat. "You have to do it, Liam. And I can help. The PTA has all sorts of mailing lists. I'm sure I can get access to them, and we can send fliers out for the show. Plus, I've got an in at the town paper, so I can guarantee review coverage. And they can mention sharing the proceeds with the school. It's a win-win!"

Gregory cackled. "By the time our show is up and running, Claude won't even know what hit him. Let's do it! It'll be like one of those old Judy Garland and Mickey Rooney MGM musicals where they're putting on a show to save the town."

J.P. looked at Liam and shrugged. "What do you say? I'm in if you're in. We could even co-direct. Less work for each of us."

Charlie held his breath, watching as Liam thought it

over. How would he be able to resist? Being involved with acting and the stage was what he was meant to do. It was a part of who he was. He wouldn't say no, would he?

"I don't know how we're going to pull this off," Liam slowly said, "but count me in. We're putting on a Christmas show!"

———

Once they were in Henderson, the strategy was to divide and conquer for the next two hours and then meet for lunch. Gregory wanted to shop for new clothes for himself and Christopher, so off he went to the high-end boutiques. Bibi was craving a new piece of jewelry, so she headed to the jewelry district, while J.P. walked toward the local bookstore.

Leaving Charlie and Liam alone in silence.

"Who's on your list?" Charlie asked, trying to break the ice and get things back to normal. Liam certainly didn't seem at all bothered or phased by what had happened yesterday. If he was acting at all strange, it was because Charlie was acting that way toward him.

"Sarah, Sarah, and Sarah. Not that I mind. Shopping for kids is much more fun than shopping for adults."

"Want to start in a toy store?"

"Sure."

As soon as they stepped into The Toy Chest, Charlie inhaled deeply. There was nothing like the smell of packaged toys. It was almost like a perfume, that combination of plastic, cellophane, and cardboard, the way it sweetly scented the air and instantly hit him. He loved it because with one sniff, it always took him back to his childhood.

"Did Sarah finally give you a list?"

"No," Liam sighed. "She's still being super secretive, so I'm winging it."

Charlie wished he could tell Liam what Sarah really wanted for Christmas. If he did, he knew Liam's heart would melt. "Let's get her something creative," he suggested. "Maybe colored pencils and paints? Markers? Some sketch pads?"

"She loves to draw."

"Great. We'll get all that stuff. How about some board games, too?"

"I'm not sure which ones she has."

"You can never go wrong with the classics. Monopoly, Parcheesi, Clue, Sorry." Charlie grabbed a shopping cart and started pushing it down the aisle they stood in. He was like a heat-seeking missile, rounding around corners in search of the aisle he always used to love visiting when he was a little boy. Finally, they reached it.

The doll aisle.

"Are you prepping me for tonight?" Liam asked with a smirk.

"No, but you do know what a Barbie is, don't you?"

"I saw the movie, so while I might not have first-hand knowledge, I'm familiar enough."

"I bet Timothy would know everything about Barbie," Charlie teased.

"No cracks about Timothy until I come back with a full report."

"You really think the date is going to be bad?" Charlie asked as he perused the selection of dolls before him. So many to choose from. It was mind-boggling. When he was a boy, there had only been blond Barbies, with an occasional brunette friend tossed into the mix. Now, there was a whole array of hair colors, hairstyles, body shapes, and skin tones.

"My track record speaks for itself. Two strike-outs."

"In your defense, they were the problem, not you."

"That's very sweet of you to say." Liam picked

up a box with a sun-tanned Ken in blue swim trunks and tossed him into their shopping cart.

"Think Ken might want a boyfriend?" Charlie asked, holding up a Ken doll clad in a tracksuit.

"Why not?"

Charlie added him to the cart. "Don't get discouraged. The right guy is out there waiting for you."

"Maybe. Or maybe it's too late for me. I don't know if I remember how to be in a relationship."

"Of course you do! Stop talking like that."

"I've never really had one," Liam confessed. "Not anything long-term."

"Neither have I," Charlie admitted. "So, I guess we have that in common. Look at it this way. We just haven't found the right person yet. He's still out there. Maybe Santa will bring him to you for Christmas."

Through me, Charlie vowed.

Liam laughed. "Dear Santa, all I want for Christmas this year is a boyfriend. But please make sure he's sane and normal."

Charlie reached for a Christmas Barbie decked out in a shimmering red gown, her hair swept up in a high swirl. "Did you want to play with dolls when you were little?"

Liam thought about it. "Not really. I was happy with my Matchbox cars and trucks. Legos and blocks. What about you?"

"Desperately!"

"Did you actually do it?"

Charlie shook his head. "Of course not! I'm sure my parents would have been fine with it if I'd asked, but somehow I knew little boys did not play with Barbies. And I so wanted to play with her! That shiny hair. Those killer outfits. And those teeny tiny shoes! Not to mention her Dreamhouse. I would have been in heaven."

"There was a girl toy I wanted," Liam confessed.

"Really? Which one?"

"An Easy-Bake Oven. The TV commercials made whipping up those desserts look so easy."

"Then, we have to get Sarah one, if they still make them. You can fulfill your childhood dream by using it with her."

"Was there anything else you wanted to play with but couldn't?"

"I wanted a Barbie styling head," Charlie answered without hesitation. "All that blonde hair, only super-sized! And let's not forget about the make-up. Sometimes, the girls on my block and I would play beauty salon. I was Mr. Pierre."

Liam laughed. "Mr. Pierre? Why weren't you, Mr. Charlie?"

"I was pretending to be French, and Mr. Pierre sounded French to me. I always came up with the best hairstyles."

"Then, let's add a Barbie styling head to the haul," Liam said, searching the shelves for one. "While I'm playing with Sarah's Easy-Bake Oven, you can play with her styling head."

"Why do I suddenly feel guilty?" Charlie asked. "Are we shopping for Sarah, or are we really shopping for ourselves?"

"Sarah," Liam instantly answered. But then, he paused. "And us, too," he said with a wink. "But I won't tell if you won't."

———

After leaving the toy store, loaded down with two shopping bags each, Charlie and Liam headed to the town square, where there were craftsmen selling their wares in booths.

"Now, this is what I live for," Liam said, his eyes sparkling with joy. "The creative, one-of-a-kind gifts."

They passed a booth where clocks were made

from hollowed-out books. Another with crocheted animals that were so adorable, Liam couldn't resist buying a penguin for Sarah. One booth had home-made jams, jellies, and sauces, while the booth next to it sold Christmas ornaments made from eggshells that were so beautifully decorated they looked like Faberge eggs.

"These are gorgeous," Charlie said, reaching for a baby blue egg decorated with a Christmas snow scene. He gazed at the tag dangling from the orna-ment's ribbon. "Yikes! A little pricey," he said, putting it back.

Liam placed his hand over Charlie's, stopping him from letting go. "I know I already bought you a wreath, but that wasn't a Christmas gift. It was more of an apology gift. Let me buy the ornament for you. As a way of saying thank you for everything you've done for me and Sarah."

"You don't have to do that," Charlie said, although he was touched by Liam's thoughtfulness.

"I know I don't have to. I want to," Liam insisted. He nodded to the clerk in the booth, handing her the egg. "We'll take this one."

"I'll always think of you when I hang it," Charlie told Liam as the young woman filled a small box with tissue paper and delicately placed the egg inside it.

Liam gave Charlie a smile. "I hope so."

CHAPTER
SIXTEEN

"I don't know why I can't have an eggnog martini," Gregory pouted.

"You're our driver!" Bibi scolded as she brought her martini glass to her lips and took a sip. "No drinking and driving."

"I know you're right, but those look so tasty," Gregory moaned as their waiter handed out the rest of the cocktails.

Bibi waved her martini under Gregory's nose. "Not only does it look great, it smells and tastes great, too. Yummy!"

"If you don't want to hitchhike back to Bramford Hills, you better take that drink out of my face," Gregory warned.

"I wonder what's keeping J.P." Charlie looked

around. "He's never late. I hope something didn't happen."

"It's Christmas," Gregory said. "He's probably stuck in a line somewhere."

They had agreed to meet for lunch at an Italian restaurant that was a favorite of theirs whenever they came to Henderson. They were sitting at a corner table with a red and white checkered tablecloth and dripping candles in wine bottles when J.P. finally arrived, storming over to their table.

"You will not believe who I ran into on the street." J.P. didn't give them a chance to answer. "Sam!"

Gregory reached for a breadstick from the basket on the table, pointing it at J.P. before taking a bite. "There was always a chance of that happening since he's performing here in that Christmas show."

J.P. pulled out a chair and joined the rest of them.

"Sam? Who's Sam?" Bibi asked.

"My ex!" J.P. exploded.

"How did he look?" Gregory asked.

Charlie groaned at the question. "Does it really matter?"

"It does if he looked bad! It gives J.P. the advantage."

"He looked great," J.P. moaned. "Even better than when I saw him on that talk show a few months ago."

"Maybe he's had a little cosmetic enhancement," Gregory suggested.

"I wish," J.P. glumly stated. "But it was all Sam." He reached for Charlie's untouched martini and took a long sip, nearly emptying the glass. "Do you know what he had the nerve to suggest to me? That we should pool our talents together. He wants to collaborate with me."

"How?" Liam asked.

"He wants me to write a play for him. Can you believe it? While his career is on the downswing and mine is on the upswing, he wants my help." J.P. snapped his fingers at a passing waiter and pointed to the empty martini glass. "Two more, please."

"Is that such a bad thing?" Charlie tentatively asked.

J.P. gave Charlie the glare of death.

"Just listen to me," Charlie said soothingly. "He's the one who's got all the Hollywood connections. Maybe you could ride his coattails. I mean, he was on TV. He does have something of a career. Why not use him to make some new connections?"

"Because that's not me." J.P. thumped the top of

the table with a finger. "I would never use someone. Besides, I've got my own connections."

"They don't seem to be doing much for you," Gregory chimed in.

"What's that supposed to mean?" an outraged J.P. asked.

"It means I agree with Charlie. I think you're incredibly talented and you should be further ahead in your career than you are, through no fault of your own. Sometimes, it's all about who you know and lucky breaks. If slithering up to slimy Sam is a way for you to get ahead, then I say go for it. It's the least he can do after walking out on you."

"But I'd be helping him!"

"You'd be helping each other," Charlie said, putting a hand on Sam's arm. "Can I give you a piece of advice? You've been carrying around all this emotional baggage for ten years. Sam hurt you. Deeply. You need to have closure with him. You have to talk with him and let him know how you felt after he walked out on you. You never had a chance to do that. Otherwise, you're never going to be able to move on. You don't have to do anything today, but give it some thought. No matter what, you know we're all on your side, right?"

"I know." J.P. closed his eyes and drained the rest

of Charlie's martini. "In the words of Katie Scarlett O'Hara, I'll think about that tomorrow."

Their waiter chose that moment to arrive at their table, sharing the specials of the day. As he went down his list, Liam leaned close to Charlie, whispering in his ear, "That was intense."

"It's been a while since J.P. has had one of his meltdowns. It was long overdue."

"This has happened before?"

"At least once a year. If he reads an article about Sam or sees him on TV. You never know what's going to set him off."

"But they broke up ten years ago, right?"

"So?" Charlie stared at Liam. "J.P. really loved him. He's gone out with other guys, but nothing has ever really lasted long-term. It's probably because every guy he's been with is measured against Sam. He's been to therapy, but that hasn't helped, which is why I think he needs to talk with Sam. He's never gotten over their break-up."

"Poor guy."

"I've tried to help him move on, but I can't tell him what to do. I've never had that kind of love, so I can't judge him for how he feels."

"Do you think there's a chance they could ever get back together?" Liam suggested. "Maybe they weren't meant to break up. Maybe they're meant to find each other again."

"I don't think you want to tell J.P. that," Charlie advised. "If you're right, he's going to need to come to the realization on his own. Whether he does or not, it's all up to him. And let's not forget the most important part of this equation—Sam. They can't get back together if he says it's still over."

CHAPTER
SEVENTEEN

They were walking back to Gregory's car when they passed a pet store called Pup Town. Immediately, Bibi stopped in her tracks to admire the frolicking puppies in the window.

"Oh! They are so adorable," she gushed, pressing her nose against the window and tapping on the glass despite the sign that urged no tapping. "If they weren't so much work, I'd get one for Annie for Christmas."

Liam gazed at the different varieties of puppies. There were Yorkies, malties, dachshunds, and beagles all playing in a jumble, nipping and pawing each other while barking. Everyone admired the pups for a few more minutes before they started walking again.

Except for Liam, who remained in front of the window, grappling with a thought.

No, he couldn't. It would be irresponsible. He knew pets were never supposed to be given as a gift. Suppose Sarah was allergic? Then what? The puppy would have to go back.

He could just see the expression on his sister's face when he showed up on Christmas Day with a puppy in a basket. She would go nuclear on him. And she would probably have the final say. Penelope was the one who ruled in her house. What she said went, and if she said no puppy, then it would be no puppy. As much as he wanted to get one for Sarah for Christmas, he couldn't risk breaking her heart. But he could just see her face lighting up with joy when she saw the puppy and learned it was for her.

"One of those puppies caught your eye?" Charlie asked, cutting into Liam's thoughts as he rejoined him at the window.

"Yes." Liam pointed to one of the dachshunds. The pup kept running from one end of the window display to the other, wiggling around the other puppies, yipping non-stop while jumping on top of them, tugging at their tails with his teeth as if exclaiming, "Hey! Pay attention to me!" He was a little ball of fire, and there was something about him that made Liam smile. "This little guy."

"When did you start thinking about getting a dog?"

"Not for me. For Sarah." Liam waited for Charlie to say something, but when he didn't, he turned to him. "You think it's a bad idea?"

Charlie held his hands up in surrender. "I didn't say that."

"You didn't have to." Liam frowned. "It's written all over your face."

"If you're asking my opinion, you should rethink this," Charlie stated. "Or at least give it some thought for a day or two."

"Why?"

"A puppy is almost like having a baby. They need a lot of attention. You have to take care of them 24/7 before they're independent."

"What's keeping you guys?" Gregory asked as he, Bibi, and J.P. returned. "We've got to hit the road. Holiday traffic is going to be murder."

Charlie pointed to the window. "Liam is thinking of getting a pup."

"Do it!" Gregory exclaimed. "Walking a dog is the perfect man magnet."

"And you know this because?" J.P. asked.

"How do you think I met Christopher? When we were in PTown, I was walking my friend's dog and that's how I caught Christopher's attention. Christopher liked the dog, and she's the friendliest little thing, scampered right up to him and started pawing at his leg. But it was what was on the other end of the leash that really caught his attention." Gregory posed. "How could he resist? Especially when I had a glowing summer tan!"

"I wouldn't be getting it to attract men," Liam said.

Gregory pouted. "Then, why bother?"

Bibi rolled her eyes. "Such an animal lover!"

"Dogs are a lot of work!" Gregory pointed out. "As Christopher keeps reminding me."

"I was thinking of one for my niece, Sarah," Liam said. "But I would need to keep the pup somewhere until Christmas." He gazed hopefully at the group. "I couldn't take it home with me."

"Don't look at me," Bibi said. "If I came home with a pup, Annie would instantly think it was for her. And when I told her the pup was for Sarah, the secret would be out of the bag the next day at school. Not to mention, Annie's been nagging me for a puppy of her own."

Gregory shook his head. "As much as I'd love to

have a trial run with a pup, the timing is all wrong. Our ugly Christmas sweater party is coming up, and it's going to be a full house. We can't have a puppy running around that might have an accident."

"I'm at school all day," J.P. said. "So, I'm out."

Liam turned to Charlie with a hopeful smile. "That just leaves you, Charlie. And you work at home all day. You'd be able to take care of a puppy until Christmas, wouldn't you?"

"Don't put me on the spot like this," Charlie said. "You know how I feel. I think it's a bad idea. Besides, I have Shadow. He might not like having a pup around."

"Shadow's a sweet cat," Liam said. "He'll get along fine with Mistletoe."

"Mistletoe?"

Liam nodded, walking toward the store's entrance. "That's what I'm going to name him."

"Liam, please," Charlie pleaded. "Rethink this. Your sister and brother-in-law both have full-time jobs. Like Gregory just said, a puppy is a lot of work. It has to be house-trained."

"My sister is rolling in dough. She can get a trainer."

"That's a little presumptuous of you, don't you

think? You don't know your sister's financial situation."

"Having a pup will teach Sarah responsibility," Liam pointed out. "How could Penelope have a problem with that?"

"What if Sarah loses interest in the pup?" Charlie asked. "It's not like it's a toy she can just abandon."

"She's not going to lose interest."

"You don't know that. She's a little girl. Little girls can be fickle!"

"It's true," Bibi chimed in. "I speak from experience both as the mother of a fickle little girl and having once been a fickle little girl myself."

"If she grows tired of the dog, I'll take it." And Liam meant it. Eventually, Penelope and her husband were going to be back, and then they'd be moving out to California with Sarah. Right now, he had the chance to spend every day with his niece. As well as with Bibi, Charlie, and everyone else he'd become close to in Bramford Hills. But soon, he'd be leaving. And when he did, he'd be alone. So, if things didn't click with Sarah and Mistletoe, if he suddenly inherited a dog, he wouldn't be alone anymore. "Does that make you feel better?"

"You're an actor," Charlie reminded Liam.

"Hopefully, you're going to be back on the road next year. What are you going to do with the pup when you're away?"

Liam didn't know why Charlie was being such a hard-ass. Okay, he hadn't given the puppy idea much thought. It had been a very spur-of-the moment idea. But now, he had a backup plan, yet Charlie was still giving him grief. "I'll take the pup with me."

"And leave it alone in a hotel room when you're rehearsing?" Charlie looked horrified. "That isn't right."

Liam had had enough of Charlie's arguing. "I wouldn't do that. I'd bring Mistletoe with me to the theatre. There are always people around. In fact, he'd probably be the center of attention. He'd never be alone."

"But–" Charlie began.

Liam cut him off. "It's lonely being out on the road with a show. Sure, you're with people during the day when you're rehearsing, and then at night, once the show is up and running, you have an audience. Maybe if you get lucky, you hook up with someone after the curtain drops, but they're usually gone by the time morning rolls around. When you're on tour with a show, you're pretty much alone. So, if Mistletoe can't live with Sarah, then he'll live with me. It would be nice to have someone with me all the time. Someone who wants to be with me because they love me and need me. Now, that's the end of it, Charlie. I'm getting the puppy, and I don't want to hear another word out of you."

With those final words, Liam walked into the pet shop.

———

Charlie was left speechless. He didn't know why it hadn't occurred to him sooner, but Liam was lonely. Even though he'd used the word alone rather than lonely, Charlie knew what he meant. He always came across as cool and confident. Independent. Not needing anyone, as evidenced by his desire not to date. But it was clear from the words he'd just said about getting a puppy that it wasn't the case.

"Looks like you hit a sore spot," Gregory said.

"What are you going to do?" Bibi asked.

Charlie shrugged. "What can I do? His mind is set. And he needs somewhere to keep the puppy hidden from Sarah. It looks like I'll be running a puppy boarding house between now and Christmas."

Wanting to prove to Charlie that he wasn't making a rash decision, Liam gave his sister a phone call before purchasing Mistletoe. Much to Liam's surprise, Penelope was okay with giving Sarah a puppy for Christmas. Not only was she feeling incredibly guilty for being away for so long, but she wanted to make things up to Sarah for the missed FaceTime call. Also, she and Steve had been discussing the possibility of getting a dog, so the timing was perfect. After hanging up with Penelope, Liam walked to the nearest clerk, brought him to the window display, and pointed to Mistletoe. "He's coming home with me," Liam happily stated.

"Don't you mean with me?" Charlie corrected as

he walked into the store, joining Liam at the window.

"Where's everyone else?" Liam asked, noticing their absence. "Still outside?"

"On their way home. I told them we'd catch an Uber. Between all the shopping bags and now this little guy," Charlie said, as the squirming dachshund was lifted out of the front window, "we didn't have enough room."

"Hey, bud," Liam cooed to Mistletoe, nestling him against his chest, "I'm your new uncle."

Mistletoe instantly raised his head and gave Liam's face a lick, causing him to laugh as they followed the clerk over to the cash register. The clerk assured Liam that, unlike other pet stores, all the pups sold at Pup Town came from reputable breeders and not puppy mills. Between the cost of the pup, not to mention his leash, collar, doggy bed, toys, and Puppy Chow, Liam's credit card was done for the day. When they left the store, their Uber was waiting at the curb, and they quickly hopped into the backseat. As they drove back to Bramford Hills, Mistletoe dozed in his carrier.

"He's very quiet," Liam said. "Is that good or bad? Aren't puppies supposed to be a bundle of energy?"

"He's probably pooped from playing with the other pups. I'm sure he'll get his second wind in a few hours."

"I really appreciate you doing this for me, Charlie. I know it's a huge imposition."

"It's only until Christmas. I'm happy to do it for you and Sarah, especially since you told me your sister is on board. It's not a big deal. How much work could one little puppy be?"

———

Sarah was doing her homework at the dining room table when Liam got home. After giving her a kiss on top of her head, he dropped his shopping bags to the floor and went to see Mrs. Morris in the kitchen, where she was stirring a pot of chili, thanking her for once again looking after Sarah.

"She's an angel," Mrs. Morris said as she bundled herself up and headed out the back door. "I'll be back in an hour before you head off to Bailey's."

"Thanks, Babs."

"My pleasure."

When Liam returned to the dining room, he found Sarah slowly inching her way toward the shopping bags he'd left behind. He could see she was grappling between looking into the bags and ignoring them.

"No peeking!" Liam scolded, rushing to grab the bags so Sarah couldn't see what was inside them.

"Are those Christmas presents for me?" Sarah asked, giving Liam her sweetest smile.

"Maybe. And for your mom and dad. But the good stuff will be coming from Santa. Like that mysterious gift you won't tell me about."

Sarah returned to the dining room table and picked up her pencil. "I'll tell you once it gets here."

"Still won't give me a hint?"

Sarah shook her head, focusing on the piece of paper she was writing on. "I want you to be surprised."

"I'm going to miss dinner with you tonight."

Sarah looked up. "How come?"

"I have to work at Bailey's, but before I go to work, I have a date."

"With who?"

"A friend of Bibi's."

Sarah started writing again. "Why don't you go on a date with Charlie?"

"Charlie?" a surprised Liam asked.

Sarah nodded. "Then, you could make him your boyfriend."

"It takes more than one date before someone becomes your boyfriend," Liam explained. "And didn't you already suggest this? Are you sure you don't want him to be *your* boyfriend?"

"Don't be silly, Uncle Liam." Sarah giggled. "Charlie is too old for me. Besides, he doesn't like girls. He likes boys. Like you do." Sarah handed Liam the piece of paper she had been writing on.

"What's this?"

"A list. It has all the reasons why I think Charlie would be a great boyfriend for you."

Liam read it over. At the top of the list was: *Charlie is cute.* Followed by: *He smells good. He knows how to bake cookies. He knows how to decorate for Christmas. He's nice. He makes people smile.*

When Liam finished reading it, he realized his niece was absolutely right. Charlie would make a great boyfriend. But for someone else. Not him. His life was too much of a mess for someone as confident and put together as Charlie. He was an adult, while there were still days when Liam felt like a screwed-up kid. The last thing Charlie needed was someone whose life had imploded and didn't know how to get their act together.

"Uncle Liam?" Sarah's voice cut into his thoughts.

"Yes, sweetie?"

"Why do you look so sad? Is it because you're missing Pablo?"

A startled Liam dropped the list as he looked at his niece.

"You remember Pablo?" he asked in shock.

Sarah nodded. "When we came to visit you in New York last year, we did all those fun things together."

Liam nodded his head, too, smiling. "We did, didn't we?"

Sarah and her parents had come down to New York City over Thanksgiving weekend last year. It was the first time they were all meeting Pablo, who had instantly charmed his sister, niece, and brother-in-law. And why not? One of the things Liam had liked about him was that he was always up for an adventure and trying something new. Over the long weekend, they had taken Sarah for afternoon tea at the American Girl café, gone ice skating at Rockefeller Center, had a carriage ride in Central Park, and then went to Radio City Music Hall to see the Rockettes and the Christmas show. After that was a visit to FAO Schwartz, where they told Sarah she could buy any toy she wanted except the twenty-five-thousand-dollar stuffed lion. After strolling through the store, she had settled on a teddy bear.

Pablo had been great with his niece, holding her hand everywhere they went and pointing out landmarks as they walked through the city: the Empire State Building, the Chrysler Building, the Flatiron Building, and Washington Square Park. Another day, they had taken a ride on the Staten Island Ferry and then visited the Statue of Liberty. Pablo had even taken Sarah to the dance studio where he rehearsed, teaching her some of his routines and calling her *mi pequena bailarina*–my little dancer. Even though they had dined out in restaurants, Pablo had also introduced Sarah to all kinds of street foods: hot dogs, knishes, gyros, and falafels. And for dessert, there had been visits to the original Magnolia Bakery in Greenwich Village for cupcakes, Schmackary's in Hell's Kitchen for huge cookies, and Serendipity 3 for their famous frozen hot chocolate. After all that, of course, Pablo had made a lasting impression.

"If I look sad, it's because I've been going on a lot of bad dates and I'm really not looking forward to tonight."

"You'd have more fun if you went on a date with Charlie," Sarah pointed out.

Liam smiled at her as he picked up her list and

handed it back. "You're probably right. But I promised to go on a date with Bibi's friend, so I'm stuck."

"Unstick yourself," Sarah wisely advised.

"Oh, I'm going to," Liam vowed. "As soon as I can. Now, put your homework away and wash up. It's time for dinner."

———

An hour later, Liam was standing on Timothy's front porch, waiting for him to answer the door. The house was decorated for the holiday, although the twinkling Christmas lights were all pink instead of the customary red and green, which was unusual. He'd never seen a house decorated in pink lights before. He was wondering how long he would have to stay at Timothy's before he could leave without seeming rude when the front door was flung open.

"Hello! You must be Liam. I'm Timothy."

Liam stared in disbelief at the man standing across from him before quickly scrambling to close his mouth and put a smile on his face.

W...T...F...

He knew there were people who were addicted to plastic surgery. If one wanted to do a little nipping and tucking, that was fine. But then, there were people who went a bit too far.

Like Timothy.

His face, his body–it was all like a work in progress, in the midst of being reshaped and redesigned. His eyebrows were plucked into high arches. His hair was dyed blond. His teeth were a dazzling white, and his eyes were such a bright blue he had to be wearing contacts. His cheekbones were defined, and his chin was dimpled. His chest was impressive, as evidenced by the clingy, short-sleeved V-neck shirt he was wearing, as were his biceps, but they all looked a little too smooth and perfect. Which meant they were probably implants. Timothy's features were all exaggerated, as well as frozen and shiny, which meant Botox. As hard as it was to believe, Timothy did look like someone Liam had seen before, although he couldn't place him.

And then, it hit him.

Timothy looked like a Ken doll.

He was going to wring Bibi's neck the next time he saw her. How did it slip her mind that her friend was transforming himself into a Mattel toy?

"It's a lot to take in, isn't it?" Timothy said. "But you get used to it. Come on in. It's cold out there."

I'm never getting used to it, Liam thought, stepping inside.

"Let me take your coat," Timothy offered.

Liam reluctantly took it off and handed it to him. "Your Christmas lights are pink." Liam didn't know why those were the first words out of his mouth. Maybe it was because he was so stupefied by Timothy's appearance.

"Aren't they fab? I got them last year when the Barbie movie came out. I love Barbie. I call this my Dreamhouse."

"You do?"

"Uh huh. Follow me. I'll give you a tour."

Liam walked behind Timothy as they went from room to room. The colors of the walls, rugs, and window treatments were bright and punchy, and the furniture was all retro from the 50s and 60s, giving the house a fun, kitschy feel. But each and every room was devoted to Timothy's doll collection.

"This is the Barbie room," Timothy said as they entered the living room. "I have Malibu Barbie, Fashion Barbie, Golden Dream Barbie, Totally Hair Barbie—which, if you didn't know, is the best-selling Barbie of all time. There were more than ten million sold worldwide. Then, we have Western Barbie, Pretty and Pink Barbie, Superstar Barbie from 1977, and a couple of bubble cut Barbies from the 1960s. Not to mention the Christmas Barbies and the Barbies wearing gowns designed by Bob Mackie. Oh! And let's not forget all the Barbies from the Barbie movie."

The list went on and on. One whole wall of the living room was nothing but a massive display case with rows and rows of Barbies, some four rows deep. There were a lot of dolls! Liam hoped he wasn't going to be quizzed because he was losing track of all the different kinds of Barbies that existed.

"This room is devoted to Barbie's friends," Timothy explained as they walked into a second room. "Francie, Christie, Midge, PJ, and Teresa." Liam nodded, none of the names registering with him, although he seemed to remember something in the Barbie movie about Midge being pregnant. "Over here, we have Barbie's little sisters, Skipper, Stacie, and Chelsea," Timothy said, pointing to a shelf. "But I don't have that many." Liam wasn't so sure about that. There were a lot of dolls crammed on the shelf.

He followed Timothy into a third room. "This is my celebrity Barbie room. Over here, we have the actresses: Audrey Hepburn, Elizabeth Taylor, Tippi Hedren, Deidre Hall, Farrah Fawcett, Lucille Ball, to name a few. Then, we have the singers: Gloria Estefan, Stevie Nicks, Tina Turner, Cher, Diana Ross, and Mariah Carey. And then, we have historical figures: Rosa Parks, Eleanor Roosevelt, Amelia Earhart, Katherine Johnson, and Frida Kahlo."

They took the stairs up to the second floor. "In my bedroom, we have the Kens: Earring Magic Ken, Sugar's Daddy Ken, Malibu Ken, Dia De Muertos Ken, Mod Hair Ken..."

Dolls, dolls, dolls, and more dolls. Liam's head was swimming. Everyone was entitled to have a hobby. But this was more than just a hobby. It was an obsession. How did he escape this dollhouse?! Even though he was never going to see this guy again, he didn't want to come across as insulting. Some other guy might be into dolls as much as Timothy, and they'd be the perfect match. And even though Timothy had morphed himself into an image of what he thought was male beauty, Liam found it fake and artificial. There was nothing real left to him.

Unlike Charlie, who suddenly popped into his mind. With Charlie, you got what you saw, and that was a sweet, funny, thoughtful guy. Everything Sarah had written on her list.

"How do you know Bibi?" Timothy asked as they walked back downstairs.

"My niece and her daughter go to the same school. How do you know her?"

"We go to the same gym. The Body Connection."

Liam made a mental note to avoid doing any workouts at The Body Connection.

"We used to take the same spin class, but I haven't seen her in months."

"How come?"

"I've been busy maintaining myself with doctors."

I wouldn't call it maintaining, Liam thought. *I'd call it living in an episode of Botched!*

Liam really didn't want to be judgmental, but obviously, something was missing from Timothy's life if he was trying to recreate himself as a Ken doll. What did he see when he looked in the mirror? Because obviously, he didn't like what he saw if he kept going under the knife.

Well, it wasn't his job to play therapist.

"Has anyone ever told you that you look a little bit like Allan?" Timothy asked when they returned to the living room.

"Allan who?"

"Ken's best friend."

"Uh, no..." To the best of Liam's recollection,

Michael Cera had played Allan in the Barbie movie, and Liam had never been told that he looked like Michael Cera. Other celebrities, yes, but not Michael. And he didn't see the resemblance at all.

Timothy put up both hands like a director and studied Liam through them. "With a little bit of enhancement, you could be a dead ringer for him. Just imagine it. Ken and Allan as a couple." He sidled closer to Liam, placing a hand on his chest and giving it a caress. "Well, you and me. I bet you have to beat men off with a stick. Until I made a few tweaks, I didn't get much attention from guys. Now, I can't keep them away. It made a big difference in my love life. But I bet you've never had that problem. What's it like being so gorgeous?"

What was it like? Insulting? Demeaning? Exhausting? It was assumed he didn't have a thought in his head because he was dismissed as just another pretty face. Early on, Liam realized if someone was going to use him because of how he looked, then why not use them? Why get to know someone when they only wanted him for his physical attributes? He could do the same thing and then move on. It resulted in a lot of sex, which he had enjoyed at first, but no emotional connection with anyone. Eventually, he became tired of it, but he had fallen into a pattern that he didn't know how to get out of. Thankfully, this time away from his life in New York City was allowing him to reset and decide what he really wanted from another guy.

And it wasn't meaningless sex.

Liam removed Timothy's hand from his chest, making it clear that there would be no Ken and Allan coupling that night. "As much as I'd like to stay and get to know you better, Tim, I've got to–"

"It's Timothy."

Liam refrained from rolling his eyes. So, Timothy was one of those gays who had to use their full first name. No nicknames allowed. "Well, *Timothy*," Liam said, "I've got to get to work."

Liam didn't want to say it had been nice meeting him because he got the sense Timothy would use it to try and set up another date, even though this one had barely qualified. It had been more of a meet-and-greet that turned into a meet-and-greet-and-beat-it. Liam grabbed his coat off the couch where Timothy had tossed it and hurried to the front door, his hand already reaching out for the handle. "Have a great holiday!"

———

Charlie was dying to know how Liam's date with Timothy had gone. Had they hit it off? Had they made plans for a second date? As much as he was tempted to text Liam, he instead sent a text to Bibi. Within seconds, she texted him back one word: *DISASTER!*

Ouch! Well, it was nice to know he wasn't the only one not having success finding a man for Liam. He wondered what could have gone wrong. Had the doll collection been too much?

Charlie tried to focus on the Christmas gifts he was wrapping, but his mind kept wandering back to Liam. Even though it was none of his business, he had to know why the date hadn't worked out. He couldn't stay home. With Timothy out of the running, it meant Liam still needed to be set up on a future date if he was going to deliver on his promise to Sarah. Liam had to have a boyfriend by Christmas. If not, what would that do to Sarah's belief in Christmas and Santa Claus?

Charlie abandoned his ribbons and wrapping paper. The gifts could wait. Right now, he needed to be somewhere else, and that place was Bailey's. Charlie went to Mistletoe's doggy bed and lifted him into his arms. "Feel like paying a visit to Uncle Liam?"

Mistletoe licked his nose in response.

"I'll take that as a yes."

———

There was a lull in Santaland when Charlie arrived. He spotted Liam sitting on his throne, looking sexily disheveled in his Santa suit, with his eyes closed. Poor guy. Did he ever get a chance to just rest? Between taking care of Sarah and working, he must never have any free time. Charlie didn't want to disturb his catnap, but who knew how long he'd have Liam all to himself before the Santa After Dark line resumed?

"Did you come to find out about my date?" Liam asked, keeping his eyes closed.

"How did you know it was me?" a surprised Charlie asked.

"I can smell your cologne. Bleu de Chanel, right?"

"Right. But I didn't come to ask about your date."

Liam opened one eye, giving Charlie a skeptical look. "You didn't?"

"Mistletoe wanted to come visit you, didn't you, Mistletoe?" Hearing his name, the puppy's head popped out of the canvas tote bag Charlie had draped over one shoulder. At the sight of Liam, he started wiggling with excitement, trying to get out of the bag until Liam left his throne and gave him a scratch behind the ears. Mistletoe closed his eyes in bliss, instantly in doggy heaven.

"The date went great," Liam said.

"Great?" Charlie exclaimed in shock. "Bibi told me it was a disaster."

"Aha! Busted!" Liam gleefully shouted.

"Okay, fine," Charlie confessed. "I came to find out what went wrong."

"It wasn't my fault."

Charlie folded his arms over his chest, a knowing expression on his face. "Uh huh."

"Really!" Liam rubbed his nose against Mistletoe's fur. "It was just too freaky for me."

"What's so freaky about a doll collector?"

"A doll collector who wants to look like one of his dolls!"

Liam then proceeded to tell Charlie about Timothy's extensive doll collection and his transformation into a human Ken. By the end of the recap, Charlie had to agree that Timothy wasn't dating material for Liam.

"Did you at least stick around long enough to

find out if he was anatomically correct?" Charlie asked.

"I did not! Although, from the bulge I spied in his jeans, I believe that's the one part of himself he left as is."

Charlie shook his head. "I don't know what I'm going to do with you. Maybe I'm the one who needs to go on a date with you."

Before Charlie could say anything else, a voice behind them said, "Who knew Santa could be tall, dark, and handsome?"

Charlie would have known that voice anywhere. He turned around, forcing himself to smile. "Claude, what are you doing here? Aren't you in the middle of rehearsals for your Christmas musical?"

"Devon is handling rehearsals tonight while I'm doing a bit of Christmas shopping." He held up his bulging shopping bags. "I heard about Bailey's Santa After Dark program and had to experience it for myself." He moved closer to Liam. "We meet again."

"Did you want a photo?" Liam politely asked, taking a step backward.

"Of course!"

As Liam walked back to his throne, Claude turned to Charlie. "I can see why you were keeping him to yourself. He ticks off all the boxes. Yum, yum, and yum!"

"I wasn't keeping him to myself," Charlie snapped. "I've introduced him to all my friends."

"Except me," Claude sniffed.

That's because you're not my friend! You're my frenemy! "It wasn't intentional. You know how crazy it can get during the holiday season."

"You seemed awfully chummy with each other. Sharing a moment?"

What was that supposed to mean? He wasn't sure what Claude was getting at. "We're friends," he explained. "Friends share moments all the time."

"I heard what you said about asking him out on a date." Claude gave Charlie a sympathetic look. "Don't take this the wrong way, but don't you think you're a little bit out of his league?"

Claude's words pressed Charlie's buttons, and he instantly saw red. Talk about insulting! What made Claude think Liam wouldn't be interested in dating him? Even though dating Liam had never entered Charlie's mind, if it had, why not? Had Claude said those words on purpose, or did he not have a filter? Charlie never knew, and so, once again, he gave him the benefit of the doubt. "What's that supposed to mean?" he asked, trying to sound calm, although he could hear the note of irritation in his voice.

"Now, don't get mad," Claude soothingly said. "I know you're a catch, and some day the right man is going to come along for you. But someone as good-looking as Liam can have any guy he wants. Why would he settle for you? He's from the big city, and you're more suited to small-town living. If you were a city guy, you would have stayed in Manhattan, right?"

Mistletoe chose that moment to seek attention. Tired of being ignored, he popped his head out of the bag again, yawning. At the sight of Charlie, his tongue unrolled and he gazed at him adoringly while panting. But when he turned his head and Claude came into his line of sight, his mouth snapped shut and he bared his teeth, growling softly.

"Keep that beast away from me!" Claude shrieked.

"Good pup," Charlie cooed, rubbing a hand over Mistletoe's head as they watched Claude turn his back on them and make his way toward Liam.

Charlie didn't know why, but seeing Claude close in on Liam...he felt jealous. Claude had a husband, so it wasn't like he was going to ask him out. Suddenly, Charlie felt like a kid again. Liam was *his* friend and he didn't want to share him. And he wanted Claude to know that. Before he lost his courage, Charlie walked up to them. "Could I have a quick word, Liam?"

"Now?" Claude groused as he settled himself on Liam's lap, draping an arm around his shoulders the same way a python would squeeze a victim. "We're about to have our photo taken."

Liam bolted from his throne as Claude fell unceremoniously to the floor. "Sorry about that," Liam said, offering a hand to help him up. "Be right back." Liam followed after Charlie. "What's up?"

"I need to prep you," Charlie declared.

"Prep me for what?"

"Dating."

Liam grinned. "I've been dating most of my life. I think I know what I'm doing."

Charlie shook his head. "Obviously, you're doing something wrong because you're still single."

"That's a matter of opinion. I choose to be single."

"You've had three dates and they've all ended badly," Charlie reminded him.

"You know why. It was because of the guys."

"Maybe. But I want to see what we have to work with."

"Work with?"

"I need to see what you're like on a date. We'll do a practice run, that way I can tell you what you're doing wrong, what you're doing right, and what you need to fix."

Liam stared at Charlie in disbelief. "Seriously?"

"Seriously."

"So, you're asking me out on a date?"

"A practice date," Charlie stressed. "That way, you'll know what to do when you go on a real date. That perfect date."

Liam threw his hands up in the air. "Sure. Why not? It'll make Sarah happy."

"Sarah? What does she have to do with this?"

"Tonight, she suggested you'd make a good boyfriend for me. She even put together a whole list of things she liked about you."

Charlie's heart melted. "Awww. I love that little munchkin."

"Let me get back to work," Liam said.

Charlie said his next words loud enough so there was no way Claude could not overhear them. "It's a date. See you on Friday night. I'll come pick you up."

The date might not be real, Charlie smugly thought to himself as he headed toward the elevators with Mistletoe, *but Claude doesn't have to know that.*

CHAPTER
NINETEEN

How much work could one little puppy be?

Famous last words.

"Mistletoe, please," Charlie begged. "Stop whimpering."

It was one o'clock in the morning, and Charlie was trying to sleep. Mistletoe was in his crate, but he wasn't happy about it. He kept whining and barking, clearly unhappy. Shadow was curled up on the dresser, his tail swishing back and forth, staring at Charlie with what could almost be described as disdain on his face. Charlie could read his mind: *You bring this creature into our home, and he keeps us up all night? Do something about it!*

Charlie knew what Mistletoe wanted. He wanted to be taken out of his crate and held. He wanted to be in bed with Charlie, nestled against his chest. But if he did that, then Mistletoe would want to do it every night, and Charlie didn't want to share his bed with the pup. He needed to set boundaries.

"Sorry, boy," Charlie said, fluffing up his pillow and turning over in bed. "But you're staying put."

Forty-five minutes later, Charlie gave up. Tossing aside the sheets, he went to the crate and removed Mistletoe, heading back to bed. "It's only for tonight," he sternly told him as the pup instantly went silent, gazing at him happily. As soon as Charlie lay back down against the mattress, Mistletoe closed his eyes, nestling against Charlie's chest, one little paw pressing on one of his pecs. Within minutes, Charlie was finally asleep, too.

When he woke in the morning, he was alone in bed. Instantly, his thoughts went to Mistletoe. Where was the pup? He lifted the sheets, looking at the bottom of the bed, thinking he had made his way down there, but there was no puppy. Had he managed to jump out of bed?

The answer was obvious as Charlie's eyes focused on the mess strewn across the bedroom floor.

When Charlie got ready for bed each night, he tossed the decorative pillows from the top of his bed onto the floor. Mistletoe, after jumping out of bed, must have bitten into one of the throw pillows and shaken it in a frenzy. The entire floor was covered with feathers, with a trail of them leading straight into his bedroom closet.

Shadow glared at Charlie from his perch on top of the dresser. *What did you expect?* his expression seemed to say.

Charlie followed the feathers, pushing open the closet door he'd left ajar. When he saw what was inside, he gasped.

There was Mistletoe, sitting in the center of his closet, casually gnawing on one of his Prada loafers. Okay, he'd gotten them on sale, but still. They were his Prada loafers!

"Bad dog!" Charlie scolded, snatching the shoe from between a startled Mistletoe's paws and shaking a finger in his face. "Bad dog!"

Mistletoe stared at him in confusion, tilting his head to one side.

"You're not supposed to eat shoes!" he lectured, waving it in the air. "No! No eating."

He scooped up the pup, tucking him under one arm while taking a quick peek at the rest of his shoes. Thankfully, they were all still intact.

"What am I going to do with you?" he asked the pup, dropping his shoe to the floor and holding him with both hands as he stared into his little face.

Mistletoe, a ball of non-stop energy, wiggled to break free. Charlie, who had to start working at nine, could only imagine what his day was going to be like. Mistletoe was going to demand Charlie's undivided attention.

Unless...

Unless he figured out a way to exhaust this pup as quickly as possible.

———

Charlie walked by the dog park all the time. Not having a dog of his own, he'd never had a reason to step inside until today.

"Okay, Mistletoe, time for you to burn off some of that energy," Charlie told him as they neared the park. "I need to work today."

As soon as Mistletoe heard and saw the other dogs, he started tugging on his leash.

"Don't worry," he told the pup. "We'll get there soon. You'll have plenty of time to play."

There were already some early morning risers with their dogs in the park, clustered together with cups of takeout coffee. Charlie found the area where

Mistletoe could be released from his leash and let him join the other dogs. Within seconds, he was running around in circles, happily barking, trying to keep up with the other dogs as Charlie sat on a bench.

"Which one is yours?"

The voice startled Charlie, who had just taken out his phone and was scrolling through work emails. He looked up to see a friendly male face smiling at him. It sort of reminded him of the Broadway actor and TV star, Jonathan Groff, who had always been a favorite of his.

Charlie pointed. "The little dachshund. Mistletoe. Actually, he belongs to a friend of mine. I'm dog-sitting."

"Cute name. Mind if I join you?"

Charlie slid over on the bench to make room. "Where's your dog?"

The guy pointed to a black Frenchy. "Her name is Mrs. Danvers."

"Like from the movie *Rebecca*?"

"Yes!" The man's green eyes lit up. "I usually have to explain it to people. I'm a huge fan of Alfred Hitchcock. It was either Mrs. Danvers or Annie Hayward."

"From *The Birds*!"

"You know your Hitchcock."

"I love his movies."

"The revival house in Henderson is doing a two-week Hitchcock festival next month. From his earliest movies all the way up to his last, *Family Plot.*"

"I'll have to check that out."

The guy held out a hand. "My name's Nick. I know your dog's name. What's yours?"

Charlie enviously noticed Nick was the kind of man who could wear short sleeves and shorts in the winter and not be cold at all. Meanwhile, Charlie was bundled up in a parka with a scarf, hat, and gloves. He took Nick's hand and shook it. "I'm Charlie."

"How long are you dog-sitting for?"

"Only until Christmas."

"Bummer. I could get used to seeing your face here every day." Nick pointed to the coffee shop across the street from the park. "I'm going to get a cup of coffee. Can I get you one?"

Coffee sounded nice. It was a bit cold, even if Nick didn't seem at all fazed by the weather. "Sure."

"How do you like it?"

"Milk, no sugar."

"Same as me!" Nick exclaimed with a smile. "That's two things we now have in common. Hitchcock and coffee. I wonder what else we'll discover as we get to know each other. Be right back."

Ten minutes later, Nick returned, coffees in hand.

"How much do I owe you?" Charlie asked, taking a cup.

Nick shook his head. "My treat. You can get them next time."

Charlie clinked his paper cup against Nick's. "Deal."

"I don't know about you," Nick said, "but this is my favorite time of year. If I could put my Christmas decorations up the day after Halloween, I would."

"Me, too!" Charlie exclaimed.

Nick laughed. "A fellow Christmas nut. I love it." His phone buzzed, and he sighed after glancing at the screen. "Looks like playtime is over. I've got to get Mrs. Danvers back home before I head to work." Nick stood up from the bench and whistled at his dog, who instantly came running over, allowing Nick to attach a leash to her collar.

"Maybe we can get together with our pups outside the park," Nick suggested. "Mrs. Danvers loves playing with other dogs. Could I get your number?"

"Sure," Charlie said, reciting his cell number as Nick put it into his phone.

"We could even catch dinner or a movie," Nick added.

That's when the light bulb went on in Charlie's head. Nick was interested in him. All this time, he'd been flirting, and Charlie had been oblivious.

Nick sent him a text. "Now, you have my number," he said with a wide smile.

Charlie stared at his phone and the smiley face text that had appeared, trying to remember the last time a guy had shown interest in him.

He couldn't remember.

———

Thirty minutes later, Charlie was leaving the dog park when he ran into Gregory. Mistletoe instantly jumped up on his legs, demanding attention. After significantly gushing over the puppy, Gregory turned to Charlie.

"Okay, who is he?" he demanded with razor-sharp intensity.

"Who?"

"You know who," Gregory confidently stated. "The guy who's got you glowing with that smile on your face."

Was he glowing? Charlie wondered. Well, maybe. Sort of. Who wouldn't when someone wanted to date them?

"I met a guy," Charlie began.

"Yes!" Gregory exclaimed. "See? I was right. Dogs are a man magnet."

"Yes, you were right," Charlie agreed, and then proceeded to fill Gregory in on his morning adventure.

"When are you seeing him again?"

"I guess tomorrow morning when I come back to the dog park."

Gregory shook his head. "No! Absolutely not! You have to reach out to him at some point today."

"Why?"

"So he knows you're interested."

"Actually, he's more interested in me than I am in him."

Nick seemed perfectly nice and charming. Friendly and cute. But the entire time Charlie had been chatting with him, that's all it had been: mindless chit-chat. No flirting. No dropping of hints. At least, on his part.

Gregory looked horrified, as if he couldn't imagine not getting back to someone who had given him his number. "Why not?"

"This all caught me off guard. I'm still processing what happened."

"Well, process! And then, give him a call."

Charlie shook his head. "I don't have time to date right now."

"Why not?"

"It's Christmas. It gets crazy busy at this time of year. Besides..."

"Besides? Besides what? Why are you hesitating and not taking my advice?" Gregory held up his hand with his engagement ring on it, waving it in Charlie's face. "Hello! Results!"

"I'm wondering if there's a way I could set him up with Liam," Charlie confessed.

It was flattering that Nick had been flirting with him, but didn't the fact that Charlie had been oblivious to it mean something? Like, maybe he wasn't attracted to him? And if he wasn't, then maybe he could set him up with someone who would be.

"What?!" Gregory shrieked so loudly Mistletoe ran to hide behind Charlie's legs. "Are you crazy?"

Gregory grabbed Charlie by the shoulders and shook him. "This guy was flirting with *you*. He asked for *your* cell number. Let Liam find his own man. Lord knows, he has more than enough experience."

"But I need to find Liam a boyfriend by Christmas."

"What? Why?"

Charlie confessed to Gregory about Sarah's letter to Santa. When he finished, Gregory succinctly said, "When you wrote her back, you told her you couldn't guarantee a boyfriend for her uncle. So, you're off the hook."

"But she's a little girl. And this means so much to her. How can I break her heart?"

"You're the one Nick wants to go out with," Gregory reminded Charlie. "It's time for Little Miss Sarah to grow up and learn not all Christmas wishes come true. When I was eight years old, I wanted a Barbie Dreamhouse. Did I get one? No. Was I disappointed? Yes. Did it scar me for life? No. She'll be fine. Besides, isn't she at the age when kids stop believing in Santa Claus?"

"I hate when that happens," Charlie glumly stated, remembering when he first realized the truth about Santa Claus not being real. He'd also been eight, and a bully in the sixth grade had told Charlie and his friends that Santa didn't exist. That their parents were lying to them. Charlie had run home in tears, throwing himself into his mother's arms. When she instantly didn't reassure him the bully was wrong, he realized he had been telling the truth. He'd been crushed, and that was the first year he didn't leave cookies and milk out for Santa on Christmas Eve.

"But don't you think if Nick got a look at how gorgeous Liam is, he'd want to go out with him?"

Gregory shrieked again. "Who cares what Liam looks like? Yes, he's a very attractive man, but it hasn't done him much good, has it? He's all alone."

"The timing isn't right," Charlie said. "Maybe in the new year I'll–"

Gregory cut him off, jabbing a finger in his chest. "Forget about the new year. The time is now. I'm not letting you throw away this man. You're inviting him to my ugly Christmas sweater party."

"Okay," Charlie readily agreed.

"That's it? Just okay?" Gregory stared at Charlie with suspicion. "No argument?"

"No argument."

"Finally! Some common sense." Gregory glanced at his watch. "I've got lots of errands to do for the party, so let me dash. I can't wait to meet Nick!"

Gregory would definitely meet him. Liam would, too. After all, Liam was also going to be at the ugly Christmas sweater party. And who was to say Liam and Nick wouldn't cross paths with a little help from Charlie?

CHAPTER
TWENTY

Liam didn't have the gift-wrapping gene.

Whenever he tried to wrap something, the end result was a package that looked messy and lopsided. The wrapping paper wasn't neatly cut, so the paper pattern didn't align, and he usually used too much Scotch tape and an excess of wrapping paper, resulting in bumps and bulges.

"What do you think?" he asked Sarah, walking into the living room where she was watching *Inside Out* on TV. He held up the first gift he had wrapped. She tore her eyes away from the TV screen and wrinkled her nose. "Are you practicing gift wrapping?" She took a sip through a straw from a can of Pepsi. "Because that package looks messy."

"What does it matter how it looks? Whenever

anyone gives you a present, you rip the wrapping paper off like a maniac to see what's inside."

Sarah's eyes returned to the movie. "Mommy says presentation is everything."

Liam sighed. Mini-Penelope had spoken.

But he knew she was right.

He went back to the dining room, determined to do better with his next gift. As he wrapped, Liam lost track of time. He knew he was still using too much paper and tape, but he wanted to get all his wrapping done. It was slow going. Some of the gift boxes were oddly sized, and he wasn't able to just fold and tape the way he would with a rectangular box. After two hours, he hadn't made much progress. He gave up and decided to get ready for his date with Charlie. Correction: his fake date. Apparently, he was going to be Eliza Doolittle to Charlie's Henry Higgins. He was curious to see what the night held in store.

He was on his way to take a shower when the doorbell rang. Sarah abandoned the couch and ran to answer it, peeking through the window beside the door. "It's Charlie!" she shrieked with excitement as she grappled with the locks and flung the door open, throwing herself at him.

"I'm happy to see you, too," Charlie said,

handing Liam a picnic basket with one arm while giving Sarah a hug.

"What's this?" Liam asked before peeking inside and inhaling an assortment of wonderful smells.

"Just a couple of meals for next week. I'm catering a few Christmas parties tomorrow, and I had leftovers."

Charlie's thoughtfulness never failed to amaze him. "Thanks."

Charlie gazed at Liam from head to toe. "Looks like someone spent the day lounging around. Did you just roll out of bed?"

"I wish." Liam, unshaved and dressed in a pair of sweatpants and a T-shirt, ran a hand through his mussed hair. "I got a little sidetracked."

"With what?"

"Wrapping presents."

Charlie's face lit up. "I love wrapping Christmas presents."

"Uncle Liam doesn't," Sarah chimed in.

"Why not?"

"He's bad at it."

"How bad?"

"Very bad."

"Hey, I'm standing right here," Liam protested.

"But it's true, Uncle Liam. Don't feel bad. Not

everyone is good at everything." Sarah took Charlie by the hand and led him into the dining room as Liam followed. When he entered the room, he could see Charlie had the same expression on his face as Sarah had earlier.

"What's wrong?" Liam asked.

"Nothing," Charlie quickly answered.

"Tell me."

Charlie studied the gifts, avoiding eye contact with him. "Your wrapping is a bit basic."

"Basic?"

"Simple. It has no style. No flair. No pizzazz! Where are the ribbons? The bows?"

"I'm lucky if I can get the wrapping paper to stay in place and not look wrinkled," Liam confessed.

"Well, there is that, too," Charlie admitted as he gingerly turned over a box covered with crinkled paper.

"I'm a horrible gift wrapper. I'm lucky Bailey's didn't put me in that department. I would have been fired on my first day."

"You want a wrapped gift to look like a work of art," Charlie explained. "You want it to be pretty. Tantalizing. You want to almost not want to rip it open."

"Not me," Sarah piped up. "I love ripping off

wrapping paper. The sooner I do, the sooner I can find out what my present is."

Charlie shrugged off his overcoat. "You go upstairs and get ready," he told Liam. "I'll handle this."

"You look really nice, Charlie," Sarah said.

"Thank you, sweetie."

Sarah was right, Liam realized. Charlie did look nice. He was dressed in olive green dress pants with an unbuttoned navy blue shirt paired with a tan suede vest. Charlie's hair was usually tousled, but tonight it was neatly brushed into place. And he was wearing his signature scent of Bleu de Chanel.

Charlie looked downright handsome.

Liam had planned on throwing on a pair of jeans and a flannel shirt, but he'd have to rethink that. Maybe Charlie had made dinner reservations at a fancy restaurant, although, wouldn't he have told him that? Liam hadn't planned to make any special effort tonight. After all, this wasn't a real date. But it looked like Charlie had put some thought into it, and now he wanted to do the same.

"Give me some time to get ready," Liam said. "I want to look nice tonight, too."

———

After Liam was gone, Charlie turned his attention to Sarah. He pointed to the gifts on the table. "How about we make like Santa's elves and help your uncle out?"

"How?"

"We unwrap these presents, and then I'll rewrap them so they look prettier. You can be my assistant and hand me what I need." Charlie started reading the tags. "I don't see your name on any of these."

"Those are presents for Mommy and Daddy and Uncle Liam's friends in New York City."

"Before we get started, we have to create some ambience," Charlie told Sarah.

"What's that?"

"It's a mood. A feeling. We're wrapping Christmas presents, right?"

"Right," Sarah agreed.

"That means we should have Christmas music playing."

Charlie called out to Alexa, asking her to play Christmas songs. Seconds later, Dean Martin could be heard singing *I'll Be Home For Christmas.*

"We should also have something baking in the oven. Preferably something made with vanilla and cinnamon so the house smells Christmasy. Want to help me make some sugar cookies?"

Sarah eagerly nodded as she followed Charlie into the kitchen, and he began gathering together the ingredients they needed. Sarah assisted Charlie with the breaking of eggs and stirring of batter while the oven preheated. Then, they used a cookie cutter to make perfectly round sugar cookies before sliding them into the oven.

"Baking is a lot of work," Sarah confessed as he loaded the dishwasher with the measuring cups and bowls they had used. "I think I like eating cookies more than making them."

"I'm always happy to make cookies for you," Charlie said as they headed back to the dining room. "Now, let's make sure we have all our wrapping supplies laid out." He searched for the wrapping paper, scissors, Scotch tape, gift tags, bows, and ribbons, placing them all in a row on the dining room table. "Great! We're all set."

With Sarah once again as his helper, Charlie set to work unwrapping the gifts Liam had already wrapped and rewrapping them with new paper. Soon, the scent of warm cookies reached their noses.

"Those smell good," Charlie said. "I bet they'll taste even better."

"Charlie, can I ask you a question?" Sarah asked while handing him a roll of tape.

"Anything you want."

"Why don't you be Uncle Liam's boyfriend?"

Even though he knew it might be coming, the suggestion still stopped him in his tracks momentarily.

"Don't you like him?" she continued.

"Of course I like him. We're friends."

"But you should be *boy*friends," Sarah stressed. "I think you would be the perfect boyfriend for him. I even made a list."

"I know," Charlie said, giving her a wide smile. "Your uncle told me you said a lot of nice things about me. But like I already told you, we're friends, sweetie. Besides, he lives in New York City and I live in Bramford Hills."

"You could move to New York City," Sarah suggested.

"I lived there once. Many years ago. But I didn't like it."

"How come?"

Charlie looked up at the sound of Liam's voice. Standing in the doorway of the dining room, the sight of him took Charlie's breath away.

Liam had cleaned himself up. He was wearing black dress pants and a fitted white shirt. He'd slicked his hair back with gel and cleaned up his five o'clock shadow so it looked like sexy stubble. The scent of his cologne filled the air. Woodsy. Musky. Intoxicating.

They were supposed to be going out on a fake date. But suddenly, the idea of being in a restaurant with Liam over a candlelit dinner seemed dangerous. He wasn't sure why he felt that way, but he did, and he always listened to his gut.

"I have an idea," Charlie said, abandoning the gift he'd been rewrapping. "Instead of going out tonight, why don't we stay in?"

Liam looked puzzled. "Are you sure?"

Charlie nodded. "I can help you wrap all these gifts, we can order a pizza, and then we'll watch a Christmas movie with Sarah. What do you say?"

Sarah began bouncing up and down on her toes, her face filled with excitement. "Please, please, please say yes, Uncle Liam. It'll be so much fun."

"Yes, please, please, please say yes, Uncle Liam," Charlie begged, joining in with Sarah's chants.

"It's two against one. How can I win?" Liam pulled his cellphone out of his pocket. "How do you like your pizza?"

———

After the pizza was ordered, Sarah went back to watching *Inside Out* while Liam followed Charlie into the kitchen. He was confused. Charlie had been so gung-ho for this date tonight, and now he was scrapping it?

"Where's Mistletoe?" Liam whispered to Charlie once they were alone in the kitchen.

"J.P. is watching him. You didn't think I'd leave a pup alone, did you? By the way, said pup destroyed one of my throw pillows and gnawed his way through a pair of my Prada loafers this morning."

Liam winced. "Ouch! Sorry. How much do I owe you?"

"I got them on sale and I've had them for a couple of years, so you're off the hook for them. The pillow was fifty dollars."

Liam took out his phone. "I'll Venmo it to you." After he put his phone back in his pocket, he asked, "Why the change in plans? I thought we were supposed to be having a practice date tonight. You were going to tell me all the things I was doing wrong."

Charlie pulled on a pair of oven mitts and opened the oven door, taking out the sugar cookies. "We'll do it another night. It's clear you're more in need of my gift-wrapping skills."

"Better hurry. I'm running out of nights in Bramford Hills. Pretty soon, Penelope and Steve will be back, and then I'll be returning to New York City."

For a second, Liam thought he saw a pained expression flash across Charlie's face. But then, it was gone.

"Why don't you stay here?" Charlie suggested.

"In Bramford Hills?" Liam laughed. "And do what? My days as a sexy Santa are numbered."

"Valentine's Day is fast approaching. You could be a sexy Cupid."

"Cupid wears only a diaper. I don't want to imagine how I'd be pawed at while being almost naked." Liam shuddered. "I'll pass."

Charlie began plating the cookies with a spatula. As Liam reached for one, Charlie lightly slapped him on the hand. "They need to cool off. You'll burn your mouth."

Liam folded his arms across his chest, leaning against the counter. "You never answered my question."

"Which one?"

"Why you didn't like living in New York City."

Charlie shrugged. "I tried big city living. I gave it five years, and it wasn't for me. I missed my family. I missed my friends. I missed the feeling of home. At heart, I guess I'm a small-town boy, so why would I want to leave? Have you ever thought of living in a place like Bramford Hills?"

Liam shook his head without hesitation. "I like the excitement of city life. There's always something to do 24/7."

"Don't you mean someone?" Charlie pointedly asked.

Liam groaned. "Maybe. When I was younger. But not anymore. It's time for me to get off that merry-go-round."

"When will you be going back?"

"Probably right after New Year's Day. Now is the worst time of year to try and find a new job." Ignoring Charlie's earlier warning, Liam reached for a cookie, taking a bite. "Your cooking and baking skills are so good. You never thought about trying to make it as a chef? Maybe open your own restaurant?"

Charlie shook his head. "That world is so competitive. It's a lot of hard work and long hours. I don't think I have what it takes."

"I disagree," Liam said. "You seem pretty focused and determined when you set your mind on something. Like trying to find me a boyfriend." Liam moved closer to Charlie. "Why is that?"

Charlie didn't answer the question. Instead, he eased himself around Liam, reaching for the plate. "Let's take some cookies to Sarah."

As they walked into the living room, Sarah jumped off the couch, pointing to the archway above them. "Kiss! Kiss! Kiss! You have to kiss each other!"

Liam gazed up and saw they were standing underneath a sprig of plastic mistletoe. He must have pinned it up there when they were decorating.

Sarah raced over to take the plate of cookies from Charlie. "Kiss him, Uncle Liam! Kiss Charlie!"

"The little lady has spoken," Liam said, taking Charlie into his arms and brushing his lips against his.

———

Charlie hadn't expected to be kissed again by Liam.

Last time, he had caught him off guard, but this time, Charlie's lips knew what to expect as soon as Liam's mouth pressed against his. And when they did, it was like they had been waiting. Eagerly. Impatiently. Charlie's lips instantly locked against his with an intensity that made him take his hands and place them against the sides of Liam's head as if to make sure he wouldn't pull away. Once again,

Charlie was lost in a whirl of sensations that kept rippling through him, only this time more acutely. Aware that they were kissing in front of Sarah, Charlie tried to keep the kiss somewhat chaste, but all his senses were on fire. Their kiss went on until finally Liam ended it and pulled away.

"Wow!" Sarah marveled, eyes wide with surprise. "That was a long kiss!"

"It was," a dazed Charlie told Sarah, his lips still tingling.

Liam blushed. "Sorry. I got carried away."

Did he? Charlie wondered. Had the kiss they'd shared affected Liam the same way it had affected him? Other than his blush of embarrassment, Liam wasn't looking at him any differently.

Why would he? Both times, the kisses hadn't been real.

Then, why did they *feel* real? Why was Charlie responding to them? And why did he want more?

Much, much more.

Charlie pushed the kiss out of his mind, telling himself it hadn't meant anything. It had only been a holiday tradition. Nothing else. There certainly wouldn't be any more kisses. After all, once New Year's Day arrived, Liam would be leaving Bramford Hills.

That kiss.

Liam hadn't had a kiss like that in a long time.

Except, of course, when he'd kissed Charlie earlier in the week. It was like he and Charlie instantly became one when their lips met.

Liam couldn't help but wonder what it would be like if they had sex together. Not that they were going to. He quickly chased that thought away. Charlie wasn't one-night-stand material, and Liam was in no place to make a commitment to anyone. Not that he was thinking of committing to Charlie.

Was he?

No, he firmly told himself. The last thing he needed was a relationship. Too much was going on in his life. He still had to take care of Sarah and get through the holiday season. A relationship required focus and attention. That person needed to be the center of his world, not an afterthought. There was no room for a boyfriend in his life right now. His professional life was still a mess, and he needed to get it back on track once he returned home. That had to come first, which meant he had to put exploring anything with Charlie on the back burner.

At least, for now. After that, however...

Liam hit the brakes on his overactive imagination. Wasn't he getting a little bit ahead of himself? He hadn't gotten any sort of vibe from Charlie that he wanted to date him. If anything, Charlie was constantly trying to set him up with other guys. If Charlie wanted to date him, wouldn't he have said something by now? Of course, he would have. Charlie was one of the most straightforward people he knew. The fact that he hadn't done or said anything made it perfectly clear they were just friends. It was as simple as that, which was fine with Liam, because, as he knew firsthand, boyfriends came and went. Friends, however, lasted forever.

While they waited for the pizza to be delivered, Charlie focused on wrapping the rest of Liam's Christmas presents. With the help of Liam and Sarah, he wrapped them in record speed, telling them he would add the bows and ribbons after dinner.

When the pizza finally arrived, ninety minutes after it had been ordered, everyone was starving. Charlie occupied himself by setting the kitchen table and placing slices on plates for everyone before starting a stream of non-stop chatter, asking Sarah to tell him her favorite Christmas movie. There was a reason for all of this. Like the first time they had kissed, Charlie once again felt awkward around Liam and wanted to distract himself from that. That was why he was constantly in motion, focusing on one task after another. By the time dinner was over, they had decided to watch three Christmas specials: *The Year Without a Santa Claus, Santa Claus is Comin' to Town,* and *Rudolph the Red-Nosed Reindeer.*

"Nothing like Rankin/Bass stop-motion animation specials to get you in the mood for the holiday season," Charlie said while cleaning off the kitchen table and loading the dishwasher.

"Leave those in the sink," Liam insisted, holding a hand out to Charlie. "We've got Christmas specials to watch."

Charlie was afraid to put his hand in Liam's. What if he felt that same jolt he experienced when they kissed? What then? Luckily, he was saved from finding out when Sarah slipped her hand into Charlie's and dragged him into the living room.

"Sit with me on the couch, Charlie," she insisted.

Charlie slid onto the end of the couch, leaning against the arm, while Sarah hopped onto his lap, pressing herself against his chest and pulling his arms around her like a blanket. Liam, taking the armchair across from them, aimed the remote at the TV. "Ready?" he asked.

"Ready!" Sarah answered.

Watching the specials, Charlie revisited his childhood. He remembered how much he had loved the campiness of the Miser Brothers during *The Year Without a Santa Claus*, while being bored out of his mind when Jessica, also known as the future Mrs. Claus, got to sing a solo in *Santa Claus is Comin' to Town*. When the Abominable Snowmonster appeared on screen during *Rudolph the Red-Nosed Reindeer*, Sarah tried not to appear scared, but he could tell she was by the way she squeezed his arms and nestled even closer to him.

"Don't worry, he can't hurt you," he whispered in her ear.

When the last special was over at ten, Charlie noticed Sarah's eyes were starting to droop.

"Looks like someone is ready for bed," Charlie observed. "And it's time I headed for home. It's almost my bedtime, too." Plus, he had a pup he needed to pick up from J.P.'s house.

Sarah yawned as she got off his lap. "Are you

going to the ice skating party at the pond tomorrow?" she asked.

"I didn't know there was an ice skating party at the pond," Charlie said as he reached for his overcoat on the other end of the couch.

"Charlie can come with us, can't he, Uncle Liam?" Sarah asked while yawning.

At first, there was silence. Then, Liam shrugged. "Charlie can come if he wants."

It wasn't the most enthusiastic invitation Charlie had ever received. In fact, Liam sounded almost reluctant to have him join them. But Sarah was staring at him expectantly, and he knew what she wanted his answer to be.

"You'll see me at the pond tomorrow if I can make it," he said, slipping into his overcoat and wrapping a blue scarf patterned with white snowflakes around his neck. He tugged on his gloves before giving Sarah a kiss goodnight. "Now, you go to bed and have sweet dreams."

"I'll be up in a bit to read you a bedtime story," Liam promised.

After Sarah disappeared up the stairs, Charlie headed for the front door. With Liam's niece gone, he didn't trust them to be alone with that mistletoe still dangling above their heads. Anything might happen, and he didn't want to find out what that might be. The sooner he left, the better.

"Goodnight," he told Liam, who was opening the front door. "Thanks for a nice evening."

He stared at Liam before walking out into the night, waiting for him to say something. To acknowledge he had felt something, too. For a kiss that powerful, Liam had to have experienced what Charlie had. It couldn't have been one-sided.

"Night," Liam said, holding the front door open for him, the expression on his face no different from what Charlie usually saw and confirming what he had suspected.

It was all in his mind. Liam didn't have any feelings for him. It had only been a kiss. Another amazing kiss, yes, but only a kiss.

Charlie hurried down the steps of the house, wanting to get as far away from Liam as possible before he somehow saw Charlie's thoughts written all over his face. He was heading toward the street when Liam came racing from behind him.

"Charlie!" he called out. "Wait!"

Despite himself, Charlie turned around with a smile on his face, his heart suddenly beating with excitement. "Yes?"

"You forgot this," Liam said, handing Charlie his

now-empty picnic basket. "Thanks again for the leftovers."

Charlie stared numbly at the basket. "Anything else?" he asked, almost hoping Liam would tell him he wanted him to stay. But if he did, what would happen next? After all, they were friends. Only friends. And Liam had made it clear he didn't want a boyfriend.

Liam shook his head, staring at Charlie in confusion. "Should there be?"

"No," Charlie said as a thought suddenly occurred to him. He didn't know why he hadn't realized it sooner. The reason why Liam was so resistant to finding a new boyfriend was because he was still getting over his old boyfriend, Pablo. After getting burned, he probably didn't want to rush into a new relationship. But Charlie had to show him it was time to move on. Maybe not with him, but definitely with someone else. "See you at the pond tomorrow."

———

Standing on the front porch, Liam watched Charlie disappear into the night, the picnic basket swinging by his side. He felt like Charlie had wanted to say something, but for whatever reason, he hadn't.

His fingers brushed slowly over his lips. He still couldn't get over their kiss. Just like the first time, it had sizzled. He was sure he didn't imagine it, but Charlie didn't seem at all fazed and acted the way he always did. Liam had wanted to discuss it, but he held himself back. Maybe it was because he was afraid of rejection. After all, he was the Viper, and his many sins could be found on the Internet with a few clicks of a keyboard.

Why would Charlie be interested in a guy like him? Charlie was special, and he deserved someone special. But something was going on between them, and Liam wasn't sure exactly what it was. He needed to process it and figure out what it meant before doing anything.

And was it his imagination, or did Charlie seem upset he hadn't invited him to the ice skating party? Even though it was a last-minute invitation, he hoped he knew he was more than welcome to join them. Liam hadn't invited him because he didn't want Charlie to feel obligated. He was already doing so much for Sarah and him, and he didn't want him to feel like they were taking him for granted. Charlie had his own life, even though it seemed like he was becoming a bigger part of Liam's life with each passing day.

He wasn't sure how he felt about that. It was nice, sure. But it was also complicated.

Like he had told Charlie earlier in the night, soon he'd be leaving Bramford Hills. And once he was gone, Charlie would be out of his life. Sure, they would still be friends, but living in two different places, it would take effort to keep their friendship growing.

He didn't know why, but the thought of no longer seeing Charlie on an almost daily basis made his heart ache. He'd come to rely so much on him these last few weeks. He was kind and nurturing, always taking such good care of the people in his life. Liam was going to miss that. Once he left Bramford Hills, there wasn't going to be anyone in his life doing that for him anymore.

CHAPTER
TWENTY-ONE

"How many marshmallows did you get in your hot chocolate, Charlie?" Sarah asked as they walked away from the park's concession stand.

"None. I'm a purist. I like my hot chocolate to just be chocolate. How many did you get?"

"Four," she said as she took a sip of the hot beverage.

"Do you feel warmer?"

Sarah nodded as she brought her cup to her mouth with mittened hands. When she pulled it away, there was a dot of foam on her nose. Charlie wiped it away with a finger as they sat on a bench looking out over the frozen pond, surrounded by towering pines. The entire scene was like something out of a winter wonderland. Christmas music floated through the air from speakers that had been set up, and there was snow everywhere from storms earlier in the month. Children built snowmen and snow forts and pelted each other with snowballs as they ran around with delighted screams. Skaters of all levels were on the ice, some moving slowly while others were more daring, showing off with spins and turns and jumps.

"It's supposed to snow again tonight," Charlie told Sarah.

"I hope we have a white Christmas," Sarah said. "I bet Santa's sled travels faster when it's snowing. Speaking of Santa…" She glanced around, making sure her uncle wasn't nearby.

Charlie spotted Liam on the other side of the pond, talking with some of his co-workers from Bailey's. He'd been with them since Charlie arrived an hour ago. Other than a quick smile and a wave of his hand when he saw Charlie, it was almost like Liam didn't want to engage with him, and that was fine. He hadn't come today for Liam, he'd come for Sarah. "What about him?"

"He still hasn't gotten Uncle Liam a boyfriend."

"It's not Christmas yet. Didn't you say you wanted your uncle to have a boyfriend for Christmas? I'm sure he's working on it."

Or at least, I am.

"Are you sure?" Sarah asked, a dubious tone in her voice.

"Trust me, he's working on it. Now, are you ready to hit the ice again?"

Sarah eagerly nodded, taking Charlie's hand as they headed back out to the pond. Once they were on the ice again, Sarah released his hand, speeding across the ice to join some of her friends. "Don't go too fast," he warned.

"I didn't know you had a daughter."

Charlie whirled around. Standing behind him was Nick, with a grin on his face.

"Sarah's not my daughter," Charlie explained. "She's my friend's niece."

"I didn't see you at the dog park this morning," he said as he began swirling around Charlie, making figure eights.

"Too much to do and not enough time. You know how it gets around the holidays. Mistletoe had to be satisfied with a walk around the block."

"Mrs. Danvers was disappointed." Nick paused and stopped skating, closing the distance between them. "I was, too. I enjoyed talking with you yesterday."

Charlie didn't know what to say to that. So, he

said nothing until Nick quickly filled the uncomfortable silence. "I'm here with some of my gay daddy friends. My own siblings don't have kids yet, so I'm an honorary guncle. I'd love to have kids of my own someday. How about you?"

Charlie loved kids. Naturally, over the years, he'd thought about having a family, but he'd never really given it a lot of thought. Before he had a family, he had to have a boyfriend, partner, or husband. He'd never had one long enough to consider that next step with, and he certainly didn't have one at the moment.

"A family would be nice," Charlie admitted.

"How many kids?" Nick asked as he skated around him again before holding a hand out. "I'd love to have three. Want to take a spin around the ice?"

Wasn't this first-date conversation? Charlie wondered. It was obvious Nick wanted to explore something with him. At any other time in his life, Charlie also would have wanted to. But something was holding him back, and he knew what that something was.

Liam.

But there was nothing going on between him and Liam! There were friends. Nothing more.

Yet, he kept thinking that perhaps there could be something more between them. Based on what, though? Two amazing kisses? Two kisses a relationship did not make, and Liam had been very clear about the fact that he wasn't looking for a new relationship despite Charlie's best efforts to find him one. Yes, they were friends, and maybe that was all they were meant to be. So, maybe, just maybe, he should give up on his thoughts of Liam and start thinking more about himself.

And about Nick. Nick was a good-looking guy. Charlie could see himself kissing him, getting naked with him, having sex with him. All those good things. More importantly, he seemed kind and thoughtful. He loved dogs and kids. He had so much going for him. Charlie hadn't felt anything for Liam when he first met him—in fact, he had despised him!—and now, he had all these strange feelings that he couldn't figure out. Who was to say the same thing wouldn't happen with Nick once they started spending more time together? The only way to find out was to explore things with him. He wouldn't know unless he gave him a chance.

At least with Nick, Charlie had a chance.

He didn't have one with Liam. After all, Liam wasn't planning to stay in town. He'd be leaving, and then he'd be back on the road with another touring show or maybe even in Los Angeles shooting a pilot or working on a movie or another reality TV show. Look at how many scandalous celebrities wound up on *Dancing with the Stars*. It was only a matter of time before the whole *Gay Househusbands* scandal was forgotten. Liam would be moving on, and Charlie would be left behind. But he'd be left behind with Nick, which wasn't such a bad thing.

His mind made up, Charlie held his hand out, giving Nick a smile. "I'd love to take a spin around the ice."

———

Liam searched the pond, looking for Sarah and Charlie. He instantly spotted Sarah with some of her friends, but where was Charlie? And then, he caught sight of him, talking with a guy.

Liam groaned as he watched them. If he knew Charlie, he was planning another set-up. When was he going to give up? How many times did he have to tell him he wasn't interested in dating?

Well, he'd better get this over with.

But as Liam skated across the ice, he began to realize something. The man Charlie was talking with was focused only on Charlie. It was like nobody else around them existed. And he couldn't miss the way his face was lit up.

Because of Charlie.

Charlie was making him feel that way.

Liam wasn't surprised. Charlie made him feel that way, too. But there was something about seeing the way he felt plastered on another guy's face that bothered Liam. It was obvious the man was interested in Charlie, and there was hardly any personal space between them.

Surprisingly, though, Charlie's face didn't mirror the guy's expression. In fact, he sort of looked disengaged. But that didn't make any sense. Why wouldn't Charlie want an attractive man who was into him?

Seconds later, Charlie's expression changed, and he smiled at the guy, reaching out for his hand. Liam knew that smile. It was the one Charlie always gave him. It was *his* smile, Liam possessively thought. What was Charlie doing, giving it to someone else?

Liam didn't know, but he intended to find out.

———

Oh, no.

No, Charlie silently wailed, dropping Nick's hand as he caught sight of Liam skating across the ice to join them. This was the last thing he wanted.

It was a recipe for disaster.

Liam stopped in front of them, spraying a shower of ice chips in the air. "Hi," he said, giving them both a smile. "Who's your friend, Charlie?"

Before he could answer, Nick held out his hand. "Nick Carerra."

Charlie watched as Liam stared at Nick's hand before reluctantly shaking it. And what was that expression on his face? He looked pissy. Like he'd tasted something sour. And then, a thought hit him that he immediately tried to dismiss, but it wouldn't go away.

Was Liam jealous of Nick?

That was the way it was coming across. As Charlie's eyes ping-ponged between Liam and Nick, he realized they were like two prize fighters sizing each other up, waiting for the bell to ring before pummeling each other. But that would mean Liam thought of Charlie as more than just a friend.

Charlie hit the brakes on his overactive imagination. He was reading more into the situation than he should. There was no jealousy going on.

"One of my friends is leaving," Nick told Charlie, breaking into his thoughts as he pointed to a bearded man with two little girls. "Let me go and say goodbye."

As Charlie watched Nick skate away, Liam said, "Is he date number four?"

"Pardon?"

"The next guy you're going to set me up with."

"Actually, no."

"No?"

Charlie watched as Liam almost did a double-take. He didn't know why he had lied. After all, he *had* planned on trying to set Liam up with Nick. But he had changed his mind. He was the one who was going to date him instead. He'd do his best to keep his promise to Sarah and find Liam a boyfriend by Christmas with what little time was left, but he was going to start thinking about his own love life, too.

"Why do you sound so disappointed?" Charlie stared at Liam expectantly. "Do you want to go out with him?"

———

Liam didn't know what to say.

He was shocked. He'd thought Charlie was going to admit to wanting to set him up with Nick, although he should have known the answer would be no. Nick had barely gazed at him, and Liam usually got at least a second look from guys.

But not Nick. He only had eyes for one man. Charlie.

Liam didn't know why, but he felt like he was losing something. Something special. All these weeks, it had been him and Charlie. And now, that was coming to an end. Well, it was always going to come to an end since he was leaving Bramford Hills. And Nick was the one who had the advantage. He lived here, so he wouldn't be leaving the way Liam would be. He was someone Charlie could develop a relationship with if he wanted.

The thought did not sit well with Liam.

"There you both are!" Sarah exclaimed as she skated up to Liam and Charlie.

"Hey, short stuff, you having a good time?" Liam asked, giving her a smile as he shook off his dark thoughts.

"The best!" Sarah exclaimed. She grabbed both Liam and Charlie by the hand and started dragging them across the ice.

"Where are we going?" Charlie asked.

"I want to go sledding," Sarah said, pointing

toward the big hill behind the pond where sledders whizzed down the slope.

"I don't know," Liam said with a frown on his face. "That looks awfully fast."

"That's the point," she explained. "It's no fun if you're going slow."

"The idea of you going down that hill so fast makes me nervous. What if you fall off and break something? Your mom will kill me if she comes home and finds you in a cast. Your dad, too."

"All the other kids are doing it."

"They're older than you," Liam patiently explained.

"What if we all sledded down the hill together?" The words slipped out of Charlie's mouth before he could stop himself. "We'll make a Sarah sandwich. I'll steer, Sarah will sit in the middle, and Uncle Liam will take care of the rear."

Uncle Liam will take care of the rear. Charlie couldn't believe the words he'd just said. He darted a peek at Liam, who gave him a devilish smile.

Dear Lord! Did he think he was flirting with him?

"I'm an expert at all things rear, if I do say so myself," Liam boasted.

Charlie was saved from saying anything else

when Nick came skating up to them. "Ready for that spin around the ice?"

Charlie stared guiltily at him. He had totally forgotten. "I've been drafted into sledding duty."

Nick casually shrugged. "That's okay. I can wait."

Charlie shook his head, aware that Liam and Sarah were watching. And listening. "No, don't wait. It's cold, and I don't know how long I'm going to be. There's a line to get up the hill for a sled, and then once we get down, I'm sure Sarah will want to go back up. I promised the day to her."

"I'll go get in line," Liam said, skating away. "Sarah, you come with Charlie."

Charlie watched Liam disappear into the crowd, wondering why he was leaving him alone with Nick. Didn't he want to hear what they were discussing? Wasn't he curious? Or did he just not care?

"I get it," Nick said with a smile. "Raincheck? Or should I say snowcheck?"

"I can do better than that," Charlie said, extending the invitation before he could change his mind. "A friend of mine is having an ugly Christmas sweater party next week. Want to come with me?"

Nick's face lit up. "I'd love to."

"I'll text you the details later."

"Guess I'd better go find myself an ugly Christmas sweater."

"Come on, Charlie," Sarah urged, impatiently tugging at his arm. "I want to go sledding."

"Bye," Charlie said to Nick before following Sarah off the ice.

"Who was that?" she asked, glancing over her shoulder at the same time as Charlie. Nick was staring at them as he waved goodbye.

"A friend."

"A boyfriend?"

"Maybe," Charlie answered, opening himself up to the idea. "Maybe."

———

Once they were at the top of the hill, they found Liam, who had gotten them a sled. Once everyone was seated–Charlie positioned at the front with Sarah nestled behind him and Liam wedged in behind Sarah–Liam's arms wrapped around Charlie's waist, locking Sarah securely in place.

"Ready?" Liam asked.

"Ready," Charlie answered, aware of Liam's strong embrace as he tightened his muscular arms around him. He wondered what those arms would feel like without so many layers of clothes between them, then quickly chased away the thought as they went down the hill.

Sarah shrieked with joy as they picked up speed, racing toward the bottom. Within seconds, the thrill ride was over, and she was eager to do it again. And again. They did it four more times until finally Sarah's enthusiasm wore out.

"I'm hungry," she declared, collapsing in the snow and making a snow angel.

Charlie joined her on the ground, arms spread wide, moving them up and down as he made his own snow angel. "I am, too."

"Me three," Liam added as he fell backward into the snow and joined them.

Charlie looked over at the concession stand and saw the line was long and winding.

"How about we go back to your house?" he suggested to Liam. "While you're getting Sarah out of those wet clothes, I can whip something up in the kitchen."

Liam turned on his side, propping his head up on his hand. "I never say no to your cooking."

Charlie gazed into Liam's eyes, wondering what he was thinking. Their gazes locked, and Liam inched himself closer. Just when Charlie thought

Liam was going to lean forward and kiss him, Sarah shouted.

"Look!" she exclaimed, pointing up at the sky as snowflakes began to fall. "It's snowing!"

Liam tore his gaze away from Charlie. He stuck out his tongue and started catching snowflakes. "Mmmm. Christmas snowflakes. They're delicious. Try one, Sarah."

Sarah stared at her uncle skeptically, but then stuck out her tongue, eyes widening. "They *are* delicious! Your turn, Charlie."

Charlie stuck out his tongue, going along with the game, but he wasn't focused on catching snowflakes. Instead, he stared at Liam's tongue, unable to take his eyes off it, imagining all the sensuous things it could do to his naked body. As his imagination soared, he could feel his cock hardening, and he blushed as Liam stared at him, his tongue curling over the top of his lips in a satisfied smile.

"The perfect end to the perfect day," Liam purred.

The snow was coming down much harder and heavier when they got back to Liam's house. While he parked the car in the garage after letting them out, Sarah started making snowballs in the front yard.

"What are you going to do with those?" Charlie asked, although he had a sneaking suspicion.

Sarah gave him a devilish smile. "You'll see."

After leaving the garage, Liam headed for the front door. The second his back was turned, Sarah grabbed a snowball and tossed it at her uncle's back, where it exploded into a burst of white confetti.

Liam whirled around in shock, just as Sarah was reaching for another snowball.

"Sarah Denise Williams, don't you dare," Liam warned.

Sarah lowered her head in shame, releasing the snowball.

Liam nodded. "Good girl."

But seconds later, as Liam was unlocking the front door, his back to them again, another snowball found its mark, causing Liam to whirl around for a second time.

"In the words of Bugs Bunny, of course, you realize this means war!" he declared, scooping up a handful of snow. He made his own snowball and threw it, but instead of hitting Sarah, it exploded across Charlie's chest.

"Oops! Sorry," Liam said. "My aim was off."

"Mine isn't," Charlie said as he reached for some snow, formed it into a ball, and aimed straight at Liam, hitting him squarely in the chest.

Soon, snowballs were flying across the front yard as Liam, Charlie, and Sarah ran around, all trying to hit each other while they ducked behind trees and hedges and the sides of the house. They laughed and shrieked with joy, their cheeks and noses turning red, their coats and hats covered with falling snow. They continued that way for almost an hour before Sarah headed into the house to use the bathroom, leaving Charlie and Liam alone. They were on opposite ends of the yard, each with a supply of snowballs, waiting for the other to make his move.

"Ready to give up?" Liam called out.

"Never!" Charlie replied.

"Don't say I didn't warn you," Liam said before letting out a battle cry as he ran directly toward Charlie and tackled him.

Caught by surprise, Charlie fell back into a mound of snow. Liam fell on top of him, pressing Charlie deeper into the snow, his face once again only inches away from Charlie's. This close, Charlie could see every bit of Liam's face. The thickness of his lashes. The deep green of his eyes. The stubble of his five o'clock shadow. And the lushness of his lips.

Those kissable lips...

———

Liam hadn't thought of his next move.

So caught up in winning their game of snow war, he'd charged at Charlie. Now, he had him pinned beneath him and he didn't know what to do next.

Except, he was staring directly at Charlie's lips. He was mesmerized by them, and before Liam could stop himself, he was lowering his head and kissing Charlie, determined to discover if the magic from the night before and the time before that would repeat itself.

As soon as their lips touched, he had his answer.

It did.

———

Charlie was stunned, and before he could lose himself in the pleasure of Liam's kiss, before he could kiss him back and prolong the experience, Sarah's voice filled the air.

"When are you guys coming inside?" she called out. "I'm tired of playing in the snow. I'm hungry. I want to eat."

Hearing Sarah, Liam pulled away, staring at Charlie as if seeing him for the first time. He looked shocked. Like he had been caught doing something he shouldn't.

Charlie wanted to reach out, to pull Liam back down, to crush his lips against his and kiss him for as long as he could. Long kisses. Slow kisses. Sloppy kisses. Deep tongue kisses. Again and again and again. He wanted more than one of Liam's kisses. He wanted multiple kisses.

Did Liam think Charlie didn't want to be kissed by him? Or that he didn't want to kiss Liam? If he did, he was wrong. So wrong. But before he could get a word out, before he could tell Liam he wanted another kiss, then another and another, Liam ran in the direction of the front porch, calling out to Sarah, "Be right there."

CHAPTER
TWENTY-TWO

The snowfall turned into a snowstorm. As the day went on, the falling snow became heavier and heavier.

Charlie was in the kitchen, making a pot of chili while cornbread baked in the oven. The mixture of spices and simmering meat filled the air with a delicious scent.

Sarah, who had been helping Charlie with various tasks, peeked out the back window. "Look at the way it's snowing. I wonder when it will stop?"

"Probably not until the middle of the night. I bet we get at least a foot of snow. Maybe more. Once the snow stops and everyone starts shoveling out their driveways and sidewalks, you'll be walking down snow corridors tomorrow. The piles of snow will be taller than you."

Sarah's eyes widened at Charlie. "Wow."

"Why don't you go wash up? Dinner is almost ready."

As Sarah left the kitchen, Liam came in. He'd been hiding out in the living room, rewatching episodes of *Schitt's Creek* as a way of avoiding Charlie, who hadn't said anything about their most recent kiss. Liam had decided if Charlie wasn't going to say anything, then he wasn't going to say anything, either.

"That smells good," Liam said, walking behind Charlie. He leaned over his shoulder, sniffing the pot of chili as Charlie stirred it. "How about a little music? It's so quiet in here."

"I like hearing the sound of the wind outside," Charlie said.

"You do?"

"It's calm and peaceful."

"I suppose." Liam glanced around the kitchen. "What can I do to help?"

"How about setting the table?"

As Liam gathered placemats, dishes, glasses, and cutlery, he kept looking over at Charlie. Why couldn't he find the courage to talk about their kiss?

Something was going on between them, and they should discuss it. What was he so afraid of?

Before he could give it any more thought, Sarah bounded back into the kitchen, holding out her freshly washed hands. "All clean!" she declared.

"Perfect timing," Charlie said as he took the pan of cornbread out of the oven. "Everyone, take a seat."

Dinner was a success, with Sarah having two bowls of chili and two slices of cornbread slathered with butter. For dessert, they had ice cream sandwiches made with the leftover sugar cookies from the other night.

"Can we watch a Christmas movie?" Sarah asked while cleaning off the table and bringing dishes to the counter.

"What were you thinking?" Charlie asked from his seat at the table.

"*How the Grinch Stole Christmas*," Sarah instantly answered. "The version with people, not the cartoon."

"I think Uncle Liam can identify with the Grinch, don't you agree?" Charlie asked.

"Uncle Liam is nothing like the Grinch!" Sarah said in her uncle's defense.

"Maybe not now, but once there was a time," Charlie teased with a twinkle in his eye.

"Guilty as charged," Liam admitted. He scooped Sarah up in his arms, flipping her upside down, much to her delight as she shrieked and giggled. "Let's leave the dishes and watch a movie. Go change into your PJs while I get the movie ready to stream."

They all settled on the couch, Sarah sitting between them. Halfway through the movie, she fell asleep, leaning her head against Charlie's arm.

"Someone's had a long day," Charlie whispered, not wanting to wake her.

"But a fun one."

Liam shut off the TV and picked Sarah up, cradling her gently as he carried her to her bedroom with Charlie following. Once they tucked her into bed, they retreated back downstairs.

"I better get on my way," Charlie said. "It's getting late. Plus, I have to relieve J.P. of Mistletoe duty."

"You can't leave. It's a blizzard out there."

Charlie waved a hand dismissively. "It's only a couple of blocks."

"There's no visibility, and none of the streetlights are on. What if you get lost?"

"It's not that long of a walk. I'll be fine," Charlie insisted as he opened the front door a crack.

Instantly, there was the sound of howling wind and whirls of thick snow making their way inside. He quickly shut the door on the chilling temperature. "On second thought, maybe I should wait a little bit and see if the weather lets up."

"We have a guest room," Liam offered. "You can stay the night."

"Are you sure?"

"Do you really want to venture out in that?"

"Not really," Charlie admitted.

"Then, you're staying. Plus, think how excited Sarah will be when she wakes up tomorrow morning and finds you still here."

"I guess I can't say no to that."

"Follow me," Liam said, leading Charlie to the guest room on the third floor. "I'll find you a T-shirt and a pair of sweatpants. You're about the same size as my brother-in-law. Be right back."

Liam went down to the second floor and rummaged through one of the dressers, grabbing the first T-shirt and pair of sweatpants he saw. When he returned to the guest room, he found Charlie shirtless, wearing just his jeans. The sight stopped him in his tracks, taking his breath away. He hadn't expected him to be in such great shape.

"Thanks," Charlie said, crossing the room and reaching out for the clothes.

As Liam handed them over, he made a decision. Before he could change his mind, he blurted out, "About that kiss."

Charlie raised an eyebrow before pulling the T-shirt over his head, much to Liam's disappointment. He liked seeing Charlie with less clothes on. "Which kiss? There've been a few."

"Three," Liam said as Charlie's mouth dropped open in shock. "You think I wasn't keeping track?"

"Frankly, I hadn't. I didn't think they meant anything to you."

"Did they mean something to you?"

"If you want to know the truth, they did. But you never said anything, so I just assumed..."

"Assumed what?"

"Assumed it was all in my head. The way I was feeling when we kissed."

"How did you feel?"

Charlie shrugged. "It's hard to explain. Just different from the way it's been when I've kissed other guys."

"Me, too," Liam whispered.

And then, before he could stop himself, he pulled Charlie into his arms and kissed him again, with one clear message: They were going to do more than kiss tonight.

It had been too long since Liam had had sex–and for Liam, that was surprising. Ever since the *Gay Househusbands* explosion, he had been living his life like a monk. But those days were now over. Tonight, he was going to have sex. Joyful, uninhibited sex with Charlie. Seeing him half-naked had turned him on like he hadn't been turned on in a long time. He wanted this. He'd been wanting this since their first kiss, but hadn't acted on it. Now, he would.

"I want you, Charlie," Liam whispered, pulling back and gazing into his eyes. "I want you now."

Charlie silently stared at him. And then, he said, "I want you, too."

It was all Liam needed to hear.

———

Were they really going to do this? Charlie wondered.

From the way Liam was devouring his mouth with his lips, from the way his hands were exploring his body, touching him everywhere before reaching for his belt and yanking it off, then pulling down his jeans and underwear, his greedy hand finding Charlie's throbbing cock and locking around it as he inched Charlie's body closer to his, he guessed they were.

And that was all Charlie needed to know.

He pulled off the T-shirt he had just put on, and within seconds his hands were exploring Liam's body, too, tearing at his clothes so there were no barriers between them, hungry for the feel of Liam's skin pressed against his. When he finally felt it, it was like liquid silk. Hot and soft and smooth. All he wanted was to be consumed by the feel of him. To wrap himself around him and surrender to his body.

Charlie arched his head back as Liam bit at his neck, his kisses strong and forceful, almost feral, as if wanting to devour Charlie. Each kiss was more intense than the last, wild and untamed, with a hunger and intensity Charlie had never before experienced. There were no words spoken, but with Liam's every touch, Charlie knew what he was saying: Liam wanted him. He wanted him with a force and passion that made Charlie want to let him do whatever he wanted. To take possession of his body and subject himself to Liam's every carnal wish. Because never before had he felt this way with another man. His entire body was on fire, his senses alive and pulsing, becoming more electrified each and every time Liam touched him. His body belonged to Liam, and he could do whatever he wanted for as long as he wanted.

Hopefully, it would be all night long.

They fell across the bed, Liam on top of him, pressing him deep into the mattress as he pulled Charlie's arms above his head with one hand while his other explored his crotch, taking hold of his hot cock and balls. He gasped with delight, his cock straining against Liam's hold. Charlie wanted more. He wanted Liam to ravage his body and do whatever he wanted as long as he kept him feeling this way.

"Fuck me," he whispered into Liam's ear. "Fuck me as hard as you can."

"I will," Liam whispered back as his tongue plunged deep into Charlie's mouth, locking with his tongue as it explored his mouth before pulling away. "I will."

Liam gave him another deep kiss and then left the room, but he was back within seconds with condoms and lube. Applying the lube made Charlie even more excited as Liam played with his hole, making it slicker, wetter, and easier to penetrate. Just the touch of Liam's fingers was enough to get Charlie's breathing to accelerate.

"Do you like that?" Liam asked as he slowly pushed his finger into Charlie's hole.

"Yes," Charlie whispered, tightly clenching around Liam's finger.

Liam swirled his finger around and around the opening, his touch making Charlie squirm from the gentle torture.

"Yes," Charlie begged. "Oh, yes."

"Wait until I fill you with my cock," Liam promised as he lifted Charlie's legs in the air, throwing them over his shoulders before pressing his face to Charlie's hole, probing gently with his tongue. At the first touch, Charlie's ass arched upward, and he twisted against the sheets. It was like all his nerve endings had been set on fire.

"Like that?" Liam asked, gazing up at him from between his legs.

Charlie nodded, his mind in a daze.

"Then, get ready for more," Liam said as he applied his tongue again, this time pressing more firmly.

Charlie moaned, feeling like he was drugged and floating on an exquisite cloud of pleasure.

"You're going to love what I have for you next," Liam promised as he slipped a condom over his cock, covered it with lube, and then entered Charlie. First slowly, and then, as he began to ease in further, with more force and speed. Soon, Liam's entire cock had filled Charlie's ass and he was pumping away with abandon. It was all Charlie could do not to scream.

"Let me know what else you want," Liam rasped as he rode Charlie.

"This," Charlie gasped. "I want this. All of this. Don't stop. Please don't stop."

Much to Charlie's delight, he didn't.

Once Liam was done, he collapsed next to Charlie, pulling him to his side as he wrapped an arm around his shoulders and covered them both with a sheet. "That was incredible."

Charlie gazed up at Liam, kissing him on the lips. Liam kissed him back. Once. Twice. Three times. Sweet kisses. Gentle kisses. Although if he wasn't careful, feeling his cock start to stir, those kisses could heat up and become something more. He resisted the urge to kiss Charlie again.

"You're very good at what you do," Charlie said.

"I've had a lot of practice."

Charlie smirked. "Have you?"

"You know I have."

"So what?" Charlie propped himself up on an elbow, brushing a lock of Liam's hair off his forehead.

"What just happened was between us and only us. It was special."

Liam wanted to believe that. He didn't want Charlie to think he was nothing more than a fuck buddy. But he didn't say anything because he didn't know what to say, and he didn't want to ruin the magic of the moment.

So many thoughts were whirling around Liam's mind. He felt something for Charlie. He really did. But he wasn't sure what it was because he hadn't felt anything for someone in such a long time. These feelings were new. Different. He was pretty sure there was more than just sex between them. But it was going to take time to sort through his feelings, and his life was already a complicated mess. Charlie was a curveball he hadn't been expecting.

"Let's get some sleep," he said, giving Charlie one last kiss. "Goodnight."

The following morning, Charlie woke up nestled against Liam. Somehow, in the middle of the night, he had found himself drawn to the warmth of his body. Charlie gazed at his sleeping form, still unable to believe they'd had sex the night before. He shouldn't have been surprised. Something had been building between them for weeks, and last night had simply been the end result. The question now was when it would happen again, or if last night had only been a one-night stand.

If Charlie had his way, it would happen again.

He'd waited too long to find a guy as special as Liam. He wasn't going to let him slip away. Even though they hadn't said those three magic words, Charlie could see himself saying *I love you* one day. Why wouldn't he? Liam was funny and sexy, caring and thoughtful. He was the kind of man he had always dreamed of meeting. All these weeks, he'd been right under his nose, and he'd been totally oblivious. Even though they hadn't discussed the future, Charlie knew they would find a way to work things out. Christmas had come early this year!

Charlie slipped out of bed, pulling on his abandoned sweatpants and T-shirt before finding a bathroom at the end of the hall. After splashing his face with water and gargling with mouthwash, he headed down to the kitchen, deciding to make a big breakfast for all of them.

He was rummaging through the refrigerator for eggs when he heard a surprised voice behind him.

"Charlie, did you sleep over?" Sarah asked.

Charlie whirled around, feeling like the Grinch caught by Cindy Lou Who while robbing her house. His mind raced for a G-rated answer and found one when he caught sight of all the whiteness outside the back window. "It was snowing so hard I couldn't get home last night. I had a sleepover."

"Was it fun?"

"A lot of fun." *More fun than I ever imagined.*

"I love sleepovers," Sarah gushed. "Do you?"

"You bet I do." *Especially with your uncle.*

The yellow landline on the kitchen wall rang, and Sarah ran to answer it, standing on her tiptoes to reach the receiver.

"Hello? Yes, he's here. Hold on."

She ran into the hall, the phone's twisty cord stretching behind her, shouting out, "Uncle Liam, it's for you."

"Who is it?" he shouted back.

"Some guy. He says he's your agent."

"Jerry?"

Charlie couldn't help but hear the note of excitement in Liam's voice. A knot of fear formed in his stomach. If Liam's agent was calling, it could only mean one thing. A job.

And a job meant Liam would be leaving.

This wasn't new information. He'd known all

along it would eventually happen. But after last night, he had been hoping Liam might have a change of plans. There was still so much to talk about. To explore. To discover.

Besides, a call from Liam's agent didn't mean there was a job offer. It could mean something else. Maybe an audition. Charlie took a deep breath, calming himself down as he began to crack eggs in a mixing bowl, adding some milk and scrambling them with a fork. He could hear Liam hurrying down the stairs, taking the phone from Sarah outside the kitchen. He tried not to eavesdrop, not that it mattered. He could only hear bits and pieces of Liam's side of the conversation, which didn't amount to much. Finally, Liam stopped talking and came into the kitchen, hanging up the phone.

"That was your agent?" Charlie blurted out, even though he'd vowed not to.

"Uh huh. I gave him Penelope's house number when I came up here because the cell reception is so spotty. Not that I actually expected him to call."

"But he did." Charlie studied Liam's face, trying to figure out what had been discussed, but he couldn't tell. "Good news?"

"Maybe."

"Maybe?"

"He got me an audition."

Charlie gasped. He put down the mixing bowl and gave Liam a hug. "That's great, isn't it?"

Liam shrugged, not hugging him back. "I guess. First one in almost a year."

"What's wrong?" Something was going on, but Charlie wasn't sure what. He put some slices of bread into the toaster and tossed a dab of butter into the slowly heating frying pan. "Isn't this what you've been waiting for? A chance to get your foot back in the door."

Liam's face turned dark. "That door never should have been slammed in my face."

Okay, it was obviously a sensitive topic. Charlie proceeded with caution. "That's the past. It's behind you. This sounds like a chance to restart your career. Don't you want that?"

"Of course I do."

"Then, what's the problem?"

"I would need to go down to the city."

"You can do the trip in a day. And if you need someone to keep an eye on Sarah, I would be happy to."

"Thanks, but I don't know if I'm going to go."

Charlie stared at Liam in disbelief. "Why not? I thought you missed acting. It's your life, isn't it?"

"It is, but…"

"But what?"

Liam began pacing the kitchen. "I'm trying not to get my hopes up. Jerry didn't tell me much when we talked. All he would say was the audition was for a musical, and if I wanted to try out for it, I needed to be in the city the day after tomorrow."

"What have you got to lose? It's a chance, right?"

"What if they don't want me?"

Charlie could hear the fear and uncertainty in Liam's voice. He turned off the gas under the frying pan and walked over to Liam, wrapping his arms around his neck and putting a hand under his chin to look him straight in the eye. "Don't do this to yourself. Don't doubt yourself. You've been acting for a long time. Just go down there and do your best. After that, it's out of your hands. Either they're going to hire you or they're not. But you can't not go. If you don't, who knows when another chance will come along?" Charlie leaned forward and gave Liam a gentle kiss. "You can do this. I know you can."

"Is breakfast ready yet?" Sarah asked, coming back into the kitchen with her iPad.

"Almost," Charlie promised as toast popped out of the toaster. He put the slices on a plate and brought them over to the table, along with a jar of strawberry jam and tub of butter.

"I'm going to go out and shovel the front walk," Liam said. "Then, I have to help J.P. with play rehearsal this afternoon."

"Don't forget I have a playdate with Annie," Sarah told her uncle.

"I haven't forgotten."

"I can take Sarah over to Bibi's," Charlie offered.

"Would you? That would help a lot."

"Anything for you, Liam. Don't you know that?"

Liam gave him a smile. Seeing that Sarah was immersed in a video game, he whispered, "I had a lot of fun last night."

Charlie nodded. "I did, too."

And then, he waited for Liam to say more. But he didn't.

CHAPTER
TWENTY-THREE

Charlie was cleaning up the kitchen when the doorbell rang.

Liam had already left for play rehearsal, and Sarah was upstairs in her bedroom. He expected to hear her running down the front stairs to answer the door, but she must not have heard the bell. Or she was still immersed in her iPad, playing a video game.

When the doorbell rang a second time, Charlie wiped his wet hands on a dishtowel and headed to the front door. Opening it, he found a stranger standing on the porch.

A tall, dark, and handsome stranger.

"Yes? Can I help you?"

Before the man could answer, Charlie heard a happy shriek from behind him. "Pablo!"

A smile spread across the stranger's face, and he bent to his knees, holding his arms wide open. "*Mi pequeña bailarina!* My little dancer."

It took a second for the name to sink in, and then Charlie remembered.

Pablo was Liam's ex-boyfriend.

Charlie gave him another look, this one more assessing, measuring himself up against him.

While Charlie had a wholesome boy-next-door look, Pablo was exactly what he would envision when he thought of a Latin lover. Sexy. Smoldering. Rich caramel skin, piercing dark eyes, and lush ebony curls. Even under his heavy winter coat, Charlie could see he had a dancer's toned physique.

This was the man Liam had been in a relationship with. What was he doing in Bramford Hills?

"You've gotten so big since the last time I saw you," Pablo said, giving Sarah a hug.

"Would you like to come in?" Charlie asked, finally remembering his manners. It was still cold outside, and frigid air was blowing into the house.

Sarah took Pablo by the hand, leading him into the living room, where he took off his coat and joined her on the couch.

"Can I get you something to drink?" Charlie asked. "Coffee? Tea?"

"No, thank you."

What are you doing here? Charlie wanted to ask.

But he didn't have to ask the question. The answer was obvious. Pablo was here because of Liam. What other reason could there be? Hadn't Charlie realized earlier in the week that the reason why Liam didn't want to move on was because he might still have feelings for Pablo? He wouldn't be surprised if Pablo still had feelings for Liam. He probably realized his mistake in choosing his career over Liam and was coming to ask him for a second chance.

"Did Santa send you?" Sarah asked.

"Santa?" Pablo looked confused.

Sarah nodded. "Are you going to be Uncle Liam's boyfriend again?"

The words were like a knife to Charlie's heart. If anyone wanted to be Liam's boyfriend this Christmas, it was him.

"Sarah wrote a letter to Santa asking him to bring Liam a new boyfriend for Christmas," Charlie explained.

"Aren't you thoughtful," Pablo said to the little girl.

"Charlie's helping Santa," Sarah said.

"Is he?" Pablo gave Charlie a sly smile. "I'll just bet he is."

What is that supposed to mean? Charlie wondered. "Liam's heart was broken earlier in the year," Charlie stated, giving Pablo a pointed look.

"Speaking of Liam, is he around?" Pablo asked.

"He's out for the day."

"Any idea when he might be back?"

Charlie shook his head. "Is there anything I can help you with? Sarah has a playdate, and we need to be heading out in a bit."

"Thanks, but I need to talk with Liam."

"About what? If you don't mind my asking."

"It's personal."

Personal. That didn't sound good. Charlie couldn't help himself. He blurted out, "Why do you want to see him after all this time?"

"That's really none of your business."

"Oh, it is," Charlie said in a tone of steel. "Liam's my friend. You hurt him once. You and those horrible producers. I'm not going to let you hurt him again."

"Take it down a notch," Pablo said, slipping his coat back on. "You're staring at me like I'm a threat."

"Aren't you? You broke Liam's heart. He doesn't need to be reminded of the past."

"Why do I think you're more than happy to help him forget his past with me? Look, I don't know what you have going on here with him. Frankly, I don't care. I just wanted to give him a heads-up about something. That's all."

Was that all, or was Pablo lying? After all, he showed up at Liam's house and found another man opening the front door. If he had a plan to get Liam back, he certainly wouldn't share it with Charlie.

"Tell him I stopped by. It's important, otherwise I wouldn't have come all this way. I'm in Henderson for the rest of the month doing a holiday show if he wants to look me up."

"*A Christmas Carol?* The show with Sam Mathis?" Charlie asked, his voice filled with surprise.

"You know him?"

"I used to."

"He's a great guy. I'll tell him you said hi. What's your last name?"

Of course Pablo would think Sam was great. They were both vain and self-centered, thinking only of themselves and not about the damage they caused to others.

"Sam and I don't need to reconnect." And then, before Charlie could change his mind, he said, "If you really need to talk with Liam, he's rehearsing a

Christmas show at The Sycamore Theatre. It's on West Holland and Ninth Street."

He didn't know why he gave the information to Pablo. Maybe he just wanted to get this all over with. End the torture.

"Bye, Pablo!" Sarah said, following after him to the front door.

Pablo gave her another hug. "Bye, Sarah." He barely gave Charlie a glance as he walked out of the house. "Bye."

"Bye," Charlie said, closing the door behind him. "And don't come back."

Sarah glanced at the closed door and then back at Charlie. "Don't you like Pablo?"

Charlie shook his head. "No, I don't think I do."

Sarah looked confused. "How come?"

Charlie chose words that Sarah would understand. "Because his name is on the naughty list."

———

No sooner had Charlie shut the door on Pablo and headed back into the kitchen, the doorbell rang again.

"I'll get it," Charlie called up to Sarah. "Start

getting ready. We'll be leaving for Bibi's in five minutes."

When he opened the front door, he expected to find Pablo again. Instead, it was Claude, who, at the sight of Charlie, arched an eyebrow.

"Well, well, well. It doesn't take a genius to figure out what you were doing last night when the weather outside was frightful." Claude's lips curled into a smirk. "Was it delightful? I didn't know you were into threesomes."

"Threesomes?"

"I got a peek at that hot Latino guy who just left."

Charlie rolled his eyes. "That was Liam's ex. He was looking for him."

"Looking for a good time?" Claude purred.

Charlie ignored the comment. "Can I help you with something, Claude?"

"Is Liam around?"

It appeared Liam was Mr. Popularity today. "He isn't."

Claude lifted his arm and waved the day's newspaper in Charlie's face. It was open to a full-page ad for *A Charlie Brown Christmas*. At the bottom were the words: Directed by J.P. Hollis and Liam West. Based on the outrage written across Claude's reddening face, the cat was out of the bag with regard to the town's second Christmas show.

"Do you know anything about this?"

"It's an ad for a Christmas show. So?"

"I've been mounting the town's Christmas show for years." He waved the open newspaper in Charlie's face again. "They're going to ruin my show."

"How?" Charlie laughed. *You're ruining it on your own without any help from anyone else. Just like you do every year.* "This town is big enough to have more than one Christmas show. Why are you getting so upset?"

Claude didn't answer. Instead, he glared at Charlie and then stormed off the porch, crumpling the newspaper in his fists as he left.

"Sarah, let's get moving," Charlie called out, wanting to get out of the house before someone else rang the doorbell and ruined his day for a third time.

CHAPTER
TWENTY-FOUR

Much to Liam's surprise, the show came together surprisingly easily. J.P. had put out the word among Bramford Hills' local theatre community that there was going to be another Christmas show. The actors who auditioned for it hadn't made the cut for Claude's show, even though they were good. But that didn't matter. It seemed, according to the grapevine, that Claude had his favorites and he chose the same actors year after year, instead of mixing things up and giving other actors a chance.

After casting the parts, they found people to do behind-the-scenes work: sets, lights, and costumes. Everyone donated their time, as well as supplies, so the costs were minimal. The rental space was a building that had a theatre and restaurant attached.

It seemed years earlier it had been popular among the dinner theatre crowd until the pandemic put an end to it. After life returned to normal, the theatre never bounced back and the building had remained empty since. They were able to rent the space for a bargain basement price, and after taking out the tables, they lined up all the chairs, creating twenty rows with ten chairs in each. Rehearsals were going smoothly, thanks to J.P. doing most of the heavy lifting and Liam helping out whenever his schedule allowed. Like today.

Everyone involved wanted the show to be a success. The other thing they all agreed on was keeping the show on the down low until the last possible minute. None of them wanted grief from Claude because they knew once he found out about *A Charlie Brown Christmas*, he was going to be upset.

So far, so good.

But their luck had run out, which they'd known was going to happen since it was the day the advertising had started for the show.

They were breaking for lunch when Claude stormed into the theatre, waving a wrinkled newspaper in the air as he hurried toward the stage. Immediately, everyone disappeared except for J.P.

and Liam. Gregory, who was playing the part of Linus, kept himself hidden backstage.

"Mind explaining this?" Claude asked, pointing to the ad.

Liam shrugged. "What's to explain?"

"Why are you putting on a Christmas show?"

J.P. joined Liam's side, staring down at Claude. "Why not?"

"I always put on the town's Christmas show."

"This year, the town is going to have two shows. And look," J.P. said, pointing to the bottom of the ad, "we made sure our show would be performing on the nights when you're dark. Everyone in town can see two Christmas shows this year."

"People can't afford two Christmas shows," Claude argued.

J.P. rolled his eyes. "Our tickets are hardly expensive. Unlike yours." J.P. gave Claude a sly smile. "Afraid our show is going to outsell yours? Maybe even get better reviews?"

Claude snorted. "That'll be the day."

"Then, you have nothing to complain about," J.P. said. "Now, please leave. We have work to do."

Liam watched as Claude left in a huff. "Something tells me you enjoyed tangling with him."

J.P. shook his head. "That guy bothers me.

Always has and always will. Whenever he's around, I regress back to high school. I'm going to grab a sandwich. Want anything?"

"A sandwich sounds good. Whatever they have. Thanks."

No sooner had J.P. left the theatre with Gregory, Liam had another visitor while he was working on some blocking.

"Liam!"

At the sound of the voice, Liam froze. Then, he slowly turned around, not sure if he'd actually heard it or if he was imagining it. He wasn't.

It was Pablo.

Liam stared at him in shock. "What are you doing here? How did you even know where to find me?"

"Your housekeeper told me," Pablo said as he walked down to the side of the stage and then up onto it.

"Housekeeper?"

"The jealous guy at your house. If looks could kill, I'd be laid out on a slab."

He must be talking about Charlie. And then, Liam realized what Pablo had just said. Charlie was jealous. The thought gave Liam a warm feeling inside. If Charlie was jealous of Pablo, it meant

Charlie felt something for him. It had to. But he couldn't think about that. He had to focus on the man in front of him. Why was Pablo here? And what did he want?

"You're kind of far from New York City. Shouldn't you be filming your show?" Liam didn't even want to say *Gay Househusbands*.

"You're impossible to get in touch with. I've been calling and texting and emailing you. No response. I finally had to call your agent, who told me where you were. I need to talk with you."

Liam's voice turned icy. "You couldn't get in touch because I blocked you. Can you blame me? And I don't think we have anything left to talk about. You said everything you had to say when you sent me that text."

Pablo stared down at his snow boots before lifting his eyes to Liam. "That was a shitty thing to do," he admitted.

"Breaking up with me, or breaking up with me via text?" Even though he hadn't had a relationship in a long time, Liam had hoped things with Pablo would develop into something more long-term. Maybe it had been being around the other married couples on *Gay Househusbands* that made him want a committed relationship. But he'd been wrong about

Pablo. He had only been using Liam because of the show.

"Both?"

"What do you want, Pablo? I'm busy."

"I need to talk to you about *Gay Househusbands*."

Liam shook his head. "Not interested. I don't want to hear it. I'm done with that show."

Pablo put a hand on Liam's arm, holding it steady. "You're going to want to hear this."

———

When everyone came back from lunch, Liam was still reeling from what Pablo had told him. Not sure what his next step was going to be, he decided to focus on the play. Gregory, who didn't have to be on stage for the next scene, took the seat next to him, dropping a paper bag onto his lap.

"Lunch time!"

"Thanks." Liam unwrapped a BLT and took a huge bite.

"How can you eat that and still look the way you do?" Gregory moaned. "All I had for lunch was yogurt and a Perrier."

"Three letters. G-Y-M," Liam said.

"How long would I have to go to the gym before I look like you?"

"Do you work out at all?" Liam asked while munching on his sandwich, licking a dab of mayonnaise off his finger.

"And get all sweaty? Ugh. No, thank you."

"There's your answer. No pain, no gain."

"Can't I just buy a new body? Like on that TV show, *Botched*."

"Did you just hear yourself? And that show fixes plastic surgery mistakes."

"Obviously, I wouldn't overdo it. Just a little fine-tuning."

"You look fine the way you are. I'm sure Christopher has no complaints."

"Of course he doesn't!"

"Okay, change of topic," Liam announced. "No more body talk. Tell me, what's it like living here all year round? You came from NYC. Huge culture shock?"

"I thought this place was going to be like Stepford. You know, everyone with perfect lawns, perfect houses, and perfect families. I couldn't have been more wrong. Would I like the place to have more gays? Yes. But they're slowly migrating from the city with their gaybies, and in a couple of years, this will be the hot town to live in. We just need to add a few antique shops, more restaurants, and a celebrity or two. Then, all the *New York Times* has to do is send a reporter to write a piece on the town and poof!" Gregory snapped his fingers. "Our real estate value will go through the roof. But for now, it's a quiet little hamlet off the beaten track. Why are you asking about living here? Thinking of relocating?"

Liam shook his head. "Why would I relocate? My sister will be moving to California in a month. There's no one here for me."

Gregory gasped, looking affronted. "How about your chosen family? Me, Christopher, J.P., Bibi. And let's not forget Charlie."

Liam realized he'd blundered. Big time. "I didn't mean for that to sound like it did. You've all come to mean a lot to me in such a short time. But my life isn't here in Bramford Hills."

"Says who?"

"I'm an actor. There aren't any acting jobs here."

"Didn't you use to tour with shows? You were barely in your NYC apartment, right? So, you make Bramford Hills your home base for when you're not out on the road."

"It's not that easy."

"Then, let's talk it out. I can tell something's on your mind."

"Just personal stuff."

"Charlie related?" Gregory hopefully asked. "Don't think I haven't noticed the sparks between you two."

Liam thought of the night before. Of the sex he and Charlie had experienced together. The wild, sweet, wonderful sex that he hadn't had enough of. It had been more than sparks between them. More like blazing fireworks.

"Actually, no."

Gregory looked disappointed. "Oh. Well, maybe, if you relocated here, something could develop between the two of you."

"I suppose."

Gregory snapped his fingers in front of Liam's face. "Hey, listen up! Charlie's a catch. Yes, he's been going through a dry spell, but he's not going to be on the market forever. Someone is going to snatch him up. Make your move before it's too late."

Instantly, Liam thought of Nick at the skating rink.

"Sometimes, the timing isn't right between two people," he told Gregory.

"Then, make it right," Gregory urged before

snatching the last bit of Liam's BLT and popping it into his mouth. "I need to go find my blanket for dress rehearsal."

After Gregory left, Liam thought about his words. He didn't want to lose Charlie, but he couldn't think about having more with him right now. There was too much going on, especially after what Pablo had just told him. After he sorted through all that, then he could figure out his next step with Charlie.

He just hoped it wouldn't be too late.

CHAPTER
TWENTY-FIVE

After rehearsal, Liam came home to an empty house. Sarah was at a slumber party at her friend Janie's and wouldn't be back until the following afternoon, and Charlie was gone. He'd left him a plate in the microwave with a note stating how long he needed to heat it up. The loneliness was a preview of what was to come once Penelope and Steve returned from California and Liam returned to living alone in New York City.

After microwaving his dinner, Liam took his plate into the living room, turned on the Christmas tree lights, and sat in front of the TV, channel surfing, picking at his food, and missing the sounds of a happy house. He had gotten used to coming home to Sarah's smiling face and her non-stop chatter. He had gotten used to relying on Charlie, turning to him when he needed help and advice, as well as his never-ending optimism. Liam hadn't had any of that in his life before coming to Bramford Hills. He'd always been a lone wolf, never relying on anyone but himself. He couldn't remember when that first started happening, but somehow it did. And then, he met Charlie, who kept pushing and prodding, getting Liam to open up. Much to his surprise, he liked it. Thanks to Charlie, he'd met a great group of people who had become his friends, and he couldn't imagine his life without them.

And he could only imagine the ways his life would get better if Charlie continued to be a part of it.

Charlie *had* to be a part of it.

But first, he had to deal with his past in New York City. Once that was taken care of, then he could focus on Charlie.

———

"You look upset," were the first words out of Gregory's mouth when Charlie opened the front door for him. Charlie was doing the catering for Gregory and Christopher's ugly Christmas sweater party, and Gregory had come over to sample the appetizers he was planning to serve. Mistletoe, who had been dropped off earlier by J.P., was super clingy, not letting Charlie out of his sight for a second, having missed him from all the time he'd spent with J.P. Right now, he was dancing between Charlie's and Gregory's legs, not sure which one he wanted to fawn all over him. He settled for Gregory, who scooped him up in his arms, placing kisses on top of his head.

"I do?" Charlie took Gregory's coat and hung it in the closet. "I'm not upset."

Gregory stared directly into Charlie's face. "Bullshit. You're upset. Tell me what's going on."

Charlie debated with himself. He loved Gregory, but he was not a keeper of secrets. If he told Gregory what he wanted to tell him, he would tell the rest of the group within twenty-four hours. That's just how he was.

"If I tell you, you have to promise not to make a big deal out of this, okay?" he called over his shoulder as they went into the kitchen.

"Promise."

"Liam and I had sex last night," Charlie said in a rush of words.

Gregory squealed with excitement, causing Mistletoe to bark.

"I'm not finished," Charlie said. "I think I'm in love with him."

Gregory squealed again, his pitch even higher. "What's the problem? Aren't you supposed to be finding a boyfriend for him for Christmas?" Gregory eyed Charlie from head to toe. "Voila! One Christmas boyfriend. I don't see a problem." He turned to the puppy in his arms. "Do you see a problem?"

"There are so many problems," Charlie groaned.

"Like?"

"We haven't talked about what happened. What it means."

Gregory waved a hand dismissively. "You'll talk later. What else?"

"He's going to be leaving soon. If this is developing into something, is he going to want to have a long-distance relationship?"

"If he's smart, he will. What else have you got?"

"I told you, I think I'm in love with him. I don't know if he's in love with me."

"Ask him," Gregory gently said.

"I couldn't."

"Why not?"

"Because what if he tells me he isn't? Or says that last night was just sex. Great sex, but just sex."

"Charlie, there's something between the two of you. I can see it. We can all see it. Maybe Liam just needs a little more time before he sees it himself."

"You think so?"

"I hope so. Any other problems you've forgotten to tell me?"

"I've saved the best for last. Pablo, his ex, showed up in Bramford Hills earlier today."

"Tall, dark, and Latino?"

Charlie stared at Gregory in shock. "How did you know?"

"He came to the theatre when we were rehearsing."

"He certainly didn't waste any time," Charlie muttered.

"You knew he would be there?"

"I told him where he could find Liam."

"What? Are you crazy?" Gregory exclaimed while Mistletoe yipped in agreement. Charlie took the puppy out of Gregory's arms and put him back down on the floor, giving him a dog biscuit, which he began happily gnawing on.

"What else was I supposed to do? He came looking for him. He would have eventually found him. I figured I might as well rip off the Band-Aid and get the pain over with."

"I need a drink." Gregory began pulling together the makings of a martini. Ice tray and bottle of vodka from the freezer, green olives out of the fridge, martini shaker and vermouth from the cabinet next to the sink. "Why don't you just serve Liam up to him on a silver platter?"

Charlie hated himself for asking the question. "Did you hear what they talked about?"

"We were leaving the theatre when he arrived. Why are you upset? You don't think Liam would take him back, do you?"

"You saw what he looked like."

Gregory began jiggling the martini shaker back and forth. "So what? He did Liam dirty. Liam's not going to forget that. I certainly wouldn't."

"They could get back together."

"Stop being so melodramatic. That's my job," Gregory said as he poured out his martini and took a sip. "You don't know that."

"You don't, either," Charlie shot back.

For once, Gregory didn't have anything to say.

———

The doorbell was ringing.

Liam struggled to wipe away the last vestiges of sleep as he stared at the time on the clock next to his bed. One in the morning. Who was ringing the doorbell at this time of night?

And then, his thoughts instantly went to Sarah. Had something happened to her while she was at Janie's? But if that was the case, wouldn't someone have called? He snatched up his cellphone as he jumped out of bed. His phone was fully charged, and there were no messages or missed calls. He hurried down the stairs, flipping on the hall light as he pulled open the front door.

He found Charlie standing with Mistletoe in his arms.

Liam's rapidly beating heart started to slow down. "Charlie!" he exclaimed with relief. "What are you doing here? It's one in the morning. I was sleeping. You scared me to death. I thought something had happened to Sarah."

"It must be nice to be able to sleep. I've been up all night. With this!" Charlie walked into the house, closed the door behind him, and placed Mistletoe in Liam's arms. Instantly, the pup nestled against Liam's bare chest before lifting his head and licking Liam's chin. "My dog-sitting days are over. I can't take care of Mistletoe anymore. Now, it's your turn to share in the joy." He gave the pup a pat on the head, talking to him soothingly. "It's time for you to live with your real daddy." He looked back at Liam. "He's getting too close to me. We're bonding, and that's not good. He needs to bond with you and Sarah."

"But I can't keep him. He's Sarah's Christmas present. If she comes home tomorrow and he's still here, it will spoil the surprise." Liam went for a low blow. "You wouldn't want to do that, would you?"

Charlie glared at him. "You're the one who wanted the dog, and yet I'm the one who's doing all the work."

"It's only temporary. Until Christmas."

"I've got a life of my own, Liam. But you keep making me a part of yours. I can't do this anymore."

"You're not here because of the dog, are you?" Liam asked as he stroked Mistletoe's ear. The pup closed his eyes in ecstasy.

"I'm not?"

Liam shook his head, sensing he was on to something. "It's not about the dog."

Charlie folded his arms across his chest. "Then, what's it about?"

"It's about you and me. Us."

"We're an us?" Charlie's tone dripped with skepticism.

"Aren't we?"

"I don't know," Charlie stated. "You tell me. We haven't even talked about what happened last night."

"What's there to talk about?"

"That's what I mean! You're so dismissive of it!" Charlie snapped, throwing his arms up in the air in frustration. "What happened last night was great. At least, I think it was. But I don't get the sense that you want it to be more than what it was. A one-night stand."

"I would never consider you a one-night stand, Charlie. Ever. What happened last night was wonderful and special. I haven't had a night like that with a guy in a long, long time," Liam truthfully said, hoping Charlie could hear the honesty in his words.

Charlie stared at him expectantly. "But?"

"But what?"

"I sense there's a but coming, isn't there?"

There were so many words Liam wanted to say, but he couldn't get them out. He meant what he had said. Last night was special. And he wanted it to happen again. He wanted Charlie. He wanted to fuck him. No, that wasn't the right word. They hadn't fucked. They'd made love, and he wanted to be the one to make love to him again and again. To make him come, to make him scream, to make him crave him, to become addicted to his touch, his lips, his kisses, his cock. He wanted Charlie to be his and nobody else's.

With that realization, Liam put Mistletoe down on the floor and pulled Charlie into his arms, kissing him hard with wild abandon and intense determination so that it was clear to Charlie he belonged to him and only him.

———

No! Charlie thought to himself. No, no, no! This could not happen again. He couldn't sleep with Liam a second time. But the thought of getting naked again with him, of having him kiss him, of having his hands explore every inch of his body, of having his cock again, instantly turned Charlie hard and all his resolve disappeared as he became powerless to Liam's carnal attention.

He wanted Liam, and he was going to have him. Now was all that mattered. He would worry about what came next after he'd gotten what he wanted.

And what he wanted was this man.

He hadn't come here tonight because of Mistletoe. Yes, the pup had been barking and whining again in his crate. Eventually, he would have settled down, but Charlie wouldn't have. He'd been awake in bed for hours as his mind kept wandering to Liam. Wondering where he was. What he was doing. And with whom. He kept imagining him with Pablo, getting hot and sweaty and sexy with him.

Finally, he couldn't take it anymore. So, he'd bundled himself up with Mistletoe and driven over to Liam's house on the pretense of not wanting to dog-sit anymore, when what he really wanted was to find out if Liam was home alone or if he was with someone else.

He knew his actions were juvenile and childish, but at least he'd gotten an answer.

And more.

He grabbed Liam's face between his hands and pressed his lips to his, opening his mouth as he sucked at Liam's tongue. Instead of going up to the bedroom, they went into the living room, in front of the fireplace. The heat of the flames added to the slow burn of the body heat igniting between them. Their clothes came off, and within minutes they fell to the carpet in front of the fire, arms and legs twisting around each other.

This time, Charlie took charge as his mouth traveled down Liam's body. He started with his face, kissing his closed eyes, cheeks, and lips, then moved from his chin down his neck before biting at his nipples, getting them hard and aroused as he sucked them before moving to his abs and then lower, to his cock, teasing its tip with his tongue, licking the underside gently, watching as Liam twitched with pleasure. He kept at it, going as slowly as possible, liking that he had Liam in his control, before finally opening his mouth and taking all of Liam inside. He sucked hard and furiously, feeling Liam's cock go deeper and deeper into his throat, wanting to take him as far as he could, wanting to drain him of every last drop until he was dry, leaving him weak and wanting more.

He could sense when Liam was ready to come. He released him from his mouth, wrapping a fist around his cock. "Not yet," Charlie said, holding tight. "Not yet."

He flipped Liam over, and with his tongue, he explored the crack of his ass, then spread his cheeks open and explored more deeply, watching as Liam shuddered with delight. Charlie loosened his grip on Liam's cock and began massaging it gently. With each touch of his hand, the throbbing of Liam's cock increased until, finally, Liam flipped himself over onto Charlie and came all over him. As he did, Liam wiped a hand across Charlie's chest and covered Charlie's cock with his cum, massaging it in.

"Now, it's your turn," Liam said as he began twisting Charlie's hard, wet cock in his grip with one hand and massaging his balls with the other.

Charlie gasped as he surrendered to the sheer pleasure of Liam's touch, knowing there was more to come and eagerly awaiting it. There was nothing else he could do.

———

Afterward, as they lay in front of the fire, nestled in each other's arms, Charlie twisting a lock of Liam's hair around his finger, he asked the question that had been on his mind all day.

"What happened with Pablo?"

Liam sighed. "I'd rather not get into it."

"But I want to."

"Charlie, just let it go. Please. What we discussed doesn't have anything to do with you. It was personal."

Charlie felt like he'd been slapped in the face. Liam couldn't be any clearer. If it was personal, it didn't have anything to do with him.

"I see," he said, disentangling himself from Liam's embrace.

"Don't get upset." Charlie could hear the exasperation in Liam's voice, which only made him angrier. "Whatever existed between Pablo and me is over."

"And yet, you won't tell me why he wanted to see you."

"I can't tell you."

"Can't or won't?"

"I can't. Not just yet. But I will, eventually. I promise."

That wasn't good enough for Charlie. If Liam couldn't tell him now, then there was a problem. A trust problem. And if he couldn't trust someone, then he couldn't love them, either.

"This was a mistake." Charlie began pulling his clothes back on. "I shouldn't have come over."

Liam placed a hand on Charlie's shoulder. "But you did. And I'm glad you did."

Charlie twisted his shoulder out from under Liam's hand and called for Mistletoe, hearing the jangling of his collar as he came running. "I'll take him back home with me." Liam had been right. He'd used Mistletoe as an excuse to come over. Because he'd wanted to have sex again and hadn't been brave enough to come right out and say it. Still, mission accomplished.

But if he'd gotten what he'd wanted, why did he feel so miserable?

"Charlie, don't leave like this."

"I have to go. I've got a lot to do tomorrow. I'm catering Gregory and Christopher's ugly Christmas sweater party."

"You have to trust me. Isn't this the season for trust and hope? Just give me a little bit of time. Please."

"Time, as you keep reminding me, Liam, is the one thing we don't have."

CHAPTER
TWENTY-SIX

Charlie spent most of the next day doing everything he could to not think about Liam. He was busy with the catering for Gregory and Christopher's ugly Christmas sweater party. It was good that he had cooking to distract him. Otherwise, he would have been obsessing over him. Not that he wasn't. He was still slightly distracted and unfocused. He'd had to scrap more than one recipe because he wasn't paying attention to the ingredients he was combining, and the end results had been a disaster.

He kept expecting Liam to call, but he didn't. Why he expected it, he didn't know. But he refused to be the one to make the first move. Yes, it was stubborn. Maybe even childish. But he'd been pretty clear to Liam last night about how he felt. He thought that would mean something to him. That he would think over what Charlie had said, have a change of heart, and call him. Obviously, he was wrong, much to his disappointment.

———

"The sweaters might be ugly," J.P. said, "but these guys are hot." He gazed appreciatively at the waiters Gregory had hired as they bustled around, getting things ready for the party. Like the guests, they were also required to wear ugly Christmas sweaters.

"A little less ogling and a little more help, please," Charlie asked as he arranged the buffet on the dining room table.

He'd made a turkey and a baked ham for those who wanted something a bit more substantial. He'd slice them up right before the party started. In addition, there was an olive and cheese appetizer that he'd created to look like a Christmas wreath. It consisted of tiny mozzarella balls, cherry tomatoes, and green olives on a bed of fresh rosemary. He'd also stuffed spinach and ricotta into puff pastry pinwheels and arranged them to resemble a Christmas tree.

During the course of the evening, the waiters

would circulate with the appetizers. There were stuffed mushrooms, mini beef Wellington bites, thin slices of prosciutto, honeyed goat cheese, and fig preserves mixed together and placed on crackers for a sweet/salty/smoky taste, as well as lobster mac and cheese bites. Last, but not least, there was the cocktail party favorite, pigs in a blanket, which was the one thing Christopher insisted on having, much to Gregory's dismay.

Dessert was simple–Christmas cookies, lemon bars, brownie bites, as well as chocolate-covered strawberries and pretzel rods.

When Charlie arrived earlier with the food, Gregory had followed him into the kitchen, insisting he mingle among the guests during the party. "I don't want you trapped in the kitchen! Yes, you made all the food, but it's just a matter of the waiters walking around the rooms with the appetizers. Put one in charge of the oven, leave him instructions, and then mingle with a cocktail!"

Speaking of cocktails, the bar was set up, along with a handsome bartender wearing a hideous snow globe sweater with white pom poms. Bibi, wearing a clingy red sweater dress with one word, VIXEN, written across the front and a provocative-looking female reindeer on it, already had a drink in hand.

"You know Gregory," she said, sipping from her martini and gazing appreciatively at the waiters. "He likes to surround himself with pretty things."

"True," J.P. agreed as he asked the bartender for a glass of white wine with a flirty smile. "But with that engagement ring on his finger, he can only look, not touch, as opposed to the rest of us who are single." J.P.'s eyes followed a swarthy waiter with bulging muscles wearing a Rudolph sweater. The glowing red nose on the sweater blinked on and off.

"A ring never stopped me before," Bibi purred. "Who's to say it would stop him?"

"Gregory and Christopher don't have an open relationship," Charlie reminded her as he arranged the cutlery and napkins on the buffet table. "They're committed to each other."

"Unlike you and a certain sexy Santa?" Bibi asked, gazing directly at Charlie.

"I don't want to discuss it," Charlie said.

"But aren't you and Liam hooking up?" Bibi innocently asked.

"Hooking up?" Charlie hissed. "Who told you that? We are not hooking up."

Bibi swirled the toothpick in her martini glass before spearing the olive and popping it into her mouth. "You're taking your clothes off and getting naked with him, aren't you?"

Charlie refused to answer.

"Aren't you?" she repeated while munching on her olive.

Charlie gave up. Bibi could be relentless when she wanted the dirt. "Yes, we are," he admitted. "Satisfied?"

"You're hooking up." She shrugged. "That wasn't so hard, was it?"

"Hooking up means it's just sex," Charlie explained.

Bibi gazed at him over the rim of her martini glass in surprise. "And it's not?"

"No, it's not. It's more than that. It's..."

"It's what?" J.P. asked, joining the conversation, all thoughts of sexy bartenders and waiters forgotten as he focused his attention on Charlie.

Charlie didn't know what it was. He wanted to say it was love, but he hadn't heard those words from Liam. And if he hadn't heard them, then who was to say Liam felt the same way that he did? He felt *something* for Liam, but was it love? Even though he'd told Gregory he thought he was in love with him, he didn't know for sure.

"I have to go check on the food," Charlie said,

done with the conversation. He headed back into the kitchen.

———

Contrary to Gregory's instructions, an hour later, Charlie was still in the kitchen. He wanted to make sure the waiter he'd put in charge knew exactly what he was doing. Well, that wasn't exactly the truth. He was also hiding, avoiding Liam, who had arrived at the party just as Charlie was getting ready to join the others. As soon as he'd caught sight of him, he'd done a U-turn and returned to the kitchen, where he'd been ever since.

Even in an ugly sweater, the man was gorgeous. And his sweater *was* ugly! It was green, decorated with red and silver tinsel, with tiny glass balls and an Elf on the Shelf smack dab in the middle of his chest. And yet, whenever Charlie looked at him, he suddenly felt strange. It sounded so cliché, but he got butterflies in his stomach and his heart began to race. It was like Liam had infected him. He'd gotten into his head and his heart, and now that he was there, he wasn't leaving. The only cure was being with him again. Not just in bed, which he had to admit he was thinking about, but all the time, in the ways that mattered most when someone became a part of his daily life.

He was explaining the order he wanted the appetizers to be served when he heard a voice from behind.

"You're not only cute, but you can also cook," Nick said, leaning against the kitchen doorway.

"Nick!" a shocked Charlie exclaimed. He had totally forgotten he'd invited Nick to the party. It was a complication he didn't need tonight, although he looked adorable in his sweater. It said Trek the Halls, featuring Mr. Spock's face surrounded by snowflakes. "I didn't realize you were here yet."

"Don't you know the rule? Always position yourself by the kitchen. That way, you have first dibs on all the food as it comes out. From the smells wafting out of there, I'm not moving."

"I did the catering," Charlie explained. "Now, I'm just overseeing everything before heading back out to the party."

"The food's great." Nick speared a sweet potato croquette from the tray of a passing waiter. "I had a nibble of everything while searching for you. I can't wait to taste the rest."

Charlie loved a man who had an appetite, although from the way Nick was staring at him,

Charlie sensed he had a hunger for more than just food.

Nick wiped his fingers on a blue napkin decorated with snowflakes and stared directly at Charlie. "Look, I'm going to lay all my cards down on the table. I like you. I'd like to go out with you and get to know you. How do you feel about that?"

Charlie's mind scrambled. He knew he had to give Nick an answer, but his mind was blank. He was saved from answering when Liam stepped from behind Nick and into the kitchen. He had an almost possessive expression on his face, flummoxing Charlie.

"I hear you're the one responsible for all the great food," Liam said.

Charlie stared at him in confusion. He was giving him compliments on the food? But he had known he was catering the party. "Thanks."

"We met at the pond the other day, didn't we?" Liam said to Nick, giving him a pointed look. No, not a look. More like a glare, Charlie decided.

Nick nodded. "We did."

Liam continued to stare at him while Nick stared back. What was going on? It was like one of them was waiting for the other to make the next move.

Charlie didn't know what to say or do. It was awkward.

"That's all I came to say," Liam said, breaking eye contact first, tearing his face away from Nick's and turning back to Charlie. "I'll see you out there." And he returned to the party without another word.

Instead of returning his attention to Nick, Charlie's eyes wandered through the doorway, following after Liam. Even though he was trying to be subtle, it didn't take Nick long to realize Charlie's attention wasn't focused on him and that it was focused elsewhere. He followed Charlie's gaze.

"Here I thought you were playing hard to get, but that wasn't it at all. You're interested in him. The Viper. It took me a while to place his face, but then I remembered." Nick's lips curled into a sneer. "Bitten by his fangs yet?"

"Don't call him that," Charlie snapped.

Nick smirked. "Looks like I hit a sore spot."

"You don't know him the way I do."

"Obviously not."

Charlie didn't want Nick to think he'd been stringing him along. Things had happened so quickly between him and Liam. He didn't even know how to explain, it was all still so new. "Liam and I are friends."

"Didn't look that way to me," Nick scoffed.

"What do you mean?"

"The way he was looking at me when I came over to talk to you. Major green-eyed monster vibes."

Liam was jealous? Charlie couldn't believe it. Although, he had been glaring at Nick... "You're wrong."

Nick shrugged. "I know what I saw. Anyway, I wouldn't have given you my number if I thought you were dating someone. I would never go after another guy's boyfriend."

"We're not dating. And he's certainly not my boyfriend." Charlie's tone was adamant.

"You could have fooled me."

"You're wrong."

"I'm just telling you what I see. And that guy is into you. The only question is, are you into him, too?"

If Nick was right, why hadn't Liam said anything? Charlie sighed. How did this all turn into such a mess? Nick was a nice guy, and now Charlie had hurt him. He felt terrible. "Look, I didn't mean to lead you on. When we met, nothing had even happened between Liam and me. But then—"

"Something happened?"

Charlie slowly nodded.

Nick sighed. "I get it. The heart wants what the heart wants. It's no big deal. We talked to each other, what, twice?"

"I'm really sorry about this. I do think you're a great guy. Maybe if the circumstances had been different..."

"I should have realized I didn't have a chance that day at the pond. You chose an eight-year-old over me, and while she's adorable, I'm pretty damn adorable, too."

"You are. Nick, I'm sorry."

"Same story, different guy," Nick said with a sad smile. "There's no need to apologize. I get it. Your heart wants Liam, and that's okay."

Charlie felt even worse. But there was nothing he could do. Liam was the guy he wanted, not Nick. "And your heart wanted me."

Nick laughed. "Well, I wouldn't go that far. My cock was more invested than my heart. You've got a nice little ass. But my heart would have eventually caught up. It's not your fault. Don't feel bad about it. My mistake is that I usually fall for a guy too fast, too soon." Nick grabbed another sweet potato croquette before leaving the kitchen. "Bye, Charlie."

————

That had been immature.

The first thing Liam had done when he'd arrived for the party was search for Charlie. When he finally caught sight of him, he was heading into the kitchen. Knowing he was busy catering the party, he figured he would wait for him to come back out, then talk to him. But he'd seen that guy from the ice skating pond head in his direction, and before Liam knew what he was doing, he was following after him, where he'd overheard their conversation.

Instantly, he had seen red. He knew it! Nick *did* want to date Charlie.

Not knowing what to say or do, he'd stepped into the kitchen and said the first thing that had popped into his head.

Smooth. Real smooth.

Charlie had stared at him in confusion. Liam was sure he'd been expecting him to say something else. Well, if he was going to say something personal, he certainly wasn't going to say it in front of Nick. Or was that what Charlie wanted? A grand, romantic gesture? Knowing the kind of guy Charlie was, he probably did.

Liam quickly left after that, but not before positioning himself across the room where he could keep an eye on things. He was pleased to see Nick leave the kitchen shortly after he did. He was even more pleased to see that he didn't just leave the kitchen, but he headed toward the front door and left the house.

Bye, bye, Nicky. Don't let the door hit you on the way out.

Liam's night had vastly improved.

———

After Nick left, Charlie decided he couldn't hide in the kitchen any longer. Grabbing a tray of stuffed mushrooms, he returned to the party and made a beeline for Liam.

"Want one?" he asked, holding out the tray. It was the only thing he could think of to get himself to cross paths with Liam again. If he didn't make the first move, the evening was going to end without the two of them saying anything else to each other.

"This is a gorgeous home," Liam said as he picked up a mushroom. "It's like something out of *House Beautiful*, don't you think?"

Charlie gazed around at the impeccably decorated rooms. "Yes, but at the same time, it's a little cold and sterile. It has a sort of 'look but don't touch' feel. Which is fine, if you're into that."

"I didn't want to say that, but yeah, it's showroom pristine. I don't think I'd be comfortable living here. I'd be afraid of breaking something. God forbid you bring in a dog or kids. There would be dirt and fur everywhere. When I get home, I want to be able to kick off my shoes, flop myself down on the couch, and cozy up with some throw pillows and an afghan. This place is just too perfect."

"Exactly," Charlie said.

"Not the way you envision your future home?"

Charlie shook his head. "I want a house that's lived in. Lots of rooms, especially guest rooms, to have people over. I love entertaining and spending time with friends."

"What else?"

"Why do you ask?"

"Just curious."

"I'd love a game room," Charlie continued. "Game nights are always fun. Monopoly. Jenga. Scrabble. Oh, and a big backyard with a swimming pool. So we could have pool parties in the summer and barbecues."

"We? You're not living alone in this house?"

"I hope not. I'd like to have a husband. Kids. How about you?" Charlie asked, staring into Liam's eyes and urging him to realize he wanted all those things with him.

"It's like you read my mind. I pretty much see my future home the same as yours, only I need someone special by my side."

Before Charlie could ask if he was that someone special, Gregory called out to him from the kitchen. "Charlie, do we have any more of those cheesy quiche things?"

"Duty calls," Charlie said, heading back in the direction of the kitchen. He arrived just in time to hear Gregory ask J.P., "How are ticket sales looking?"

"Actually, they're through the roof," J.P. said, sounding surprised. "Who knew there was so much nostalgia for *A Charlie Brown Christmas*?"

"You're welcome," Gregory smugly replied.

"What do you mean, you're welcome?" Charlie asked as he began putting some mini quiches on a baking tray and then into the oven.

"People were going to come to the show, but let's say I goosed them a bit."

"How?" J.P. asked, his eyes narrowing with suspicion.

"I might have placed a few anonymous nuggets on the Bramford Hills Neighborhood message board about Claude's visit to the theatre the other day and his little hissy fit. I might have...embellished things a bit."

"Wait, how much?" Charlie asked while J.P. groaned.

Gregory shrugged and waved a hand in the air while sipping from his eggnog martini. "Who doesn't love a little bit of drama? I mentioned that Claude might have threatened to make a scene on opening night. Of course, we know he didn't, but they don't, and it got them to buy tickets in the hopes of seeing a little bit of live drama."

J.P. groaned again.

"What?" Gregory exclaimed in his defense. "The first night is a sell-out, isn't it? Once everyone sees us perform, word of mouth will be great and the rest of the run will sell out, too."

"I wish you hadn't done that," J.P. said.

"Why? You think Claude isn't planning on playing dirty if he can? Grow up, J.P."

Sensing a change of topic was necessary, Charlie asked Gregory why he wasn't wearing an ugly Christmas sweater like the rest of them. J.P.'s sweater featured a Yeti surrounded by Christmas lights, while Charlie's sweater had a row of dancing gingerbread men with their arms linked together, kicking up their legs.

Gregory rolled his eyes. "I'm wearing an unflattering color and channeling Bing Crosby," he said, pointing to his tan pants, V-neck tan sweater, and tan Bally loafers. "Isn't that enough ugly for you?"

"Then, why are you having an ugly Christmas sweater party?" Charlie asked.

"Because my darling Christopher wanted to."

"I'm going to go mingle with your guests," J.P. said. "But do me a favor. No more blind items. I don't want a war with Claude."

Gregory stuck his tongue out as J.P. departed. "Spoilsport."

"You are so bad," Charlie told Gregory.

Gregory gave him an impish smile while taking another sip of his eggnog martini. "I know."

Seconds later, as Charlie was removing the mini quiches from the oven, he could hear an outraged J.P. exclaim, "What are you doing here?"

Charlie and Gregory rushed to the kitchen doorway. Standing across the dining room was Claude, and by his side was J.P.'s least favorite person in the world: Sam.

"Who invited them?" Charlie hissed to Gregory.

"We invited Claude to the party," Gregory reluctantly admitted. "But not Sam."

Charlie stared at him in disbelief. "Why would you invite Claude? You despise him!"

"Don't blame me!" Gregory said in his defense. "It was Christopher's idea. Sort of an olive branch to show everyone that two theatre groups can get along and co-exist in the same town."

"And Sam?"

"It must be Claude's way of sticking it to J.P. He had to have known J.P. would be here. How hard would it be to hunt Sam down in Henderson and invite him as his plus one?"

Charlie reached for Gregory's eggnog martini and downed it for strength. He knew how upset J.P. could get when it came to Sam, and the last thing he wanted was for him to have a meltdown with his ex.

"Sam," he said, a cordial tone in his voice as he walked over and gave him a hug. "It's been a long time."

"Hey, Charlie. You're looking good."

"Thanks. I'm surprised to see you here. Considering..." He didn't have to say the rest.

Claude rolled his eyes. "How many years ago did these two break up? If J.P. is still carrying a torch for him, it's not Sam's fault."

"I'm not carrying a torch for him," J.P. said between gritted teeth.

"Are you sure?" Claude purred. "Otherwise, you wouldn't be so upset."

"He's not upset," Charlie snapped before J.P. could say anything. "He was caught by surprise. As anyone would be by the return of their past."

"Isn't that what Christmas is all about?" Claude smirked. "Ghosts of Christmas past?"

"Actually, I didn't know you would all be here," Sam said, nodding his head at J.P. and Charlie. "I wouldn't have come if I'd known."

J.P. snorted. "Right."

"It's the truth. Why would I want to make you upset?"

"That's never bothered you before." J.P. handed Charlie his martini glass. "I'm out of here."

"Wait," Charlie called out, watching as J.P. stormed out the front door. He turned to Claude. "Just when I think you can't go any lower, you do," Charlie hissed, tempted to throw the remainder of J.P.'s eggnog martini in his face. Instead, he downed it and returned to the kitchen.

———

As the night went on, Charlie lost count of the number of martinis he had. It seemed whenever his glass was empty, a freshly filled glass took its place. He alternated between circulating through the party and popping into the kitchen once every hour to make sure the food was making its way out with assembly line precision. Toward the end, he was in the kitchen by himself, arranging the desserts on trays, when Claude came in.

"Your nibbles are so tasty," he said.

"But not tasty enough for your party, right?" Charlie asked, unable to resist giving him a zinger, still angry over his stunt with Sam, who had left right after J.P. "What do you want? Did you need something?"

"I wanted to apologize. For earlier."

Charlie glanced up from the cookies he was arranging. "Shouldn't you be apologizing to J.P. instead?"

"I will. The next time I see him. But I wanted to apologize to you, too."

"Why?"

"Because I don't like you thinking the worst of me."

That train left the station years ago, Charlie thought to himself. Then, he noticed Claude had the drink of the night in his hand: an eggnog martini. And from the way he was swaying on his feet, glass wobbling in his hand, he'd had a few. More than a few.

Charlie sighed. "You need some coffee." He found the electric percolator in a cabinet over the sink, next to a can of Maxwell House.

"I don't want coffee." Claude closed the distance between them. "I want you."

Charlie stopped spooning coffee into the percolator's filter. He didn't want to acknowledge what he'd just heard, so he pretended he didn't hear it while he reached for a mug.

"Did you hear me?" Claude asked in a louder tone of voice. "I want you."

Charlie sighed, turning around. "Claude, you've had too much to drink. You don't know what you're saying."

Claude shook his head. "I do. I've always been mad about you."

Charlie stared at him skeptically, remembering all the catty comments Claude had said to him over the years. The backhanded compliments. The smirks and sneers. They'd never had a real friendship, and instead of turning his back on Claude, he'd allowed himself to remain frozen in time, with Claude still in the role of high school bully/frenemy. "You have a funny way of showing it."

"I never thought I was good enough for you," Claude said, grabbing Charlie by the shoulders.

Charlie laughed, breaking free of his grip. "You've always thought you were too good for everyone!" He didn't know what kind of game Claude was playing, but he was done with it. "You've had too much to drink. Let's sober you up."

Claude shook his head. "It's not the liquor talking." He stared into his martini glass. "Well, maybe it is. It's giving me courage. I've always had feelings for you, but I've never been able to tell you."

"You're married to Devon," Charlie reminded him.

"We have an open relationship. Lately, we've discussed adding a third, and I thought, maybe..."

Was that what this was all about? Claude and Devon wanted to have a throuple? Charlie knew there were many gay couples who had open relationships, but that wasn't for him. When he committed to someone, his commitment was to that person alone. No one else.

Charlie decided to be more blunt. "Claude, you're drunk. I don't have feelings for you, and you don't have feelings for me. It's the vodka talking."

"I do!" Claude insisted before grabbing Charlie

and pressing him against the kitchen wall, giving him a deep kiss, shoving his tongue down his throat.

Charlie was caught completely by surprise, and Claude had the advantage, using the weight of his body to keep him immobile.

"Claude, no! Stop!" Charlie protested, struggling to break free.

Suddenly, Claude was gone and he could move again. To Charlie's surprise, Liam had Claude by the scruff of his shirt collar and was shaking him in the air.

"What kind of an idiot are you?" Liam raged. "No means no. If someone tells you they're not interested, you back off! Understand?"

"Let go of me!" Claude shrieked, swatting at Liam with his hands as he dangled in the air.

"With pleasure." Liam dropped him to the floor, where he fell with an *oomph*. "I don't like you," Liam added, glaring down at him. "I don't think I've liked you since the moment I first met you. Charlie and his friends, when they told me about you, tried to give you the benefit of the doubt, but they shouldn't have. You're not a nice person. I don't know why they even go out of their way to be polite to you. Get the hell out of here."

"Or what?" Claude sneered, getting to his feet and wiping off the bottom of his pants.

"I'm directing *A Charlie Brown Christmas*, remember?" Liam gave him a dangerous grin. "In the words of Lucy Van Pelt, I'm going to give you five reasons." Liam held up his hand and started counting backward from five, folding down his fingers until he had made a fist. He shook it in Claude's face. "Got it?"

Claude glared at Liam before making his exit from the kitchen, leaving Liam and Charlie alone.

"Are you okay?" Liam asked, going over to Charlie's side, his voice filled with concern. "When I saw that guy slink in here, I figured he was up to no good."

Charlie wasn't exactly drunk. More like pleasantly buzzed. So, he didn't know if it was all the martinis he'd had, being alone with Liam, or the fact that Liam had come to his rescue, but Charlie threw his arms around him and crashed his lips against Liam's before he could stop himself.

"My hero," he exclaimed, breaking the kiss.

Liam just stood there, almost as if he was in shock, as Charlie nestled against his chest as if he was burrowing into him, before lifting his head up and giving him another deep kiss.

This time, much to Charlie's joy, Liam returned his kiss.

———

They kissed, long and slow, until Liam finally came up for air and realized it was time to get Charlie home. In the condition he was in, there was no way he could drive, and Liam wanted to make sure Charlie got home safely. After pouring him a cup of coffee from the percolator on the counter, he went to find Gregory, explaining he would be taking Charlie home.

"Make sure you tuck him into bed," Gregory whispered, giving Liam a knowing wink.

Liam ignored the innuendo, but once the seed was planted, it was hard to forget...as evidenced by the sudden hardness of his cock.

"Time to go home," he told Charlie when he returned to the kitchen, helping him into his overcoat and leading him out the front door. Charlie leaned against him as they walked, brushing his cheek against the side of Liam's leather jacket. "I bet you would look hot in just a pair of black leather jeans," Charlie murmured. "Super tight. Glued to the skin with your rock-hard cock straining against the zipper. And then, I would pull down that zipper and your cock would spring free and I would–"

"Here we are!" Liam cut him off, opening the passenger door of his car and getting Charlie settled inside, locking the seatbelt in place.

Thankfully, the drive went smoothly–Charlie pretty much dozed the whole way, head against the window and eyes closed, so there were no more X-rated stories–but once they were on the front porch of Charlie's house, it was like he got his second wind, and his hands were suddenly all over Liam. Hugging. Tugging. Unbuttoning.

"You need to make sure I make it up to my bed," Charlie told him over his shoulder as he began unlocking the front door.

"I don't think that's such a good idea."

"Why not?"

"You know why."

"Because I might do this?" Charlie turned, wrapping a hand around the end of Liam's scarf and drawing him close. "Or this?" he asked, pulling Liam's head closer to his.

"Charlie..." Liam moaned.

"How about this?" he whispered into Liam's ear as he began nibbling on his earlobe before pressing his lips to his.

Liam surrendered to Charlie's kiss as all his resistance melted away. He wanted this. He wanted to have sex with Charlie again.

Charlie opened the front door and they stumbled inside, still locked in an embrace, still kissing. From the living room, Liam could hear Mistletoe excitedly barking from his crate.

"Someone's happy we're home," Charlie murmured, pulling away from Liam and turning on the lights before going to let Mistletoe out of his crate. Immediately, the pup ran into the front hall, dancing around Liam's legs. Before Liam could give Mistletoe any attention, Charlie grabbed him by the scarf again, leading him upstairs to his bedroom. Once they were inside, Charlie pushed Liam backward onto his bed, tore off his overcoat, and fell on top of him.

———

Charlie began stripping off his clothes and tugging at Liam's, desperate to feel his flesh pressing against his. He might have been slightly buzzed, but he knew exactly what he was doing, and exactly what he wanted. He was going to have sex with Liam again. He was absolutely clear-minded and determined about that.

And besides, if Liam didn't want him as much as he wanted Liam, he would have just tucked Charlie into bed and left. But he stayed.

Charlie kept pressing himself against Liam, holding tight and tearing at his clothes, wanting Liam to know that he wanted to be with him again. Liam listened and surrendered to Charlie, giving in to his own desire.

As he kissed him, Charlie realized there was a desperation to his kiss. He was trying to make it last for as long as possible. This might be the last time he and Liam had sex, and he wanted to create memories. He wanted to have something to remember when Liam was gone and he was alone. He wanted to be able to recall Liam's scent. His touch. His kiss. His cock. Because he didn't know if this would ever happen again, and memories would be all that he had left.

Liam flipped himself over so that Charlie was the one being pressed into the mattress. Taking a suddenly helpless Charlie by both arms, he spread them wide across the mattress, pinning him into place with his body as he began a slow and sensual assault with his mouth and tongue.

His five o'clock shadow was rough as he rubbed

his cheek across Charlie's before moving down his neck, his chest, and further downward. Each touch sent jolts of pleasure rippling through Charlie's body. He struggled to escape Liam's grip, but Liam was too strong and Charlie was powerless to Liam's exquisite sexual torture. Not that he wanted to escape. He didn't. He wanted more.

Liam slowly licked Charlie's nipples, teasing them into hard pebbles as he bit at them, causing Charlie to arch his back, silently begging Liam to continue. He wanted harder bites. Longer bites. Then, Liam's tongue went to Charlie's armpits as he inhaled their scent before one hand made its way to Charlie's crotch, where his throbbing cock waited.

He wanted to come, but he didn't. He wouldn't. He wanted this night to last for as long as possible. He thrust his cock upward, and Liam looked into his eyes before dropping his head and opening his mouth, inhaling Charlie's cock as he began to suck. He kept sucking, and Charlie kept writhing, wanting to put his hands around Liam's head, locking it in place, but he was powerless against Liam's hold on his arms. Then, just when Charlie thought he couldn't hold out any longer, Liam released him from his mouth and started sucking his balls, before moving on with gentle licks and poking at the crevice of his ass with his tongue.

Charlie's body jolted. It was like thousands of sparks had traveled through his body. A satisfied Liam grinned up at him, then probed deeper with his tongue.

Charlie gasped, whispering, "Nightstand. Condoms. Lube."

Liam didn't have to be told twice. He opened the drawer of the nightstand, finding the lube. He caressed the cold liquid in and around Charlie's hole, unable to resist slipping in a finger. At the first touch of penetration, Charlie jerked against the mattress, whimpering.

"Soon," Liam whispered, pressing his mouth against Charlie's, smothering his cries of pleasure. "Very soon."

He slipped on a condom and covered his sheathed cock with lube. Then, spreading Charlie's legs wide, Liam slowly made his way into him, gasping as Charlie's legs locked around him, pulling him closer. Liam began a rocking motion, slipping in and out of Charlie, slowly at first, then with more speed, causing Charlie to gasp again and again until Liam came hard, allowing Charlie to do the same.

When they were both spent, Liam released his hold on Charlie, collapsing on top of him. Instinctively, Charlie's arms wrapped around him in a hug, resting his head on his shoulder before closing his eyes and falling asleep.

———

An hour later, Liam tried not to wake Charlie. He moved through the bedroom quietly, picking up his clothes as he headed downstairs. He needed to get home for a shower and a change of clothes before catching the five o'clock train to New York City. Today was the day he met with his agent. He would also deal with what Pablo had told him.

He was getting ready to slip out of the house when Mistletoe trotted into the hallway. At the sight of Liam, he gave a short bark.

"Shhh," he softly scolded the dog. "Quiet. We don't want to wake up Charlie."

Hearing Charlie's name, Mistletoe cocked his head at Liam. Then, as he headed for the front door, Mistletoe began to whimper. Then bark. Once. Twice. Three times.

"Bad dog!" Liam said. "Bad!"

Mistletoe raced into the living room, coming back with a stuffed lamb that he dropped at Liam's feet. He looked up at Liam expectantly.

"What do you want me to do?" Liam whispered. "Throw it?"

Mistletoe barked in response, tongue hanging out of his mouth.

"Okay, okay," Liam said, picking up the lamb and tossing it back into the living room.

As Mistletoe happily ran after it, Liam made his escape out of the warm, cozy house and into the freezing cold night.

———

Sunlight was streaming into his bedroom when Charlie woke up with a monster hangover. His head throbbed, and he never wanted to see, smell, or taste eggnog again. Vodka, either. He rolled over in bed, draping himself in the warmth of the sheets. He could still smell Liam in them. It was the first time they'd had sex in his bed, and he was going to sleep in these sheets for weeks. Every time he turned over, he would be swaddled by Liam's scent. It was a wild, intoxicating aroma, and it turned him on. Of course, nestling against the real thing would be even better. He reached out to feel Liam, to pull him close, but discovered the space next to him was empty. And then, it sank in.

He was alone.

Charlie lifted his throbbing head off the pillow, gazing around the bedroom. He saw his clothes still on the floor, but Liam's were gone. He dropped his head back down, groaning. Was there anything more depressing after a night of sex than finding yourself alone in bed? He glanced at the nightstands and dresser. Liam hadn't even left him a note. He'd just slunk out of his bed in the middle of the night.

Now, Charlie was angry. He deserved better than this. And yet, he kept going back to Liam for more of the same.

He'd had enough.

Contrary to what he'd just thought about the sheets, he jumped out of bed and immediately began stripping the bed. He would have had to be a masochist to keep sleeping in them. He then headed straight for the laundry room, tossing the sheets into the washer and dumping a cup of laundry detergent on top of them before turning the machine on.

CHAPTER
TWENTY-SEVEN

It was weird being back in New York City. Liam had to admit, he had missed its crazy energy, rush of people, bright lights, noise, and non-stop action. But at the same time, the city lacked the leisurely pace of Bramford Hills. He didn't see friendly faces when he walked down the streets. People were either scowling or frowning or hurrying with their heads bent down, rushing to wherever they needed to be. These weren't people he was used to seeing every day, who went out of their way to say hello and ask about him and Sarah and how they were doing. He was back in a city of strangers and found himself pining for the small town warmth and charm of Bramford Hills.

Well, he wasn't going to be here very long. He'd

taken the five o'clock train down to meet with his agent and then go out for his audition. After that, he would make a Pablo-related pitstop. His mind was still reeling from everything Pablo had told him the other day, which was explosive.

After arriving in the city, he had swung by his apartment to check the mail–nothing but junk and a few magazines–and it had been exactly as he'd been expecting when he'd gone upstairs. Lonely. Empty. Liam hadn't stayed for more than ten minutes, eager to leave, but he was mindful that he'd be returning in a few weeks. When he and Sebastian had been roommates, the apartment had been warm and inviting. Then, Sebastian and Dominick got married, and Sebastian moved out. Liam didn't begrudge them their happiness, but when his friend moved out, the warmth of the apartment had gone with him. Sebastian had always been the one to make their apartment a home, either through his decorative touches or his non-stop cooking and baking in the kitchen. Being Italian, 'food equals love' had always been Sebastian's motto. Now, he had a home of his own with Dominick. They were deliriously happy, and Liam wanted that same happiness for himself. If everything went the way he was hoping, he was one step closer to making that happen after he talked to the lawyer he had come to see.

Liam hadn't come to New York just for an audition.

He'd also come to settle a score with *The Gay Househusbands of New York City.*

————

Liam always loved walking into Sebastian's bakery. As soon as he opened the door, he was embraced by the smell of baked goods. There were so many delicious scents vying for attention–chocolate, vanilla, cinnamon, sugar, caramel, yeast, butter. It was hard to know which one to inhale first. Or what to taste! There was so much yumminess on display. Case after case of cookies, cupcakes, pies, cakes, brownies, and other delectable treats were everywhere.

Sebastian's bakery was exactly the way Sebastian had always envisioned it. Liam remembered the nights when he would show him sketches of the interior and tell him the colors of the walls, the type of floor he wanted, where the display cases would be, how the bags and boxes and logo (a heart-shaped cookie) for his baked goods would be designed. Like Liam, Sebastian had also started out as an actor, but little by little, he had branched out into baking until it eventually became his passion, then his dream, and finally a reality.

Liam's dream had always been to be an actor. And he had made it come true. He hadn't been a brand name, but he'd been on his way. All he'd needed was a little more time, a few more breaks, and a bit of luck to get to the next level.

But now, he wasn't so sure. Now, he wanted something else.

When he looked at Sebastian, he saw that his friend finally had what he had always wanted: someone to love, a home, and his bakery, all in the order of importance. There had never been any doubt in Liam's mind that Sebastian would make it all happen.

If Sebastian could do it, couldn't he?

Sticking his head through the swinging door of the kitchen, he called out, "Need a taste tester?"

Sebastian abandoned the cupcakes he had been frosting, rushing across the room and jumping into Liam's open arms, embracing him in a hug. "What brings you down to the big city? I thought you had babysitting duty until the end of the month."

"I still do, but I had an audition. That's where I just came from."

Sebastian's eyes lit up. "Liam, that's great. How do you think it went?"

Liam shrugged. "Okay, I guess."

"Why aren't you more excited?"

Liam sighed. "It felt sort of cheap."

"This from the man who used to drape himself all over my husband as a way of making me jealous."

"I was doing that to get the two of you together," Liam said in his defense. "Not that I minded. Your husband is a dead-ringer for Matt Bomer. And it worked, didn't it?"

"I'm just teasing. Tell me about this role you auditioned for."

Liam rolled his eyes. "It's another beefcake part. Eye candy. It's for a musical that's supposed to be a cross between *Naked Boys Singing* and *The Full Monty*."

"Why do you sound so down about it?"

"Bash, I'm thirty-two years old. Am I going to be playing the beefcake role forever?"

"You do have the body for it," Sebastian pointed out.

"That's not the point."

"Then, what is?"

"I would think at this stage of my career, I would have advanced to something a little more substantial.

These kinds of roles were fine when I was starting out, but I'm not starting out anymore."

"But you are kind of getting a do-over," Sebastian gently reminded him. "This is your first audition in over a year, right?"

"I shouldn't have to be getting a do-over, and after the meeting I'm having later this afternoon, I won't. I'll be back where I was before this whole mess started. In fact, I might be even better off."

"What are you talking about?"

"There's another reason I came back. It has to do with Pablo."

"Pablo?" Sebastian scowled. "What the hell does he have to do with anything?"

"He's making amends."

"How? Don't keep me in suspense. Fill me in."

At the end of Liam's story, Sebastian stared at him with wide eyes. "Wow. Your name really is going to be cleared. In fact, you're going to be getting so much attention, the offers will be pouring in, and you'll get to cherry-pick what you want to do next. Talk about jumpstarting your career. You're not the villain anymore, and you're going to show that network that this viper has fangs!"

"You got that right," Liam vowed. "Can you believe what they did to me?"

"Actually, I can. The Viva network's always been down and dirty. But there's something else going on." Sebastian stared at Liam intently. "Tell me."

"What do you mean?"

"I can't put my finger on it, but something about you has changed. Something is different."

"I look exactly the same."

Sebastian shook his head. "No, it's something internal. You seem more at peace with yourself."

Liam laughed. "I wish that were the truth. Actually, I'm a ball of knots."

"About your meeting with the lawyer?"

Liam shook his head. "It's not that."

"Then what? Tell me," he urged.

"I've met this guy," Liam admitted.

Sebastian's eyes widened with surprise. "You met someone?"

Liam folded his arms across his chest. "Why do you sound so shocked and surprised?"

"Because you said you met a guy. I can't remember the last time you used those words. Usually, you say you had a trick, a one-night stand, a snack."

"Charlie's not like that."

"Sorry. I stand corrected. Continue."

"I mean, we have had sex," Liam sheepishly

admitted. "But there's more than that between us. At least, on my part. I'm not exactly sure how he feels."

"Have you asked him?"

"No."

"Why not?"

Good question. Maybe it was because Liam was afraid of Charlie's answer. For all he knew, Charlie was having a little bit of fun. A Christmas fling before Liam left Bramford Hills.

As soon as the thought popped into Liam's head, he chased it away. No, that wasn't right. He knew Charlie wasn't a fling type of guy. Charlie didn't use and discard people the way Liam used to do. Liam had never intended to hurt anyone, and he had always been upfront and honest, telling the men he hooked up with that there were no strings attached and he wasn't looking for anything long-term or serious. Some were fine with that, but others thought they could change his mind with time. Those were the ones whose hearts he eventually broke. Because instead of ending things as soon as he realized they were starting to get serious with talk of moving in together or meeting their family, he kept sleeping with them, sending the wrong message, until finally he had no choice but to bail.

That had all changed with Charlie. With Charlie, he wanted it all. His body, his heart, and most importantly, his love.

"I think I might have feelings for Charlie."

"You think, or you know?"

"I know," Liam admitted. "I love him. I do."

"Have you told him how you feel?"

"No."

"Why not?"

"Because he's the perfect guy and I'm so imperfect."

"You're not imperfect."

"Look at the mess I've made of my life."

"But you didn't make a mess of it," Sebastian pointed out. "You were manipulated and tricked and abused by that network, and now they're going to pay."

"I'm damaged goods."

"Hey! You are *not* damaged goods." Sebastian took Liam by the shoulders and shook him firmly. "If Charlie means so much to you, then you have to tell him. You don't want to lose him, do you?"

"I almost did, to another guy."

"Almost?" Sebastian exclaimed. "Start at the beginning and tell me the entire story."

When Liam finished, Sebastian said, "Charlie sounds wonderful. I can't wait to meet him."

"But I don't know what I should do next."

"Yes, you do," Sebastian firmly stated. "You have to go back to Bramford Hills and let him know how you feel."

"I don't know if I can. What if he rejects me?"

"You're an actor. You're used to rejection."

"Yes, but if I don't get a role I've gone out for, there's usually another one waiting. But there's only one Charlie. My Charlie."

And it was true, Liam realized. Charlie was his, and he didn't want anyone else in his life or his heart.

He only wanted Charlie.

CHAPTER
TWENTY-EIGHT

Charlie was supposed to be working. It was getting to the end of the year, and his office was always closed between Christmas and New Year's. He was being slammed with ads that needed to be designed, and instead of focusing on his deadlines, he was playing with Mistletoe. How could he not? The pup was too adorable to resist.

Just like someone else in his life.

Charlie had spent the entire day thinking about Liam, and he'd come to a decision. He was going to break up with him. Although, seriously, how could they break up? They never really had a relationship. Still, he needed closure. He needed to put this behind him and move on. The only problem was that he didn't know how to do it.

Luckily, between his day job and his catering, he had enough work to keep him busy. So, he could avoid Liam for the next week. By that time, Christmas would be here, and Liam would be on his way back to New York City. Which meant he could avoid any sort of uncomfortable conversation. Whatever had existed between them would just end. Wither. Die. Sarah's Christmas wish for her uncle wouldn't come true, but it wouldn't be because Charlie hadn't tried. He'd tried as hard as he could, but when someone's heart was closed to love, it made falling in love impossible.

Unable to focus, Charlie decided to wrap things up for the day and tackle the last of his Christmas shopping. After putting Mistletoe into his crate, he headed to Bailey's. In the elevator, he resisted the urge to press the button for Liam's floor. Instead, he headed to the housewares department. The last time he was here, he'd seen some nice ceramic serving bowls from Italy and was thinking of getting one for Gregory and Christopher.

When the doors opened, he began walking through the jewelry department in the direction of housewares. But then, he stopped in his tracks when he caught sight of who was standing in front of one of the display cases while having an animated conversation with the sales clerk.

It was Liam, looking adorable in his elf costume. He must have been on a break.

Charlie quickly ducked behind a pillar, not wanting to be seen, cautiously peeking his head out. Liam was now studying an arrangement of rings on a black velvet tray, picking one up and studying it, then putting it down and picking up another. All thoughts of Christmas shopping were instantly forgotten as Charlie focused on what he was witnessing.

Liam was buying a ring.

Charlie certainly wasn't going to fool himself into thinking it was for him. Which meant it was intended for only one other person.

Pablo.

They'd been involved, and with Pablo's return and Liam not wanting to talk about him, it was clear they were picking up where they left off.

Charlie hid himself back behind the pillar. It looked like Sarah's Christmas wish would be coming true. Not only was her uncle going to have a boyfriend again, but he might also be getting a husband.

"Charlie? What are you doing?"

At the sound of his name, Charlie whirled around, finding himself facing J.P., loaded down with shopping bags filled with wrapped Christmas gifts. J.P. gave him a knowing smirk as his gaze traveled over to the jewelry section. "Spying on someone?"

"Of course not!" Charlie quickly denied.

"Looks that way to me. You're hiding behind a pillar watching Liam's every move."

"I'm not watching his every move!" Charlie said. "I'm doing Christmas shopping."

"I don't see any bags," J.P. pointed out as he glanced at Charlie's empty hands.

"Because I just got here! And where have you been hiding yourself? I've been calling and texting, and you haven't gotten back to me. After that scene with Sam, I've been worried."

J.P. rolled his eyes. "There's nothing to worry about."

Charlie raised an eyebrow. "Then, why did you storm off?"

"I was caught off guard. I needed to process what I was feeling, and I couldn't do it at the party. So, I left."

"You need to talk with him," Charlie encouraged. "You need to clear the air and put this behind you once and for all."

"The way you're doing with Liam?"

"What's that supposed to mean?"

"Something is going on between the two of you, but it's not smooth sailing, is it? Otherwise, you wouldn't be hiding from him."

"It's complicated."

"Uncomplicate it."

"You should take your own advice," Charlie shot back.

"We're not talking about me, and my situation with Sam is different. We were in love, and I thought we were going to spend the rest of our lives together until he blindsided me and walked out." J.P. looked down at the floor and then up at Charlie. "I've never been able to trust another guy because of that. Maybe I never will."

Charlie's heart broke for his friend, and he wanted to give him a hug. "Oh, J.P." He started to step forward, arms outstretched.

J.P. held up a hand, stopping him in his tracks. "No hugs. Not today. We're focusing on you, not me. The situation with you and Liam is different, don't you see? You could have something special with him. There's a connection between the two of you. I can see it, and I know you feel it."

"Maybe I'm the only one who feels it," Charlie said in a small voice.

"How do you know that? If you don't talk with Liam, if you don't tell him how you feel, if you keep avoiding him, then your love life is going to be in limbo. Just like mine has been since Sam broke up with me. Think about it." With those final words, J.P. left to continue his Christmas shopping.

Hearing the ding of the elevator behind him, Charlie quickly ran from behind the pillar and into it before the doors closed.

"Merry Christmas to me," Charlie whispered, wishing he hadn't decided to come to Bailey's at all.

———

Was that Charlie's voice he had heard?

Liam looked around, but he didn't see Charlie anywhere. It must have been his imagination. He turned his attention back to the tray of rings on the counter in front of him, but was unable to make up his mind. He liked all of them, but none of them was a clear winner.

"Let me think about it," Liam told the clerk. "I'll be back."

As Liam walked away from the counter, he

pulled out his phone and sent Charlie a text, wanting to see him. Wanting to talk with him. Wanting to tell him everything that was going on in his life.

He just wanted him, like he'd never wanted anything else before.

———

Charlie was exiting Bailey's when his phone buzzed. He pulled it out and saw there was a text from Liam.

Instead of answering the text, he ignored it.

———

Over the next week, Liam kept calling Charlie and leaving messages. But instead of Charlie calling him back, he got nothing but silence. It was the same with texting.

He tried not to be obvious about it, but when he was around J.P. and Gregory at the theatre during rehearsals, he would casually ask about Charlie. The answers they both gave him were the same: He was slammed with deadlines from his day job and also juggling a few catering jobs. They hadn't heard from him in days, either, but that wasn't unusual at this time of year.

Liam knew it was more than that. Charlie was avoiding him, and it was going to take more than a phone call to get him to talk to him.

And that was fine, because Liam wasn't ready to give up just yet.

———

Charlie was in the kitchen making cream puffs for a party, Mistletoe by his feet, shaking his lambie by the ear, when the front door bell rang. At the sound of it, the puppy abandoned his toy and went racing out of the kitchen, barking loudly. Charlie followed, scolding him. "We don't bark when the doorbell rings, Mistletoe. No! No barking!"

Without thinking, Charlie opened the front door and found himself facing Liam. It had been a week since the last time he had seen him, and he missed him so much. His first instinct was to throw his arms around him, pull him close, and inhale his scent before pressing his lips to his. But he resisted. He had to. Because if he gave even an inch, his resolve to end things would be gone, and he'd be right back where he started, hopelessly in love with him. Not that he still wasn't, but he was trying to move on.

"You're starting to give me a complex," Liam

began with a teasing smile. "You won't return my calls. You won't answer my texts. I haven't seen you in days. Something's going on."

Charlie shrugged. "Between my day job and catering gigs, I've been busy. That's all. How did your audition go?"

Liam shrugged. "Still waiting to hear back. I think it went well, but you never know until they call and offer you the job." Mistletoe ran out onto the porch and put his paws up on Liam's legs, begging for attention. "Looks like someone's missed me."

He's not the only one, Charlie thought.

"Have I done something to make you upset?" Liam asked after giving Mistletoe a few pats on the head before the pup raced back inside. "I'm getting the sense you're trying to avoid me."

"Why would I want to do that?"

"I don't know. Sarah misses you."

"I miss her, too. But like I already told you, I've been busy," Charlie explained. "Tell her I'll stop by for a visit soon. I've got a Christmas present for her. So, what's up? What brings you by?"

"I wanted to share some news with you. Good news. The Viva network is in major hot water. It turns out, I never slept with Jason."

Charlie's mouth dropped open. "You didn't? But I thought...didn't Jason say you did?"

"It was all a set-up. They drugged my wine," Liam explained. "When I passed out, they put me in bed with him, and then Jason pretended we had slept together."

Charlie was horrified. "Why would he do something like that?"

"He and Mark figured if they came across as victims, they would garner public sympathy. Their businesses were bleeding cash, and they needed to do something to stop it. What better way than to make me the bad guy who almost destroyed their marriage? The public ate it up and started buying their merch again."

"That's low."

"There's more," Liam continued. "The idea didn't come from them."

"Who did it come from?"

"Ollie, who, it turns out, has pulled some nasty stunts on Viva's other reality shows. Now, the lawsuits are piling up. Racial discrimination, sexual harassment, supplying cast members with too much liquor, physical assault. Steroids and drug use. Practically every reality show on the network has some sort of scandal connected with it. And it all leads back to Ollie and his desire for increased ratings."

"How did this all come out?"

"One of the interns at the network leaked a memo to a blog. He found it when he was doing some filing. When word got out, a number of cast members from different shows got together and hired a lawyer. He's filed a huge lawsuit, which I'm part of. Not only am I getting my reputation back, but probably also a hefty settlement."

"And after that?"

Liam smiled. "It means my career is back on track."

That's what Charlie knew he was going to say. "Congratulations. Hopefully, you can make up for lost time."

"My agent is starting to get calls. TV. Theatre. Movies. Talk shows and podcasts."

"That's great. I'm really happy for you."

Liam studied Charlie's face, as if he were searching for something, but Charlie didn't know what. "You don't sound happy."

"How am I supposed to sound?" Charlie's voice was sharp. "This is what you've always wanted, right? To have your career back. Well, now you have it."

"Yes, but–"

Charlie cut him off. "Let me ask you a question. How did you find out about all this? The memo, the lawyer, the lawsuit." Charlie didn't give Liam a chance to answer. "It was Pablo, wasn't it?"

"Yes."

Charlie found himself getting worked up, and he found himself bubbling with anger. Anger was better than love. Anger would keep him focused on what he was planning to do. "Any particular reason why you couldn't tell me that? It was the reason he came to town looking for you."

"There was a timeline for everything. The lawyer wanted to blindside the network by filing the lawsuit the day the *New York Times* was publishing a huge front-page article on the scandal. Everything needed to be hush-hush. He also wanted to get as many people as possible to join the lawsuit, and he asked Pablo if he could track me down."

"I know how to keep a secret," Charlie said. "You could have trusted me. But you didn't."

"Of course I trust you." Liam took a step forward, reaching for him, but Charlie pulled himself out of Liam's reach, shaking his head.

"No, you didn't. You didn't say anything to me because you wanted to make sure everything would go the way it was supposed to, so you could get your career back. Because that's what matters to you most—your career. You've been counting down the days since you got here, eager to leave Bramford Hills."

"That's not true."

"It is. Admit it."

"Maybe in the beginning..."

"We had our fun, our fling, but we always knew it was going to have an end date. Now, that date has come, maybe a little sooner than expected." Charlie sniffed the air. "My pudding for the cream puffs I'm making is burning. I've got to go." Charlie reached out and placed a hand on Liam's chest. He really wanted to put it on his cheek, but that was too dangerous. He would want to caress it and then, within seconds, he would be pulling Liam's face close to his, his lips only inches away. "I really am happy for you. When you become a big star, I can tell everyone I knew you when. Bye, Liam."

Charlie then closed the door on Liam and raced into the kitchen. He grabbed a potholder and threw the pot of burning pudding into the sink while asking himself what had just happened.

But he knew. He had ended things with Liam.

What just happened? Liam asked himself.

He'd come to Charlie's house ready to declare his love and let him know he wanted to have a future with him, and Charlie had broken up with him. He was kind of stunned. He was so caught off guard and surprised, he hadn't known what to say. Instead, Charlie had said everything and shut the door in his face.

He thought about ringing the doorbell again, but what good would it do? It sounded like Charlie's mind was made up.

Liam's hand went into this pocket. To the box with the ring in it. He'd gone back to Bailey's and bought what he thought was the perfect ring for Charlie. Why hadn't he taken it out? Why hadn't he given it to him?

Because in his gut, he knew he had to do more than just give Charlie a ring.

Charlie, Mr. Christmas, Mr. Sentimental, Mr. Always Thinking of Everyone Before Himself, needed a grand, romantic gesture to see that Liam loved him with all his heart.

The only question was how he was going to do it.

CHAPTER
TWENTY-NINE

"We need to talk," Liam said to Bibi when they went for coffee the following morning after dropping the girls off at school.

"About what?"

"Charlie."

"And you're coming to me because?" she asked, pushing her Versace sunglasses to the top of her head while adding some milk to her coffee and stirring in some sugar. "Have I recently become an advice columnist and no one's told me?"

"You're tight with Gregory, and Gregory is tight with Charlie. I need you to go to Gregory and see what you can find out."

"About?"

"Why Charlie broke up with me last night."

"Charlie broke up with you?" Bibi gasped. "I didn't even know the two of you were an item."

"How could you not?" Liam asked while sipping his latte.

"It's not like the two of you were dating."

"Then what were we doing?"

"Duh. Having sex."

"It was more than that."

"Was it?" Bibi asked, a tone of skepticism in her voice.

"Of course it was!"

"Did Charlie know that? Did you ever tell him? Did the two of you ever go out on a date?"

The questions came fast and furious. "Slow down! Give me a chance to answer. One question at a time, please."

"Did the two of you ever go out on a date?" Bibi repeated.

"No, but we spent a lot of time together. He kept trying to fix me up with other guys, but all the dates were disasters. And we were always doing something with Sarah. We weren't officially dating, but we got to know each other–"

Bibi cut him off. "He's not a mind reader. Maybe on some level you thought you were dating him, but maybe he didn't think the two of you were."

"What did he think was going on between us?"

"Exactly what I said before. Sex." Bibi nibbled on her coffee stirrer. "But maybe he wanted more than that."

"Then, why didn't he tell me?"

"Why didn't you tell him?" Bibi countered.

Liam was getting confused. He didn't want to hear any more of Bibi's theories. "Will you please talk to Gregory for me?"

"Aren't you directing him in your Christmas show?" Bibi pointed out. "Can't you talk with him yourself?"

"I've tried, but I keep hitting a brick wall. Same with J.P. I don't know if it's on purpose or they just don't know anything. I'm hoping you'll have better luck."

Bibi sighed, finishing her coffee and sliding her sunglasses back over her eyes. "I'll see what I can do, but I'm not talking to Gregory. I'm going straight to the source."

———

Charlie opened his front door in surprise. "Bibi. What are you doing here?"

Bibi gave him an assessing look as she stepped

inside, unbelting her black leather jacket while Mistletoe danced around her, eager for attention. "You know what I'm doing here."

"No, I don't."

She walked into the living room and settled on the couch, Mistletoe nestling at her feet. She gave him a quick pat on the head before focusing on Charlie. "We've got to figure out a way to get Liam not to leave Bramford Hills. He's too fabulous. He has to stay, and you're the key to his staying."

Charlie laughed bitterly. "Oh, come on! Are you serious? Liam has wanted to leave since the day he arrived. And in case you haven't heard, he finally got his golden ticket."

"Yes, I heard, but wake up!" Bibi snapped. "Something is going on between the two of you. We've all picked up on it. Me, Gregory, Christopher, even Mr. Cynical, J.P., isn't it worth exploring? The only way to find out is if Liam doesn't leave."

"It's too late."

"What do you mean? It's never too late."

"He's moving on with his ex."

"How do you know that?"

"Because Pablo came to find him. To get him to join a lawsuit that's being launched against the Viva network for all their dirty deeds."

"And you're jealous because of that? Pablo might be Liam's ex, but that's all he's ever going to be. Liam would never get back with him. You know what he did after Liam was dropped from that show."

"So? Couples break up and get back together all the time."

"But you don't know if that's happening with them," Bibi stressed. "You're theorizing."

"I also saw Liam buying him a ring at Bailey's."

"Liam's never once mentioned his ex to me," Bibi said, tapping a fingernail painted to look like a candy cane against her lower lip. "And he's said nothing about getting back together with him. Something is not adding up. Did you ever stop to think that maybe he was buying the ring for you?"

"Why would he buy a ring for me?" Charlie scoffed.

Bibi stared at him in disbelief. "Has it not crossed your mind that maybe Liam has feelings for you?"

"If that's the case, he has a funny way of showing it. He hasn't even said that he wants a relationship with me."

"Have you given him a chance? I heard you slammed the door in his face last night."

Charlie's eyes narrowed. "Did Liam send you here?"

"Liam didn't send me," Bibi said, crossing her heart with a finger.

"Then, why did you stop by? Why all the questions about him?"

"Because I'm Liam's friend. I'm looking out for him. Selfishly, I don't want him to leave. I like having him in my life, and you do, too. Admit it, you don't want him to leave town, either."

"It's not about what I want. It's what he wants. And he wants his acting career back. He's always been very clear about that."

"Maybe Liam's realized that there are other things in life that are more important than just a career," Bibi suggested.

"Are you playing messenger? Did he say that to you?"

Bibi squirmed on the couch. "Not exactly."

"What does that mean? Either he did or he didn't."

"He cares about you. I know he does," Bibi stressed.

"If he cares about me, shouldn't he be the one telling me and not you?" Charlie countered. "I'm not getting the point of this conversation, Bibi."

"I'm trying to figure out what's going on. You and Liam were joined at the hip, and now there's this distance between the two of you. You used to spend so much time together, and now you've ghosted him."

"That was my mistake," Charlie explained. "I was making too much time for Liam and Sarah. I was getting too close to them, too attached."

"Was that a bad thing?" Bibi asked.

"It is when only one person feels that way. I needed to take a step back. To protect myself."

"Protect yourself from what?"

"Liam." Charlie decided to just say it. "There was something developing between us, but he never acknowledged it. He never said what was going to happen once he left town."

"Maybe he was planning to. With that ring!" Bibi triumphantly exclaimed.

"He wasn't buying the ring for me," Charlie repeated. "He was buying it for Pablo."

Bibi screamed in frustration, causing a dozing Mistletoe to lift his head up in surprise. "Stop saying that! You don't know if that's true, so stop driving yourself crazy. You're clinging to this fantasy of Liam getting back together with Pablo, and I'm telling you, it's not going to happen. Do you want to believe it so you won't have to give Liam a second chance?"

"I know what I saw," Charlie stubbornly said. "I

know what I feel." And what Charlie felt was hurt. Overlooked. Dismissed.

"You're wrong," Bibi said. "Somehow, Liam's messed up, and you're angry about that. I get it. But don't you at least owe him the chance to explain himself?"

Could Bibi be right? Could Liam have been buying the ring for him?

As if reading his mind, Bibi said, "Friday night is the opening night of J.P. and Liam's show. Let's go together."

"I don't know," Charlie said.

Bibi got off the couch, putting her jacket back on. "At least think about it?"

Charlie nodded as he walked her to the front door, Mistletoe following after them. "Fine. I'll think about it."

CHAPTER
THIRTY

"I still don't know what I'm doing here," Charlie grumbled as he took the seat next to Bibi.

"You're here to support your friends at the premiere of their Christmas show. Isn't that what friends do?"

"Yes, but–"

"But what? Are you saying you're not friends with Liam? I've been friends with many of my exes."

"We weren't dating, so we're not really exes. I don't know what I am to him." Charlie gazed around the crowded room, even though he knew Liam was probably backstage. "What if I run into him tonight?"

"Darling, of course you're going to run into him

tonight. We're invited to the after-party at Gregory and Christopher's house."

Charlie's eyes widened with panic. "I said I'd come to the show with you. I didn't say I'd go to the after party."

"This isn't only Liam's big night," Bibi reminded him. "It's also Gregory and J.P.'s. Think how disappointed they'll be if you don't show up."

"They'll understand if I skip it."

"Look, you have to deal with Liam eventually. You can't keep running away, trying to avoid him. This town is too small. Besides, you have to do the puppy hand-off with him so that Mistletoe is under the tree for Sarah on Christmas morning. Face it, it's inevitable. You're going to have to talk with him one more time. Just get it over with."

Charlie had thought he could do this, but he couldn't. The idea of seeing Liam again was too overwhelming. If he was going to move on, he needed to make a clean break. He couldn't backslide, and that's what he was afraid of happening. If he saw Liam again, he would allow himself to spend time with him during his last few days in Bramford Hills. That would be both in and out of the bedroom. And then, he would be left with nothing but heartache once he was gone.

"This was a bad idea. I should go." Charlie started to get out of his seat when Sarah came running over, with Mrs. Morris trailing behind. "Charlie! Charlie! Charlie!" she squealed in excitement at the sight of him, her entire face lighting up. "I haven't seen you in so long. I missed you." She threw her arms around him, hugging him fiercely.

Charlie wrapped his arms around the little girl, giving her a long, tight hug. "I missed you, too, sweetie."

She looked up at him with adoration. "Are you here to see Uncle Liam's play?"

"You bet he is," Bibi said. "In fact, you can take the seat next to him, if you want."

Sarah instantly slipped into the seat next to Charlie, taking his hand in hers while Mrs. Morris sat on her other side. "Did you know Uncle Liam is much happier since he came back from New York City?" she asked.

"Really? Do you know why?" The words slipped out before Charlie could stop himself.

"He met with his agent."

"I did hear about that. Anyone else?" he casually asked, unable to believe he was pumping a child for information.

"His friend, Sebastian. He owns a bakery."

"No visit with Pablo?" he asked, immediately regretting the question the second after he asked it. How much lower was he going to go? Bibi, hearing the question, jabbed him in the side with her elbow. "Ouch!"

Bibi gave him a sweet smile. "Sorry. These seats are too close together."

"Okay, I deserved that," Charlie whispered, rubbing his side. But he wouldn't be asking these questions if he still didn't have feelings for Liam, as much as he hated to admit it.

"No visit with Pablo," Sarah answered as she leaned closer to Charlie. "Can I tell you a secret?"

"Sure."

"I wrote another letter to Santa," she whispered.

"How come?"

"I wanted to remind him that he needs to bring Uncle Liam a boyfriend by Christmas."

"But I thought he already did," Charlie said. "Pablo."

Sarah laughed. "Pablo's not Uncle Liam's boyfriend."

"He's not?"

"No, silly! They broke up last year."

"But he came to the house."

"Just that one time," Sarah said. "I really wish you would be Uncle Liam's boyfriend, Charlie."

Bibi leaned across Charlie and gave Sarah a wink. "I do, too!"

"Me, too," Mrs. Morris added.

Three sets of eyes turned to him, waiting for his answer.

So do I, he thought, not wanting to say it out loud. If he did, it wouldn't happen, he superstitiously believed. But if he kept it a secret, maybe, just maybe, if there really was a Santa, like he once believed when he was a little boy, he would make Charlie's Christmas wish come true, and Liam would be his boyfriend.

"Uncle Liam's backstage," Sarah said. "He's the director. He said I could watch backstage with him if I wanted. I bet he'd let you watch, too, Charlie."

"That's a great idea," Bibi exclaimed.

"No, it isn't," Charlie said. "I'm fine watching the show from here."

"Why don't you take Charlie backstage?" Bibi suggested.

Sarah jumped to her feet, pulling Charlie by the hand. "Come on!"

Charlie glowered at Bibi, but he followed Sarah just the same.

Liam was helping the actors find their spots while waiting for the curtain to rise when he spotted Sarah.

"There you are!" he exclaimed. "I knew you were here with Mrs. Morris, but I couldn't find you out in the audience."

"Look who I found, Uncle Liam!"

Sarah tugged Charlie by the hand, pulling him out of the shadows.

"You came," Liam said, giving him a tentative smile, hoping Charlie would smile back.

Liam knew Bibi was bringing Charlie to the show, but that's all she had promised. The rest would be up to him, she said, and that this was probably going to be his one shot with Charlie. She'd told him Charlie not only thought he was back together with Pablo, but that he'd also bought him a ring. It had boggled Liam's mind. As if that would ever happen! How could Charlie think he would go back to Pablo, ring in hand, after spending the best weeks of his life with him, here in Bramford Hills?

"Bibi can be persistent," Charlie said. "She wouldn't take no for an answer. Plus, I'm a sucker for *A Charlie Brown Christmas.*"

"We're going to watch it with you, Uncle Liam," Sarah piped up. "Is that okay?"

"That would be wonderful," Liam said, taking Sarah by the hand and leading her to the side of the stage, making sure Charlie followed. He didn't want to let him out of his sight, afraid that if he did, he would disappear before he had a chance to say what he wanted. Seconds later, the curtain rose and the play began as the 'Linus and Lucy' theme started.

Charlie and Sarah were both focused on the actors on stage, but Liam was focused on Charlie. There was so much he wanted to say, but the words wouldn't come. Why was it so hard?

When the first act ended, there was a twenty-minute intermission. Sarah went off to the concession stand to get a snack, leaving Liam and Charlie alone. An uncomfortable silence developed between the two of them until finally Liam asked, "Have you ever heard that expression, 'be careful what you wish for'?"

"Yes. But what does that have to do with anything?"

"I have my career back, but I'm not sure I want it."

"Not sure?" Charlie looked confused. "Why?"

"There are more important things than a career.

Like a home. A family. Finding someone special to love." Liam stared directly into Charlie's eyes as he said those last words.

"Are you saying you love me?" Charlie asked, staring right back.

"What do you think I'm saying?"

Charlie shook his head. "I don't know. Sometimes, you have to hear the words in order to believe them. To know that they're real."

"Of course they're real."

"Are they?"

It was time for Liam's grand, romantic gesture. He got down on one knee, reaching into his pocket and pulling out the velvet box he'd been carrying for days. He heard Charlie gasp as he opened it and held it out. The ring was white gold with a diamond chip in its center. "This ring is a symbol of my love and deep feelings for you, Charlie Fisher. It's a symbol of the hope I have that what I feel exists between us can grow and become something even more special. I love you, Charlie," Liam said as he slipped the ring on Charlie's finger. "So, do you take this ring? More importantly, do you take my heart?"

He stared at Charlie with hope in his eyes, waiting for his answer.

———

Charlie was caught totally by surprise. This was not what he'd been expecting.

He stared at the ring in disbelief, not knowing what to say until finally he found his voice. "You bought this ring for me?"

"Of course I did. Who else would I buy it for? Pablo?" Liam teased.

Charlie blushed.

"You really thought I would go back to him after the way he treated me?"

Charlie shrugged. "He is hot."

"You think I'm that shallow?"

"You do have a history with him."

"Ancient history," Liam countered.

"He did loop you in on the lawsuit."

"And what? I owed him something? With or without Pablo, I would have eventually found out about it."

"I guess I was feeling insecure."

"Why?" Liam gently asked.

"Because I never really knew how you felt. You know, if you had feelings for me or if it was just sex."

"It was never just sex." Liam gave Charlie a grin, showing off his dimples. "Don't get me wrong, I love having sex with you, but I love everything else, too. I've never had that with someone."

"That's because you weren't looking in the right places," Charlie said, a cocky tone in his voice.

"Oh yeah?"

"Yeah." Charlie pulled Liam back up to his feet, drawing him close. "Maybe the guy you've been looking for has been right under your nose and you just didn't know it."

Liam gazed down at Charlie. "You know, you never told me how you felt, either."

"True," Charlie admitted. "I guess I was afraid."

"Of what?"

"Look at you! You can have any man you want."

"But I don't want any man. I want you, Charlie. I've always wanted you. But I wasn't brave enough to say it."

"I also thought your career came first," Charlie admitted. "I know how important it is to you."

"Yes, it's important to me, but not as important as you." Liam lifted Charlie's hand with his ring on it. "You still haven't answered my question."

"Yes. I'll take your ring. And your heart. I'll take whatever you want to give me because I love you, too, Liam. I think I've loved you since your first Scroogy moment in the elevator at Bailey's."

And with those words, Charlie kissed Liam as the cast of *A Charlie Brown Christmas* gathered around them, happily clapping.

"It's about time!" Gregory exclaimed, swinging his Linus blanket in the air like a lasso as the actor playing Snoopy began doing the Snoopy happy dance around everyone.

"Woo hoo!" J.P. shouted. "It's a Christmas miracle."

"Why is everyone clapping?" Sarah asked as she rejoined the group, sucking on a candy cane.

"Sarah, guess what?" Charlie exclaimed. "Santa answered your letter!"

"What?" Sarah's eyes widened with delight. "He did?"

"Letter?" Liam asked. "What letter?"

"The one I wrote to Santa, asking him to find you a new boyfriend by Christmas," Sarah explained. "Charlie was helping him."

"Oh, he was, was he?"

"You know how busy Santa can be," Charlie said. "Just call me Santa's Little Helper."

"Now all those horrible dates are starting to make sense," Liam whispered into Charlie's ear.

"Where's Uncle Liam's new boyfriend?" Sarah asked, looking around. "I want to meet him."

"You already have," Liam said.

"I have? Who is it?"

"It's Charlie."

Sarah let out a shriek of delight. "Yay! That's what I wanted all along. Does that make Charlie my uncle?"

"Not yet," Liam said. "But if I have my way, by this time next year you'll be calling him Uncle Charlie and I'll be calling him Mr. West."

"Don't you think Mr. Fisher-West has a better ring to it?" Charlie suggested with a mischievous smile.

Liam pulled Charlie into his arms and gave him a deep, long kiss. "You can call yourself anything you want as long as you say you're mine."

CHAPTER
THIRTY-ONE

The best part of breaking up was making up, and who didn't love make-up sex?

The after-party at Gregory and Christopher's had been a double celebration. The first performance of *A Charlie Brown Christmas* had gone off without a hitch, and Liam and Charlie were officially a couple. Bottles of champagne had been popped at the theatre before the celebration moved to Gregory and Christopher's house, where there was even more champagne to be had. At the end of the night, Bibi had taken Sarah for a sleepover with Annie, leaving Liam and Charlie by themselves and quickly making up for all the days and nights they'd spent apart. While they'd enjoyed getting naked again, they both agreed the very best part of make-up sex was afterward, in bed together, snuggling in each other's arms.

"As wonderful as this has all been, we haven't discussed what comes next," Charlie said, resting his head against Liam's chest.

"Haven't we?"

"Nope."

Liam threaded his fingers through Charlie's hair, playing with the strands. "We're going to live happily ever after. Isn't that how all romances end?"

"Seriously."

"I am serious." Liam pulled Charlie closer to him. "I'm going to do everything I can to make you happy every single day that we're together."

"But we're not going to be together every day."

"Says who? Where are you going to be?"

Charlie felt like he'd walked into a room during the middle of a movie and was missing plot details. "You're going to be working wherever your acting jobs take you. And I'll be here in Bramford Hills. Missing you."

"You won't have to miss me," Liam announced. "I'll be here in Bramford Hills, too."

"Doing what? Has the town suddenly become a TV and film capital?"

"No, but it is going to be the home of a new dinner theatre."

"Pardon?"

Liam nodded. "My lawyer called me today. The network wants to settle as soon as possible, and they're offering a check with lots of zeros that we're going to accept. After I got off the phone with them, I put an offer in for the old dinner theatre where we're doing the play. It was a real bargain."

"Why did you buy it?"

"I thought we could bring it back to life."

"We? As in us?"

"Yes," Liam said, his voice filled with excitement. "Us. Think of all the fun we'd have bringing in shows or mounting our own productions. And I know you love to cook. You could plan out all the menus and oversee the cooking. It would be like running your own restaurant."

Charlie's head was spinning. Was he hearing what he thought he was hearing? Liam wasn't going to leave Bramford Hills. He was staying. And he wanted the two of them to work together.

"But you love being an actor," Charlie pointed out.

"I can still do that," Liam said. "New York City isn't that far away. TV shows and movies are always filming down there, and if I got a part, I could commute back and forth. We could even get a little place in the city. How does that sound?"

It sounded wonderful. Almost too good to be true.

"Are you sure about this?" Charlie asked. "It would be a big commitment."

"And an adventure," Liam added. "And there's no one else I'd rather commit to having an adventure with than you. What do you say? Want to run a dinner theatre with me?"

Charlie didn't even have to give it a second thought. "Yes!" he exclaimed. "Absolutely."

———

The following morning, Liam and Charlie hosted a brunch for the cast. Charlie was in the kitchen making waffles from scratch and frying bacon, while Liam was in the dining room mixing up mimosas. The food was all ready to be served when Gregory arrived with a huge grin on his face.

"The suspense is over," he announced, holding up a stack of local newspapers. "Our show's a hit! We got a rave review." Everyone gathered around Gregory with excitement as he handed out newspapers, eagerly turning to the page with the review. "Now, if you turn the page, you'll see there's also a review for that other Christmas show in town." Gregory wrinkled his nose in disdain. "It opened the night before ours."

"What does it say?" Charlie asked.

"The headline says the show is wonderful... wonderfully awful!" Gregory laughed. "The reviewer even made a few suggestions for improving the show. He said if you added a couple of drag queens, it was destined to become a camp classic." Gregory cackled with glee. "I'm sure that's not the review Claude was looking for!"

"Poor Claude," Charlie said.

Gregory snapped his fingers in the air. "It's about time he got cut down to size. Money can't buy you everything. Definitely not a good review! Hopefully, this will be the end of Claude's monopoly and reign of bad taste on the town's Christmas shows, and the directing team of West and Hollis will be bringing more plays to Bramford Hills."

"Actually, they will," Liam said, holding up his champagne flute. "Gather around. Charlie and I have an announcement."

"You've set a wedding date!" Gregory happily

squealed. "Oh, let's have a double wedding! Christopher and I will share our day with you."

"But I don't want to share our special day with anyone else," Christopher said in a rare moment of rebellion. "I want it to be just ours."

"You are sooo romantic," Gregory cooed, giving Christopher a kiss on the lips.

"As lovely as that sounds," Liam said, "Charlie and I haven't set a wedding date yet. We haven't even talked about moving in together. But we are going to be bringing back the Bramford Hills dinner theatre next year. I just bought the building, and Charlie is going to run it with me."

Cheers erupted, and everyone congratulated Liam and Charlie.

"What did I miss?" Bibi asked as she walked through the front door with Sarah and Annie. The two little girls instantly made a beeline for the waffles, stacking their plates and pouring syrup.

"You're looking at the new owner of the soon-to-be-reopened Bramford Hills dinner theatre," Liam answered, pouring Bibi a flute of champagne.

"Fabulous!" she exclaimed, taking the filled flute from Liam and sipping at the bubbles. "That means you'll be sticking around to help me wreak more havoc at Bramford Hills Elementary."

Liam raised his flute and toasted Bibi. "I wouldn't miss it."

Suddenly, there was the sound of honking outside the house. Sarah ran to the front window and pushed back the curtains, gasping with delight.

"It's Mommy and Daddy!"

She abandoned her plate of waffles and rushed out the front door and into the arms of her approaching mother. "Mommy, Mommy, Mommy!" Sarah shrieked, her voice filled with joy. "Daddy! You're back!"

Penelope lifted Sarah up into her arms, twirling her around. "Oh my goodness, you've gotten so big! How could you have grown so much in only a month? I missed you so much." She began kissing Sarah all over her face.

"I missed you, too, but Uncle Liam took great care of me. Charlie, too."

"Who's Charlie?"

"Uncle Liam's new boyfriend. Santa brought him."

"He did?"

"It's a long story," Liam explained, as he came out to help his brother-in-law unload the taxi of suitcases, Charlie following behind. "I'll tell you all about it. In the meantime, Penelope, this is Charlie.

Charlie, meet my sister, Penelope, and her husband, Steve."

Sophisticated. Chic. Glamorous. Those were all the words running through Charlie's mind as he introduced himself to Penelope, a cool, sleek brunette with a shoulder-length bob, cheekbones to die for, and the same killer dimples as Liam. She instantly pulled him into a hug.

"You must be something special," she gushed with a huge smile on her face. "I haven't seen my brother this happy in ages."

"Charlie makes everyone happy, Mommy. He's the best."

"That's right, he is," Liam agreed.

"Let me help with those bags," Charlie offered as Steve, a dead-ringer for Channing Tatum, joined them, juggling luggage.

"We have an announcement," Penelope said, slipping her arm through Liam's as they walked into the house. "Two, actually."

"What's the first?"

"We're not moving."

Liam gasped. "You're not? Did the new job fall through?"

Penelope shook her head. "No."

"You couldn't find a house?"

"No."

"Then, what happened?"

"We realized something when we were out in California," Penelope said. "We were missing out. Missing Sarah. The amount of hours we were working was ridiculous, and being remote made us realize it even more. It jolted us awake and made us realize life is too short. So, we've rejiggered our priorities and decided that our family comes first. Steve turned down the new job, and I'm going to cut back on my hours at the brokerage firm."

"I'll toast to that," Charlie said, as he carried two champagne flutes to Penelope and Steve. "To family time." Steve accepted his flute and took a sip, but Penelope waved hers away.

"What's the matter?" Liam asked. "You always love a glass of bubbly."

"I still do. Except..." Penelope gently touched her belly. "In my condition, there will be no bubbly for the next couple of months."

Liam gasped. "You're pregnant?"

Penelope swatted her brother. "Don't sound so shocked! You're not the only one in this family who hits the sheets. I'm not saying this was planned, but it's a happy Christmas surprise." Penelope turned to Sarah, who was glued to her mother's side. Penelope knelt down so she was eye level with her daughter. "Guess what, sweetie? You're going to be a big sister by this time next year."

Sarah stared at her mother in amazement. "Really?"

Penelope nodded. "Yep! Mommy's having a baby. What do you think of that?"

"Oh, boy!" Sarah exclaimed, giving her mother a hug. "I can't wait!"

"Let's go upstairs," Penelope told her daughter, hugging her back. "Mommy and Daddy brought back some presents for you. Ones you can open before Christmas."

Charlie watched as Penelope, Steve, and Sarah headed up the stairs for their own little reunion. "With a new baby on the way, do you think your sister is still going to want a puppy for Sarah?" he asked Liam as they headed back to the dining room and the cast brunch.

"What do you mean?"

"Well, I've gotten pretty attached to Mistletoe. And I think you have, too. Even Shadow tolerates him now. I can't imagine saying goodbye to him. Maybe he could stay with us, and we could get Sarah another puppy next Christmas. It's not like she knew about Mistletoe. I was thinking maybe a maltipoo? They're so adorable and girly."

"Stay with us?" Liam asked.

"Live with us. You know, when you move in with me."

"Is that an invitation?"

"You don't have a place of your own in Bramford Hills, do you?"

"No, I don't. Other than my sister's house. And now that she's back, my babysitting duties are over."

"Then, I'm officially inviting you to move in with me. What do you say?"

Liam's eyes lit up. "I would say that's the best Christmas present ever."

"Good." Charlie wrapped his arms around him, leaning close as they kissed. "Because you're the best Christmas present I've ever gotten. I don't think even Santa could improve on this."

Liam gave Charlie a slow, lingering kiss while pretending to give it some thought. "I don't know. I bet next year's Christmas will be better than this one. And the one after that will be even better."

"Promise?" Charlie asked.

"Promise," Liam said. "Because all I'll ever want for Christmas is you. As long as I have you, every

Christmas and every day we're together will be perfect. That's a promise I'll keep all year long."

The
HITMAN'S
Love
Contract
RACHEL DOVE

ABOUT THE AUTHOR

Author photo taken by Kevin Mathis

John Salzone grew up in Bensonhurst, Brooklyn. His father was one of eight and he was lucky enough to have both sets of grandparents living next door, as well as two sets of aunts, uncles and cousins living on the same block. Growing up he had twenty-four cousins and his fondest memories are of family gatherings and vacations when everyone would be together, talking in a combination of English and Italian. John has worked in publishing as an editor, published a number of *New York Times* bestselling authors and written a variety of adult and young adult novels under the names John Hall (*Home-*

coming Queen; Killer Christmas; Is He or Isn't He?), Sabrina James (*Secret Santa; Party Girl*) and Jennifer Hall (*Star Quality*). He's also the author of *An Offer He Can't Refuse,* which is Sebastian and Dom's story. He loves hearing from readers and you can email him at: sjamesauthor@yahoo.com

ABOUT THE PUBLISHER

Harbor Lane Books, LLC is a US-based independent digital publisher of commercial fiction, non-fiction, and poetry.

Connect with Harbor Lane Books on their website (www.harborlanebooks.com) and social media @harborlanebooks.

facebook.com/harborlanebooks

x.com/harborlanebooks

instagram.com/harborlanebooks

bsky.app/profile/harborlanebooks.bsky.social

tiktok.com/@harborlanebooks

threads.com/harborlanebooks

youtube.com/harborlanebooks

pinterest.com/harborlanebooks

9 781963 705256